BELLA

A Woman of Courage

1863-1953

LYN THOMPSON

BELLA: A WOMAN OF COURAGE 1863-1953
Copyright © 2013 by Lyn Thompson

Printed in Canada

ISBN: 978-1-77069-775-1

Word Alive Press
131 Cordite Road, Winnipeg, MB R3W 1S1
www.wordalivepress.ca

Library and Archives Canada Cataloguing in Publication

Thompson, Lyn
          Bella, a woman of courage, 1863-1953 / Lyn Thompson.

ISBN 978-1-77069-775-1

          I. Title.

PS8639.H628B45 2013   C813'.6   C2012-907555-8

This book is dedicated to those of you who
knew and loved
Nana and her three boys.

TABLE OF CONTENTS

FOREWORD

This is a story still poignant even though it took place one hundred years ago. Events that shaped Bella's life may sometimes make the reader doubt the story's credibility, but these things did happen. I know, for Bella was my grandmother; her eldest son, my father; and the two younger boys, my uncles. I knew Grandma well and spent many hours listening, in awe of her incredible life. I feel her story of love, happiness, agony and hard work needs to be told because, like our forefathers who came to the New World to find a better life, her faith in God and the future remained unshaken despite overwhelming odds.

All dates, geographical locations and addresses are exact. The signal turning points in her life are here. The family characters in the story are real. Bella and Shauna are their true names, but by author's licence I changed the names of some family members. Her story will make you recognize the pressures of Victorian culture that are still with us today, although they are now less obvious because women like Bella helped to prove that women could succeed in business.

Despite having lifelong physical disabilities from rickets, the causes of which were not then understood, Grandma gave birth to three children and lived a productive life to the amazing age of ninety, feats as medically remarkable as her colourful life.

Enjoy *Bella: A Woman of Courage 1863–1953.*

ACKNOWLEDGEMENTS

I thank Bella (my grandmother), my father and my two uncles for their lifetime of stories that form the framework for this story of Bella's life.

A most delightful part of this book came in researching the Cambridge years that my father knew at the turn of the twentieth century. I thank Marta Pardee-King and Patricia Feeley of the Boston Library for their helpful links that introduced me to Old Boston, and Ted Hansen of the Cambridge Historical Society, who answered e-mail questions. I especially want to thank Kathleen Rawlins of the Cambridge Historical Commission. When I gave her the addresses, she sent me old maps, census information and historical pictures taken of the houses where Bella and her family lived one hundred years ago. She alerted me to the importance of Agassiz Grammar School and its first principal, Maria Baldwin, who taught my father. Through her I learned of Bella's signature in Cambridge's Blue Book.

Of most importance, I thank my family and relatives for their gems of information. One brother provided me with copies of letters and maps originating in the colonial days of Surinam. Another brother gave me details from his extensive genealogy records.

Thanks to my writing friends, and in particular, Mark Kirtland, Bob Stallworthy and all those who have helped me visit the past in a most remarkable, insightful and real manner.

1

PLYMOUTH, VICTORIAN ENGLAND 1887

"**M**rs. Bowen," said the doctor, "Bella will die from lung congestion before she's thirty if she doesn't move away from Plymouth's damp weather. You must choose a warm British colony and ship her off as soon as possible."

Dutifully, Bella followed her mother from the doctor's office. In silence, she gathered her skirts and climbed into their carriage. She sat with her gloved hands clenched in her lap. Eyes unfocussed and narrowed with indignation, her thoughts relived her past while she tried to grasp the magnitude of the doctor's words.

The doctor always talks to my stepmother! Why doesn't he talk to me? I'm twenty-four years old and quite able to determine my own future. We started visiting the doctor right after my new tutor went clattering down the stairs to bring my parents. How I remember that day! I was six. "Rickets!" my stepmother cried when she lifted my skirts. She clutched at Father's shoulder in a swoon and they left the room. "No wonder she grew so slowly," Father said as he closed the door behind him. How was I to know that bowed legs were not normal? Warm colony! On my own? Who will care for me when I'm ill?

***

When they reached home, Mrs. Bowen said, "Bella, you haven't spoken a word since we left the doctor's office. Are you lost in the pages of one of your books again?"

"Lost? No, Mother; I'm thinking about the doctor's remark. I'm old enough to determine my own future and it doesn't include being shipped off to some British colony."

"Tut, tut, Bella. We'll discuss this with your father in the parlour after dinner."

***

"I don't see that there's anything to discuss," said Father. "What parents would stand idle and let their daughter die? The doctor said to leave as soon as possible, so that must be our goal. I have connections with ships that sail to British Guiana. I'm told there is a fine colonial life there. Details, details. You'll need a guardian to accompany you on board ship so you'll be safe. I'll have him carry money for you, help you open a bank account in Georgetown and find a place for you to live that's to your liking. You are sure to enjoy the warm weather and palm trees."

"But Father, just think, I may die in five years anyway—with or without palm trees. I might die alone. I'd rather be home with my family."

"The doctor said that a warm climate would improve your health, and that's the important thing to Mother and me. The decision has been made by your health, Bella. You must go to South America. You'd do best to see the excitement in sailing off to a land of wild bananas and flaming bougainvillaea instead of arguing over this decision."

***

Bella discovered that her atlas showed British colonies in pink and soon found British Guiana on the northern shore of South America. Father brought home books about British Guiana and she read them all, even the ones the librarian slipped in about romance, sex and the naughty behaviour of men. *Travelling sounds dangerous. Why would I go so far away from England? The idea is preposterous!*

2

***

Bella felt a flush of uneasiness the first time she saw the SS *Balfour* moored in Plymouth Harbour. It seemed strange to see a bulky steamship in the bay amid the tall masted sailing ships. She ran her gaze over the grey-painted metal hull trimmed in white above the deck and red below the water line. *In just ten days I'll be leaving my family and living on board that ship. Why are they so adamant about my leaving? For my health, they say. Must I go or be forever sickly? What a cruel choice.*

***

The days passed quickly and soon Bella found herself calling and waving to her family as the ship pulled away from the pier with its horn blasting a long single note. She dabbed at her eyes. Mr. Scott-Wallace, her guardian, stood at the railing some fifteen feet away while other men grouped together and lit cigars to mark the beginning of the trip. None of them looked her way or tipped their hats. *Are they unhappy to have a woman on board? If they insist on ignoring me, I shall go below, inspect my cabin and hope they become more civil out at sea. I can't imagine five weeks of travel if no one speaks to me.*

Bella crossed the metal decking to look over a railing meant to restrain passengers from entering the fore deck. Below, she saw a hoist for transferring cargo into one of three cargo hatches. She passed through a door in the stern of the superstructure. Down a few steps, she came upon the dining room and twelve cabins. She opened the door of Number Eight, the cabin designated on her ticket.

She saw a narrow wooden bunk, a desk with a straight-backed chair and an area along the wall with pegs for hanging clothes and space below them to store her trunk. She recognized hardship when she saw a small red carpet beside the bed to moderate the cold of the metal floor. *The room is nothing like home, but the Spartan furnishings must be accepted. I don't want to go, but I'm determined to survive.*

***

Days out at sea, Bella stood at the railing of the SS *Balfour*, her eyes glued to the horizon. She saw only rough waves and a leaden sky, yet she continued to stand there, huddled in her heavy wool shawl and bonnet. Aunt Kate had told her fresh air and keeping her eyes on the horizon would prevent seasickness. She wished the other eleven passengers had heard this same advice. Instead, they took to their bunks the first day the ship crashed through the daunting waves of the open Atlantic. Two boat hands reported to the passenger cabins to clean up after those who had lost their breakfast.

Bella found herself the only passenger in the dining room at lunch that day. *Tramp steamer? I heard those two shipmates call the Balfour a tramp steamer when they were scrubbing down the cabins. Father called it a steamship. I do not consider myself a tramp. The men in my books are more interesting than the passengers on board. I'll go to my room and finish* Wuthering Heights, *and after that I'll start on* The Scarlet Letter. *Queen Victoria must be very proud of our new romance novelists.*

***

Now two weeks at sea, some of the men walked the deck for a smoke, but they passed her as if she were not there. *Let them ignore me! I won't stop taking my walks on deck. The fresh air lifts my spirits after a morning of reading.* While she stood at the railing watching the grey horizon, reality shook her little body free of fantasizing. *What will become of me so far from home? I have no training, no mind for money. Must I live on Father's stipend forever? What if he dies? Dear God, I might never see him again!* She blotted the thoughts from her mind and went below.

***

On the high seas the ship tossed like a cork, but Bella, undaunted, continued to go on deck and watch the horizon. Her cheeks caught the cold salt spray as the rough waves roared in long furrows of curling foam. The metal hull pounded with ill humour as it humped through the waves. Standing there in the wind, she had never felt so alone.

Where is my guardian when I need him? He ignores me. What a fop, wearing a diamond stickpin even for breakfast that first day out of Plymouth. Perhaps he doesn't want the other passengers to know that he is travelling with the only woman on board. Then again, maybe he thinks me

4

an embarrassment. After all, he stands more than six feet tall, and with my stunted growth, my chin could hang on his vest chain. What man would want a woman just four-foot nine with intense eyes set in the sockets of a sallow face?

"Stop this nonsense, Bella!" she shouted to the deaf waves. She knew she must not think of herself as imperfect. She was a woman, she told herself, perhaps plain, but she had a fine mind. Upset by her troublesome thoughts, Bella squared her shoulders and assumed the countenance shown in pictures of dignified British colonials. Even this did not allow her to control her innermost feelings. Because of illness, her black hair hung limp and her peaked face looked pinched. She felt as if she wore the head of a witch attached to the body of a child.

With thoughts of Scott-Wallace and her father, Bella looked to the northeast as if to see Plymouth—to see her father and stepmother and two older sisters waving goodbye to her—to see them smiling as if glad to be rid of her.

"Glad to be rid of me!" Bella screamed to the wind. "Good Lord! How did that dreadful thought crowd into my mind?"

At first it shocked her. She knew the answer if she wanted to be honest. Having an adult sickly daughter about the house carried a certain stigma for her Victorian parents. They considered themselves to be among the emerging middle class of the late eighteen hundreds— neither royalty nor rich, but certainly not poor. Bella winced. She knew her constant illness and her ability to gain attention and get her way tried the family's patience. *Yes, with my departure, they could very well think that a household burden has been lifted.*

Bella tried to erase this thought by thinking pleasant thoughts about her father, her only true parent. *Right now he'll be at his warehouse, or maybe he and his men are out loading a ship using our handsome flat-bottomed barges.*

Bella looked at her white knuckles on the railing. She didn't want to continue with her next thoughts, but still they came. *He named the first barge after my eldest sister, "Althea," and our second barge bears the name "Constance," for my second sister. Not even our fishing dinghy proclaims the name "Isabella" after me. Isabella! I'm just plain Isabella Bowen! If my real mother loved me, why didn't she give me a second name like the double names of my older sisters? Everyone calls me "Bella" because of my size, as if I'm still a baby. Then my stepmother gave birth to little Flora Mae and she became the baby.* Bella pounded her fists on the railing and stared at the ship's wake. *Why do my happy thoughts always change to heartache?*

***

Bella grew accustomed to the roll of the ship. When the sea chose to be calm, she increased her daily walks around the passenger deck while the men played cards in the dining room. She liked to feel the sun on her face and the growing warmth of the winds as the steamship plugged away to the south. During these walks it amazed her how often she thought of home. *Does the cat still sleep on my bed? Did the roses bloom without my dose of milk? Have any of Althea's three boyfriends asked her to marry? Did sailors, swimming to shore from the Spanish Armada, really start generations of raven-haired beauties? Like my sisters—not me.* She stared so desperately at the horizon that tears welled in her eyes. *Everyone notices Althea and Constance. They're both much taller than I am and their black hair falls in soft waves against rose-tinted cheeks. I'll never grow tall and beautiful like them.*

***

Even as she tried to drop off to sleep, Bella's active mind troubled her. *I know my parents bought Sadie, the Jersey cow, so I'd have milk, but who could like warm raw fatty milk? I shouldn't have poured it on the fern or out the window. Even though I know now, because of my reading, about bones needing milk, I cannot change the past.*

Bella readjusted her bedcovers and turned over. "But," Bella shouted to the darkened cabin, "understanding why I have rickets makes no difference to the present! I have bowed legs and the deformity will never change. Now please, dear God, let me go to sleep and be done with these tiresome thoughts!"

She nestled her head into the pillow and thought of her dear Aunt Kate's parting words: "Bella, don't allow yourself to waste energy on a past you cannot change." Drifting off to sleep, Bella realized what her aunt's message meant and determined that she would not waste the rest of the voyage on despairing thoughts—or worse, waste the rest of her life with inactivity. In the morning she felt refreshed, uplifted in some way, and with the days growing warmer she felt an improvement in her health.

***

One day Bella chose to relax in a canvas deckchair. She chuckled. *Ah, the "stout" day! How I remember the look on my stepmother's face when the doctor said, "And even though she's only seven, as she is underweight, to build her strength she is to have a jar of stout every day."*

How shocked my stepmother looked. Liquor in the house! The thought of what people might think if they discovered this travesty likely concerned my stepmother more than did my health. That's when they gave Flora Mae her own nursery. "She might catch your cold," my stepmother said, but I imagine she meant, "She might see you drinking stout." Even when I grew older, they insisted that I drink my daily half-pint in the nursery so friends would not see that they kept liquor in the house. The stout lifts my spirits, has a wonderful flavour and makes me feel delightfully outrageous. My parents don't know what they're missing.

***

As the sun climbed to directly overhead and the metal deck burned her feet through the soles of her shoes, Bella knew they were nearing the equator and British Guiana. *I will stand at the forward railing, watch for land and look forward to my new life. Perhaps, in Georgetown there will be a shortage of women my age and the men will not mind my small bony figure.*

***

The next two days brought no sight of land, but even when the sun blinded her eyes, Bella persisted in standing at the railing facing the south. She dreamed marvelous dreams of the cocktail party she would hold in her new home with servants attending the guests. *Oh, it will all be such fun and I will shock them by having my tankard of stout!*

7

Stout, thought Bella with one last look at the sun dipping into the waves. *It is time for my daily stout.* She made her way to the tearoom, now a beverage room after five o'clock. The men, lounging in the chairs, looked askance when she arrived each day to order her jar of the strong black beer, for women with culture did not drink in public. Mr. Scott-Wallace always came early and sat facing the portholes so he would not have to acknowledge her presence. Bella found the whole performance rather amusing and enjoyed ruining their sense of "men only" in the "club lounge" by bidding a loud "Good afternoon," to them as she entered.

The same thing happened at dinner. The men would crowd together and the only chair left for her would be at the captain's table near the potted philodendrons. This amused her too, for she hardly considered the male passengers worthy of advances. They were all too old, fat or generally intoxicated. The more she studied them (her first prolonged contact with men she did not know), the more she decided they were totally infatuated with themselves—*the poise required to smoke a cigarette or lift a gold watch and chain from a vest pocket. Really, they are a knavish lot with their expansive claims of business successes, their favourite vintage of wine, women they have bedded and how they plan to leave Guiana with gold in their pockets.*

She could hear their conversations as she sat quietly by the philodendrons with her stout while the men imbibed successive drams of whiskey or rum. *Without Scott-Wallace, would these men act like the men in the librarian's naughty books? Would they?*

***

One day, while walking her rounds on deck before taking her position at the bow, Bella paused at the stern of the ship to watch the wake boil up in white foam that traced their passage from Plymouth. Suddenly, a seagull dived into the wake.

"A seagull!" she cried to no one in particular. She screened the horizon but saw no land, yet she knew that there must be land if the seagull came in search of the refuse that Cook dumped through the galley window.

The next day after lunch, while immersed in *Lady Audley's Secret*, Bella answered a sharp knock on her cabin door. *It sounds like the silver knob of Scott-Wallace's ridiculous walking stick.*

"Good afternoon, Miss Bowen."

She had guessed correctly. After weeks of ignoring her, when she opened the door there stood her guardian.

"Please come to the tearoom, Miss Bowen. It would be improper for me to enter your room." Bella felt awkward as she followed him down the passageway past open cabin doors to the empty tearoom.

"Miss Bowen," he began once they were seated, "in two days we will reach Georgetown in British Guiana. We must be ready to disembark on that day in the morning at nine o'clock. Tomorrow your trunk must be packed and ready for removal by the ship's crew. In your small valise I want you to pack a gown suitable for dinner at the finest hotel in the country. Leave your packed valise outside your cabin door when we disembark and it will be delivered to the foot of the pier."

Does he never need to take a breath?

"I have booked two rooms for us in the hotel. In the evening of that first night we will have dinner together at seven-thirty. The following morning, I will take you to the bank to deposit the money I carry from your father. After that, I will show you some houses. When we have found your lodgings, I will note the address and take it to your father on my return trip next week. Your trunk will be delivered to that address the following day. Am I clear?"

At least he thinks I have a fine memory for details.

Bella nodded her head and had just parted her lips to speak when Mr. Scott-Wallace rose, stiff as a stick, and said, "Good afternoon, then," and marched out of the tearoom.

Well, she thought, *he was clear. What a codfish. I suppose I shall pack my blue taffeta for dinner. Tomorrow I must ask for a pitcher of warm water to wash my hair and see if I can twist it up on the top of my head against this heat. "The finest hotel in Guiana," he said. At last my dreams of romance might come true!*

She rose and approached the waiter.

"Please, may I have my jar of stout?"

"But, Miss Bowen, it is not yet five o'clock."

"I plan to drink it in my cabin, good man, and I promise I won't drink one drop of it before the sun passes over the yard arm or whatever phrase it is that you men use."

She left with a stoneware jar of stout, its metal spring fastener still clipped in the down position. Once in her room, Bella flung off her hat, grasped the pottery jar in both hands and, with her bottom teeth, flipped the tight spring that held the lid. *Thought I wouldn't get it open, didn't you, barkeep? Didn't expect me to know how to keep my upper teeth out of the way. Well, dear boy, I used to practice so I could shock my stepmother's friends. 'Course I never got the chance.* She guffawed. *Too bad—it would have been great fun!* With this she swigged half of the beer straight from the jar, allowed the chuckle to escalate into uproarious laughter and flopped down on the edge of her bunk to enjoy her moment of outrageousness.

What's wrong with celebrating my arrival in British Guiana? She took another swig, put the jar on the desk and, with a burst of energy, started to pack. *I'll have my trunk ready and my valise will be stuffed with the blue taffeta gown and its full crinoline, if nothing else. After such a long voyage, I feel ready for change. In two days,* she fantasized with a final quaff of stout, *I will walk down the pier into Georgetown, prepared to meet my new country. And in the evening, I will be ready for dinner looking demure in my prettiest gown—and I will enter the dining room on the arm of a man, even if it's only my codfish, Scott-Wallace.*

2

GEORGETOWN, DEMERARA
1887

The following morning Bella looked for the Guiana coastline. *That grey smudge—is that land?* With a spring in her step, she walked ten circuits of the deck and went to the dining room for lunch. The young second officer waved her over with a big smile. *Too bad he will always be at sea. There's not much point in casting my eyes at him. Georgetown is sure to have many eligible bachelors. Trust yourself, my dear; the right one will come along.* Bella returned his smile and joined him.

***

By sundown she saw a rough outline to the grey smudge. *When this voyage is over, I won't allow myself to be alone ever again. Surely, other men won't be as cold as my codfish.*

***

That evening at dinner, Bella walked over to Scott-Wallace's table. Despite his apparent inability to look up as she approached, she said in a pleasant voice loud enough for all to hear, "Mr. Scott-Wallace, don't look for me in my cabin in the morning." She paused for a second, like an actress timing her line for the benefit of the audience. "I plan to be on deck in time to see our approach and passage into Georgetown. Will you be joining me?"

The room fell silent. The men lowered their forks and flashed puzzled glances at Scott-Wallace, yet no one dared ask what kind of business awaited him in this woman's room. Much to her pleasure, as she turned to leave Bella saw a rosy blush rising up her guardian's neck. *Good! His unfriendliness brought it on himself.*

***

At seven-thirty the next morning, Bella smoothed her pale-yellow gown in front of the mirror. She combed her hair into an upsweep and covered the bun with the crown of a wide-brimmed straw hat. For the first time she recognized the lovely shape of her head and neck.

Enough preening. It is time to see our arrival in Georgetown.

The thermometer on the aft deck already registered 80 degrees Fahrenheit, yet the brisk southwesterly caused Bella to wrap her white silk shawl around her shoulders. The horizon now revealed a low line of green mangrove swamps on either end of a concrete seawall. Near one end of this she saw a light flashing. Clasping her hands together under her chin, she murmured, "There's the lighthouse that I saw in my book back home."

The closer they approached, the more Bella saw of Georgetown. Lofty palm trees dotted the horizon. Buildings began to take shape. She discerned a finger of grey stretching out from the seawall.

"Why, that is the pier where we shall land," she said triumphantly in a small voice meant only for the wind. *I wonder where my codfish is.*

Mr. Scott-Wallace came for her exactly at nine. Together they walked down the gangplank towards the foot of the pier. With the ship in port, the ocean breezes were stilled. The smell of the jungle and the draining powers of heat and humidity descended on her like a cloak. She missed the roll of the ship and questioned her balance as men with handcarts and children selling trinkets crowded her path. For support, she reached up and grasped the crook of her guardian's elbow. To her surprise, he did not pull free. *The dutiful guardian,* she thought with a wry smile.

She could see her dreams coming to life in a collage of colour. Horse-drawn carriages waited for the ship's passengers. Sweating cargo hands wheeled valises to the foot of the pier. Lured by the loud blast of the ship's horn, a multi-coloured crowd of town's people bustled towards them with wagons and braying donkeys. Three Creoles with guitars added to the cacophony of sounds. Bella found this infectious and tripped along on Mr. Scott-Wallace's arm while she struggled to see every detail of the scene.

A coachman came forward to claim their bags. The carriage pulled away from the pier and climbed the street that came down to the waterfront. Everything she had read in her books presented itself like a homecoming. Palm trees waved against blue sky, and along the oceanfront stood white houses wrapped with bougainvillea in flaming pinks and burgundies. Among the adults on the street ran sweet-faced children. *Yes! Georgetown will make my life come alive.*

The carriage pulled under the portico of a handsome brick building with etched glass in its double front doors. A uniformed doorman awaited them. Bella's guardian guided her up a short flight of stairs and across the blue ceramic tile of the foyer. Bella's eyes swept across white plaster walls, colourful woven hangings, a picture of Queen Victoria and a painting of an austere gentleman.

"Right this way," said a man in hotel livery. He led them down a hallway to a hotel guest room, entered with the valises and stood back just inside the doorway to wait for the couple to enter.

"Do as you wish with the day, Miss Bowen," said Scott-Wallace. "I shall come for you at seven-thirty for dinner." He nodded to the porter to recover one valise, and the door closed behind him. *What a man, so curt. Not even a goodbye!*

She rather liked the idea of being on her own until dinner, for back in England, with her poor health, she had never gone anywhere by herself. She pulled the blue taffeta dress from her valise, smoothed it flat on the bed, shook the crinoline and left the room with plans to stroll down the main streets of Georgetown. *I'll check the dress shops, have lunch in some quaint restaurant and find a place to have my five o'clock stout.*

Bella pushed aside the heavy hotel door and descended to street level. In front of her a wide street, lined with colourful shops interspersed by tall palms, stretched both left and right. At the street corner she saw a large sign pointing left to River Street. *If it has a special sign, it's important—perhaps the shopping district, parallel to the Demerara River.*

With her bowed legs and small-heeled shoes, walking on the uneven red gravel proved difficult. Most of the buildings she passed were built of wood and not the white stone of her dreams. They were raised on brick pillars three to four feet above ground level depending on their proximity to the ocean. Bella concluded that high storm tides must have regularly swept over the low-lying land to flood the city before they built the seawall. She struggled up the steps of the first ladies' shop.

"Good morning, Madame," came the soft voice of a mulatto woman at the rear of the shop. Bella explained the clothes and size she wanted. The woman slowly shook her head from side to side. "No, Madame, but we will sew it for you." *What kind of gown would they sew? I see nothing of London fashions. Must I sew my own clothes to be in style?* She pulled herself up the steps of two more shops to no avail.

To rest, Bella seated herself on a shaded bench beside the river and watched people moving along the street. Horses trotted past carrying white-suited gentlemen. Ladies carried parasols to protect them from the sun, and peasants smiled her way as they pulled their laden carts.

She continued her sightseeing tour, with one street leading to another until before her stood the enclosed market pictured in one of her Plymouth books—Stabroek Market, with its tall pointed tower trimmed in bright red on white walls. How cool it felt under the solid dark roof as she strolled past the various vendors. The abundance of colourful fruits, vegetables, dried fish and live caged chickens amazed her. *Must I buy live chickens and kill them while they squawk?*

She left the market by another entrance and continued her walk under the noonday sun. *What am I doing out in this relentless heat? It's beating on my shoulders while the road reflects heat up under my skirts.* In a near faint, she steadied herself against a building. *I must find shade. Yes, Englishmen must not go out in the noonday sun. I have learned my first lesson. A cup of tea will revive me.*

Bella pushed on past a crude sidewalk stand-up bar selling strong Indian curry. In desperation, she tried to find her bearings. *I do believe I'm lost! Which way is the main street? With the sun directly overhead I can't determine directions.*

She noticed a mahogany-stained door with brass fittings. Instinctively, she moved towards it because the polished brass suggested a place for refined people to enter. A man in livery held the door open for her as she approached, and she entered with a polite "Thank you," as if she knew exactly where she was going. *This looks like a men's club, yet that fellow held the door for me.*

Bella walked into the anteroom with its wooden chairs and potted plants. She could hear chatter coming from a room to her right and with it she discerned the clatter of dishes. Leading with her chin at just the proper angle, Bella walked into the room and crossed the floor to a corner table where she could survey the people in the room without drawing too much attention to herself.

"Shrimp salad with a piece of dry toast and a pot of tea," she ordered from the waiter who attended her. Engraved on his brass badge she read, "Georgetown Club."

She cast her eyes over the other customers. Near her sat three women in large hats and gracious gowns. Farther along the wall, two gentlemen hissed in the heat of a negative discussion. A lone fellow sat closer to the windows. As he faced away from her, Bella allowed her eyes to linger while she studied him. *About my age or maybe a couple of years older, polished riding boots, a tall body under that white riding habit and all topped with a mop of wavy red hair that glints in the sunlight—*

Her idle stare ceased as the man's chair scraped backwards. He repositioned himself sideways to the table. As she averted her eyes, Bella caught a glimpse of a teapot and cup that had been pushed away as if finished.

Ladies do not stare—but he's so handsome—perhaps another peek—but what if he looks my way? I don't want to be taken for a loose woman. After several seconds and a nonchalant sip of tea, Bella glanced up. She found the fellow looking right at her. Their eyes met! He stood and walked directly towards her.

Bella could not imagine what this forward advance would mean in the colonies. She stiffened. With unwavering eyes on the approaching stranger, she hoped to keep him in his place.

"Miss Isabella Bowen, I believe. My name is Donald Macdonald. You may not remember me, but I visited your home in Plymouth some years ago with my father. May I join you?"

Bella could not believe that a prince charming had entered her life on her very first day in Georgetown—a handsome man with a fashionable five-inch rust-coloured moustache and a delightful Scottish brogue. *Such a kind face with laughing eyes, but what does he want?* She smiled and waved her dainty hand, inviting him to be seated.

Donald Macdonald continued, "I remember the occasion at your home because your long lacy gown and diminutive size, for eight years old, made you look like a Dresden doll. At sixteen, with brothers, I admired your spunk and the delight you showed in holding your own with your two older sisters." He paused to pay the bill for his tea and Bella's lunch and continued, "Last week I received a letter from my father saying you would arrive on the SS *Balfour*. It seems he heard of your adventure through business connections. Your date of arrival coincided with my business trip here, so I've been watching for you even though I missed seeing you disembark. Whatever brings you to Demerara? Father didn't say."

After answering his question, Bella inquired about his business trip and they chatted while she finished her tea.

"I don't live in Demerara. My work is in Paramaribo, in Surinam, where I manage a sugar plantation when I'm not prospecting for gold. My business in Demerara will take another few days. Would you care to have dinner with me this evening?"

Bella wanted to say "yes" but knew she must continue under Mr. Scott-Wallace's care until tomorrow, or whenever they found her a house.

"I'm sorry, Mr. Macdonald. This evening must be spent with a man whom Father hired to be my guardian for the trip. We are having dinner at the hotel at seven-thirty." She followed this with a devilish grin and went on with a coy tone in her voice. "However, I always have a half pint of stout every day at five o'clock. If you have the time, perhaps you might escort me to a lounge or pub that serves women and we can continue getting acquainted."

Again, Bella saw laughter in his eyes. "Do you wish a lounge or a drinking hole, dear lady?" *He has read me through and through.* With a flourish, he offered his arm and off she teetered in little steps, her chin just inches above his waist. Boldly, they entered the Wild Boar Pub.

Donald called out in a preemptive way, "A stout for the lady and rum for me." The pub went quiet when the drinks were brought to the table. Bella delighted in the fact that every eye in the place watched her as she reached for the beer. Donald lifted his glass to Bella, smiled at her and nodded his respects to the onlookers. *He's joining in the show. He's as outrageous as I am. What fun!* They talked of themselves and the tropics until their drinks were finished.

During the conversation, Bella realized that most people called the city Demerara, the regions' historic name, rather than the British name of Georgetown, and Surinam supplanted the name Dutch Guiana. She also realized that she liked Donald Macdonald's attention.

Donald escorted Bella to her hotel and they agreed to have dinner the following night.

***

Frustrated with her lopsided bun, Bella grasped her hair at the crown, braided it and coiled the braid into an elegant topknot. *Much better and fashionable.* She buttoned on her mid-calf shoes and freshened her hands with a splash of water from the bowl on the dressing table. While adjusting the blue taffeta gown over her crinoline, the image in the mirror surprised her, fascinated her. *Can I possibly look that elegant? The weeks on board have tanned my skin from paste white to light bronze. The tan makes my marsh-green eyes appear as bright as green chrysoprase. My upswept hair marks me as a short adult, not a child.* She pinched her cheeks to a soft pink and waited for the seven-thirty arrival of her guardian.

***

Scott-Wallace dipped his head in acknowledgement of the door opening, offered his arm and they left for the dining room. Once seated, claiming to know the menu well, he ordered for the two of them. First came an appetizer of shrimp salad.

Bella smiled and murmured, "How nice." *Identical to my lunch.*

While enjoying lamb chops with fresh mint sauce, she surveyed the dining room. Paraffin lamps, spreading soft light, lined each wall. Potted plants tempered the abrupt corners of the room. In the centre of each white tablecloth a candle reflected its glow on interesting faces and elegant clothes. Bella couldn't believe how happy she felt.

A gentleman appeared beside their table. His surly voice barked, "Scott-Wallace!" Bella eyed the rough-spoken man. "Our business must take place tomorrow," he ordered.

"I will be free by noon," came her partner's dry answer, with a quick tip of his head towards Bella.

Before the man left, he cast his eyes across the room to the dance floor, where a small orchestra played the latest dance tunes mixed with Creole rhythms.

"Come, Scott-Wallace, ask your dinner partner to dance," the man goaded. "I know you dance well. Up now; lead her to the dance floor." He seemed to have some sort of command over her guardian. *Perhaps a senior business partner—and so insistent!*

Bella saw a hand extended. Her guardian said, "Would you care to dance?"

Then she heard her own voice responding, "Why, thank you. I'd love to."

Mr. Scott-Wallace actually dancing! Her feet swirled with his in a waltz. The instant the gruff fellow left the dining room, their dancing ceased. Moments later, Bella found herself back in the hotel corridor that led to their rooms.

Scott-Wallace turned to face Bella. "Breakfast at nine. I shall call for you. Then we will go to the bank. I have ordered a carriage for eleven to take you to some houses you might like. Bring your valise in case you find a suitable place." He turned his key and vanished behind his hotel room door. *Same Scott-Wallace. He nodded, but failed to say goodnight.*

Very clear and very terse. Certainly, if Father asks if the man lived up to his commitment as guardian, I will have to say yes. He's civil enough, but he makes me feel no more feminine than a garden slug.

***

The next morning, his voice all business, they finished breakfast, and with her valise, they walked across the street to the bank. Mr. Scott-Wallace deposited Mr. Bowen's note in an account bearing the name "Isabella Bowen." She added her signature to the bank's registry and trailed her guardian to the waiting carriage.

The carriage descended the main street towards the pier and turned right along the waterfront. The red crushed-gravel road jostled the coach as it passed the white homes that Bella had seen the day before. The farther they went, the less dramatic the houses. *Don't judge them too soon,* she told herself, trying to be positive—*they are well kept two-storey houses, and they face the ocean.*

As the carriage bumped along beside the seawall, she wondered how one reached the shops. At that moment, the carriage stopped its shaking. Bella heard the latch on the carriage door lift. They had arrived at a house named "Sunningdale." Before alighting, Mr. Scott-Wallace turned her way and said, "Your father did not want you to live alone. He suggested a good boarding house."

At that moment Bella realized for the first time that she would not be living in her own grand house like the family home in Plymouth. *Boarding houses offer one room and perhaps a nasty landlord. What was Father thinking?* She knew that her guardian would follow her father's wishes to the letter, and in despair she backed herself into the corner of the carriage, totally deflated.

"I have located three boarding houses that fit within your income," Scott-Wallace continued. "I have brought you to the nicest one first."

A wide flagstone walk led straight towards the raised house painted in white.

"Don't step off the walk, Miss Bowen. The green groundcover harbours poisonous insects." Bella cringed and dutifully walked behind her guardian as they approached the house and climbed the steps. The instant Scott-Wallace cracked the head of his walking stick on the door it opened to reveal a middle-aged woman framed in the entrance. Without waiting for the woman to say a word, Bella's guardian took over the introductions.

"I am Scott-Wallace. I sent you a message that we would call on you this morning. Miss Bowen, I present Gabriella Wilton, owner of this house. Mrs. Wilton, please meet Isabella Bowen of Plymouth, your new boarder."

Bella stepped forward and extended her hand to the lady, even though she felt confused by Scott-Wallace's pronouncement. *"New boarder," did he say? Why, I haven't seen the other two homes, nor any of the rooms in this house.* Her eyes swept over the hallway to determine what she could of the house. *What a man! That rude fellow who appeared beside our table last night put him up to this in order to be free of me by noon.*

Bella wanted to get angry with Mr. Scott-Wallace but she knew it would do no good. Her hands clenched into fists that pressed together below her small bosom. She knew they would not strike out. *Ladies do not have temper tantrums.* Nonetheless, in an act of defiance, her right foot stamped once when she saw that Scott-Wallace had already waved to the coachman to bring in her valise.

"Good day, Mrs. Wilton. Goodbye, Miss Bowen. I am glad you arrived safely." With this he turned and left, having never entered the house past the threshold of the front entrance.

The door bumped shut, cutting off the sunshine. In the grey light of the foyer, Bella felt loneliness invade her spirit. *The future*, she said to herself, thinking of Aunt Kate's words, *look to the future.*

"Well, Mrs. Wilton," said Bella, "Mr. Scott-Wallace has left and somehow I doubt that he plans to return. As I am to be your new boarder, please show me to my room."

3

SUNNINGDALE

From the front entrance of Sunningdale, in an effort to follow Mrs. Wilton upstairs, Bella took the handle of her valise and found she did not have the strength to carry it upstairs. *Oh God, I am too much of a weakling to survive in this country!*

"Here, Miss Bowen, let me carry your bag," said Bella's new landlady, "and please call me Gabby."

"Then you must call me Bella; everyone does," said Bella, somehow sensing that with the adult look of her upswept hair she no longer minded her childhood name.

Bella smiled. *Why do I like this woman already? She's hardly the way I've thought of landladies. But then, how would I know? I've only known landladies in books.*

Gabby lifted the valise with ease and started up the staircase. In silence, Bella followed behind her. *Perhaps forty to forty-five, a pleasant face, medium-brown hair and in good health.* They climbed the stairs and followed the curve of the mahogany railing as it turned towards the front of the house. Gabby entered the front bedroom on the left.

"Sunningdale is not a boarding house, Bella. The grapevine told me that you came to Demerara for your health and needed a place to live. I answered the grapevine. There will be just you and I living here. I use the master bedroom across the hall. Now that I am a widow, I've returned to teaching school. My desk is in the bedroom behind mine. The fourth bedroom is for storage. Put your trunk there if you wish. Have you had lunch?"

Bella admitted that Scott-Wallace had not allowed for lunch in his schedule.

Gabby laughed. "He certainly left in a hurry, didn't he?"

Bella nodded. "Last evening at dinner, he told a man that he would be free by noon, but I didn't expect him to abandon me at the first door that opened."

Gabby grinned. "Never mind, I'm glad you're here. I don't keep any servants, so give me fifteen minutes and then come down to the kitchen and we'll get acquainted over a lunch of cheese, fruit and dry toast." *Just the lunch I like. I must tell her that I will be out for dinner this evening.*

Bella turned to inspect the room. Serviceable described it: dark mahogany furniture and ugly green shutters to keep out the heat. She pushed at the shutters and beheld a view of the ocean sparkling with sunshine. The view made up for any shortcomings of the room. She stood mesmerized by the rolling sea, with each wave throwing white spray to the winds as it crashed against the seawall. *Do those waves travel on the Gulf Stream to rock Father's barges? Does my family miss me?* Eyes misting, she watched the waves and wondered. Unrewarded with an answer, practical thoughts forced her to open her valise, unpack and return to the main floor for lunch.

"Gabby," said Bella, carrying a jar of beer into the kitchen. "I drink a half-pint of stout every day for my health. The ship gave me the few remaining jars of my father's supply for the voyage. May I keep them in your icebox?"

Gabby smiled and said, "Then I'll join you each day with my bit of wine."

***

After lunch Bella rested. She wanted to be fresh and perfectly groomed for the arrival of Donald Macdonald. Fantasies filled her head with

Prince Charming escorting her to parties, teaching her to ride astride a horse—she laughed—*perhaps riding a horse is the one thing for which my bowed legs are well suited. I hope Gabby is right when she says that he'll know how to find me at Sunningdale.*

***

Knowing that nightfall drops like a dark robe at six o'clock on the equator, Bella lit the parlour lamp. With the living.room windows open to catch the onshore breeze, she heard the rattle of carriage wheels on gravel long before she could see its outline against the phosphorescent glow of the ocean. Her prince arrived exactly at seven. She answered his soft drum on the door, and there he stood, in a pristine white suit set off with a royal blue cravat. *Oh my! I believe I am in love, but how would I know so soon? Quit gawping, Bella. Say something.*

"How ever did you know to come to Sunningdale?" Bella's face radiated a beauty that she did not know she possessed.

Donald chuckled. "I noted the carriage you hired this morning and asked a young Creole to watch for its return; then I asked the coachman where he had taken you."

Gabby appeared at the end of the hall leading from the back of the house.

"Gabby," called Bella. "Come and meet my friend from back home, Mr. Donald Macdonald." Turning towards Donald she added, "And this is Gabriella Wilton, who wishes to be known as Gabby."

With introductions over, Donald Macdonald, with Bella on his arm, said goodnight to Gabby. Soon the clip-clop of horse's hooves broke the stillness as the carriage jiggled its way into town. Through the carriage window Bella could see a black velvet sky sprinkled with a thousand pinpoints of light. She had to control herself to keep from squeezing tight to the warm body next to her as lovers in books would do. Her emotions had never felt like this before. She forcibly put her hands in her lap and tried to think of something to say besides blurting, "My dearest, I love you."

Donald saved the situation by asking about Sunningdale and Mrs. Wilton. The carriage rumbled on and he told her of things she must see while living in Georgetown. She found his conversation had no emotion compared to her thoughts. *I wonder if he knows that this is my first evening engagement.*

When the carriage stopped she could see that they were on a side street about to enter an inn painted blue and white. The interior was dark and smoky. When her eyes became accustomed to the dim light she could see plank tables, worn from years of use, and heavy wooden chairs. By the lamp shining on the waiter's desk Bella saw a small Dutch flag, the flag of Paramaribo, and knew that Donald had brought her to his favourite Dutch restaurant.

Much to her surprise and delight, Bella found it easy to carry on a conversation with this man she hardly knew. They spoke of his trip up the coast from Paramaribo on the *Schooner Van Dam*, of his home near Inverurie, Scotland, and of how his education as a mining engineer had brought him to Surinam in search of gold.

"When you are tramping through the jungle," said Donald, "you might see cute armadillos and monkeys, or killer jaguars and labaria rattle snakes."

Is he joking or being serious? Why does this matter? Why doesn't he talk about the future? Maybe invite me to Surinam? Bella turned the subject back to Paramaribo.

Donald explained that he managed a sugar plantation, as dictated by need for income during the rainy seasons while he continued his search for a goldmine in the hills beyond the jungle a few months at a time when the rain stopped.

Maybe this is my introduction to Paramaribo, just small talk to acquaint me with Surinam. Bella did not interrupt his long stretches of dialogue.

"The original German planter named the plantation 'Reiche Ernte,' meaning 'Rich Harvest.' Then, like many German immigrants in the 1830s, he died of jungle fever. A Dutchman in the old country owns the plantation now." A waiter refilled their glasses with white wine. ·

"Ernte stretches back from the Surinam River side by side with other plantations all along the river's west bank. Ernte is fairly close to Paramaribo."

Perhaps if I place my left hand nonchalantly on the table he might hold it.

"Even today," exclaimed Donald as he sipped his wine, "the silt of the great Amazon River floods into the ocean and then . . ." *Is my hand not close enough? He just keeps on talking.* ". . . during high tides and storms the current sweeps north along the coast and washes the silt ashore onto the low coastal plains." *Isn't attracting a man's attention an attribute of all women? Why, he hasn't even noticed my pretty gown.*

Bella found the geography lesson interesting but wondered when he would talk of them, of what they might do together tomorrow and the night after.

When he told her that he lived right in the centre of Paramaribo rather than in the big house on the plantation she became more excited and lifted her chin a little so that the candlelight might enhance her shining green eyes. She listened even more intently when he claimed that the social life of the plantation elite delighted the wives of the managers. She found it difficult to concentrate on his melodic voice while wondering *What about us? Does he not realize I adore him?*

The evening grew late and Donald became serious. "I had hoped to show you lovely areas of Georgetown on other evenings, Bella, but today I received word that I must return to the plantation tomorrow. The indentured workers from India are giving the overseer a bit of trouble. I leave for Paramaribo on the SS *Balfour* at daybreak. I will write to see how you are getting along. If you wish to write me, address it to Reiche Ernte, Paramaribo, and Dirk, my stable boy, will bring it to me from the post office."

Donald's news came as such a jolt that Bella's former ability to converse evaporated. Her mouth opened in a little "oh" and failed to close. The stardust vanished from her world. Donald continued to talk but Bella could only think of his departure. *The evening has been cordial. He has not tried to hold my hand. His actions seem more like that of an older brother.* She chastised herself for being foolish enough to fall in love with this man. They drove back to Sunningdale still talking of nothings. Bella felt as if her heart had been wrung out like a common dishrag.

"Good night, sweet Bella. It feels like we've been close ever since we met years ago. I won't forget you, I promise." Donald escorted her to the door of Sunningdale and returned to town in the carriage. *Sweet Bella! Does he say that to all the girls? I'm fooling myself to think he admired me when at our house years ago and still admires me. Why can't I remember him? I hope he writes soon. But what if he doesn't?*

***

Bella's trunk arrived the next day. With little enthusiasm, she folded underthings into drawers, hung gowns in the wardrobe and took her meals with Gabby. Finally, at evening tea Gabby said with candour, "You are unhappy, Bella. If we are going to live in the same house, I think it wise to confide in each other. Sharing your problems will help you find a life in British Guiana—a life with satisfaction, security and happiness."

How can I tell this woman that my heart aches? Bella looked down at her hands, rubbing one against the other, and started to explain her confused emotions.

"On board ship I felt so alone, but when I saw the shores of the tropics come into view, my spirits burst with happiness because I felt sure that my life would have a new beginning. Then I couldn't lift my suitcase and realized my weakness would never allow me to succeed in this country." Tears came. Gabby guided Bella to the settee and put her arm around the sobbing bit of a woman. Bella continued.

"Excitement raced through my body when Mr. Scott-Wallace told me that we were going to look at 'houses' until he divulged that we would be looking at 'boarding houses.' Only then did I realize that I would not own a nice home like the houses of women in my books." Bella wiped her eyes and spoke between sobs. "Just as I was adjusting to the idea of looking at three boarding houses, Scott-Wallace dumped me on the doorstep of Sunningdale without letting me make the choice as promised." Bella's sobs shook her whole body. "I felt so alone standing there as the door closed. I feel so alone . . ."

Gabby hugged the heaving shoulders to relieve her new boarder's distress.

"Last night, I . . ." Bella sobbed, "I thought . . . This sounds so foolish. Gabby, please don't laugh. I've never gone out with a man before and I've fallen in love with the first decent one I've met and he doesn't love me. How do you make a man realize you love him? He walked out of my life in a minute." The sobbing started afresh.

"Oh Gabby," she wailed. "He's gone, and it's all because I am so plain and sickly. I am too short for him. I bob along when I walk because I have rickets." A fresh cascade of sobbing filled the room. "And it's all because I didn't drink my milk."

Gabby consoled her for a few minutes to stop the crying, then, in her kindly but insistent schoolteacher's voice, she said, "There is more to life than men, my dear. You are here now—learn to enjoy it. Plan little goals, achieve them and you will find happiness wherever you live."

To Bella she sounded like Aunt Kate saying, "Look to the future."

***

Over the next week, in the endless hours of the day when Gabby taught at the primary school, Bella considered Gabby's advice about planning and achieving little goals. *It's good advice but quite useless. If my goal is to see Donald, how can I plan that?*

Instead of seeing the sun as a thing of beauty, painting the bougainvillea in many shades of pink, she rejected the rays of the sun as hot—too hot—and the air, too humid and quite unbearable. Most of her dresses were too warm for temperatures in the low eighties. *I have nothing to wear and nothing to read. Even if I wanted to go to town, I have no way to summon a carriage. Nothing good will come from living in British Guiana. Why did I refuse to drink my milk? Were those I left in Plymouth really happy to see me leave?* Endless questions with no answers. Endless thoughts, all negative.

***

Gabby allowed Bella to rest and fuss until the weekend. Then on Sunday, at breakfast, she confided her own story to Bella.

"I know the pain of suddenly being wrenched away from one life and dropped into a new one through no decision of your own making.

27

Bella, you are beset with rickets and I, with instant widowhood. One year ago my husband, a professional engineer for the Demerara Railroad Company, fell between two coaches of a train while testing new trackage going east out of Georgetown. Poor Clifford leaned over the barrier guarding a coach hitch. Suddenly, the handrail gave way. His body pitched forward under the wheels. They brought him home in pieces."

Bella's head swung in tiny movements of disbelief as she stretched forth a consoling hand to cover Gabby's hand. After a quiet moment, Gabby resumed their conversation with a lighter tone.

"Bella, as you can see, I do all my own work around the house. I have to because the remuneration for teachers is very low, yet I want to stay in my home. Rather than have servants, I find it very satisfying to be able to cook, clean, test the water cistern or shop in the market—whatever job presents itself. I think you should follow me around and learn to do these chores too. Some day when you have servants in your own home you will need to know how to manage a household in the tropics."

Bella had no choice but to oblige her, for she had nothing else to do. She felt degraded from her days in Plymouth—wearing a kitchen apron, cooking with the landlady, washing dishes and her clothes, cleaning the house and sweeping the flagstone walk where neighbours might see her. Yet, she recognized that with the stigma of servants' work came improvements in her health. Even though she added no weight to her body, her appetite and strength increased. At night she went to bed bone-weary and slept until well after Gabby left for school.

***

One Saturday at the breakfast table, with sunshine highlighting the flowers at the windowsill, Gabby put down her teacup and turned to Bella.

"Before he died, Clifford gave me one of those newly invented treadle sewing machines. It lies idle in the storage room. Could you sew clothes suitable for the tropics?"

I can do needlework but certainly not sew clothes! That's work for a seamstress. But Gabby's question needs an answer, and to say that I cannot sew would be a lie. So be it. If I must live here for my health and die an old maid wearing hand-made clothes, that must be what God intends for me.

Bella flapped her eyes shut for a moment. *Perhaps it is an opportunity I must accept if I am to look to the future, not the past.* She squared her shoulders and thanked Gabby for her suggestion. "I have never worked on clothing. Maybe I can try to design and sew a summer gown, but how do I get to town to buy material, buttons and thread?"

"Quite simply," said Gabby. "You use my trap and the dapple-grey mare that I call my pony because she isn't very big. Come, we'll walk down the trail to the end of my property, and in the trees back there, you will meet Strawberry. Dominic, the neighbour's manservant, looks after her. I'll teach you how to drive the trap and you can go to town whenever you please. A friend will drive me to work when you wish to use it."

With Gabby chatting all the way, Bella followed after her down the narrow path worn through the matted tropical growth by Strawberry and the trap.

"Don't wander off the path, Bella. Poisonous insects, fungi and all sorts of nasty things live in that undergrowth."

Adrenaline coursed through Bella's body. She looked at the wall of green leaves and black shadows crowding her on either side and wondered how Gabby could continue towards the tall palms quite unconcerned by the dangers surrounding them. Despite her fearful jungle fantasies, she willed herself to walk in Gabby's footsteps farther and farther from the safety of the house.

"Today we have high thin cloud, Bella; it won't be quite so hot. It's a perfect day to go into town and look in the shops. If Dominic isn't there, we'll have to brush down Strawberry and harness her ourselves."

Now I'm to be a common stable boy, Bella said to herself when she saw the pony's rough wooden shelter. The thought of walking near enough to touch Strawberry, let alone brush or harness the horse, terrified her. Still, she stayed resolutely behind Gabby as they approached. Strawberry neighed and came galloping over for her treat. Bella flinched but stood her ground as the pounding hooves came straight for her.

"Strawberry, meet Bella," called Gabby, with a tug on Bella's arm to have her step closer to the rambunctious mare. "Stroke her nose, Bella.

Here is a carrot. Hold it in the flattened palm of your hand close to her lips. Her gentle nibble will tickle, so don't pull your hand away. That would tell her that you're frightened. You'll soon get to know her."

Bella held out her hand as directed and squeezed her eyes shut as she saw Strawberry's lips curl back to take the carrot with yellowed teeth.

"Here's a brush. You take that side and I'll take this side. Start with the neck."

It's a good thing Strawberry is short or I'd be reduced to polishing her hooves. Bella and Gabby harnessed the pony, added the trap, gathered the market baskets and headed parallel to the seawall into town. As they drove along Gabby started teaching Bella how to drive the trap. At one point she handed the reins to Bella. Strawberry stopped in her tracks.

"She knew that the reins changed hands!" cried Bella.

Once Gabby took over the reins, Strawberry continued into the centre of Demerara, where Gabby showed Bella her favourite shops. After lunch at the Georgetown Club, they visited the market. On the way home, the trap bumped along, loaded down with overflowing market baskets, a case of stout and things for Bella's sewing. *With Gabby's kindness and the beauty of my surroundings, I must be more positive. If this is to be my life, then so be it. I shouldn't have expected Donald to reappear at the Club.*

***

Rainy season came upon them. Every day, rain streamed down the windows and pounded the flowers at the rear of the house. Humidity rose like a fog when the sun did appear. The leaden sky compelled Bella to spend many lonely hours indoors. She kept her hands busy making a set of lace collar and cuffs to give Gabby on Christmas Day. Although her hands flew through the motions, her thoughts were of Plymouth. *I must write a letter now so they have it by Christmas—one that sounds cheerful! I'll wish them Good Health and Good Fortune for the New Year. In January, I'll write again to tell them about the happy Christmas I had here in the tropics, even if it isn't.* She sat down at her dresser, ready to write the first Christmas letter.

"Dear Mother and Father, Althea, Constance and Flora," she wrote.

Now what can I say? I certainly won't tell them that I have learned to cook or shovel out Strawberry's stall. They would never understand the feeling of accomplishment that I have when working around Sunningdale. No, I must tell them all about Georgetown and what it has accomplished in fifty years.

She made a list of suitable subjects. *My sisters will want to know about eligible bachelors. I'll have to find a way to get around that subject. Perhaps if I went to St. George's Church of England more often, I might meet somebody, but Gabby doesn't care to go. She thinks God took "dear Clifford" away from her far too soon. I feel down. I must talk Gabby into going out somewhere.*

Bella put God and Clifford aside and wrote a masterfully happy letter, even though she yearned for her family. She stood the letter on the dresser for the next time she went into town. She heard Gabby come in from school and joined her for tea.

"We must do something for Christmas, Gabby. What do you usually do?"

Gabby lifted her shoulders in a slight shrug. "Since dear Clifford died, I haven't done anything. Colonists' parties seldom include single people or widows."

"Well!" said Bella, mimicking Gabby's stern teacher's voice, "we are going to do something, you and I, together. First, I would like to go to the midnight service on Christmas Eve. The next day, I propose that we dress in our finest gowns and jewellery and have Christmas dinner at the hotel."

By this time Gabby had a big smile on her face. "You think you might spy a bachelor in church or be asked to dance at the hotel. Is that it?" She broke out laughing.

"Never mind my motives, Gabby. I think it would be nice to do these two things. You are not officially in mourning any more, no matter how you feel personally. We'll hire a carriage and go to dinner in style." After a moment, Bella squeaked with delight: "Do you want to have the pleasure of being ogled in an all-men's establishment? We can stop for our drinks right there in the men's lounge before dinner."

***

The church service brought serenity, but Bella could see no eager young bachelors in attendance. As promised, in the hotel lounge the men all stared at the two lovely ladies who put their elbows on the bar. To tease the onlookers, Bella lifted her skirt and placed her dainty foot on the brass foot-rail. The bartender brought one woman red wine and the other—horror of horrors—a half-pint of black stout. Bella's eyes noted the reaction of the men in the lounge and smiled. *This is no longer an all-men's lounge.* After dinner, no gentleman asked them to dance. Bella felt as if their two outings had been failures.

On December the thirty-first, they welcomed in the New Year by themselves at Sunningdale. The clock struck twelve times.

"Bella," said Gabby as they toasted each other with red wine. *Oh dear, that's her serious voice; she has something on her mind.* "It is now January the 1st, 1888, and time to start a New Year. You've been here six months and you have struggled valiantly to cope with your new life by learning skills to exist here in the tropics. Emotional stress comes with learning new ways that are contrary to your old ways. At first life is exciting and fun. By three months everything seems bleak. The person either throws herself into work or cries the hours away. If a newcomer finds things to do, by six months they start to appreciate each day. You have come through your six months admirably. I drink to your success." Bella threw her arms around Gabby for her motherly lecture.

"Emotional stress?" said Bella. "That was my problem? I didn't know. I just thought I wasn't able to cope—thought I would always be a failure, an unwanted old maid. Why didn't you explain this to me earlier?"

Gabby clasped her hands. "It doesn't work that way, Bella. You have to come through on your own. Some day you will meet a newcomer and help her to accept change or wave her goodbye at the docks if she's found no way to keep her brain and hands busy."

Bella moved back a pace, mystified by Gabby's words. "You make it sound like I've accomplished something when I've done nothing extraordinary."

"That's not so, Bella!" exploded Gabby. "You have allowed yourself to drop old customs and to learn many things that will help you cope.

The real healing shows in the pride and enjoyment you derive from your accomplishments. You will be fine now. Goodnight. I'll see you in the morning."

***

1888, thought Bella as she turned back the covers on her bed. *I may have learned to cope, but I shall turn twenty-six on the twentieth of May—one year older and still a spinster. Why don't men choose the plain girls, like me?*

She set the mosquito netting to guard against mosquitoes that spread yellow fever, blew out the lamp and stretched out on the bed, thinking of Gabby's words about emotions. *If I'm ready for change, what will 1888 bring?*

4

LIFE IN THE TROPICS

In January the sun returned to glint off the abundance of green leaves that formed the wall of jungle at the back of the house. Bella went to her room to face writing the second letter. "Dear Family," she started. After a long pause, she added, "I must tell you about the lovely Christmas Gabby and I shared here in Georgetown, but first I hope all is well in Plymouth, for I have not yet received a Christmas letter from you." She wrote about the book called *Plants and Animals of the Tropics* that she received from Gabby. She did not tell them that she, herself, would harness the horse and trap for the trip to town to post the letter. She knew they would never understand.

For this one short month of sunshine, the days passed easily. Bella's persistence with learning how to be independent sent her to bed each night with a happy tiredness instead of the former weariness. During the day, with Gabby at school, concentration on the household jobs left little time to think of Donald, but those moments before she fell asleep were agony. ·

That's it! I'll write to him and tell him that I love him. No, I had better say that he continues to be in my thoughts. Bella sat down at her vanity with paper and pen. Thoughts from her heart would not form properly into words in her mind. *Perhaps I should merely write of all the things that I have learned to do for myself.* That thought didn't please her either, for it held no emotion. Finally, exasperated with the difficulty of writing of loving desires, she threw the pen down with tears in her eyes and crushed the paper. *I must lose myself in sewing. The concentration required for sewing will drown Donald Macdonald from my thoughts!*

***

Gabby took Bella's measurements one evening after work. Bella sucked in her breath as she dropped the final petticoat. Gabby didn't say a word when she saw Bella's dreadfully curved legs, narrow hips and tiny pigeon-breasted chest. *Now she knows how deformed I am. Would Donald want me this way? Not likely. Sewing must wipe him from my mind.*

Bella measured the cut of the simplest gown she owned. With her eye for design and hard work on the treadle, the finished sea-green gown could easily have come from a London shop. Spurred on by her success, Bella designed five more dresses and used the dry month of January to visit the market for suitable materials.

February and the beginning of the next rainy season will give me ample time to sew. Today, I'll try walking to the end of the seawall.

The gravel surface of the road pressed against the thin soles of her shoes and she cursed the "knobblies." The constant splash and sucking roar of the waves against the seawall brought thoughts of home. She still hadn't had a letter from her family, despite her many letters to them. "No letter," she whispered out to sea. Without conscious expectation, the thought of a letter forced the handsome face of Donald Macdonald to form in her mind. *Will I never forget him! Is it not obvious that he has no interest in me? Enough of walking—I shall sew.*

Bella spent her days at the treadle machine, forcing her thin bowed legs to pump until they ached. She continued this self-destruction until she owned three new summer gowns. Thoughts of Donald Macdonald receded as she worked every moment of the day to make it so. *Even an old maid with no place to go must have clothes!*

The sun shone a few hours every day, but Bella continued her insular life of pumping furiously on the sewing machine's treadle. In her state of personal punishment she barely noticed the rain that whipped across her window, pressured by strong winds.

One evening after tea she blurted: "Gabby, in all the months since I arrived here no one has come to the house. I don't even know your neighbours. Let's have a party. I'm working on the fifth gown and when it's finished I will have nothing to keep me busy. I think we should have a magnificent party. What do you think?"

Gabby puckered her brow in thought. "I suppose we could invite some of the teachers from school, perhaps have four in for the evening meal."

"We can do that too, but I mean a big party."

Subconsciously, Gabby rubbed her fingers over her wedding ring. "That might be difficult," she said. "Somehow, society overlooks inviting widows to parties held for couples. I haven't been to a mixed social event since my husband's accident a year and a half ago. Perhaps we could have a Sunday afternoon tea."

Bella opened her eyes wide with a hopeful look on her face and asked, "After that could we hold a mixed party?"

Gabby smiled. "I can see what you are after. You're still looking for eligible bachelors. My friends are all married and quite unavailable."

"You mean you don't know any bachelors? That's the whole point of the party—to mix them in with the guests and see if they notice me. I don't want to be an old maid."

***

Bella met four ladies when they had Gabby's teacher-friends over for dinner one night. The evening passed pleasantly with fine food, wine and conversation, but she felt unfulfilled despite her success at planning and cooking for the event.

***

Bella started to badger Gabby to make a list of the ladies they could invite for tea.

"Afternoon tea," said Gabby thoughtfully. She counted the chairs in the parlour and added six more with the dining room chairs. "We can seat twelve people in the parlour; less you and me, that makes ten. I'll invite the neighbours from each side. I might be able to think of eight more women who would like to come. I'll work on a list."

Once Gabby gave Bella the list, she wrote ten personal invitations and drove into Demerara to drop the letters at the post office. She checked for mail addressed to Sunningdale. There were no letters. She thought that she had wiped Donald Macdonald from her thoughts, yet her disappointment at finding no letter from him proved that he still dwelled in her mind. The crushed rock in the road seemed twice as bumpy as Bella brooded all the way home. *You are miserable, Bella. Don't blame the road. Donald has forgotten you, so you must forget him and make a life for yourself in Demerara, starting with this party. It's in two weeks and you must be ready for it. Forget Donald!*

Bella and the trap jogged on towards Sunningdale. *I refuse to serve dainty sandwiches or strawberries and clotted cream on a baking powder biscuit. No, my party will be different, unique.*

Planning, organizing and making arrangements allowed Bella to experience, for the first time, the personal freedom of her new life in the tropics—*making* the plans this time instead of following someone else's directions. That evening, Bella used the word "emancipated" when discussing this new sense of direction with Gabby.

"You are right, Gabby—set little goals, accomplish them and life looks brighter."

***

On the Saturday night before the Sunday afternoon tea party, Bella checked the flowers in the dining room and parlour. At the front entrance she admired the two bouquets of long-stemmed roses to be placed on either side of the front steps. Finally, she checked the nosegay she had placed in the private room—the "privy," as everyone called it.

"Gabby, I'm ready, except for a few last minute hors d'oeuvres to prepare in the morning. Come and see."

There, on a white linen tablecloth in the dining room, sat Gabby's gleaming silver tea service, free of tarnish. Between the tea service and a vase of daisies at the other end of the table, Bella had set out twelve wine glasses, six beer glasses and twelve teacups.

"Why the wine and beer glasses, Bella?"

"Why not? They all think of me as that wild woman who drinks stout in their pubs, so why shouldn't I drink stout? Maybe some of them would like to try it but have never had the opportunity." For the first time, Gabby noticed a determined tone to Bella's voice.

"And wine?" asked Gabby. "It's supposed to be a *tea* party."

"Watch and see. With no men around, I'm quite sure the ladies will all have wine or beer before they have tea. It will loosen their tongues and they'll have a grand time. You might say that, instead of a tea party, I've planned a 'party' party just for women. The wine will do wonders for their inhibitions."

"Bella, Bella, aren't you the sly one? Maybe my two teacher-friends might choose wine or stout, and likely one of the next door neighbours. I know she drinks by the way I hear her carousing around their property on her horse." Then, with her arms extended, Gabby slapped imaginary reins and shouted, "Gedda move on. Yer as shlow azh a mule. Yee-haw!" Bella laughed at this candid description of their neighbour to the east.

"What if your stout shocks everyone?" asked Gabby.

"Then I will have lived up to their opinion of me and nothing will have changed."

***

On Sunday morning white fluffy clouds drifted over the ocean. Bella did not notice the onshore breeze when she placed the two urns of flowers outside the front door. Soon, the scudding clouds cut off the sun as they blew inland. Darker clouds waited out at sea while Bella bustled around in the kitchen preparing her *pièce de résistance*. From the icebox she removed the crustless three-inch square pieces of thinly sliced white bread. She coated the slices with a tasty cream sauce made from fresh mushrooms and rolled each piece of bread into a dainty log, spiked through with a toothpick to hold it rolled until they went into the oven. She knew that once the rolls were toasted to a golden brown in the cook-stove they would flare out in a dainty fashion at the ends and stay rolled without the toothpicks. While still hot from the oven, she planned to serve them peeking out of a white napkin folded on a silver tray. After lunch she and Gabby went to dress in the gowns that each had prepared for the occasion.

***

"Did you hear that loud noise outside, Gabby? It didn't sound like the blast of a foghorn." Rain slashed across Bella's big front window. Like a snapping mast, another crack of thunder rattled the shutters.

"Pretend this isn't happening," Bella murmured aloud. She rushed into Gabby's room in her crinoline and threw herself across Gabby's feather bed and sobbed. Out at sea, shards of lightning streaked into the rebellious waves. The cascading roar of thunder rumbled as the rain pounded the road below.

"The ladies will not venture this far from town in this storm," cried Bella. "My party will be a disaster!"

"Maybe the rain will stop," said Gabby. "My neighbours and the teachers live close by. You'll have to be ready for them, so dry your eyes and finish dressing." Again, Gabby had used her determined teacher's voice that always made Bella feel that she must obey.

***

At two o'clock the two teachers came up the walk, protected from the steady rain by oversized umbrellas. When Bella opened the door for them, she noticed that the earlier sudden torrent of rain had pounded the roses and scattered pink petals in the ladies' path. *A carpet of fresh flower petals to welcome our guests like royalty.* She opened the door wide for Susan Lorry and Kathryn O'Toole, two of the teachers Bella had met when they came for dinner. They took seats in the parlour and the doorknocker clacked again. The horse-riding neighbour from the east, all smiles, flounced into the front entrance.

"Mrs. Schultema, please meet Isabella Bowen, from Plymouth," said Gabby. "Bella, this is my neighbour, Gussie." Gabby escorted Gussie into the parlour to meet the teachers while Bella waited for the carriage pulling up in front of the house. Dominic carried an umbrella above the lady's head as she held her skirts high and scurried up the steps. Seeing Dominic, Bella knew that the lady lived on the west side of them.

"Come in, come in," said Bella, raising her head to engage the neighbour's eyes. "You must be Elizabeth Neville. I'm Bella, the woman from Plymouth who drinks stout." She laughed. "I say that because everyone in town seems to know. The doctor ordered it for my health and I find it delightful. Let me take your shawl."

After introductions, Bella allowed the ladies to visit. When no other guests came knocking to join the six of them, she stood in the dining room archway and announced that, as Sunningdale did not use servants, she would like them to pass into the dining room and choose their own refreshment. The ladies saw the frosted stout glasses—more than just one for Bella.

"May I have stout?" asked Kathryn O'Toole. "I always stole a sip of my grandfather's stout in Dublin and I rather like it."

"I'll try it too," said Gussie Schultima with a sly glance. "I've never tasted it before." Bella doubted this. Gabby and the other two chose red wine.

"How did you know they would choose spirits over tea?" Gabby whispered to Bella.

"Women behave differently without their husbands. At the club, I noticed that women with their husbands have tea, but with only women they have wine."

Soon the ladies' gloves were off so that they could dip their fingers into the dishes of roasted nuts that Bella had placed on the side-tables. The mushroom rolls were a great success and the women were having a splendid time chatting about the local gossip and their health problems. After one drink, as Bella expected, they had no inhibitions about going to the dining room table for refills. Mrs. Schultema asked if she might remove her large hat. In no time, four elegant hats were stacked on the small server in the hall. In high spirits, the ladies returned the six dining room chairs to the dining room and seated themselves around the table. When they switched to tea, Bella placed three plates of sweets in the centre of the table.

"Ah-fer all, we should 'ave tea," slurred Gussie Schultima. "Bella invited us to a tea party and this's the finesht one I've ever atten'ed. Do you serve *tea* offen, Bella? My huzshban, Izsak, wouldn' allow me to hold a ladies' tea party like this even though he hazsh drinking parties for men all the time. Yesh, now we'll 'ave tea—strong black tea."

Bella's tea party lasted until six o'clock. Sitting around the table, the guests had a lively visit over many cups of tea and the sweets that disappeared from the plates. All went home sober (to the eye) and were profuse in their appreciation of the lovely party.

"Bella," cried Gabby, "your party pleased everyone, although the grapevine might never know that you served stout and wine."

"It won't?" said Bella. "How will word get around to all of the young bachelors that I'm a new kind of woman in their midst—one that likes to take risks and have fun—one that they should take out for dinner?"

Gabby laughed and poured herself another wine. "We'll just have to listen to the grapevine and discover if news of this party leaks into the gossip. If it does, perhaps you will have a caller."

A week went by, and no gentleman called on either Bella or Gabby.

***

Three days later, Bella drove into town. By the time she returned home, Gabby had finished school for the day. She came out to help Bella remove Strawberry's harness.

"Strawberry can wait," squealed Bella. "Look what waited for me at the post office!" She waved a square white envelope, and despite her bowed legs, she jumped from the trap in her excitement. "It's a letter from Donald Macdonald," she cooed. "He hasn't forgotten me. He says he's coming to Demerara in a month, on April 14, and he wants to see me—wants to take me out for dinner. He says he will be in town for two weeks, says to write him if I'll be free those weeks. Imagine, two weeks!" Clutching the letter, she twirled around and around in Strawberry's paddock as best she could in her small-heeled shoes, happy as a schoolgirl.

5

THE RETURN OF DONALD MACDONALD

Bella heard the grandfather clock of Sunningdale chime seven times. Once again, she rose from the wicker chair and stared through the living room window into darkness.

"For goodness' sake, Bella!" said Gabby in her teacher's voice. "You answered his letter and told him you would count the days until his arrival—or whatever you said—and posted it to Paramaribo. Quit fussing; he'll be along."

Bella fidgeted as she stood at the window in her newest gown, a burgundy satin. A string of her mother's pearls rested on her bosom and the matching bracelet, strung around her braided topknot, glowed in an iridescent white against her black hair.

"I should have met the boat," murmured Bella.

"Bella, you look absolutely stunning except for that dreadful scowl. Go to the mirror in the privy and smile at yourself until the twinkle returns to your eyes. He could arrive at any moment." Like a chick following the cluck of a mother hen, Bella left for the privy to smile into the mirror and tweak her cheeks to a rosy red. "Bella! Come quickly. Someone's coming up the walk!"

Bella checked the mirror for a beautiful smile and rushed to the foyer in time for the doorknocker. She threw the door open and held out her hands to welcome her love.

"Why, Bella," said Gussie Schultema, "aren't you the pretty one this evening. I thought this might be a good time to drop by for cards, but I see that perhaps it isn't. Maybe just one little drink together, then. How about that?"

Bella wanted to shoo her out as fast as she could, but Gussie had already moved into the parlour. Gabby came to Bella's rescue by offering Gussie a glass of wine.

"Here you are, Gussie. Sit and chat with me. You're lucky; that is the last drop of wine in the bottle," said Gabby. Bella returned to the window. The clock chimed a short set of notes. *Seven-thirty. He's not coming.* She excused herself and ran up to her room. Mrs. Schultema and her wine disappeared as quickly as her unannounced visit.

"Bella," Gabby called up the stairs. "Gussie's gone. Come down! Don't go ruining your pretty face with tears. Maybe he had work to finish before he could come." Gabby climbed the first stair and repeated herself. Bella grimaced in the mirror and appeared at the head of the stairs, working on a weak smile. A soft knock sent Gabby scurrying across the foyer to the door. She clutched at the brass door handle and stepped aside with the swing of the door. There stood Bella's Prince Charming in a white suit.

Bella floated down the stairs and rushed across the foyer towards Donald with the poise and emotion of a well-rehearsed theatre drama. Smiling, Donald brought forth a huge bouquet of roses. He winked and pitched the paper cone of flowers to Gabby just in time to bend down and sweep Bella into his arms for a kiss. *A kiss so tender my heart is pounding, even my toes are tingling. How magical is love! I wish I could twirl forever in his arms, my lips on his. Oh Donald, I am yours; I pray that you notice.*

"You wrote me such a lovely letter, Bella, that I didn't think you would mind me giving you a first kiss."

Bella wagged her head. "Not at all, moustache included; I rather thought you'd write again," she smiled.

"I'm a bachelor, Bella, inexperienced in writing letters to women." He laughed, "But I knew enough to bring you flowers." He retrieved the bouquet from Gabby and settled the cone of roses into the crook of Bella's arm.

"For you, little princess."

"Why, thank you, Donald," she said with an upward tilt of the head, a teasing smile and a vamp-like beckon. "Come down here and I'll give you another hug and kiss for the roses." Donald went down on his knees and they kissed and hugged again. "Donald, however did you choose this colour—a deep burgundy? They are exactly the same colour as my dress." Donald tipped his head towards one shoulder for an answer so Bella wouldn't see him wink at Gabby.

Bella pulled at one of the roses, and with the help of Donald's penknife, she snapped off most of the stem. Centering the rose near the back of her head, she slid it under the white pearls and secured it with the small curved comb. With her black upsweep and a rose matching her dress tucked beside the pearls, Bella looked stunning.

"Look at you, Bella!" cried Donald. "You are so vibrant and full of energy. Whatever have you been doing with yourself for the past eight months?"

"What have I been doing?" she answered in a strong voice like Gabby's. "I've been mucking the stables, clipping undergrowth on Strawberry's path, washing dishes, weeding, cleaning and making the meals. This landlady of mine is always at me."

Bella sounded so serious that Donald's expression didn't change until Gabby hooted with laughter. "That's right, Donald. Bella followed me around until she learned to do all those things and more."

Bella lifted her skirt a smidgen, enough to see only her ankle but suggestive of a leg show. "Just call me 'Muscles' from rocking the treadle on Gabby's sewing machine." Bella took a turn to model her gown. "I designed and sewed my gown just for this evening." She fluttered her dark eyelashes in a big act to look coy and asked, "Do you like it?" While Donald laughed at her playfulness, he remembered the fire of life that he saw in Bella back in Plymouth and again when they went drinking at the Wild Boar Pub.

"I'll put the roses in the crystal vase," said Gabby. "You two make yourself comfortable in the parlour."

"Thanks, but no, we won't stay, Gabby," said Donald. "I have a reservation at the hotel dining room this evening and we must be on our way." Bella retrieved her evening bag from the living room and returned with a white stole draped over her shoulders. Gabby reappeared with the roses to see the pair standing together, hand in hand, with mutual adoration shining in their eyes. With Gabby's reappearance, the couple said good evening and stepped out into a moonlit night.

***

The hotel maître d' led Bella and Donald to a table beside the dance floor marked "Reserved." Without a word, a waiter arrived, carrying a silver stand filled with ice and a bottle of champagne.

"To my Rosebud," Donald said, raising his glass.

"If I am your Rosebud, what would you like to be called? Prince Charming? Squire McDee? Duke?" The banter played back and forth while they gazed into each other's eyes. Finally, they looked at the menu.

"In celebration of your return," said Bella, "I shall have pan-fried queriman and a small salad." Donald concurred. Shortly, the waiter arrived with two dinners that included rice and asparagus as well. Donald refilled their glasses and, with a boyish grin, tied the linen napkin under his chin and patted it into place.

Many times over, the whole evening far surpassed the night Bella had dined and danced with Mr. Scott-Wallace. The plants, the lamps, the table candles shining on faces and fancy clothing were all the same, yet tonight felt special, quite magical. They finished the champagne and danced to the music until they exhausted their energies.

Back at the table, Donald took Bella's hand and asked in a serious voice, "Do you mind that I am eight years older than you?"

With eyes twinkling, Bella replied, "Do you mind that I am half your height?"

"Come, come," laughed Donald, "two-thirds my height, perhaps, but not one half. With a comeback like that, you can represent quality and I'll represent quantity."

The evening grew late and they travelled home in the carriage with Bella snuggled up to Donald's shoulder. The carriage stopped at Sunningdale, but the driver did not jump down and open the carriage door. Experience had taught him to give some couples a little time.

"Bella, would you like to go for a picnic tomorrow?"

"Splendid idea, Donald; I shall pack the lunch. What time will you arrive?" They settled on eleven o'clock.

"Wear something simple," said Donald, "and bring a parasol, for I'll be driving the carriage and you'll be up front on the seat with me." Donald smiled the smile of a mystic and continued. "I borrowed the carriage from a friend. You wouldn't want a carriage driver watching over our private picnic, would you?"

With an embrace at the door, Bella's evening came to an end. In total euphoria, she crept up the stairs in the darkened house and fell into a happy, contented sleep.

***

"Do you have a picnic basket, Gabby?" asked Bella. "Donald wants to take me on a picnic today."

"Yes, I do," said Gabby with the look of the proverbial Cheshire cat. "Lucky for you, there's more red wine in the cupboard. I'll get the basket and the wine. You are glowing, Bella, so I won't ask if you had a lovely time last night."

Bella looked in the icebox and found cold ham, various salad makings and soft rolls but not much more. *It looks like we will have ham and potato salad, rolls, sliced tomatoes and black olives. I wonder if he likes chocolate. There is some of yesterday's cake on the counter.* With lunch packed, she turned to the question of a suitable gown. The pale green gown, she decided, with her flowered parasol. When ready, she folded the pink blanket from her bed and put it with the picnic basket at the front door.

***

With Bella sitting close to Donald, the carriage left downtown and rattled through smaller streets in a southwesterly direction. From her high perch on the driver's bench, she saw the people of fancy homes and poor homes, the beauty of the foliage and the luster of a clean blue sky. Donald turned onto a rural road parallel to the Demerara River. After a few minutes he stopped at a gate bearing the name "Henker." He led the horse and carriage through the opening and closed the gate again, refusing to tell her their destination.

At first they passed tall green stalks on either side. Ahead Bella saw a thick wall of jungle. The horse followed along the narrow trail and came to a stop beside a huge palm tree. A footpath parted the heavy foliage and beyond that she saw the glint of water and a rowboat pulled up on shore.

"A picnic with a boat ride!" she cried out with delight.

"There, Bella. Isn't a surprise better than knowing?"

Bella gave him a quick hug and picked her way down the jungle path until she stood by the boat. Colourful birds flitted above the strip of jungle that separated the river from the sugarcane fields. Green vines that clung to palm trees curving over the river hung their trailing tendrils down to the water. Orchids showed splashes of pink against the thick undergrowth. Donald attended to the horse and joined Bella at the river.

"Sit here on the stern seat, Bella. I've fixed the blanket where I can see you while I row." Donald helped Bella into the boat, pushed off and jumped in as it slid free into the clear mountain water.

"This is the most romantic spot I know for a picnic," Donald said with an engaging smile. "You remember my restaurant friend, Simon Henker? He owns this plantation, the carriage and the boat."

Donald headed upstream, claiming that if he rowed upstream first they could float back on the current. He kept close to shore to catch some of the shade from the lofty palms. At times the green tendrils brushed against them while a cheery mix of sounds emanated from the jungle. Fish jumped with a splash and a roosting ibis rose up into the endless blue sky. Bella sat entranced with the beauty of the scene that surrounded her while Donald pulled strongly on the oars.

"You look very happy, Bella. Do you like my jungle treat?"

Bella smiled, mouthed a kiss and asked, "Is it like this around your house?"

"No. I rent a house in the middle of Paramaribo, and the plantation home is surrounded by sugar cane. I ride my horse out there when I have to attend to business."

"Will you teach me to ride a horse? I would like to ride astride the horse rather than sitting side saddle, but I have no jodhpurs or boots to dress like you. Do you think I could find riding boots small enough to fit me?"

"No, but it isn't hard to order things from London or Paris if you have the patience to wait for your order to arrive. In the meantime, how about a split riding skirt?"

"I want a riding habit." *Will he want me to look like his Dresden doll all the time?*

"Very well, then, a tailor will sew you some jodhpurs." *A tailor? Aha.*

Times of conversation alternated with quietly gazing at each other or the passing riverbank while Donald rowed the boat upstream. Rounding a bend in the river brought them to a small clearing in the jungle. Bella could see that the jungle growth had been recently hacked away and guessed why Donald had been late for dinner the night before. He brought the boat to shore and jumped out with the painter in hand to tie up.

"Sit tight, Bella, until I drag the boat up on shore." With amazing strength, Donald lifted and pulled at the bow to slide the boat onto dry land. He helped Bella out of the boat and led her to the clearing, where he spread the pink blanket and plunked the picnic basket in the middle of it. He swept Bella into his arms and placed her gently at one side of the basket, then he seated himself on the other side and flipped open the lid.

"I'm starved, Bella. How about you?" His hands reached into the basket. "Wine and linen napkins!" he exclaimed. Plates, knives and forks came forth, followed by potato salad and ham. After devouring the chocolate cake, Donald leaned down on one elbow to bring his shoulder closer to Bella. She turned her face towards his and received a gentle kiss on her forehead.

"You cut away the jungle just so we could have our own little picnic spot, didn't you, Donald?" Bella murmured.

"Certainly, my Princess. Remember, I am a jungle man—strong as a boa," and he playfully flexed his biceps.

Both laid back and gazed at the sky. Bella snuck her hand over Donald's. "Yes, strong as a boa," she said, "and brave too. Will you take me to Reich Ernte?"

"Of course, and I will have the workers plant a rose arbour for you, my sweet, but no one will know it is our picnic spot." They talked of little things. Donald's life in Paramaribo continually found its way into their musings.

"I may manage the Ernte Plantation, but I'd rather pack up and ride off through the jungle to the hills beyond to prospect for gold." *My goodness, he actually rides through that dreadful jungle. However does he survive?*

"By being a sugar plantation manager, I am part of the socially elite with grand parties to attend." Bella smiled at this nugget of information. "Would you like to attend the governor's ball, my little one?" Bella nodded agreement and offered Donald a kiss.

He's back talking about the jungle again—talking about pumas and how to tell if they're stalking you. He actually sounds like he enjoys the danger.

"And alligators," said Donald. "We have those too." Bella did not want to know more and spoke of a nearby flowering vine. Donald stirred. At first Bella wondered why. She sat up when he rose and came to her side. He kneeled down before her on one knee.

"Dear Bella, will you marry me?" The simple question floated on the air. *Oh my, he's proposing! I've dreamed of this moment so often; I must not shed tears of happiness.*

Donald continued his plight. "I fell in love with you when I visited your home in Plymouth. I wanted to ask you to marry me while drinking at the Wild Boar Pub but I thought you might not be prepared to answer, so I waited until now. Will life as my wife please you? I purposely told you of my jungle trips and social life so you'd understand your possible future and say yes right away."

Bella wished he would stop talking so that she might cry out, "Yes, yes!" which she did the moment he took a breath.

"Oh, Bella, I do adore you. I promise that I will make you happy." He reached into his pocket and brought forth a small leather box with a red velvet lining. "A Brazilian diamond for you, my love." And he placed it on her left hand.

"Forever and ever," Bella whispered and leaned forward to hug him.

In a heartbeat, Donald moved the basket aside and the two of them lay in each others' arms with a canopy of jungle green overhead. At that instant the magical reality of love flowed between them while they held each other.

"I planned this outing long ago, over and over in my mind, until I felt sure it would please you, Bella. Remember, I wrote that I would be in Demerara for two weeks. In fact, my business will be concluded in two days. The other days are for you."

"I pined for you all winter," Bella confessed. "To be your wife filled all of my thoughts. I believe we were meant for each other. You are a kind and loving man and I will be happy with you wherever life takes us."

"What do you say to eloping?" asked Donald. Bella recognized the serious tone in his voice. "In two days you could pack your trunk and then we could travel back to Paramaribo on the *Schooner Van Dam* and honeymoon for a week at the New Palace Hotel. The boat sails in three days."

Bella almost swooned. All her life she had wanted adventure— wanted to escape being considered less than whole or imperfect because of the rickets. She had always had to tone down her love of being outrageous, and now the idea of eloping with her prince in a sailing boat past miles of jungle seemed a most magnificent way to start married life.

"As long as I may have my stout each day," she teased.

The sun continued to arc overhead. When it reached the west, its rays penetrated the shade of their love nest, and with the humidity and heat, the two moved to return to the boat. Donald settled Bella in the stern as before, shipped the oars and sat on the floor of the boat beside her while it floated downstream as predicted.

***

"Gabby, Gabby!" Bella cried out as she rushed into Sunningdale near eight o'clock. "You are going to lose your boarder in two days. Donald and I are eloping!"

Gabby rushed from the kitchen and threw her arms around Bella's neck, turned and did the same thing to Donald. Gabby admired the large diamond and went to the liquor cabinet to celebrate with drinks.

Over wine, the three of them discussed all the details covering the next two days so that the couple would be ready to board the *Van Dam* early on the third morning. At ten o'clock Donald suggested he leave. Gabby feigned a need for the privy, said her goodbyes and retreated down the hall. She returned when the front door thumped shut.

"When are you planning to be married?" asked Gabby.

"I have no idea," said Bella. "Why, I haven't even thought of a marriage ceremony. I'm sure that sooner or later it will happen," she laughed as if the matter was inconsequential. Gabby raised her eyebrows as if a marriage ceremony did indeed matter. "Don't worry, Gabby, I plan to be an honest woman. Perhaps there's a church near the New Palace Hotel in Paramaribo. With this, Bella poured them more wine and repeated all she knew about Donald's life in Paramaribo.

"Oh yes," remembered Bella as they parted before going to bed. "Tomorrow, he has invited the two of us to dinner at his favourite Dutch restaurant. Goodnight."

***

Bella divided her belongings between those for the trunk and things for her valise. A carriage driver came for the trunk at four in the afternoon for delivery to the *Van Dam*. An hour later, Donald arrived to take Gabby and Bella for dinner at the Dutch restaurant, and again, they were expected. The waiter ushered them to a table set for four.

"I have asked my Dutch friend, the owner of this restaurant, to dine with us tonight, Bella, in celebration of our engagement," said Donald when Bella noticed the settings for four.

Presently, a handsome fellow with silver-blond hair came from a doorway at the back of the restaurant. Donald rose to welcome him to their table.

"Bella, you met Simon when we had dinner here before," said Donald. "Gabby, this is my friend, Simon Henker. Simon, may I present Gabby Wilton of Demerara." Everyone shook hands, but before Simon seated himself beside Gabby, he raised his wineglass in a toast to Bella and Donald. Again, conversation came easily for Bella. She noticed it seemed to flow equally well for Gabby and Simon.

**

The next morning, Bella packed her valise, except for the dark-green chiffon, her white stole and the straw hat that she would wear to board the ship. She spent the rest of the day puttering in the kitchen and visiting with Gabby until close to dinnertime.

"I told Donald that tonight he must put his feet under your table, Gabby, and that I planned to cook this last meal for both of you." Bella's voice softened. "I am going to miss you, Gabby. How I have changed with your gentle persuasion and goodness. You turned me around last winter and taught me how to live with understanding, and I shall be forever grateful to you." She rushed to Gabby and hugged her.

"No tears, Bella. We will always be good friends. It is not difficult to take the tramp steamer or the schooner back and forth between Demerara and Surinam. We will see each other again and often."

**

Donald arrived for dinner. Bella began the evening in the parlour with drinks and her marvelous toasted mushroom log hors d'oeuvres. She invited them into the dining room, where Gabby's silver and crystal reflected the vibrant colours of the red poinsettia at the unused end of the table. Donald lit the two candles and Bella lowered the lamp.

"Now, if you will excuse me," Bella announced grandly, "I'll ask the maid to bring in the salad."

Bella returned wearing a small white apron. She carried a tray with three plates of salad: greens, cashews, peeled sections of fresh oranges and a sprinkling of chopped parsley, all marinated with a touch of pineapple vinaigrette. Bella disappeared into the kitchen for a moment and then returned to her place at the table, minus the tray and apron. She turned her head toward the door of the kitchen.

"Thank you, Ethelyn. I will ring when we are ready for the main course."

Donald laughed at her charade. Next, Bella rang the little dinner bell and excused herself a second time. Soon, complete with apron and tray holding three plates, she served creamed shrimp over rice, stuffed baked tomatoes and a mélange of colourful vegetables fried in butter.

"Bella, my love," called Donald, "you didn't tell me you could cook so divinely."

"I never taught her to cook like this," said Gabby. "She keeps inventing new ways to combine colours, flavours and textures, and just months ago she couldn't cook at all."

The next time Bella entered the room, she wore a common kitchen apron and carried three crockery bowls stacked along one arm. Using a cockney accent, she plunked down bowls of pudding in front of Donald and Gabby, saying, "'ere's yer Spotted Dick, luvs." Bella's sudden switch to acting like a waitress in a lowly British pub and her perfect cockney accent caused the two of them to bend over with laughter. Neither had been served Spotted Dick since leaving Britain, and indeed it tasted every bit as good as the start of the meal.

Donald raised his glass of wine and said, "Here's to the cheff-ess!"

Gabby then raised her glass and added, "To a long and happy life together. I will miss you both."

***

At seven o'clock the next morning, Donald arrived with a carriage to collect Bella. With tearful good-byes and promises to write, Gabby and Bella held each other in a long tearful embrace. Donald kissed Gabby goodbye and, arm-in-arm in the light of early morning, Donald and Bella walked out to the carriage.

"Goodbye, my lovers," Gabby called after them. "May you have many happy years."

Bella could not bear to look back for fear she would cry again. While the clip-clop of the horse's hooves carried her away from Sunningdale, she could only hold tight to her prince and think of Aunt Kate's words, "The future, Bella, look to the future."

6

NICKERIE

The *Schooner Van Dam* left Demerara on time at ten a.m. heading for Paramaribo. Bella stood at the rail, Donald's hand over hers. With a lump in her throat, she thought of Gabby. She moved closer to Donald and wondered if Paramaribo would be the same as Demerara. *The future, Bella; it awaits you.*

"Let's stay on deck, Donald. The haze in the sky reduces the heat of the sun, and the light breeze makes it a heavenly day." They walked around the deck of scrubbed wooden planks, under sails and past sailors hauling on ropes. Again, she walked among men only, but the men did not eye her with disdain because, on this trip, she looked to be Donald's wife.

Finally, the two of them clambered through a hatch and down wooden steps to their cabin below. It had one double bunk. *I promised Gabby to remain an honest woman, but perhaps unusual circumstances are allowed. Who will know if I break the code of Victorian society? What can one do with only one bunk?* Bella paused in thought for only a second. *Yes, I know exactly what I will do.*

On the bedside table a dozen red roses claimed her attention with a card reading, "Always yours, my Rosebud. Love, Donald."

Bella wheeled and looked up at Donald with outstretched arms. Donald knew the signal and lifted her up for the hug and kisses she wanted to bestow on him.

"You think of everything, Donald!"

After a tender kiss on both cheeks, he placed her feet back on the floor, unlocked the trunk and lifted back the heavy lid. Bella started to unpack by hanging two gowns on the pegs, with the hope that the humid air would have them wrinkle-free when she needed them.

"Do you mind if I step out for a moment, Bella? Usually the men gather in the dining room for a smoke about now. It's their way of finding out who is on board."

Bella used the time to freshen up and check her hair before lunch and then stretched on the bed to rest her legs. "Just think," she murmured aloud to the ceiling, "I am to be Mrs. Donald Macdonald. Married at age twenty-five!" Bella furrowed her brows. *Surely we'll be married before my birthday on May twentieth! What will my parents think of me, "the sickly one," becoming their first daughter to be married? Me, the one that seemed doomed to die before I turned thirty.* With this thought, Bella sat up and spoke to the mirror across from her in the cabin. "Look to the future, Mrs. Macdonald. Follow Aunt Kate's advice and the future will be more magical than you can imagine." A sudden surge of happiness and energy enveloped her. She stood and twirled herself around.

Just then Donald returned to find Bella in the centre of the room with a glow on her face radiating happiness and adoration.

"You are so beautiful, my dear," he whispered with hugs, kisses and love murmurs. "It's lunchtime; I suggest a cordial of pineapple juice and rum."

***

After lunch, to allow for a few puffs on his cigar, Donald and Bella walked hand-in-hand on deck. They basked in the soft sun and admired the curl of the waves and the green coastline creeping past the starboard bow. Bella reached up for Donald's cigar and dragged the acrid smoke into her mouth.

"Aaagh! What a dreadful taste. I won't be adding that to my collection of outrageous habits. No wonder your tobacco plantations were the first to go bankrupt."

"You are right, Bella. Tobacco plantations did go first, but it wasn't because people stopped smoking tobacco. Europeans preferred the essence of American tobacco more than ours and stopped buying ours."

Bella left the cigar industry and asked a new question.

"Why are there three Guianas—British, Dutch and French?"

"Why these questions when you're eloping, Bella?" For an answer, Bella lifted her shoulders and grinned with a playful tilt of her head.

"I know, I know—you're curious and new to South America. Well, it's this way. Originally, this miserable area of rivers, swamp and jungle beckoned men from those three motherlands to search for gold and plant their country's flag. Guiana means 'Land of Many Waters' and so the name Guiana applies equally to all three colonies. Now, may we retire to our cabin and curl up for a nap?"

***

At five o'clock, as they seated themselves in the dining room, now the bar, Bella wondered if the ship would stock stout. With no orders given, the waiter arrived with a slender glass and a jar of stout, cool and ready for her.

"Donald, you thought of this, didn't you?" The twinkle in his eyes could tell no lie. "Love, you think of everything. I am so lucky that you found me." After a quiet stout and rum, with all the male voices blending in jocular storytelling around them, they went along to their cabin to dress for dinner.

***

"Bella, have I seen a white summer gown in your collection? Don't you think white would go nicely with my red hair?" he teased. The white gown with its frills of lace lay deep in the trunk. She shook it out and held it up against her at the shoulders.

"Perhaps it's too fussy for dinner on board a ship. What do you think, Donald?"

"I think it will make you look exactly how I would want you to look. Here, let me find white shoes to go with it."

Dressing took a little longer than Bella expected, but finally she had the braided topknot encircled with pearls in perfect symmetry. She turned to Donald. Her smile changed into a look of surprise when she saw that he had lopped off the stem of a rose and put it in the buttonhole of his fresh white suit. She noticed that he wore a white bow tie instead of a cravat but assumed that on a Dutch boat you dressed in the Dutch mode.

"If you are going to wear a rose," said Bella, mimicking a spoiled child, "then I will wear three of them." She placed the roses that Donald clipped for her over a sprig of green leaves and tied it with a piece of blue ribbon from her hat tie. Next, she took a hatpin and added the roses to the neckline of her dress in her own statement of elegance.

"You look beautiful, my darling Bella, just like the Dresden doll that I fell in love with so many years ago in Plymouth." Gallantly, he offered his arm and they walked along the passageway towards the dining room.

As they approached the archway into the end of the dining room, Bella noted that the room ahead seemed very quiet. She looked up at Donald to mention it but they were nearly there. She matched his happy smile and continued the last pace into the room.

A violin chord burst the silence the moment they came under the archway. Everyone stood. They formed a corridor of men, facing each other a few feet apart, which led all the way to the other end of the room. *Oh dear! What is happening? Is this because I am the only woman on board? Why is the captain dressed so formally?*

Captain DeJong, who usually wore white shorts and shirt, appeared at the other end of the room in whites—his full dress uniform. Sweat poured from his brow. He pinned his gold-braided captain's cap between his elbow and body and clutched a small leather book in his hand. Donald paused. He looked down at Bella's quizzical upturned face. The violin burst forth with a vigorous bridal march. Donald urged Bella forward. "An honour guard, my sweet, for our wedding."

Our wedding? Why didn't he warn me! How divine.

The "honour guard" smiled upon them as they made their way past passengers in fine suits, senior staff in whites and deck hands straight from their duties despite grime and sweat. When the couple stood in front of Captain DeJong, he asked the "guests" to be seated, and all took seats at the tables or stood along the wall. On each white tablecloth a nosegay of red roses surrounded a flickering white candle to add atmosphere to the room.

"Dearly Beloved," the captain began in English with a heavy Dutch accent, "we are gathered here to witness the wedding of Donald Alexander Macdonald and Isabella Bowen. Who gives this bride?"

"We do," chorused the wedding guests. The Captain nodded approval and read his own abbreviated version of the marriage ceremony. It still managed to include the opportunity for each of them to say "I do" and a request for the ring. Donald took a wide gold band from his side pocket and slipped it onto the fourth finger of Bella's left hand to rest beside her diamond engagement ring.

"For you, dear Bella, until death do us part," Donald spoke out. Bella radiated happiness with the sudden surprise of the whole event. *Donald could not have planned it with more perfection. Why, he makes life outrageous too. Just the way I like it.*

"Yes, dear Donald, until death do us part."

"You may now kiss the bride," Captain DeJong intoned.

In a flash, Donald reached down and took Bella like a child being raised to the sky. He brought her back down to where their arms could entwine each other and they kissed. Everybody cheered.

"Drinks on the bride and groom, my friends," Donald shouted out.

"Just a moment, please," called the captain. "I have a marriage certificate for the bride and groom to sign and I need the signature of two witnesses."

The nearest two men rose immediately and the marriage certificate soon bore the signatures of a ship's hand, S. Van Brinket, and that of the cook, a German by the name of Manfred Kolb. The guests filed past to shake Donald's hand and kiss the bride while drinks were served. *Sweat, grime and aftershave cologne—I will kiss them all.*

Soon the evening meal arrived: salad, tender roast of beef, rich brown gravy, Yorkshire pudding, asparagus tips, creamed potatoes and honey-browned carrots. *Wherever did they find this tasty roast beef? Donald must have imported it somehow. Considering all of the details necessary to plan this wedding to please me, no wonder it took him so many months to come forth with his intentions. Too bad we didn't elope a year ago, but no matter; in Donald I have found true love.*

The violinist, usually the ship's mate, played chamber music during dinner under the glow of the room's two lanterns and the four candles. *How did Donald know that the ship's mate played so divinely? It could easily have been the bo's'n and his squeeze box that I heard playing this afternoon. That would have fit the occasion too.*

When the plates were cleared, Cook arrived in a clean white apron and tall chef's hat, holding high a masterful wedding cake that he'd prepared. It gleamed with white icing, and into the centre of the slab he'd half-buried a small glass filled with red roses.

"Make vish," Cook said in Dutch with a guttural German accent. "Cut cake," he added, his pale blue eyes dancing with merriment. Donald picked up the knife, offered it to Bella with his hand over hers and they made the first cut into the cake. Bella nearly laughed aloud at the cook. His wide smile and little bows to his shipmates showed that he enjoyed every moment of his importance in the wedding—enjoyed being out in the dining room presenting his talents rather than closeted in the galley.

The men pushed back the tables and rearranged the chairs to create a small dance floor, and the evening continued with more drinks and violin music for dancing. After Donald and Bella whirled through the first waltz, with the all-male guests smiling their approval, the violinist offered an Irish jig. One of the sailors jumped onto the dance floor and danced a jig while the rest clapped to the music and stomped their feet. *Surely with all that stomping the deck of this boat is vibrating against its ribs. What a jolly bunch.*

The violinist switched to a Scottish strathspey tune, "Weel May the Keel Row." Donald recognized that he must consider this a cue. He bowed to Bella with a Scottish flourish and proceeded to dance what he could remember of the Highland fling, toes pointing and arms above his head. He bowed to Bella and the crowd before sitting down, and everyone clapped their hands and pounded the tables at his unexpected performance. A voice with a Dutch accent yelled "Hoot, Mon, where did ye learn t' dance?"

Bella heard strange music. The room fell silent. *Why, that is either music for belly dancing or some sort of an African tribal dance.* The sailors began a rhythmic clapping. Bella saw all eyes riveted on her. *My goodness! They think that I am supposed to perform next.* She rose, dipped a perfect curtsey to Donald and then did her best to swivel her tiny hips and wave her arms suggestively in acceptance of their cry for a belly dance. Eyes wide with fun, she looked into the face of each man as she circled with erotic gyrations. The clapping turned from its rhythmic beginning to applause. Bella finished with a flurry, curtsied to left and right and returned to Donald amidst cries for more from the boat hands.

Next came music for a hornpipe, and a thick-bodied sailor, who looked least likely to be a dancer, pranced and dipped his way through its many intricate steps.

Glasses were refilled more than once. With each refill the wedding became more boisterous. The bo's'n appeared with his fingered squeeze box and the cacophony of happy men's voices grew even louder as they joined him with lusty singing.

With all the drinks, one guest became bold enough to ask Bella to dance. The violinist began to play dance music for them. Bella, the only woman, attracted one guest after another until Donald strode onto the dance floor and shouted, "Enough! She's mine." He swept her off her feet, and holding Bella cuddled across his arms like a rag doll, the fullness of her white "wedding gown" flowing elegantly below, he called, "Goodnight, my friends. Bella and I thank you for a wonderful wedding. My bride and I are off to bed." This caused Bella to blush and the guests to clap and yell their approval. *With such a fine wedding, I shall be an honest woman after all. Bravo, my prince!*

As the couple went down the hall they could hear the party start up again with raucous singing and laughter.

***

Back in their cabin, Donald gently placed Bella on the bed.

"I'm exhausted," sighed Bella. "You have given me a heavenly evening—just the kind of wedding for me—but I am so tired. Donald, would you mind pulling off my kid boots?"

With one shoe off, when Donald gently pulled at the other, he heard a quiet coy voice saying, ". . . and undressing me?"

***

And so their wedding night together commenced. It surprised no one when they didn't turn up for breakfast and had lunch and dinner served in their cabin. The third day they emerged to the knowing glances of the other passengers and the smirks of the young deckhands. To satisfy the stares of onlookers, Bella curtsied and Donald gave an elaborate bow. At dinner they received a round of applause when they entered the dining room. *Applause? Is it a facetious greeting to acknowledge that we've finally come out of our cabin or a thank you for the fine wedding dinner and copious drinks? We'll never know which.*

***

Two days later, the *Schooner Van Dam* docked at the seacoast town of Nickerie.

"Mr. Macdonald," said Captain DeJong, "take your *Van Dam* marriage certificate to the government office on the main street and register it. Their office is in the biggest building on the street so it's easy to find." He added with a sly grin, "Take Mrs. Macdonald with you so she'll remember the place where your certificate claims you were married. You will have time; we won't sail until six in the morning."

***

With the sun overhead and high humidity, Bella opened her parasol to prepare for their walk into town. For the first time, Bella saw Donald in his white pith helmet.

"Donald, just look at us; we look the full part of British colonials shown in my books back in Plymouth—me wearing a full summer gown with a parasol and you looking grand in white, pith helmet and all."

"And so we should, my dear, for indeed, we *are* British colonials! People will stare. Do you mind being the centre of attention?" Donald quizzed, quite happy to have it that way. Bella answered by setting her parasol at a saucy angle and taking Donald's arm.

Tripping along like a pair of youngsters on their first date, Bella and Donald reached the government building at eleven a.m. They entered the cool, dank building and registered their marriage with the elderly European clerk.

"Congratulations, Mr. and Mrs. Macdonald," said the clerk in accented English. He chuckled and added, "I'm amazed that Captain DeJong knew where to find his book containing the ceremony." The clerk registered their Dutch ship's certificate, returned it to Donald and produced a second copy. He patted the document on the counter and said, "Someday you'll need a copy in English." They offered their thanks and proceeded down the street, looking for an eatery. On a side path Donald led her to a quaint café, a very simple version of the sidewalk restaurant that Bella dreamed of finding some day.

A green and white tattered awning offered shade over the crude clay floor. They sat at one of three small tables and ordered lemon tea and a fruit plate. Creole music played in the distance while they ate and watched the passers-by. Drivers with rustic carts stood by their horses, hoping to be summoned for a small fee. Mules with bundles on their backs waited at the edge of the road, tethered by a rope attached to a large lead weight. Handsome dogs trotted behind owners who looked masterful astride their sleek bay horses. *I wonder if they are well-trained guard dogs accompanying their masters for security.* Bella abandoned this thought, for everyone she saw seemed warm and friendly.

"Remember this town, Bella. I come to Nickerie every time I go to the jungle to prospect for gold. The ship's harbour is the mouth of the Corentyne River, and in the headwaters of this river I find gold nuggets in the sand."

"Really, Donald? That's why you seem so at home here. You were speaking their language, not Dutch. So many words sounded familiar. Why can't I understand them?"

"Because," said Donald, "they are speaking Sranan, a language handed down since the time of the slave trade. It is a mixture of English and African words with their own ideas of grammar, and over time words from India were mixed in as well. Sranan is the language of the Creoles. In the Guianas, Creole refers to locally born people with mixed ancestry of European and African or Indian decent. But, my dear, you are far too serious for a honeymoon."

***

After a second lemon tea, they realized that further sightseeing in Nickerie with the heat and humidity would be ill advised, so they ambled past the weathered little shops towards the Nickerie pier and up the gangplank of the *Schooner Van Dam*.

A light breeze freshened the air on the ship's poop deck. They sank into two canvas chairs to cool themselves and rest. Bella looked out at the wide river and, musing to herself, turned her head and raised her twinkling gaze to meet the agate-brown eyes of her husband.

"Donald, I am the luckiest woman in the world. I never dreamed that I would ever be this happy, and it is all because of you." She lifted his hand from the armrest and kissed it. He in turn drew her hand his way and smothered it in kisses.

"We sail tomorrow morning," said Donald, "and in three days after that, if the winds and current are willing, we will dock in Paramaribo just after you finish your five o'clock stout." With a wink, he added, "And then you can write Gabby with the news that you were an 'honest' woman after all."

That Gabby! She told him what I said!

7

PARAMARIBO, SURINAM

onald carried their drinks up on deck so that she wouldn't miss anything in their approach to Paramaribo. He insisted that they sit in deck chairs at the forward railing facing the bow. Sunset colours filled the sky behind them. The sea looked murky-grey with silt. As the sun sank closer to the horizon, the square-masted ship left the Atlantic coastline and entered the Surinam River heading in a southerly direction.

"If we've turned into the river, why can't I see the riverbanks?" asked Bella.

"The river is too wide to see either of them," Donald said as he squeezed Bella's hand.

Bella's shoulders shuddered. "It's growing dark. This is eerie, inching our way by sail up a river with no banks. I can't tell where the water ends and the sky starts."

Donald kissed Bella on the nose. "Don't worry, Button. Paramaribo is upstream twenty-three miles on the west shore of the river. You won't see anything in this gloom until we dock."

"Look, Donald! Something's on fire over there." Bella pointed into the blanketing darkness where huge flames leapt into the air as if a building were burning.

Donald leaned forward in his chair to focus on the flames glowing brightly in the darkness. "So far out here on the river it's hard to tell if it's a building or a bonfire." Bella crowded closer to him as he spoke again. "As a matter of fact, that fire has to be very close to Ernte." He laughed, sat back and said, "I hope it's the Ernte plantation house that's burning—and good riddance. It's full of termites."

Despite Donald's apparent disinterest, Bella continued to watch the flames in dismay. He closed his hand over hers on the armrest and at that very moment, above the fire, she saw bursts of fireworks.

"How do you like the fireworks, Bella?"

"Donald! You planned that fire and the fireworks to welcome me to Surinam," and she clapped her hands together in delight followed by a long hug.

"Why do you think we are up here sitting in the dark?" he chuckled. "I've been watching for the bonfire. Now, if you don't mind, I have the captain's permission to fire my gun so the workers know that you saw their welcome."

"A gun! You have a gun with you?" *I've married a man who carries a gun? I must speak to him about that! Why is no one on deck objecting? Donald is trying to please me with a moment of fun; I must control my voice so I don't lose it when I speak.* Bella strained to settle herself and asked, "Won't that scare the passengers and crew?"

Donald laughed. "Where do you think I was that first day on board the *Van Dam* when I said that I had to go to the dining room for a smoke with the fellows? I did go there, that's true, but of more importance, I told everyone of our wedding plans and this welcoming. Look around you; everybody is on deck enjoying your surprise." With that, Donald took his gun from an inside pocket. She saw his arm raise—a flash, followed by an ear-splitting crack!

While Bella trembled, everyone cheered, as if gunfire occurred regularly. Bella said nothing, but her inner self shook in disbelief at the strange acceptance that the other passengers had regarding Donald carrying a gun in his pocket. She had never seen the gun or felt a shoulder holster. *Do all colonists carry guns? Why did I never suspect that carrying a gun was commonplace to local residents—perhaps necessary for safety? It didn't seem dangerous in Demerara. Has Donald brought me to a place where I must fear for my life, his life?* With these thoughts whirling through her head, Bella clung to Donald in a stupour and found herself going below for dinner.

***

By the time the boat docked in Paramaribo, the smell of jungle humidity permeated the air. A half moon dodged the clouds. With a lamp held high, the ship's maître d' led the passengers down the pier to waiting carriages. On the way to the hotel the streets and buildings lay shrouded in darkness except for intermittent moonlight that outlined buildings in shades of grey. *Surely, it will look more hospitable in the morning. I mustn't be afraid.*

From the little that Bella could discern, the New Palace Hotel appeared to be quite tall and built of white painted wood. In darkness, they stepped from the carriage and entered the hotel. Gloom pervaded the corners of the foyer. Bella saw only a clerk standing behind the counter, then in the shadows, a man in hotel livery slipped silently past them. Donald tugged on Bella's arm to come along, for the man had returned with their bags and expected them to follow him.

Why, we haven't registered our names with the clerk and the man with our luggage appeared on cue. Donald must have arranged everything before he left Paramaribo. What a man, so perfect for me. But the gun? How can I hug a man with a gun in his pocket and not worry? There is nothing else for it. I must ask him what this new discovery about my husband means.

At that very moment, the hotel man stopped to unlock a door. He swung it open and stepped back. Without warning, Donald swept Bella into his arms and carried her across the threshold of a large room. He turned in every direction to show her the room he had chosen for their first nights in Paramaribo.

"Donald!" she exclaimed. "This is so grand! And look—a vase of red roses."

He stopped her talking with a kiss that held such passion that the hotel man dropped the bags where he stood and backed out of the room before they might tear off their clothes and fall into bed. Donald set her feet down on the white carpet and watched the magic in Bella's face as she turned in a circle to view the room once more.

Bella marvelled at the length of the sashed royal blue tapestry drapes hanging on either side of white lace covering the window. She turned toward the blue chesterfield with white satin cushions at either end. Surrounding the spotless white carpet, Bella could see wide polished mahogany floorboards pegged down at the ends with dark walnut studs. Polished brass lamps, all alight, cast a golden glow in the room and highlighted the gold embossed crests of the wallpaper. Bella's eyes rested on a serving wagon fashioned in simple elegance from hand carved wood.

How divine! Champagne on ice in a bucket, cheese, dry toast and a basket of fruit.

Very happy, Bella turned towards Donald. He took her hand and, leading her to the matching blue chair, he knelt beside her.

"Bella, I want you to be very happy here in Surinam. If there is anything your heart desires, I will try to get it for you." With a kiss on her hand, Donald's serious demeanour vanished. He stood, smiled and asked, "What do you think of our lodgings for the next few days?"

Bella finally found her voice after she had taken in the beauty of the room again and marvelled at Donald's thoughtful attention to the things on the serving wagon.

"My dear Donald, you are spoiling me completely and I love every second of it." Next, she teased in her cockney voice, "Let's 'ave a swig-a champagne and find the bed. I don't see one."

Donald laughed. Always, she found a way to be his outrageous little princess, his Rosebud, his Dresden doll. "There is another room, Bella. Come, it's right through this doorway."

There she beheld a huge canopied bed swagged in sheer cotton for the mosquito season. The attached bathroom showed a marble sink boasting brass faucets that looked like gold. Bella turned the taps. Instantly, they produced hot and cold running water. *How wonderful, but where does that door over there go?*

Off to one side in its own little room Bella found a new Crapper, straight from England. Clapping her hands, she announced. "Thomas

Crapper has saved the universe from a most unpleasant part of life. I think Queen Victoria should give him a medal."

"This surely is the Governor's Suite, Donald. However did you manage to wangle it for tonight?" Her intense green eyes would not allow him to lie.

"You are right, Bella. It is the Governor's Suite. He is in Holland on business and I know the hotel owner very well. A little money for the staff to keep the manager's secret of loaning it out to a person like me with a new bride, and here we are."

With all Donald's charm, Bella let the thought of a gun in his pocket fade further from her mind. He carried their bags into the bedroom and reappeared to enjoy the cheese, toast and champagne with Bella before they retired to the bedroom.

***

"Why, Donald, you have turned down the covers to welcome me."

"Bella . . ." Donald started to speak. *That serious voice of his again. Last time he sounded like that he left me for eight months. Oh God, please shine on us tonight.*

"Bella, I don't want to shock you, but I usually sleep with my gun under the pillow, especially in the Governor's Suite." Bella's eyelids opened with the focus of an owl. Donald continued. "I am fairly well-to-do and a visible European colonial. I am sure your guardian, Scott-Wallace, carried a gun in Demerara and that your father hired him to protect you until you were settled in a better part of the city." Donald paused to consider his choice of words. "Daytime is safe, but you never know about the night. The law is quite primitive in South America. The poor in any of the Guianas can cause trouble." Again he paused for her reaction to this unsavoury truth.

How did he know the gun worried me? Here he is, making it sound like a very civilized thing to do—a gun in his pocket and under his pillow! If carrying a gun is so commonplace, then I must learn to steel myself against knowing that any pocket can produce one. I might even have to know how to use one. I must say something; he's waiting.

"When you ride to the plantation, are you safe, Donald? In Nickerie,

I saw two large dogs trotting after their master's horse. The thought crossed my mind that the rider had guard dogs but I told myself not to think such silly thoughts. Were they guard dogs?"

"I suppose so, but the dogs would be guarding the horse and fine saddle during daylight if the man wanted to enter a building. Maybe the rider planned to return home after dark, but I don't ride at night and I don't see the need of a guard dog. There, does that settle your worries?" Bella nodded, but his comments did not wash away her uncertainty. She smiled and cocked her head, ready to change the subject.

"Who's undressing whom tonight, my ducky?" she said, to lighten the moment. *After all, I'm still on my honeymoon and I plan to make the most of it—gun under the pillow or not.*

***

The sun already rode high in the sky when they rose at ten. Bella chose her pale green gown. Donald wore white jodhpurs and jacket with black riding boots. When Bella entered the main room, they eyed each other with approval. Bella picked up the bowl of fruit and plunked herself down on the chesterfield beside Donald with the fruit bowl in her lap. Without asking, she popped a strawberry into his mouth and took one for herself.

"The rains will start later in the day, Bella. What would you like to do before then? We can see Paramaribo and find a restaurant for tea, or take the carriage out to Ernte, or drive to the house where I live in town and meet my stallion, Cobus."

"So many choices, Donald—have another strawberry—I want to do them all."

"Ah, but which one first?" asked Donald.

"If Cobus resides in the back garden of your Paramaribo house, then I choose meeting Cobus first, which just happens to let me see your house. And then I wish to drive out to Ernte by some pleasant route that shows me part of Paramaribo."

"Bella! Gabby told me that you were a sly one. Why, you have chosen to do all of my suggestions instead of one of them for your first day here." Bella cocked her head and tossed a strawberry into the air. She caught it in her teeth to show off a feat that she had practised all of her childhood when alone in the nursery.

When that seemed to be her only comment on what they would choose to do, Donald said, "Fine, we'll hire a carriage and keep it all day. You can meet Cobus and view the outside of the house. After lunch at the club, we'll drive out to Ernte and pray that we don't get caught in a downpour."

***

When they passed through the foyer of the hotel, Bella could tell that the clerk had already spread the word that Donald Macdonald had arrived back in Paramaribo with a wife. Unlike the evening before, people were sitting in the chairs grouped in the corners of the room with tea trays on little tables in front of them or reading newspapers by the pillars and generally trying to hide their curiosity.

Donald seems to be well known. Perhaps I have wed the most eligible bachelor in town. I must give them something to please their curiosity, but what?

Bella slipped her hand into the crook of Donald's elbow with a joyous smile and called back to the clerk. "We will be back for dinner. At five o'clock, I will have a glass of stout in the foyer."

Donald smiled and added to the act by patting Bella's hand as it rested on his arm. He expected that Bella would make some gesture for the onlookers, and she didn't let him down. Subtle, but there nonetheless, she had announced to the curious when to return to see the new bride again, and drinking stout in public at that. Donald and Bella stepped from the cool of the hotel interior into blazing heat and high humidity.

"What's that gorgeous building across the street with the four white columns, grand tower and cupola," she cried out, "and the huge garden surrounding it?"

"That green garden is known as 'Oranjeplein,' but you may call it Orange Square," answered Donald. "The building is the Governor's Palace. It houses government offices and has a lovely ballroom. That's where we'll go to the Governor's Ball."

"Really? We'll dance the night away. When is it?"

"Near the end of the summer dry season."

While Donald watched for a carriage, Bella looked up and down the street.

"Isn't the sun glorious, Donald? Look at the way it paints the buildings in light and shadow with a background of lofty palms and colourful parrots. Smell the scent of the flowers in Orange Square. Heavenly! Is this not paradise?"

As in Demerara, from what she could see, the streets of red cracked bauxite gravel stretched in wide ribbons at right angles to each other at the intersections, copying the Dutch tradition. Paint of various bright colours decorated the street signs and buildings. An open carriage drew up in front of them. Donald asked the driver to lower the half-carriage sunshade so they might see the city more easily. Donald gave the driver some directions in Dutch that Bella could not understand, then picked up his Rosebud and placed her in the carriage. The carriage rocked along on the street in front of the hotel. *Mr. Lim A Postraat*, she read. *I must remember that street sign in case I get lost shopping. And just look at those mahogany trees!*

"We are catching the eye of people on the street, Donald. I feel like royalty riding along in my Landau. Do you think I should give them a queenly wave?" she teased. Donald guessed that she would do it anyway and did his part by smiling and nodding to the people staring at them. *Am I imaging it, or is Donald known to half the people in Paramaribo? Something makes us attract attention; otherwise, why would people stop and stare? Why, I do believe Donald likes to attract attention as much as I do. He knew this would happen. What fun!*

"A penny for your thoughts, my dear," said Donald.

Bella returned her attention to Donald's running commentary of "Waterkant," a street running parallel to the river, and said, "So many of the buildings are made of brick. Does Surinam have a brick factory?"

"No, Bella. The bricks arrive as ballast in empty ships that load sugarcane for the return trip. With the arrival of each successive ship, Paramaribo soon had mountains of bricks, so the government used them to build their civic buildings. But I don't think that is what you were thinking about." Bella ignored his added comment.

The carriage turned left, and across the street a yellow brick church stood with red bricks set elegantly into the corners of the building all the way up to the bell tower. Donald pointed.

"They've been building St. Petrus and St. Paulus Catholic Church for eight years."

"Can you imagine, Donald! Building a church that big, brick by brick, with both Creoles and those other workers."

"All those with darker shades of skin, we call Creoles," said Donald. "Some are of African descent and some East Indian. They all get along with each other, even though they follow their own cultural traditions at home and in church." The carriage bumped along. "Do you see the shops that we're passing, Bella? You'll be able to walk to them from our house." The carriage returned to Waterkant.

"Donald, I can't imagine how civilized and cultured I find Paramaribo. Naïvely, I expected it of Demerara, but this is truly a handsome city tucked away in this no-man's-land of mangroves and swamps."

They passed two sets of piers and then the driver turned right down Jodenbreestraat into a residential area salted with old Victorian houses on deep lots.

"My house is down this next street, Dominiestraat," said Donald, and he called out to the driver in Dutch. *I must learn to speak Dutch quickly to manage in this country.*

"Now, Bella, you said you wanted to meet Cobus first, so close your eyes while the carriage reaches my house and goes down the long driveway to the back of the lot." Bella liked games and immediately closed her eyes. She felt the carriage make a left turn and heard the sound of gravel crunching under its wheels. Donald took her hand.

"When we stop, I'm going to lift you out of the carriage and carry you to the paddock. No peeking." When he put her down, Bella popped open her eyes.

"He's beautiful, Donald!" Bella squealed, no longer afraid of horses. "Just look at his lovely chestnut colouring with black mane and tail and the black legs shading to chestnut at the hocks."

Cobus gave a whiney of recognition and trotted over to them in a most gentlemanly manner. Donald stroked Cobus's neck and said soft words into his ear.

"I'll get him saddled for you, Bella."

Donald called out, "Dirk, are you back there?" Bella saw the same kind of stable as Strawberry's—two walls with a straw roof for shade and palm trees sighing overhead in the freshening breeze. Bella heard a door close behind the stable. A young man, a Creole, came from the back of the building.

"Goedn dag!" the mulatto called out with pleasure at the sight of his master.

"Halo, Dirk," Donald answered in Dutch. Then in English he added, "Your English will soon improve, Dirk, because my wife cannot speak Dutch. May I introduce Mrs. Donald Macdonald, my bride!" Dirk's curious eyes fluttered shut as he dipped his head in acknowledgement. "And Bella, when I'm busy at my desk, Dirk will teach you to ride. Dirk, please saddle Cobus so my wife can ride him."

"Donald, what kind of name is Cobus for a horse?"

"It's Dutch, Bella—short for Jacobus, with the inflection on the 'o.' Here, let me lift you into the saddle." In wild abandonment, Bella gathered her gown up above her knees like a can-can dancer, and up she went. Dirk's eyes closed, embarrassed by the view. He had never seen legs like that before. His sister's legs were straight.

"Oh, Donald! Your horse is so broad my hips are about to split apart. Please take me down before I rip right up my middle."

Donald started to laugh. Bella's hips were so narrow, and her legs so short, that they stuck straight out on either side of Cobus's wide back and hung there, curving down, like wilted rhubarb. "I guess you're not going to ride my stallion. We'll find you an Arabian horse to ride. An Arabian can pull a trap to take you to the market and the shops as well."

The palm trees bent and the fronds fluttered as a cold gust of wind raked the sky.

"Quick, Bella. We are in for a cloudburst!" cried Donald. Dirk hurried Cobus into his shelter while Donald pounded towards the house with Bella in his arms. They reached its overhanging roof as the first big drops of rain splatted around them.

"The wind is driving the rain onto my skirt, Donald. Why don't we go inside?"

"Remember, Bella? I told you that we would only see the outside of the house today. I'm sure you won't dissolve with a little rain. It should be over soon."

"You must have a good reason to be so adamant, Donald."

"I have two good reasons. First, I gave my housekeeper some days off so she could visit her parents, and an empty house attracts bugs in this climate. Second, seeing the house from the scullery is hardly how I want to introduce you to your new home."

Bella crowded near to the back door in an effort to find more protection from the tropical downpour. The carriage driver turned the carriage around and hauled the canvas sunshade into position to give him cover on the passengers' bench.

"That may be so, my dear," said Bella equally as adamant, "but we are both getting soaked and logic says that we would be dry inside."

Donald unlocked the back door. They hurried inside and slammed the door against the rain. Donald went forward and shut the door to the kitchen.

"You wanted in to be dry, so here we are, but you will go no farther, my love. This way, we both have our wishes."

Bella heard a little snap. Her shoes felt like they were stepping on something.

"Donald, what are all these bugs on the floor! They will climb up my petticoats." With both hands she lifted her skirts and rustled them back and forth to knock off any bugs already clinging to the hem.

"They are cockroaches, Bella. As I told you, bugs take over an empty house in this climate. They seem to creep out from every crack at night. Don't worry; the housekeeper will look after them tomorrow."

'Well!" said Bella. "Sunningdale taught me how to deal with household problems!" She spied the scullery straw broom and attacked the cockroaches at a feverish pace until she had them swept into a pile. Before they could run off again, she pushed the door open, flicked at the bugs until they were all swished over the door sill and slammed the door against them. Donald stood quietly by, smiling at Bella's spark of independence—the same independence he had seen in her on that day back in Plymouth when she refused to be intimidated by her older sisters.

"That takes care of that," said Bella, putting the broom back in the corner and dusting one hand against the other to signify "done."

"You are right, Donald. I shall wait to see the house rather than encounter a whole army of creatures."

**

They talked of the housekeeper while they waited for the storm to abate.

"The housekeeper's name sounds like 'Shauna,' but in Dutch it is spelled 'Jeanne.' Spell it the English way; she won't mind because she doesn't read English. She speaks it well enough to be understood, so I'm sure the two of you will manage to communicate."

"Is she taller than me, Donald?" asked Bella in a small voice.

"As a matter of fact, for a girl of mixed East Indian and Dutch blood, she is quite tall, maybe five feet six inches and spare. She's fifteen and very loyal. Let's just say that I helped her once and now she craves the security of my home and would do anything for me. I trust her implicitly. I'm sure you two will enjoy working together. Now, I suggest we check on the storm. I can't hear the rain lashing the trees."

Donald pushed the door open. Ominous clouds still bristled in the overcast sky. The palm leaves, wet and slickery, hung their heads in dismay. Water dripped from the eaves, but the downpour had moved on. They ran out to the carriage and climbed in to sit on the wet bench. The driver roused the horse and it plodded forth.

"That concludes your travels for today, Bella. We are wet and may get doused again on the ride home. We must go back to the hotel and change out of these clothes. By then it will be near five and time for our drinks."

"And tomorrow?" Bella asked.

"No, not the house. I can tell what you are thinking. I'll take you back there the day after tomorrow when Shauna is ready for us." Donald finished with a big smile. "Tomorrow, how would you like to go shopping for an Arabian mare and a trap?"

8

MISCHIEF

Donald stopped at the bedroom door in polished brown riding boots, tan jodhpurs and a matching shirt.

"Dress yourself for horse hunting, Bella. I am going to the hotel desk to pick up a newspaper and order breakfast in our room."

Horse hunting! You'd think that we plan to go out with reatas and capture the beastie. I will wear a skirt and blouse and insist that we purchase some jodhpurs or at least buy a pair of boy's pants before we leave downtown.

Bella went to the bathroom mirror to fix her hair in a French roll. *Why don't I try the Crapper again? It is such a marvellous invention, and to think that they have one in this hotel! Why, this place is as modern as a London hotel. But that tub—it's huge! I don't think I'll try it unless Donald is here to save me from drowning. Perhaps I'll try it this afternoon when we have finished "horse hunting."*

Bella finished her morning routine by dabbing perfume on her ear lobes and the hem of her skirt. She took her parasol from the wardrobe and placed it near the door. Donald and the breakfast trolley arrived at the same moment. Bella wheeled it over to the small inlaid table at the window.

"Two bowls of oatmeal and three eggs?" squealed Bella. "Donald have you not noticed that I am just a little woman? I simply do not need so much food."

"Two of the eggs are for me," Donald explained with a grin. "If you don't wish the porridge, I'll eat both bowls of it and you can enjoy your dry toast and preserves after you eat an egg. You must eat something, Bella." Donald held out two letters. "Here, I went to the post office as well. The one must have been forwarded on today's ship."

Bella looked at the stamps and pronounced, "One from home and one from Gabby." She opened the letter from home first. "It's from my sister Constance. Oh my, Althea is marrying George Smith. He's the one who works in a bank." Bella read on to herself for a bit. "Their wedding date is set for next week. They won't get my letter for six weeks. Won't they be surprised." Bella started to chuckle. "He's so sober, I'm sure he'll consider our wedding outrageous. Here, you can read it later."

Bella ripped at Gabby's letter. "My, my, Donald. She's giving us her treadle sewing machine for a wedding present! She says, 'What a perfect wedding for the two of you. I can just imagine the fun it must have been. Donald did a splendid job of reaching so many people with all his planning.'" Bella cocked her head at Donald. "Pray, tell me, Donald, how did she know of our wedding plans? We've only been in Paramaribo for two days. This letter travelled on the same ship as we did. Were you and Gabby keeping secrets from me?"

Donald raised his newspaper a little higher to suggest that he wasn't about to discuss what Gabby knew or didn't know. Bella finished reading the letter and placed it on the table for Donald. "She says she's shipping the sewing machine on the next sailing of the SS *Balfour* from Demerara. We'll have to check the schedules and meet the boat."

From behind his newspaper Donald reached out a hand and offered a newspaper to Bella. "I bought one in English for you and this one in Dutch for me. As you can see, I read at the table. It is hard to break a bachelor's habits. To make it fair, while I read this one in Dutch, you can read the English paper." Donald turned to the back pages of his newspaper to look at the list of ads.

"I've circled two ads showing Arabians for sale, Bella. We'll have to drive out and see what they have to offer."

"Please, Donald. I can't make a spectacle of myself again, trying to ride a standard saddle in a skirt. Did you not see the look in Dirk's eyes when you lifted me on to Cobus's back and he saw my legs sticking out right in front of his nose?" Donald smiled in a knowing way and tipped his head a fraction sideways rather than answer. Bella continued, "We must go to the shops before we attend to the horse ads."

"Why jodhpurs, Bella? Some ladies wear split riding skirts."

"Why jodhpurs? Because I want to wear jodhpurs—white ones with black boots and a green silk blouse. With my black hair, it will look stunning. Whether I ride well or not, I'll look like a jockey."

"Fine. There are a few clothing shops grouped together near here." Donald put the breakfast trolley in the hallway and they started on their quest.

***

An hour later, Bella had shed her skirt in favour of a pair of boys' pants. In the mirror, Bella eyed her lacy blouse and the plain cotton pants with her high button shoes protruding below the hems of the pant legs.

"Could I help it if I had to buy pants too short in order to get a size small enough to fit my waist?" protested Bella.

"Don't worry, my sweet. I will have a tailor make you some proper riding clothes as soon as we have time to visit his shop. I suspect you feel quite happy in your present get-up—happy to conjure up what the horse traders will think when they see you."

***

Bella could tell that they travelled west to the outskirts of town. The houses were in atrocious states of disrepair, with unpainted weathered boards turning silver-grey from rain and sun. Bella thought that most of the people they saw along the way were Creoles of various shades of skin, yet here and there were Muslims facing the east, bowed down on their prayer mats. In one window she saw a brass candlestick with seven sockets, a Menorah, to be lit for Hanukkah. She spoke of these differences.

"Some families have been here for generations," said Donald. "They work at anything that makes a little money. Everyone may have different coloured skin, but European colonists look different too. We stand out because we are white."

Donald is trying to tell me that our white skin is a liability, the reason he carries a gun—not needed by day but, like he said, "darkness might bring trouble." I can see it's going to take me some time to understand this country. How can it be so beautiful to me yet offer such sad conditions for the poor? I suppose Demerara had slums and troubles too. I just never saw them.

***

They came to a modest house with unruly grass and bushes. The carriage passed down the gravel lane beside the house to stop behind a large cart, used perhaps for delivering kegs of beer. Three horses stood in the paddock. A dark fellow sat on the back two legs of a chair, leaning against the barn with a cigar in his mouth.

"Ya saw my ad, did ya? I'm selling that little one with the dark coat." The man spat tobacco juice on the dirt in front of him and rocked the chair forward before standing. "She's a nice quiet horse, pulls a trap, easy to ride." Donald could see that the horse had a little Arabian blood, but something bothered him about the animal.

The creature in the frilly blouse and pants that had come to the paddock fence spoke up. "What are those worn spots on her shoulders, bare of hair?" The man looked askance at her to show she had no business in horse dealings.

"Not too old—give ya lots of years yet," he said.

Donald climbed through the fence and strode over to the mare. She didn't move a muscle. Donald lifted a lip and looked at her teeth. Still no reaction. Her head hung down and her eyes looked dull. The worn spots suggested an ill-fitting harness.

"Have you been pulling that heavy cart teamed with this horse?" asked Donald. "She looks plumb worn out. Maybe has worms." The man shrugged his shoulders.

"She's cheap, what do ya want for a few guilders?"

"Come, Donald. I don't like his attitude. He's ruined that horse." As they walked back to the carriage, they heard another splat of tobacco juice land behind them.

"I'm getting hungry, Bella. Let's look for the restaurant with a green striped awning that you thought you'd find in Demerara."

"Do you know of one in this end of town?" she answered coyly, like a youngster that wanted her dad to find a candy shop. "Have you been keeping secrets from me?"

The journey back into the city seemed twice as long to Bella. The iron rims of the wheels on gravel jolted every bone in her body. She rested her head on Donald's shoulder and said, "I do believe my ribs have come unbuttoned."

The vignettes they passed presented the same poor neighbourhoods as before. She saw little children, naked and barefoot, as they played while their mama sat rocking on the porch seeking a little respite for her pregnant tummy. Bella bowed her head with a slight turn back and forth. *What is the government doing for these people? Do the rich ever see these conditions? Do they care? Should I care?* She never answered herself. Bella reached for Donald's hand to gain assurance that she would never be poor.

The carriage rumbled on while Bella watched for the promised sidewalk restaurant that would relieve them from the scorching rays of the sun. Then she saw it! Reaching her hands to the sky with the fluttering of her fingers she called aloud, "Hallelujah! We're here." Everyone on the street stared in disbelief at such outlandish actions. The carriage stopped, and with no regard for her short boys' pants that showed her ankles and boots, Bella leapt from the carriage and made her way to a back table. She sat in a chair that faced the other customers and waited for Donald to join her.

So everyone is staring. Do I care? Why can't people loosen up and show a little joy or be ridiculous now and then just for the fun of it? Perhaps I shall start a new fashion with my pants. I imagine those women over there, whispering behind their fans, are wondering if I am one of them. The clothes women wear in this hot country are far too cumbersome with their long skirts swishing along in the gravel. That's it! I'll design a gown that suits me and it will not drag on the ground.

Donald seated himself next to Bella so they would have the same view in case she started to pass humorous comments for diversion during lunch.

"I'll have iced tea, Donald, and a fruit plate with cheddar cheese and dry toast."

"I doubt that they have an icebox to keep cheese or iced tea," said Donald. He gave the waiter an order for mixed fruits, two pineapple cordials topped with rum, one serving of hot Indian curry and two servings of dry toast.

A toff passed by with his walking stick held ever so elegantly. "Perhaps, Donald, I have a better understanding for men with their cudgels. It is a safety measure. It is no different than ladies relying on their brooms to threaten unwanted intruders."

"Bravo, Bella," said Donald. Their lunch arrived and Bella's comments started.

"Donald, you say men wear riding boots to protect themselves from snakes. Funny, I haven't seen a single snake. I guess the rustle of long gowns scares them away."

"I'm sure the snakes are afraid they'll get lost in your petticoats and die of heat exhaustion," answered Donald.

I'll have to be careful; Donald might outwit me at people watching. Bella's attention turned to the three fashionable ladies talking behind their fans. "Why is it that ladies have fun gossiping during lunch, while men scowl with heated discussions?"

"Because men don't know how to gossip."

Bella guffawed and changed the topic.

"Remind me never to dress in black with a black hat. That lady on the right looks ready for a coffin. A little colour in her attire would do wonders for her looks."

"Quite right," Donald agreed, ready to end their game. "I've never seen you without a touch of flamboyant colour in your outfit. Take today. You have a vivid red straw purse to highlight those ugly brown pants." They finished their drinks.

"Shall we check on the second horse?" asked Donald. "The address will take us through a better part of town that's not too far from Dominiestraat."

***

Soon they reached the river road and were proceeding down a side street under a canopy framed by mahogany trees on either side of the road. The driver found the house named "Somersby" and turned into the lane that circled past the front door. The old Victorian home had a charm about it that made Bella envision what a Victorian home should look like, and she vowed to change the look of Donald's house.

A tall gangling man in his fifties answered the door. Donald enquired about his ad in the paper. They shook hands and exchanged names—Donald Macdonald and Richard Whitaker. *Men! My name is not important to men doing business.*

"Yes," said Richard, "I have a small horse—too small for you, sir. She's an Arabian mare." He paused as if in sorrow. "My wife loved that horse, but Mary died last month. I don't want to sell the little filly, but no one is riding her and she's become too much of a burden for me to keep as a pet."

While he loped along towards the back of the house he told them of his poor wife who had died of botulism. From what the police could tell of the kitchen, the botulism came from a pot full of reheated beans. "I had business in Georgetown that week. No one knew of her illness or how she struggled to call for help. I found her behind the front door, where she died from exhaustion as much as from food poisoning." They rounded the corner of the house, and there in a paddock down at the back of the garden Bella saw a golden horse prancing in front of a mass of green undergrowth. As the mare came running for her treat, her creamy mane and tail floated like chiffon in the wind.

Bella stood transfixed.

"The mare is seven years old now, but my Mary raised her from a foal," said Richard. Donald asked about a saddle and the man produced his wife's saddle.

"We were thinking of an English saddle to ride astride the horse," said Bella.

The man continued to direct his conversation towards Donald. "My son owns a small saddle like that—used it when a boy, but he's an adult now and back in England." He lowered his eyes to the ground. "Might as well sell it. Dick will never use it again."

The saddle, made from tan-coloured leather, shone in the sunlight. It appeared to be brand new. Richard threw a deep-green blanket over the horse, added the saddle and cinched the belly strap.

"Is the horse for your son?" asked Richard. "Sorry, I didn't catch his name."

Donald guffawed. "Richard, please meet my wife, Bella. She insists on riding astride a horse but hasn't a riding habit. We bought the boys' pants today so she wouldn't have to gather up her skirts." With that, Donald lifted Bella into the saddle, they shortened the stirrups and Richard handed her the reins.

"What do I do now?" asked Bella. "I can drive a trap but I have no idea how to drive a horse."

"That's *ride* a horse, Bella," said Donald. "Here, I'll lead her around with my hand on the bridle." The mare stood still. *Not again. Please go, horse.*

Richard called after them. "She will stand still until she feels a little bump from your knees. She doesn't use many voice commands; just lean the direction you want to turn and apply a little pressure to the stirrup on the same side as you're leaning. Move your hand holding the reins towards the direction you wish to go and the rein will rest against the opposite side of her neck. Stay with her, Donald, but let Bella try as well."

My first riding lesson and the horse is doing what I tell her to do, not like Strawberry. Bella leaned forward and stroked the mare's neck.

"I think you have sold us a horse, Richard," said Donald. "I saw a trap at the back of the house as we came in. Does the mare pull it?" Indeed she did, and the men worked out a price for the mare, her saddle and the trap.

"What's her name?" asked Bella.

"Mary called her Mischief because, as a colt, she always got into things that annoyed us as well as made us laugh."

"What a lovely name—Mischief!" cried Bella, clapping her hands together. "Donald, are we taking her now?"

"Let's see her harnessed to the trap," said Donald. While Richard and Donald adjusted the trap's harness, Bella climbed into the driver's seat and picked up the reins. When the men were finished, she started up and circled the garden in perfect control.

"Well done, Bella. I can see you have driven a trap before," cried Richard. Bella took a long jump to exit the trap without waiting for any help from Donald. *Now he knows for sure that I'll be fine with Mischief and the trap.*

"With a performance like that, Bella, I will send the carriage on its way and we'll drive home with your new mare and trap."

They put the saddle into the back of the trap with the other bits of the mare's paraphernalia, and off they went, with Bella grinning as she held the reins.

After the first turn, Donald cried out, "Bella, think of what we are doing! It's springtime and we are taking a mare home with a stallion already in the paddock."

"Is a pregnant mare difficult to handle?" asked Bella.

"You have to know what you're doing when the horses get wind of each other. I suppose Dirk knows what it's all about."

"Then I suggest that you have Dirk take on the extra work if Mischief gets pregnant and give him the foal. As for me, I adore Mischief and I intend to take her home right now, with or without your stallion ogling her."

"I think we should stop at the front of the house and consult Dirk first," said Donald. "We don't want Cobus coming on to Mischief while she's trussed up in the trap harness. Dirk will know if Mischief's in heat. I gather you don't mind if we have a baby."

"Why, Donald, we've never discussed having babies. Whatever makes you bring that up now?"

"I thought we were talking about Mischief and Cobus, not you and me, but you never know what might happen."

"You are right, Donald. One never knows what might happen."

9

MOORCROFT

Dirk came running at Donald's call. "Bring a long rope with you. We have a surprise boarder."

"Is she yours, Mr. McD?" Dirk asked, his face beaming. "She's lovely." Dirk's eyes blinked when he saw Bella's boy's pants, but he pretended not to notice.

"She's Bella's horse and her name is Mischief," said Donald.

Mischief did not care for having the trap harness removed out on the street. She laid back her ears and kicked out at them. With Dirk's ability to commune with horses, he soon had her under control and out of the trap harness. Donald hitched her to a porch post at the front of the house. "What do you think Cobus will think of her?" Donald asked Dirk as they strode off down the side of the house, pulling the trap to the back garden.

"With her ears flat back and kicking out like that, she's not in season, Mr. McD."

Men! They ignored me, but what do I know about horses? Quite a bit, I'd say!

Bella turned to look at 31 Dominiestraat. *So this is Donald's rented house that I said needed work. Whoever painted the house dark grey had no respect for Victorian architecture, and the shrubs are intent on taking over the road. It isn't the biggest house on the street but it has character. I wonder if the house has a name.* Bella probed the bushes for a name plate and found nothing. *I must ask Donald to offer his ideas for one.*

Donald came around the corner of the house. "Bella, Dirk and I have made a crude fence across our carriage pathway between the house and the fence to the neighbour's property. It might be interesting to see the attention the horses show each other. Come, I'm going to lead her around now."

Dirk stood off by the stable, holding a restraining rope tied around Cobus's neck just in case he tried to vault the fence. The second the mare came in sight, Cobus whinnied, pranced to the paddock fence and strutted like a rooster.

"It appears," said Bella, "that Cobus is a true-blooded stallion, quick to proclaim his amorous intentions." Mischief stood where they untied her tether. Her glance passed over Cobus as if he were just another bush in the garden.

"It's nearly five o'clock," said Donald. "We'll have to get back to the hotel in time for your stout. It's not very far. Do you feel like walking?"

"Society will disown us if I parade into the lounge in disagreeable attire. So, which do you prefer, Donald: clean ridiculous pants or a terribly wrinkled skirt?"

"Frankly, I don't care what society thinks," Donald replied. "Shall we go?" and he offered Bella his arm. Together they swaggered down Dominiestraat, enjoying the audacity of it all.

As they entered the hotel everyone began to stare. The pair seated themselves in the foyer lounge. A waiter brought Bella her stout and Donald, a rum. The couple didn't look up to see who might be staring nor did they try to read the waiter's inscrutable eyes.

After the first quaff of stout slid down her throat, Bella started on her next project.

"Donald, while you and Dirk were fixing the fence for Mischief, I discovered that your house doesn't have a name. I think we should name it, don't you?"

"What are you thinking?" asked Donald. "A Dutch name for the Dutch owner?"

"Of course not, silly. I want an English name that suits us. Other Victorian homes in that area have names, like Mischief's "Somersby," so we should have one too."

"Alright. How about Raven's Crag, for all of the angled roofs on the dormers?"

Bella stopped sipping her stout. "Good heavens, Donald! That is so masculine. We must find a name that represents both of us." Donald nodded his agreement. The waiter took Donald's nod to mean a second rum for him.

"Donald, what comes into your mind when you think of Scotland? Where did you spend your happiest days?"

"Out on the moors around Aberdeen. As a youth, I felt a wonderful feeling of freedom and peace with the wind in my hair and the perfume of heather. Why?"

"And," said Bella, "I always liked Dartmoor, near Plymouth. You see? We both like moors." Bella finally looked around the lounge and surveyed the sly glances they were getting, but she did not lose her train of thought. "Let me think, now. Your house is a rental property. That makes me think of us as crofters—running our horses on a tiny rented farm. What do you think of the name Moorcroft?"

"Moorcroft," Donald repeated, rolling the *rrs* of his Scottish brogue." With a broad smile, he slapped his knee and said, "Then we have it. The house will be named Moorcroft. Moorrrcrrroft. The name sounds equally Scottish and English. Now let us have dinner. Tomorrow you will meet Shauna and see the inside of the house."

Together they walked into the dining room with the elegance of royalty, even though the queen wore short cheap cotton trousers and showed her ankles for all to see.

***

When Donald and Bella arrived at Dominiestraat, a smiling Shauna stood at the front door to greet them. Just as Donald had said, Shauna looked tall and spare. Bella could see through the open door. *Spotless and polished. Not a single bug in sight.*

"Shauna, please meet my bride, Mrs. Donald Macdonald." Shauna did not extend her hand like a colonial. Instead, she gave a type of curtsey that involved a slight dip in the head and knees. A smile spread across her face as she stood aside and said, "Come. See your new home, Mrs. Macdonald."

"Please, Shauna, I don't need the formality of Mrs. Macdonald. Call me Bella."

"Oh, I no do that, Ma'am. Wouldn't be proper."

Donald said, "Shauna, call her Mrs. McD when it is just the three of us. That will do very nicely to go with Mr. McD." Shauna smiled a toothy grin.

So I am to be Mrs. McD. Shauna is happy with that name and so am I. Good heavens, I am ten years older than she is and she looks at me as if she wants to be my mama and take care of me. She is likely beaming down at me so I will like her. Yes, we'll get along well.

Donald led the way into the house. Excited with the thought of finally seeing their home, Bella hurried after her husband and Shauna.

Typical Victorian—an entrance and hallway past the stairs and on through to the kitchen, with the parlour off the hall and the dining room beyond through an archway. No, I'm wrong. The parlour and the dining room are switched so that the windows of the parlour look out on the back garden and here, through these French doors beside me, is the dining room. Perhaps Donald merely prefers to reverse the role of the two rooms.

"The dining room, my dear," Donald intoned with a sweep of his hand towards the French doors. *A table polished like a shiny penny, a bouquet of flowers and six chairs. Has he no cabinet? Shauna must have all of the dishes and cutlery in the kitchen. Light brown walls! It looks like the painter started with white paint and spat tobacco juice into it for colour, perhaps even for texture. Roses again. Donald has had a hand in this.*

Bella smiled as Donald pulled her along through an archway to the parlour. *Must have had only one can of paint!*

"Do you like my magnificent furnishings?" asked Donald in a serious tone.

Bella laughed out loud. "Why, Donald, you have only one wooden rocking chair, a footstool and a side table with a paraffin lamp on it!

This is a man's creation." Bella went right over to the chair and took possession of it, leaving the others to stand.

"I am the only person that lived here, Bella. This is all I needed. Just think, it is perfect for you to decorate the way you wish."

I suspect he had more furniture than this but removed it for lack of décor. She could not tell by looking at his face. Shauna looked at the floor to hide a grin. *I am right, but I'll let him keep his little secret. At least the windows have a lovely view of the horses.*

Through a standard door on the left wall of the living room, Bella entered the kitchen. *At last, some cupboards; no, they are shelves with no doors. Stale green walls! That door goes to the scullery. The other door must lead to Shauna's bedroom.*

"Will you have tea, Mrs. McD?" asked Shauna.

She obviously wants to serve us tea and something she's baked for my arrival.

"That would be delightful, Shauna. We will have it in the dining room with the lovely roses," said Bella before Donald could speak.

"Why tea now?" Donald whispered to Bella when they passed into the dining room. "I wanted to take you upstairs to see our bedroom."

"Because, Donald, that poor girl is dying to show me some of her capabilities."

Tea and cookies with orange skin and coconut bits in them arrived on a gilt edged plate together with fragile teacups and linen napkins, all placed on an inlaid mahogany tray. After warm words of approval to Shauna from both Donald and Bella, Donald finally took Bella upstairs so he could show off the master bedroom.

"A vanity table with a stool and two wardrobes, Donald? Now I know you bought some new things for the house, for you would never have spent time gazing into a vanity mirror or had need of two wardrobes." Bella took Donald's hand and together they circled the room. "What a beautiful rose and blue patchwork quilt on that mahogany bed, my sweet."

"The bedroom is charming, Donald." *He must have bought the whole suite from someone going back to Britain. If I want any living room furniture, I must meet other colonials and get on the grapevine to know who might be selling off their furniture. Perhaps the servants' grapevine is even more direct. Yes, Shauna and I are going to make a fine team.* Bella's thoughts came so quickly, one after another, that her head swirled. *I must ask Dirk and Shauna if they want to make extra money by being my house painters. The paint work here, both inside and outside, is disgraceful.*

Donald and Bella stepped back into the upstairs hall. *Odd, he didn't show me the rooms behind those other two doors. The far one smells horsy. I suppose he keeps his jungle gear in there.* They returned to the main floor.

"Thank you for tea, Shauna. The house looks lovely. I look forward to coming back tomorrow with our things," said Bella as they left for the hotel.

***

"Have you finished packing your valise, Bella?" Donald called from the little table by the window in the hotel room. "Your breakfast is here."

Bella swished out of the bedroom in her blue taffeta dress, carrying a large brimmed hat thick with pink silk peonies around the crown.

"You look gorgeous, Bella, but why are you dressed so exquisitely? This is moving day, the day we are leaving the New Palace Hotel and having your trunk delivered to Dominiestraat."

"I'm improving my reputation, Donald—yours too, for that matter. The other day everyone saw me in pants, improper and uncaring in my ways, an item for the grapevine among colonials. Today, the grapevine will report that I am ravishing and, no doubt, quite proper. I will be a curiosity item whom colonials wish to meet. Mark my words; the women will come calling, one or two at a time, tomorrow or soon after to have afternoon tea."

"Your slyness is showing again, Bella."

"Of course. You wouldn't want me any other way. I learned a lot in Demerara, and my nanny in Plymouth would have called me sly too. When you are as small as I am, you discover alternate ways to achieve your goals, and I plan to be well known for the right reasons—as the charming wife of Mr. Donald Macdonald."

Donald put his hands together and registered a short applause.

"Well said, my Princess. When we finish breakfast, we'll go to the bank and set up an account for you so you have a source of money when I go away in three days."

"Away, Donald? This soon?"

"No, not away, away. I must go out to Ernte and see how things are. I usually stay overnight and travel back before the late afternoon rain. Then, in two months, when the rains stop, I will truly be away—up in the mountains prospecting for gold. Remember, I told you about this before we were engaged. I panned a large number of nuggets last fall. That's where I make most of my money."

Bella dug a little more papaya from its skin and held the spoonful as if in thought.

"You pan for gold? I thought you prospected for it—you know, went around looking for outcroppings of the right type of rock to have a seam of gold in it."

"I do both, Bella. The sands of the riverbed along the Corantyne River can be panned successfully if you find a good spot. That means there has to be gold enough for a gold mine in the hills above. The gold I pan pays for my prospecting and will hopefully allow me to save enough to start up a gold mine some day. I've given ten years of my life to find it and I don't intend them to be wasted because someone else finds it first, which means I must go to the jungle every time it stops raining. In short, my dearest, I plan to be very rich. If you're finished here, let's be off to the bank. We'll drop your design for jodhpurs at the tailor's shop and then we'll move into our house."

By the time Bella and Donald reached Moorcroft, Dirk had picked up their baggage at the hotel and, with the help of a neighbouring stable boy, carried the trunk up to the master bedroom. A vase of fresh red roses sat on the dining room table.

"Roses again, Donald! They're lovely. How do you manage to give me roses when you haven't had two minutes away from my side to arrange for them?"

"Careful planning, my dear." Donald winked at Shauna.

For lunch, Shauna arranged two chairs in the garden and served them shrimp sandwiches, cordial and cookies.

"Donald, tonight we must eat at home, our home. Are you as excited about our home and us as I am?" In answer to her question, Donald took Bella by the hand, led her to the stairs and suggested that they should have an afternoon nap.

"My dear, sweet Bella," Donald said when they had the privacy of their room. "Every day is an anniversary of our wedding. I will cherish you each morning I awaken at your side and hold you tight each night when we retire. This evening at dinner, I'll have the flicker of candlelight dancing in your eyes and you will have my strong arms to adjust your chair at our table."

***

Three days later, Donald arrived at the breakfast table dressed in a khaki riding habit with polished brown boots. He wore a sidearm on his belt for all to see.

Oh dear. I'd rather not see the gun. "Good morning, Donald," Bella said, rising to give him a hug, "I came down early so Shauna and I could plan our day. She has made you a big breakfast. Sit and enjoy it."

"I'm glad that you have plans, Bella," said Donald when he had finished eating. "I'm sure you won't miss me at all with the way you fill every hour. Here is a purse with money in case you go shopping. I see Dirk has saddled Cobus, so I'll be on my way."

Hand in hand, they walked to the scullery door. There stood Cobus, tossing his head as if anxious to get underway. Dirk had tied a roll behind the saddle. *Jacket and raincoat,* guessed Bella. Then she saw it—a rifle sheath strapped on the right in front of the saddle. Donald paused in the scullery, opened a tall cupboard and removed a rifle. Dirk stepped forward to receive it, then slid it into its scabbard.

"All these guns, Donald. They frighten me."

"The rifle is for shooting poisonous snakes that bar my passing, little one. I am not setting out on a dangerous mission. Cobus and I will merely trot along a road that passes several plantations until we arrive at Ernte." Donald kissed Bella and mounted his stallion. Bella forced a smile and waved as he passed around the back corner of the house. She stood and listened as Cobus trotted down their carriageway to the street.

When she could hear only the birds in the trees, she turned and walked to the dining room window facing onto the front street. With misty eyes she sought to regain her composure. *Don't be afraid, Bella. Donald will return just as he said he would. You'll be fine on your own. This is the future.* Her hankie went back into its pocket.

***

While Shauna tidied up after breakfast and readied the market baskets, Bella paced out the size of the main floor rooms and noted her calculations on a piece of paper.

"What colour would you like the kitchen, Shauna?" asked Bella.

"Whatever you like, Mrs. McD. It is not for me to say."

"Nonsense, Shauna. You work here all day. It should be a colour that pleases you."

Shauna stood in thought for a moment. "This yellow-green makes me feel hot. I can show you the colour at the store."

***

Dirk, Shauna and Bella piled into the trap. "I'm only a pint-sized person," said Bella. "Mischief should be able to handle two and a half people."

After dropping the women off to buy paint, Dirk stopped at the lumberyard with Donald's list of required building materials for Mischief's paddock and stable. Bella bought paintbrushes and enough white, rose and mint-green paint for the downstairs rooms, kitchen and scullery. At the market, while Shauna purchased produce, Bella sought out shears to trim the shrubbery, pencils and three tablets of lined paper. With Dirk to care for the trap and carry the parcels, Bella found it easy to shop.

An early morning trip like this is delightful. By mid-morning I'll be able to put on my boy's pants, ready to start work whether Shauna thinks it's 'fittin' or not. Gabby did me a great service when she taught me to be self-reliant and capable of almost anything.

By suppertime, Dirk and Shauna, with the help of the kitchen stool and a stable box, had painted the ceilings white while Bella had thoroughly sanded and dusted the walls in the hall, dining room and parlour. Bella took Donald's stack of overseas newspapers and placed them on the floor in single sheets around the dining room.

"Tomorrow morning, Shauna," said Bella, "the three of us will start painting. We'll complete the hall, parlour and dining room before Donald comes home at five."

Buoyant with their progress, while covered with splashes of paint on their hands and face, Bella heard someone knocking at the front door.

"I'll go," said Bella. With paintbrush in hand, her hair covered with a sugar-sack cloth against paint splashes and wearing her short boy's pants, Bella answered the door.

"May I speak with Mrs. Macdonald, please?" said a pleasant English lady. "I've brought her some cookies to welcome her onto Dominiestraat. I live three doors away."

"I'm sorry, Ma'am," said Bella, trying to disguise her voice and looking at her feet so her face was not too easy to see. "Mrs. Macdonald isn't here right now, jus' us three painters. I'll give her the cookies. Thank you. Whom should I say called?"

When the lady, Mrs. Aston, had left, Bella whooped with laughter while Shauna and Dirk didn't know what to make of their mistress's lie.

"I couldn't have her telling the grapevine that she met me painting my living room," said Bella. "This is our secret. Have a cookie."

By the time Donald came home, the house smelled of wet paint but looked elegant in a light shade of dusty-rose.

"It's looks so clean and lively, Bella. How did you accomplish this in two days?"

"Organization, my dear, and a fine group of painters."

Donald handed Bella her stout, took his rum from Shauna's tray and motioned to the dining room chair beside his rocking chair. "Which chair would you prefer tonight, my beautiful Bella, so elegant in your burgundy gown?"

10

COLONIAL GRAPEVINE

"Donald, before we go downstairs, I'd like to discuss what you keep in the rooms behind those two closed doors." Bella's hand signaled that she meant the one straight across the upstairs hall from their bedroom and the door hiding the horsy odor.

"The first is a billiard room," said Donald, making no move to open the door. When Bella raised her eyebrows, Donald added, "I don't have a billiard table, so the room can stay empty until I get one. The other room has the paraphernalia for my trips into the hills." Bella opened the billiard room door.

"If this is the only empty room in the house and so large, I think it will do very well as a nursery for several children."

"Are you trying to tell me something, Bella?" Donald cried out.

"No, but maybe someday. As you said yourself about babies, one never knows."

Donald heaved a sigh and they went down to the dining room.

I wonder if that sigh was a sigh of relief. Men can be so quick to climb into bed and so slow to realize that sex carries responsibilities. He would likely die of embarrassment if I tried to discuss sex with him.

***

Donald put aside his paper and looked across the breakfast table. "Today, Dirk and I are building the paddock for Mischief. When the lumber arrives, it might help if you and Shauna took the trap to town to get Mischief out of the way."

"Fine, I'll let Shauna know. In the meantime I want Dirk and Shauna here in the dining room with clean hands at 8:30. Please tell Dirk. We are going to have our first English/Dutch lesson. Sit in on it if you wish. Your Dutch is more complete than theirs."

Bella placed three tablets of paper on one side of the table and matched the papers with three chairs, side-by-side. She moved the flowers back and placed a chair at the end of the table for Donald. She had just finished sharpening the pencils with a silver penknife when Dirk and Shauna arrived with puzzled looks on their faces. Bella sat on the centre chair and asked Shauna and Dirk to sit on each side of her.

"Do you both know how to write the Dutch alphabet and numbers?" asked Bella. Dirk and Shauna both said they did. "Then," said Bella in Gabby's teaching voice, "we will start with simple greetings and replies. First, draw two lines down the page dividing it into three columns. The first column will be English, the second, Dutch and the third is for your language, Sranan. Is that right? Or perhaps you call it Surinaams? I understand it is an English-based Creole language that suits everyone. I want to learn it as well as Dutch. Let's start with 'good day.' Copy my book for the correct spelling of the English words."

"You write 'Goedn dag,' Mrs. McD," said Dirk. They all knew what it meant so they went on to 'hello,' which turned out to be 'halo' in Dutch.

"Perhaps we should add the Sranan another day," said Bella. I plan to have a class every day except Sunday until we are all proficient with English and Dutch at least." They went through "thank you," "excuse me," "pardon me," "please let me pass," and how to ask the price of things. Bella had them write the words correctly in English and practice pronouncing them while they helped her with the Dutch.

"If we think of more useful phrases tomorrow, we will add them to this page. On the next page write 'Body Parts' and we will see how many you know. I will certainly have to study this evening with the Dutch words you tell me." Donald put down his morning paper with reluctance and came to help them with the Dutch spelling.

After Dirk and Shauna had returned to their duties, Bella looked at Donald with her chin lowered and her eyes focused from high in her eye sockets. She spoke quietly to Donald in a reproachful manner. "I believe those of us who have been fortunate enough to learn to read and write should help those less fortunate, Donald."

"You are perfectly right," said Donald. "And, as we are sharing our talents, I believe it is time for your riding lesson. I have asked Dirk to saddle Mischief."

***

Two days later, with the paddock for Mischief finished, Donald suggested that the two of them walk to town for lunch and see what the post office might have for them.

At lunch, Donald sorted through the mail.

"All business letters except for one. Here, you open this one, Bella."

"Someone named 'Aston' has invited us to an evening cocktail party," said Bella. "Why, that is the lady who called at our house the other day when I was…ah…indisposed. She left some cookies. Very nice of her. She says she wants us to meet some of their friends. Do you know her?"

"No, not really. I have to admit I know the men better. Percy Aston manages a sugar plantation down the road from Ernte. I've only met him socially—never had any business dealings with him. He's a nice enough fellow. When is the party?"

"In two weeks," said Bella. "The invitation is signed 'Rachel Aston,' so it is Percy and Rachel. You will have to help me choose the right gown to wear." Donald pulled a note pad from his pocket to check his list of appointments. He jotted down the date for the party. When he looked up from his notes he said: "I see here that the SS *Balfour* arrives tomorrow night. Dirk and I will go to the docks for your sewing machine. One of the business letters I just received is from two men who are interested in prospecting for gold. Now, who would give them my name and why did they choose me for a lunch partner tomorrow?"

"Do you think they're trying to pry on your prospecting?" asked Bella.

"Maybe. Likely. But I won't judge them until I meet them." Donald put the letter in his pocket. "I must have lunch with them in order to know what they have in mind, or 'on their minds,' in case it threatens my interests on the Corentyne River. I'll walk over tomorrow if you need the trap. The hotel isn't far."

***

The next morning Bella sat at her vanity and wrote three letters. The first letter thanked Mrs. Aston for her invitation and assured her that they would attend. The second letter, to her parents, described the highlights of moving into 31 Dominiestraat, their two servants, Shauna and Dirk, and the two horses. *There! Mother will like the idea that we have servants, and father will be happy that we have horses and a trap to make travel easier. They don't need to know about my painting spree or the fact that we have hardly any furniture. They'll hear bit by bit when the time is right. I'll tell them about the party in my next letter.* Bella addressed the two envelopes, added stamps and set them aside for Dirk to post. *What a simple and organized life I have with Donald. It is truly paradise.*

Bella did not intend that anyone in the household should see the third letter. When finished, it read:

Dear Sir,

Your tenant in 31 Dominiestraat, Paramaribo, Mr. Donald Macdonald, recently married. May I introduce myself, his wife, Isabella Macdonald. At this time my husband is quite busy with affairs of the sugar plantation, so I have taken it upon myself to write to you about an important matter. As I do not have your name and address, I hope to reach you by giving the bank this letter and asking them to forward it to you.

My husband has been at this address for ten years. When I brought to his attention that your house needed painting, he smiled and said he wasn't the type to notice things like that. However, upon inspection, he agreed that the sun has dried the south facing walls and the rain has played havoc with exposed areas already beaten by the nor' westerlies. Indeed, if the house does not receive attention, moss and ants will start to invade the seams of the wood.

I have enclosed a statement from the local paint shop, giving the cost of paint for this size of house. The shop owner told me to double the cost of the paint to approximate the cost of labour needed to execute the work.

As my husband has his monthly rent transferred from his account at the bank to an account that you no doubt have there, I suggest the following:

I will gladly make arrangements to have your house painted and then present two invoices to the bank—one for paint and one for labour. You, in turn, will inform the bank and me that you have made this arrangement with me, so the bank knows to reimburse my husband's account when I present the two invoices to them. The dry season comes in August, which is two months away. I trust that I will hear from you by September and that you will be in favour of my proposal.

Sincerely…

She signed it Isabella Macdonald, and fitted it into an envelope with no recipient's address. She added her return address on the back of the envelope and placed it in her purse.

As soon as Donald has had time to meet those men at the hotel, I'll walk to the bank and ask the bank manager to put it in the bank's mail pouch. Not even Shauna and Dirk will know my destination. Bella checked her watch to be sure that she had waited long enough, then she set out on her walk.

"Just a walk," she told Shauna. "I need the exercise. I should be back for lunch in twenty-five minutes." In ten minutes she reached the bank. The bank manager had no trouble with agreeing to Bella's request, and she arrived home in time for lunch, quite pleased with herself. *It is simply ridiculous that women must fill their time with small undertakings around the home when they are quite capable of organizing things of bigger magnitude. Donald has no interest in planning for the house to be painted, but he will be pleased to see it done. I can't see the owner refusing me. The neighbours don't have to know that I planned it, if that is what society demands. I must remember to ask Donald about Paramaribo cocktail parties. I suspect that I should look demure and leave my outrageousness at home. I will ask him if he thinks the pink gown is the right one to wear.*

***

"How very nice to meet you, Mrs. Macdonald," Rachel Aston intoned when her butler brought Donald and Bella to his mistress. "Percy," Rachel called to her husband, "Mr. and Mrs. Macdonald have arrived. Do come and meet Donald's new wife." *New wife—do people ever have old wives? Are all colonials this proper?*

Donald shook hands with the host and hostess. "Please meet my bride, Isabella."

"Bella," interjected Bella. "Everyone calls me Bella, Mrs. Aston."

I'd have thought she would have invited us to call them Rachel and Percy. No matter, I will anyway. Their parlour is so formal it looks like a hotel foyer. If she recognized me as the painter that she spoke to at our door, she didn't show it.

Rachel escorted the Macdonalds around the room to introduce them. "Stephanie and Ronald Lyon, please meet Isabella and Donald Macdonald. Isabella is new to Paramaribo. The Macdonalds are my neighbours, three doors away." Rachel went on to the next couple, Sarah and Edward Hargrave, and made exactly the same introduction. On around the room they went until they had met all five couples.

There's Rachel, Stephanie, Sarah, Marie and Evelyn, pronounced Eevlyn.

"Yes, thank you. I will have a glass of white wine," Bella said to the butler and continued her thoughts. *I shall engage them all in conversation and find out their favourite pastimes. I'm sure I will find someone who sews, knows tropical plants or rides. Now, a rider might be Rachel because I've seen her butler down by our stable with Dirk. Their butler likely looks after the horses. I'll train Dirk the same way.*

"What a lovely party, Rachel," Bella said as Rachel passed by.

"Thank you, Isabella." Rachel nodded and swept past as if on a mission. *Well, la-dee-daw, ain't she the "praw-pa" one! I told her to call me Bella and she introduced me to everyone in the room as Isabella. Surely she didn't hold this party to show me off as a trophy, the pip-squeak Donald landed. I shall be bigger than life, a perfect charmer, and show her that size doesn't matter.*

Bella moved towards Stephanie. "I hear you live in this area of town, Stephanie." Bella had no idea where Stephanie lived, but at least it started a conversation. Bella offered her friendship by saying that all her friends called her Bella and that she should too. The conversation came around to playing bridge.

"Would you like to come to our bridge club?" asked Stephanie. *What better way to look for furniture, even though I detest bridge.*

After a suitable length of conversation, Bella moved on to Sarah.

"What a charming gown, Sarah. Where should I go shopping for gowns? I can't find anything small enough to fit me." *From the simplicity and fit of the gown, my guess is that she sews.*

"Why, thank you, Isabella. Would you like a letter from me to introduce you to my couturier in Paris?" replied Sarah. *Oh dear. Bad guess. She must have gained a pound.* Again, Bella visited for a bit, asked Sarah to call her Bella and moved on to Marie.

By this time the men had grouped themselves near the archway to the dining room and the ladies were taking over the rattan chairs. *Before the places to sit are all taken, I must sit in the middle of the group. If I am lucky, Marie or Evelyn will sit beside me.* Marie chose the chair next to Bella. *Hmmm, a bit short. Maybe she sews.*

"Marie Stevenson, I believe," said Bella. "My husband has a friend by the name of Stevenson back in Scotland. Yes, I remember now, they live in Moffat, close to the English border. He sells those newly designed prams—or is it treadle sewing machines?—something like that. I know his wife has a treadle sewing machine and sews."

Within minutes Marie and Bella had exchanged the information that both liked to sew and, in fact, both had the newly invented Singer sewing machine.

"I must make some drapes for our home. Perhaps we could go to town together in my trap and you could show me where the fabric shops are located."

"Did I hear that you drive the trap yourself?" asked the lady still to be met, Evelyn Peterson. *Uh-oh, is she going to be pleased or negative about me, a lady, driving her own trap?* Evelyn continued. "I ride, but Olaf, my husband, won't teach me how to drive our trap. He says it isn't proper. Will you teach me how to drive?" Evelyn sounded so excited by the whole idea that Bella agreed and they set a date.

By the time the hors d'oeuvres appeared on the dining room table, causing people to circulate again, Bella had a date with Sarah, who showed an interest in gardening. Stephanie named the next Wednesday for bridge, where Bella hoped to find someone with furniture for sale. On Monday, Bella and Marie were having lunch at the club and visiting the fabric shops. Evelyn and Olaf decided that horseback riding with Bella and Donald would fit very nicely in the cooler part of Sunday morning. *I have visited with every one of the ladies except Rachel.*

Bella smiled sweetly as she passed four men still discussing business near the archway. Donald stood beside the dining room table, enjoying the shrimp. She paused and chatted for a few minutes.

"Donald," she asked quietly, "am I fitting in properly?" Donald smiled, winked and nodded. Others came to the table and their private conversation ended. Bella stayed near the table, sampling cut fruit with a pineapple dip until she saw Rachel coming towards her on her way to the kitchen.

"Rachel, the hors d'oeuvres are so tasty. Where do you find things like these?" *Do I see a frosty stare coming my way? What did I say that she could find offensive?*

"My dear Isabella, I don't 'find things like this,' I make them." *She said that courteously but I don't think she meant it to be all that friendly. What do I say now?*

"Really, Rachel! How talented of you. You must be a connoisseur of tropical delights. The pineapple dip with the fruit plate tempted my taste buds completely." *It's true, a sincere compliment. Maybe now is when*

I should ask her to call me Bella. Now that she's smiling, I'm certainly not going to ask her if she shares her recipes.

Bella noticed that, except for short greetings, none of the women visited with the men. *How strange? Surely the ladies know their friends' husbands. I'd think the women would find men's conversation stimulating. I know I do, so why should I not visit with them? If visiting with the men is improper, then I must do it without being forward.*

Bella walked up to the nearest group of men with a smile and her hand extended.

"I'm Donald's wife, Bella, and you are Ronald Lyon, husband of Stephanie?" She raised her eyebrows with the question. "Stephanie has invited me to play bridge next Wednesday so that I may meet more of the colonials." Bella moved on to the next man. "Edward Hargrave? I understand you have a beautiful garden. Sarah has asked me over to see it." Bella smiled at the next two men standing in the group. "I am pleased to meet you too, Hamish Stevenson. Now there's a Scottish name. Your wife, Marie, and I both enjoy sewing. And Olaf Peterson," Bella said as she took his hand. "When I asked Evelyn to call me Bella instead of Isabella, she confided that she preferred Eve. Do folks call you Olie?" The men all laughed. The women stared. Men seldom laughed about business.

Ronald said, "You just shook hands with Ron, Ed, Jim and Olie." The men were smiling and chuckling with good humour while their wives continued to look on in amazement. "Our host, Percy Aston, is still Percy," Ron added.

"And sometimes we call Rachel 'the Duchess'—to her face, mind you. It's in fun, not meant to be mean," said Ed.

Hamish spoke up. "I prefer Jim, for James, the Anglicized name for Hamish. Jim sounds much better than Ham." Again the men chuckled.

Bella found it easy to laugh and talk with the men. They seemed happy to leave the topics of business and made inquiries like, "Where did you meet Donald?"…"What brought you to Paramaribo?"…"Demerara first?"…"You are from Plymouth? My uncle lives in Stanton, not far away." Finally, Rachel and Percy came to listen to the men and Bella chitchat. *Now things are getting more civilized. The wine and rum are making the guests lose their inhibitions about mixing with each other. Just wives visiting with wives and husbands talking business doesn't make much of a party. I hope the women don't think I have my eye on their husbands. I would hate to have them think that I am a troublemaker. Imagine, skinny me stealing their husbands! I must go and pay some attention to Donald so they know I am a loyal wife.*

Donald had his own group with three ladies gazing up at his earnest face. *They seem spellbound with his monologue about the dangers of the jungle, or perhaps they're entranced by the curious twitchings of his red moustache as he speaks.* Bella caught his eye as she worked her way through the guests to his side.

The Aston's party continued much later than expected, for everyone enjoyed the funny comebacks that the men offered and the times when the conversation began to expose stories of embarrassing moments during colonial life.

Donald finally whispered to Bella, "It's one o'clock in the morning. House parties never last this long. I think we should be going." Bella noticed the other men were pairing up with their wives the same way and agreed that they should begin the exodus.

"If we leave first, Donald," Bella whispered, "they will all stay a little longer to pass on the information about me that the first four men heard before the rest joined us. Won't they have a lovely time trying to guess why I am so short? I assure you, Donald, soon the grapevine will know I talk to men, drive a trap and every other scrap of information they heard this evening. Men gossip just as much as women do." Donald and Bella moved towards the front door. "In return for feeding the grapevine, I have four new friends who plan to spend time with me and perhaps Rachel will break down and call me 'Bella.' We might even be invited out to dinner by some of these couples, which means I had better work on 31 Dominiestraat so we, too, can entertain."

"Thank you for a wonderful party, Rachel, Percy," said Donald. "It's been a pleasure to meet everyone. I hope we meet again soon. Good night."

"Yes, thank you, my friends," said Bella, and they turned and stepped from the bright lights of the party into South American darkness.

The stars danced overhead as Bella and Donald walked arm in arm towards their house. Halfway home, Bella stopped to stare at the sky between two mahogany trees. With no lights in the homes at one a.m. and no moon, the never-ending depths of blackness were laced with multitudes of stars, more than she had ever imagined.

"That, my little Rosebud, is the Southern Cross," said Donald, with his hand pointing into the heavens. "It is the constellation that the British and Dutch ships used to sail the Caribbean and find their colonies of mangrove swamps and monkeys."

"Donald! You can be so infuriating," said Bella. "Here you go wasting a perfect opportunity for a hug and kiss under the stars by joking about mangrove swamps and monkeys, can you imagine!" With that, now in the light shining from their window, she turned and held up both arms. Donald swept her upwards into a tender embrace just as the other guests left the Aston's house.

Bella hugged a little longer for all to see under the veil of soft light. She giggled into Donald's ear, "More grist for the grapevine, my dear. By tomorrow morning we will be well known as a pleasant couple, ardently in love, talented and handsome." For the onlookers, Donald twirled in a circle with Bella's feet on the fly. Once the twirl ended, he cuddled her into his arms like a baby and carried her into their house.

11

PARAMARIBO SOCIETY

Again, Bella heard pounding and sawing in the back garden.
"What are you building with all that lumber?" she asked.
"Two things," said Donald. "First, a lean-to for the trap. There is no need for it to be cooked by the sun and drenched in the rain. And secondly, we're building a mouse-tight storage shed for my 'smelly' prospecting paraphernalia so you will have a sewing and ironing room. I envision you sewing up yards of draperies while I'm away, and I thought you should have a permanent place for your machine." For that, Donald earned a kiss. Embarrassed at sharing this private moment, Dirk looked away.

"There's no need to look away, Dirk," said Donald. "One of these days you'll find the right woman and fall in love too."

**

Over the next week, Bella kept her dates with her new friends and came home with samples of material, a better idea of tropical plants and a few leads on buying furniture. At dinner, she asked, "Donald, would you like to go riding with Eve and Olie Peterson again on Sunday? If we go early we should be home before the sun bakes our brains."

"Good idea, Bella. Cobus needs the exercise before I leave for the hills."

***

On Sunday, when they arrived at the Stevenson house, a third couple rode up. Eve, astride her mare, Midnight, spoke up.

"Bella and Donald, allow me to introduce you to Angelique and Mitchell ter Keer. That's Ange and Mitch," Eve added. "Mitch is an accountant in government affairs. He's planned a different route for our ride today."

The congeniality of colonials is most amazing! Maybe it takes a special sort of person to go wandering around the world—an adventurer, someone who laughs at change, someone who will try new things? And isn't it nice that I am one of them.

Bella joggled along at the trot on the crushed gravel streets, her backbone lurching forward with each landing. Soon, verdant shrubs dotting open land on clay soil lay ahead. The scene looked serene and the air smelled clean.

"Turn off here," called Mitch. "We can pick up the pace on this clay path."

Look at me! I'm going fast enough to make my hair fly in the wind. I do believe it's easier to gallop than pop up and down in the saddle, trotting. I feel as if Mischief and I are one.

They arrived at a small creek. By travelling in single file, exactly where Mitch guided them through the water, they forded the rivulet and continued on a path with sugar cane to the right and jungle to the left. After a few minutes, the fields of sugar cane opened to reveal first a barn, then the rooftop of the plantation manor with the river and dock ahead. A man hailed them in Dutch.

"I've brought along company, Connie," Mitch called back in his native Dutch. Edwina, Connie's wife, came from the house to greet the riders.

"Come in, come in," said Connie. "Call my wife Ed, instead of Edwina," said Connie in Dutch.

I must listen carefully to know what they're saying. Why, I do believe I am thinking in Dutch! I am following along quite well. I'll have to add my bit now and then to see if they laugh at my pronunciation. This must be the first time I've had to converse in Dutch. How fascinating.

***

"Stephanie's bridge club has asked me to be a permanent substitute," Bella said to Donald a few days later. Donald nodded. Bella rocked her chair a few times and continued. "I will say 'yes' because they are the only ladies I've met that gossip, and I learn a great deal that way." From his hard chair next to the rocker, Donald nodded again and sipped his gin and tonic. Bella suspected that Donald wasn't listening, but carried on. "If I fill in at bridge, perhaps I will find a lead on some furniture through the gossip."

"Furniture?" Donald came alive. "What kind? I suppose any kind is useful, especially another soft chair."

***

At bridge, the foursomes spoke English. When Bella mentioned having met Rachel Aston, two women at her table, Hildebrand and Faye, claimed to know her.

"What a great coincidence," said Hildebrand. "We're having lunch with Rachel on Thursday. Please join us. I'm sure we will all become fast friends."

"If Rachel and I need transportation, I drive a trap," offered Bella.

Hildebrand frowned and said, "No, that won't be necessary. I'll have my driver pick you up at twelve sharp after we have collected Rachel." *It seems Hildebrand is the spokesman for this pair.*

***

On their way to bed that night, Bella asked Donald if he knew of Hildebrand or Faye. "I met them at the bridge club."

"I don't know a Faye, but I've heard the name Hildebrand. If I'm right, you are going to be in high company. Her husband is the local manager of the Dutch East India Line—Fenton and Hildebrand Leppard. Faye's husband is likely with shipping too."

***

Thursday arrived. Bella chose her new turquoise dress and planned to carry a parasol. *Ruffled petticoats are just too hot, and hats are a nuisance when dining. I'll put my hair in a French roll and nestle white daisies next to the roll. If I am improperly dressed, I am not one to worry. At least I will be comfortable.*

When she came downstairs, Shauna saw Bella from the kitchen.

"My, Mrs. McD, you look pretty and ever so comfortable in that slim line."

"Thank you, Shauna. Your English is as good as my Dutch. Three cheers for us."

Hildebrand's driver arrived punctually at noon with the three other ladies seated in a covered carriage. Bella could see that all three wore large hats. Bella held her folded parasol and small purse in one hand and stepped into the carriage a might too fast for the driver to assist her. A silent second followed. Rachel spoke first while Bella searched among the faces for a smile.

"Good afternoon, Isabella," said Rachel, accenting the name Isabella, as if Bella should learn to use her full name. *I wonder if it is the lack of a hat or my ability to step into the carriage with no assistance that has caught their eyes. If I continue to break the rules, I wonder who will change—them or me?*

"How nice to see you all," Bella bubbled sincerely and held out her hand to gently grasp each set of limp fingers. Bella leaned back in her carriage seat and looked out of the open window to match the actions of the other ladies.

The three friends marched into the New Palace Hotel dining room one after the other, looking straight ahead with their noses held high. Bella, bringing up the rear, smiled and waved at the man behind the counter to show that she remembered him.

During the chatter that went along with lunch, Faye said, "Isabella, I hear that you are teaching your servants to speak, read and write English. Whatever for? They are both Creoles!" *My, my. It sounds like she rehearsed that line.*

"You ask why?" said Bella and followed it with, "I ask, why not?"

Hildebrand jumped into the conversation. "Mark my words, if you give these half breeds any education, they will take over the country."

Is this why they asked me to lunch—to explain to me the rules of being a colonial in Paramaribo? I think I will answer their questions with questions and see how long it takes them to be frustrated with me. I doubt they will recognize that I am amusing myself.

"Rachel, do you have horses?" said Bella while they waited for their desserts to arrive. "Yesterday, I met your butler out at our paddock visiting with Dirk, our man. Your fellow seemed to know a lot about horses."

"He may, I wouldn't know," said Rachel with a disagreeable look.

"Didn't I see a stable and paddock through your dining room window the other evening?" said Bella, as innocently as she could manage.

"I suppose you did. We have a cow," said Rachel before she could stop herself.

"How wise of you, Rachel. My parents kept a cow. And you, Hildebrand and Faye, does your butler—oh excuse me, I mean your driver—care for your horses?"

"My husband's company has the stable," said Hildebrand with a haughty demeanour. "I wouldn't have a horse smelling up my back garden."

Bella smiled sweetly. "I love horses. They have personalities all of their own. Since I arrived in Paramaribo, Donald has taught me to ride astride my Arabian mare. Do any of you ride?" From their blank expressions, the women hadn't yet digested the word "astride." Bella decided to return to the subject of servants who speak English.

"Hildebrand, your driver asked me very politely to come down to the carriage when you stopped by for me. Where did he learn his English?"

"My husband would not have hired him if he could not speak English. I have no idea where he learned it," said Hildebrand, her head tipped up towards the ceiling.

"Faye," started Bella. "Wouldn't it be helpful if your maid spoke English?"

"My maid, like me, speaks Dutch," answered Faye. "In fact, I prefer it if she can't understand our English conversations." *I wonder who is fooling whom. One cannot be around another language without understanding some of what is said.*

Faye then asked Bella, "Isabella, why do you find it so important for your servants to speak English?" Her tone of voice showed that the matter was not finished.

"It goes both ways, my dear," said Bella in a pleasant tone. "In their efforts to learn English, I have learned to speak Dutch quite well in the three and a half months I have lived in Surinam. If you would rather speak Dutch now, that's fine with me."

"No, we'll not speak Dutch," said Rachel emphatically. "I am told that colonials from England should not give in to these people." *I suspect she has not bothered to learn Dutch. I wonder if Percy taught the stable boy to speak English so he could be a butler to out-do the other colonials. No one else seems to have a butler.*

"Well," said Bella, "when our Dirk can manage English sufficiently, I plan to teach him to be a butler. That way, he'll have experience in another line of work and get on better in life as he grows older." Hildebrand and Faye flapped their eyelids at each other. Rachel's face burned red. Her eyes shot a hateful look at Bella.

I am right. Percy must have tutored their stable boy to serve as the butler. Nothing wrong in that, except she doesn't want those other two to know that her household has broken the unspoken rules of helping darker skinned people to learn something. I wonder if the indentured plantation workers on Ernte get any schooling.

"Hildebrand, I know you through bridge," said Bella. "What do you do on other days? Do you have a hobby? Music, perhaps, or sewing?" Bella saw a touch of perspiration run down the side of Hildebrand's face, starting at the headband of her big hat. Bella glanced at the other two. Faye had a quaint Japanese fan in motion and Rachel's face burned red.

At first Hildebrand seemed lost for an answer. "What do I do, Isabella? Well, I'm having lunch with you today, am I not?" Bella said nothing, knowing that silence might urge Hildebrand to dig deeper for an answer. "My husband has a great number of social occasions to which I must accompany him." Again Bella waited. Finally, Hildebrand blurted, "Why would I sew? That's work for the servants!" *I needn't go on baiting them to know that these three women are prissy, self-righteous and opinionated. I do not need them for friends. Well, perhaps Rachel might become a friend. She's my closest neighbour. She brought me cookies and introduced me to four other women who are very friendly. It is time to break up this luncheon.*

"This has been delightful, ladies," Bella said cheerily. "It's a shame to go home in the heat of the day when it is so cool in here. You know, I designed and sewed this gown myself specifically to find a cooler way to dress. She stood and twirled around to show them the back of her dress accented by a short peplum and skirt free of hot ruffled petticoats. *Surely they will envy how fashionable I am in this new style. I do believe they are speechless.*

Hildebrand wagged her finger for the luncheon cheques and the waiter came running. "Tell the porter to have my driver come to the front door of the hotel. We wish to leave," said Hildebrand to the waiter who bowed over and over in his retreat from her crisp demands. Each lady left money on the table to cover her bill. Bella remembered Simon Henker's remark in Demerara, "If you have the money to eat out, you have enough to give these poor waiters a proper gratuity." Bella allowed the other ladies to see her last "indecent act" by putting coins at the top of her plate as well as beside the bill.

They rode home in silence. Bella found herself first to be dropped off. She jumped down by herself, like a gazelle, to add insult to their ideas of propriety. *Those three don't approve of me, but it doesn't matter; I don't approve of them. Donald will burst out laughing when I tell him about today's lunch.*

***

"Does it suit your schedule if I take the trap, Bella?" asked Donald the following week. "I must find out which ships stop in at Nickerie that will board Cobus and a pack mule. Then there's the farm where I rent the mule and an outfitter where I buy blasting charges, paraffin for my lamp and other things that I'll need. I may not get it all done today, so count on me using the trap for two or three days."

***

During that week, Donald's business kept him away all day. Concerns about his departure in search of gold in the jungle began to creep into Bella's mind.

July's wet weather will soon give way to a dry season and Donald will be off prospecting for two, maybe four months, if the rain stays away. I'm glad I have Shauna and Dirk and some friends or I'd find the weeks ahead unbearable. Perhaps I can sew drapes late into the night so I don't notice the empty bed. With my wardrobe so full, I'll teach Shauna to sew. She might like sewing for her family. If she makes them all something, she will be an experienced seamstress. And Dirk, I must remember his butler lessons. Keep thinking, Bella. Maybe you'll talk yourself out of being lonely. You'll have to. You knew before you married him that he would go prospecting.

With her self-lecture over, Bella decided to place the drapery samples in the different rooms. She hoped their eye-catching colour would drag Donald's attention away from his jungle trip for a moment. *I must know his choices before he leaves if I wish to complete the drapes while he is away.*

***

Two evenings later, Donald noticed the bolts of material in the dining room.

"Ah yes, the drapery materials, Bella. Not the one on the right. It is too dark. That leaves a choice between stripes and one that looks like a Monet painting of pink and white flowers on mauvish-blue." Donald went over to inspect the samples of material more carefully. "I like the blue Monet. Stripes are too harsh for my dainty Dresden doll. Which is your favourite among the three samples?"

"We are lucky, you and I, Donald. We think alike and choose alike. The mauvish-blue, called periwinkle blue, is my favourite too. I am going to let Shauna choose the kitchen curtains; it's her room. The upstairs drapes will wait until we go to bed." *Project number two is ready for the days ahead. With house painting, the Dutch/English lessons, teaching Shauna to sew and training Dirk to be a butler, I'll be fine. Yes, the future, Mrs. McD, is in your hands. All will be well.*

***

The rains came to an end. Donald had his travel plans for Nickerie and a mule waited in the back garden.

"I leave in two days, Bella. What would you like to do? We have been so busy making friends and preparing for my absence that you haven't been to Ernte yet. Would you like us to travel there in the trap and have a picnic at the plantation? All of the indentured employees will be curious to see the boss's new wife. It would be a good idea for you to meet the overseer. Or we could go to the New Palace Hotel for a night. The governor is out of town again." He winked at her with a knowing look. "Choose whatever you like, even if it is just a night out for dinner and dancing."

"It's hard to make a choice," said Bella. She furrowed her forehead in thought. "I have it. We'll leave for Ernte in the early cool of the morning, see the plantation house with its termites, call the workers and their families together to meet me, have a picnic, come home, have stout time and leave for the hotel with dinner clothes in a valise. Then," Bella emphasized, "I'll run a tub of lovely warm water for us in the governor's deep bathtub and after that we'll dress for dinner and dancing. The next morning we'll come home so you can prepare the load for the pack mule, and on your last evening, we'll enjoy each other's company over a candlelight dinner at home. How's that for a plan?"

"Bella, you have done it again. You have taken all of my ideas and built them into one plan. I suppose it could work." He smiled as he thought about the full day ahead. "Fine, let's do it. You tell Shauna and I'll tell Dirk."

***

"This is like the road to Connie's plantation, only down river," said Bella.

Bella moved closer to Donald's shoulder. "The countryside is so serene, Donald, with just our trap wheels quietly rolling on clay, rhythmic hoof beats, wind sighing in the palms and birds calling to each other. You must enjoy your rides to Ernte very much."

Donald changed the reins to his left hand and put his right arm around Bella.

"I've been meaning to tell you something, Bella. This seems to be a good time."

Bella froze. She always feared when he spoke in this sombre voice. *I don't want to hear about the dangers of the jungle or of what I should do if you fail to come home. I just want happy thoughts. Please don't lecture me!*

"Bella, I want you to know that going off to the hills to prospect for gold is much harder this year than ever before. It is hard because I have you, your companionship and your love, and I am trading it for material wealth as if you didn't matter to me." He leaned over and kissed her forehead. "You will always be with me in my mind. I will see you in the beauties of nature that you always enjoy—the shafts of sunlight breaking through to the forest floor, the soft moving clouds overhead and the bright colour of an orchid nestled on the trunk of a fallen tree. And when I clip a wild banana for my lunch, I will taste your sweet lips and savour every moment."

Bella reached over and pulled on the reins to stop the trap so that the two of them could hug and have a silent moment for their strengths to join as one.

"We will both be fine, my love," murmured Bella, "just fine." She paused to snuggle closer. "I have been searching my soul for the strength to carry me through this time of separation, and you have just given it to me. The smell of your cologne still lingering on your pillow, the manly odour of your cigars, the rattle of the newspaper at breakfast and your patient silence will be with me every moment. Despite the distance, our love will be complete and you will come home satisfied to have worked on your passion. I will do the same—sewing drapes, learning Dutch and several other little projects I have planned to keep me from worrying about you in that awesome jungle."

"You mustn't worry about me, Bella. I am one of the best jungle men out there. I can take care of my safety; I eat well off the land and I don't get lost because I have a sextant and know the sun and the stars."

"And I have Shauna and Dirk and good friends to watch over me, my dearest. We will both be fine during this first parting," Bella added, with passion in her arms and kisses until their quiet space again included the songs of birds and wind in the palms.

In this quiet companionship, they passed several fields of cane. The silence of love and their nearness to each other filled their hearts completely.

"We are here, Bella," Donald said softly. Bella lifted her head from Donald's shoulder. At the entrance of the next narrow side road, a brand new sign emblazoned with red lettering on a golden background proclaimed "Reich Ernte." Below, in black neat lettering, it read "Manager – Donald Macdonald, Overseer – Ken O'Reilly."

Bella asked, "You have an Irish overseer? You have never mentioned him."

"Maybe yes, maybe no," Donald teased. "I didn't want to mention him until you met him. He'll come as soon as he hears the trap." *Another one of Donald's surprises. I wonder if the overseer is a reformed pirate with a black patch over one eye, a whip-cracking monster or a little man with leprechaun ears and a twinkle in his eyes. Wherever do I get these ridiculous thoughts? Most times my mind is quite sane.*

12

REICHE ERNTE

Mischief balked at making the turn into the narrow plantation pathway leading to Reiche Ernte. Bella jumped from the trap, spoke softly to the mare, then stepped aside. The horse took a few steps and waited for Bella to climb on again before continuing on.

"Well done, Bella. You won't have any trouble reaching Ernte when I'm gone." They jiggled down the narrow pathway through the green fields of sugar cane until Donald said, "Behold, Termite Mansion! I'm sure Ken O'Reilly will be waiting for us."

The dormers of a large house appeared over the sugarcanes. Like Connie's plantation home, it faced the riverbank with a dock stretching out into the river. The front veranda had pillars that held a wide sloping roof with a dormer to the front and rear. Its white paint peeled from weather or termites. A dark-skinned Creole came towards them, a tall man with soft brown eyes, a gentle smile and powerful shoulders.

The two men shook hands and clapped each other on the back like old school buddies. "Kehinde, may I present my wife, Isabella Macdonald," said Donald.

"My pleasure," said Kehinde, in perfect English with an outstretched hand. Bella took the brown hand in hers and patted their clasped hands with her left hand. She looked up and up. *I've never seen such a tall Creole, and his skin feels just like mine. He seems important. I wonder what job he holds on the plantation.*

"Bella, please meet my overseer, Kehinde O'Reilly." *This Mulatto is the Irish overseer?* Donald continued: "The workers and the women call him Ken. The children say Mr. O." Bella smiled her warmest smile and hoped astonishment didn't show on her face. Donald asked Ken to tell all the workers and their families to come to the grassy area at the back of the big house.

"Bella, while the families assemble I'll give you a quick tour of the house. The termite-riddled wood doesn't show, but I don't think the stairway to the upper floor is safe." They climbed the three steps to the veranda and paused at the front door. "Did meeting my overseer surprise you? In the 1830s, when the African slaves were given equality and freedom, a colonial in Surinam named Sam O'Reilly married an African slave girl. He and Daisy, as Sam called her, started several generations with the O'Reilly name. By birthright, Ken and his family are Irish."

Donald and Bella passed through French doors into the parlour. "Why, Donald, the house looks very comfortable. It's even furnished. If we don't want to live here, why not take this lovely rattan furniture to Moorcroft?"

"Because," Donald warned, "you will infect our home with termites, that's why."

"The house seems nice and clean," Bella offered.

"That's because Ken's daughter, Wumi, sweeps it every day. Omowumi is her full name but everyone calls her Wumi. Her mother, Asha, is from India. Wumi is a beautiful, intelligent eighteen-year-old who speaks English, Dutch and Sranan."

"Really!" marvelled Bella. "If we can't use the house, Donald, would you mind if I used this room for a classroom to help the families learn good hygiene and proper Dutch? As a child, I yearned to be in school like other children. At home reading books, I probably received an even better education, but somehow it wasn't the same. Perhaps I could help your people."

They moved through the ancient kitchen towards the rear of the house.

"Dear Bella, you are so soft hearted. If you can figure out a way to use the house, by all means teach my workers to read and write. I taught Ken everything he knows about the plantation because I recognized his ability to lead his people. I trust him implicitly and you may too. If I find my gold mine and leave Ernte, I'll ask the owner to choose Ken O'Reilly for his next manager. Let's go outside; the families have gathered."

***

The workers and their families stood quietly in a large semi-circle. No one smiled.

They are not particularly clean or mended in their manner of dress. The children are hiding behind their mothers' saris, afraid of me. I can't tell from the women's faces what they think of me. Can they scrutinise my face? Do they know I think they are dirty?

"Donald," Bella whispered, "I don't think they like me. My skin is too white; I am too small. What am I to do?"

"I'm sure you will think of something, my dear. Be positive, like you always are."

Perhaps they don't know how to act in front of this new important white woman that the boss has brought among them. Are they afraid that I'll act as if they're inferior? Then I shall not, for each one is a person like me. I must try to put them at ease. We are in the shade; I'll take off my hat. That should make me look less superior.

Donald led Bella forward in a courteous way and said in Dutch, "My wife, Mrs. Macdonald." The women gave their typical half curtsey. The men nodded and the curious eyes of the children continued to peek out from behind their parents.

Bella stepped forward to reduce the distance between her and the families. In her few Sranan words and wearing a wide smile she said, "Families of Ernte, you must call me Mrs. McD." She then went around the half-circle and shook hands with the man of each family, met the wives and children and found pleasant remarks for everyone. *Perhaps shaking hands is a European custom, but they all offered their hands and smiled in approval. I hope I did the right thing.*

"Thank you, Mrs. McD," Ken said aside to Bella. "Treating them as people with value has made them smile. Do you see that?"

Five women started to sing and dance to a rhythm strange to Bella's ears.

"They dance to welcome you, Mrs. McD," said Ken.

"Thank you," Bella called out when she thought they were finished, but the women were not finished. They stayed in front of the others and danced an Irish jig with three little children in their midst trying to copy their mothers' moves while the rest of the women sang "The Irish Washer Woman" in an odd version of English. When the dancing finished, Bella rushed up and squeezed their hands two at a time with her little white ones. The closed look on their faces vanished. Bella's magic had spread among them.

"I'm so proud of you, Bella," said Donald. "Everything you said and the way you moved among the families pleased them as if you were a goddess. Come, I will introduce you to Ken's wife, Asha, and Wumi. Then we will go to the river for our picnic."

***

Back at Moorcroft after "stout time" as Donald called it, they continued with Bella's plan for the day. Valise in hand, Donald and Bella walked to the New Palace Hotel, waved good day to the registry clerk and went to the Governor's Suite.

***

"Do you think we will ever have warm water coming from a tap like this?" asked Bella as they stepped into the oversized bathtub.

"If we keep track of the governor's timetable, we can enjoy this big tub as often as he goes out of the country on business. Will that do, my Princess?"

"Yes, now climb in and catch me if I float away."

***

"Champagne, like last time?" asked Donald under the soft glow of candlelight.

"I want us to copy everything we did last time," crooned Bella, "the love light in your eyes, the menu, the dancing—everything, until we've used our last ounce of energy.

No, *nearly* our last ounce of energy. There's still bedtime," said Bella with a coy grin.

***

The next day Donald and Dirk attended to the mule's packs. Just before five p.m., Donald assembled his khaki jungle breaches, a matching shirt and khaki pith helmet on the bedroom chair. Bella watched his preparations.

Tomorrow will come just as surely as the darkness falls after sundown. Be joyful for him tonight, Bella. This is no time for tears. Under that manly appearance he is struggling with emotions too. I must dress in my burgundy gown and wear the pearls in memory of that happy evening in Demerara when he came back to collect me.

Choosing a white suit, Donald finished dressing for dinner and went downstairs, carrying the pith helmet. A few minutes later, Bella came floating down the stairs into his arms as she had done at Sunningdale. He lifted her into the air and finished with kisses.

"Come, my love, drinks first and then we'll have dinner." *Donald chose a blue cravat; he remembers Demerara, too! And look, red roses. I must have Donald cut one for my hair. Then he'll know that we are both thinking of our first dinner date.*

"Your choice, Bella," Donald asked with a grin. "Do you wish to sit in the rocker or on my lap in the rocker?"

"I don't find much choice in your offer," said Bella as she stood aside and made a grand gesture with her hand, inviting Donald to sit in the rocker. The second Donald sat down, Bella said, "You can hardly fit on my tiny lap, can you?" Before he could settle himself, she landed in his lap and hugged him around the neck.

Shauna served their drinks and later lit two candles on the dining room table and announced, "Dinner is served, Ma'am." She brought the steaming plates to the table and turned the paraffin lamp low as she left the dining room.

"I am glad we are having dinner at home, Bella," said Donald. "When I am away, these moments with you will always be with me. I will picture you right here, dining as we are tonight, just you and I."

I must lighten the moment or I will cry. That would never do.

"And what am I to picture?" countered Bella as she paused to feign thinking. "I shall think of a hairy man in a loincloth endeavouring to get some meat from under the shell of an armadillo he caught with his bare hands. And as the sunset turns the jungle to black velvet with the screams of pumas and the rustling of poisonous snakes, my bushman will leap into the trees and hang like a sloth, content in every way."

Donald let out a deep belly laugh before adding to Bella's story. "And in the morning sunrise, I will see the gold I seek, reflected by the sunshine on the very cliff beside me. In an instant, I will swing through the vines with my booty all the way to Nickerie and home to you, my dearest." Donald poured wine and they started what Bella knew would be their last dinner together until the rains came again.

"Come, let us go up to bed," said Donald.

***

At sunrise, Donald awakened Bella. "Today is the day, my darling. Dress like my Dresden doll to bid me goodbye."

The first time he thought of me as his Dresden doll happened when I was eight years old and in lacy white. Is that what he means? He wants me to wear white? What a dear, sweet man he is. They dressed in silence, for they had said it all the night before.

***

At breakfast, through the parlour windows, Bella could see Dirk saddling Cobus. Behind the saddle he strapped on Donald's roll of the most important items he must have with him: the sextant, the flint stones, a small food bundle with a metal pot and his hammock and mosquito netting all rolled into his slickers. Dirk brought Donald's rifle sheath from the stable and buckled it to the right front of the saddle. Bella took a quick look at Donald, who sat at the table with her.

He hasn't put on his gun belt and pistol yet. How thoughtful of him not to wear it for breakfast. I see that Dirk has the pack mule ready too. Ginger—what a name for a mule! It makes one wonder if he is full of courage or bound to be trouble. Bella, you are thinking idle thoughts to blot out the moment. She squared her shoulders. *What if the day of departure has arrived? We are both ready for it! Yes, today is the first day of the future, Aunt Kate. You will be proud of me.* And she sipped her last drop of tea.

In these last moments of solitude, Donald patted her hand. "It will be fine, Bella. Come, it is time for me to go. The schooner sails for Nickerie at eight and I must get the animals settled on deck before we weigh anchor." Holding her hand, he invited her to rise. He lifted her to stand on a chair for a final embrace in the privacy of their home.

"Yes, I know all will go well," Bella whispered near his ear. "I shall wait for the rains to start again and hasten your return, my love."

They walked to the scullery. Donald accepted the water canteen that Shauna offered him. He buckled on his Sam Brown belt with bullets in the slots and leather strap over his shoulder. As Bella knew he would, Donald opened the long, narrow gun cupboard. He jammed a revolver into its holster and lifted down the rifle.

"Bella, my pistol and the bullets are in the cupboard. Without me in the house, I would like you to know how to use it. Dirk will load it for you and explain the trigger mechanism. Carry it in your purse and sleep with it under your pillow, as I have done."

With a sudden sense of fear Bella cried out: "Donald, why didn't you tell me this before? I don't want any part of guns!"

"The gun I have always carried is not very large or heavy. I suspect your lady friends know how to shoot one. Perhaps you don't need it by day or when you are shopping with Shauna or Dirk, but I would advise you to take it if you are out at night or on the road to Ernte. The grapevine will tell many people that I'm away in the jungle."

Poor Donald. He's using his serious voice. He wasn't looking forward to this part of leaving. He's only trying to protect me. Well, I have to protect myself, so smile!

"Thank you, Donald. I didn't expect this turn of events, but I suppose I should have realized the possibility since you have always carried a gun in your pocket. I will discuss the sidearm with Dirk after you leave." Bella renewed her smile with a little bob of her head to finish the subject, and they stepped out into the garden.

"Goodbye, Mr. McD," said Shauna from the back door. "Dirk and I will look after Mrs McD while you are away; don't you worry. Have a safe time in the jungle."

Dirk held the reins while Donald sheathed the rifle. "Have a good journey, Mr. McD. May your God go with you."

"Thank you, both of you, for your good wishes," said Donald to Shauna and Dirk. He circled back around Cobus to where Bella stood. "If things don't always go as you expect, my Princess, remember 'the sun always rises in the morning,'" and with that, Donald bent over and kissed Bella one last time before mounting his stallion with the mule tethered to his saddle.

Bella blew Donald a kiss and called, "Reiche Ernte, my love. Good Harvest in your quest for a gold mine."

With that, Donald gave a salute-like wave from the brim of his helmet and rode out of the back garden. Bella held her gaze at the spot where he disappeared from view at the corner of the house, determined to remember how gallant and happy he looked to be on his way. The coarse green grass and paddocks looked the same, but an early breeze sighed with his leaving and Mischief stood with her head over the paddock fence as if mourning the departure of Cobus and her master.

From her sleeve Bella recovered a small white hankie and left for their bedroom to weep in private. Tears, far more that her hankie could control, washed down her cheeks. She dropped her head onto Donald's pillow. Huge sobs wracked her tiny chest. *Be strong, Bella. You have made plans for this moment; you have things to do!* But the sobbing came anyway until the emotional stress had passed. *That's better—splash cold water on your eyes. The servants will be worried if you stay up here too long.*

***

Twenty minutes later, Bella returned to the main floor of the house and called from the scullery: "Dirk, my husband wants you to explain his gun to me. Now is a good time to do it." Dirk opened the long cupboard door to retrieve the gun. Bella removed and replaced the bullets as Dirk instructed. She cocked and un-cocked the gun, promised to fire it sometime when out riding with her friends, and returned it to the cupboard until she planned to go out or retire to bed. She called the servants to the dining room.

"Shauna and Dirk, today started so early that we have plenty of the morning left for shopping. We need paint and brushes for painting the outside of the house, as we discussed earlier, and I wish to go to a stationery shop. While you paint, I'll sew the drapes and outline my projects for next week."

13

WAITING FOR THE AUTUMN RAINS

The next morning, Bella rose with the sun, put on her boy's pants, wound her hair into a bun and added a kerchief to cover her hair similar to the style of local workmen.

"Mrs. McD," said an astounded Shauna, "you mustn't paint the house with us. If people see you dressed that way and working with us, they will talk!"

"They won't even dream it is me in these pants," said Bella with assurance. "We must get started before the walls heat in the sun. The wood must be cool or the paint will be hard to apply." With that, Bella gulped her tea and trotted outside through the scullery. Soon all three of them were working on the front of the house in the shade.

"Bella? Bella, is that you?" came a voice from three doors down. *Rachel Aston! I never expected her to be up this early. What will she think? I made this predicament, so I must face her and talk my way out of it. She's sure to tell everyone. What rule says that men paint and ladies knit? I must stand my ground.* Bella stepped back from the half-painted wall and faced the woman who hurried towards her.

"Yes, Rachel, it is I, in my painting clothes. I tried to fool you the last time you caught me dressed this way, but I shan't worry about it this time. I just happen to like painting. In fact, I like using my muscles and my brain at almost anything."

Dressed in a pale blue robe and pink slippers, Rachel approached Bella with a puzzled look on her face. Then she started to giggle like a schoolgirl with a secret.

"Bella, if you can dress like that for all of the neighbours to see, then I should be able to retrieve our newspaper in my dressing gown and not give a snuff."

"That's right, Rachel. People should be allowed the freedom to do what they want to do if it is within the law, and right now I want to paint." Rachel stood in silence while Bella waited for a tirade on propriety. Finally, Rachel spoke.

"Have you another brush, Bella? It looks like fun. Percy is so strict about being proper that I sometimes feel hemmed in. He'd be furious if he caught me, so I'll wait until he's off to the plantation and then I'll return. Imagine—me in pants! Percy has an old pair; I'll just belt in the waist." Rachel winked at Bella and hurried home.

What a complete change of character. How could I have judged her so differently the other night? If she really likes to follow her own aspirations, then I think I have found a friend who won't judge me when I do the things Gabby taught me to do. With this turn of events, I doubt that either of us will make the grapevine twitter.

***

One afternoon, with the paint job complete, Rachel joined Bella, Dirk and Shauna in admiring the shining white house with its Dutch-blue door and blue front steps. She noticed the board stating "Moorcroft" neatly hung just below the edge of the roof.

"Your Moorcroft sign looks lovely, Bella. Who painted that handsome script?"

"I did," answered Bella. "Come, our success calls for iced tea in the back garden."

Bella and Rachel chatted in the shade until Rachel returned home. *How interesting that Rachel mentioned Morgan's Ice Company. Let me think on that; it's where Dirk buys ice for the ice box and chipped ice for drinks.*

Bella stretched back in her chair. *What a divine afternoon! I feel so happy and pampered—so different from my useless life in Plymouth. Rachel's visit helped me make plans for another project, but tomorrow I'll sew drapes. When the drapes are finished, I'll write to Aunt Kate. If Rachel's comment about Morgan's Ice Company and my plan works out, Moorcroft will have furniture. I wonder who rents large carts.*

***

Early in the morning of the second week with Donald away in the jungle, Shauna, Dirk, Bella and the "pistol" left for Ernte, seated on the rough board that served as the seat of a large cart. Mischief acted like an elephant in the traces— slow, but still moving. The three sat enjoying the green wilderness on the left, clicking away with its cricket-like sounds, and the silent eight-foot sugar canes on the right. During the journey, the mare's mood improved as she became accustomed to the heavier load. They turned in at Ernte.

"Good morning, Ken," Bella called out in her musical voice with Ken's approach. "I would like to start a school for the women and children. With the help of Wumi and my two servants, I think we could teach them Dutch, good hygiene and horsemanship." Wumi and Asha came from the overseer's house and Bella told them her plan. Ken left to ask the women and children to gather at the house.

"Dirk," said Bella, "come with me and I'll point out the pieces of furniture to load onto the cart before I announce that we're going to start a school at Ernte. Then you can saddle Mischief for your class"

***

Bella divided the women and children into three groups. The first group of women stayed with Shauna at the back of the house. In Sranan, Shauna taught them basic hygiene— the importance of washing their hands to avoid intestinal upsets and how to boil water for drinking. She talked about soap and washing their bodies and their clothes, and then she gave each family a bar of soap, a metal basin and two towels.

"No more washing in the river," Shauna explained.

"Hmph! River washes clothes good," an older woman grumbled in Sranan. Shauna smiled and went on with the class.

***

Dirk took his group of older children to the front of the house to meet Mischief. With trepidation, they all stroked her nose and fingered her mane. Dirk taught them about safety and the students took turns brushing her coat and sitting in the saddle.

"Next week, you'll all ride the horse," promised Dirk.

***

Bella asked the younger children to sit on the floor in the parlour of the house. She gave each child a tablet of paper and six crayons.

"Draw a picture of me, children," said Bella in Dutch with Wumi translating Bella's words in Sranan. "Now, draw yourself standing beside me." Bella admired the pictures and said, "Hold up a finger like I am doing; that's one finger." Wumi wrote the numeral "1" on her paper and had them copy it. This continued with fingers up to three. Wumi wrote the numeral "2," then "3" to go with Bella's fingers. Wumi knew a song with the words "one, two, three" in it and taught them the tune and words.

"Wumi,' said Bella, "I do believe you were born to be a teacher!"

After the first twenty minutes of classes, everyone gathered at the back of the house for lemonade. The groups changed location. The women learned about horses, the older children about numbers and the younger children about hygiene. After another twenty minutes they gathered together again for cookies. The classes changed location a third time.

"When we are not here, Wumi, do you think you can manage them all at once in the parlour of the big house like we did today? Keep them busy learning colours, more numbers and Creole songs and dances. Ask how many washed their hands before eating. When they get restless, tell them how well they have done and let them go home."

The "new teachers from Paramaribo" waved goodbye to the students and left to enjoy their picnic lunches in the shade of a date palm by the river before returning home.

***

"What a long day, Shauna," said Bella as she collapsed into Donald's chair with her stout. "Do you think they enjoyed having lessons?"

"Oh yes, Mrs. McD. They jabbered with pleasure in Sranan in my classes."

"Today is Wednesday," Bella mused aloud. "We will go out to Ernte every Wednesday until the rains return."

***

The second visit to Ernte for lessons showed how quickly the adults and children could learn. Wumi had them counting to ten in Dutch and Sranan. They learned about clean homes, started on the letters of the alphabet and enjoyed more horseback riding. Their smiling faces told Bella all she needed to know about their hunger for knowledge.

"Teaching is fun," said Wumi. "I'm sure the children and adults enjoy learning things as much as I enjoy teaching them."

"You must urge the women and children to teach the men and older children who are working in the fields," said Bella. "Mention it in different ways next week. Little ones might sing their number songs with their dad holding up the right number of fingers. The older children could talk about horses. The women might dress up in clean clothes and hold a bonfire and dance for their husbands. Do you think that would work?" Wumi grinned so wide her cheeks rose like tender dumplings under her smooth olive skin. Her brown eyes sparkled in the sun as she nodded her head up and down.

***

The next week Dirk went to fetch the plantation furniture from Morgan's Ice Company, where he had delivered it the week before when he brought it in from Ernte.

"Why did Sam Morgan smile and thank me so much, Mrs. McD?" asked Dirk.

"Because, Dirk, we showed him a new way to make money. I had Sam Morgan keep our furniture frozen for a week in his icehouse. Termites can't stand the cold and they all died right where they lived in their burrowed holes. It may sound gruesome, but if people freeze their things every year, their furniture won't disintegrate into sawdust." Dirk nodded and smiled as Bella went on. "I am quite sure that Mr. Morgan will start up an icehouse for furnishings. Freezing termites should make him a flourishing business, for he owns the only fast ship with a hold prepared for transporting ice from Boston. For a time, Sam will know a secret about termites that, I have to presume, no one has thought of before."

"My goodness," said Bella. "I said 'Boston.' You two don't know about Boston and America. I must buy an atlas with pictures called maps and teach you about the world."

"Mrs. McD," wailed Shauna. "You say those white slugs are still inside our furniture, but dead? I hope you're right or we'll be in big trouble with them."

Bella considered where she wished to position the living room pieces of rattan they had brought from Ernte. *I'll leave Donald's chair, table and lamp exactly where they are in that corner and design the parlour around them. I'll sew padded cushions in a cheerful colour for all the furniture, like Gabby had at Sunningdale. By the time Donald returns I'll have potted plants where I think the room needs a little life.*

She lifted her gaze to the window. The plain blue sky did not cheer her like the splashing waves had done at Sunningdale. All the projects in the world could not make up for her loneliness. *Cheer up, Bella. The rains will come and Donald will arrive home on Cobus, just as he promised.* Bella returned her eyes to the parlour. The pleasant effect offered by the new furniture spurred her on to adjust the positioning of the pieces that Dirk had left in the dining room and upstairs. *The furniture cushions can wait for a bit. I must start Shauna's class in sewing and Dirk's class in learning to be a butler.*

***

"Today, after lessons, we three will go to town," Bella announced after breakfast. But she did not tell them why. She wanted to see surprise on their faces. Although the thermometer read eighty-three degrees Fahrenheit, a soft breeze blew as they turned from their carriageway into Dominiestraat, towards the shops. The leaves of the mahogany trees along each side of the street offered shade until they reached Spunhoek Keizerstraat and turned left toward Heerenstraat and the downtown shopping area.

"Shauna and I will go to the fabric shop to buy material for her to sew a lungi for each boy, a ghagga and polaa for the little girls and saris for the older girls and women. Shauna, you may also pick material for a sari for yourself. After the fabric shop we'll go to the men's wear shop. If you are going to be a butler, Dirk you must have a pair of black pants, a white shirt, a black bow tie and black shoes."

Dirk's face flushed and Bella sensed his discomfort. "Do you not want to be a butler, Dirk?"

"Oh yes, Mrs. McD. I want to learn to be a house servant." Dirk said no more. Bella could tell from his inability to look her in the eye that he had a problem unknown to her. *I must deal with the problem or it will grow bigger,* so she asked what troubled him.

When he finally spoke, he blurted out: "Please, Mrs. McD, just give me a note saying you want me to have the clothes and that the clerk may put the cost on Mr. McD's bill." Dirk dropped his eyes. "It wouldn't be fitting for you to come with me into the men's shop. I would be embarrassed." *Poor Dirk. It took courage to tell me that no women, not even wives, go shopping with their men in that shop.*

"I do believe," said Bella to Dirk, "that Shauna and I may be a long time at the fabric shop. Drop us off at the shop and come back in an hour" Bella scribbled some words. "Use this note if you make any purchases."

With a wide grin, Dirk took the piece of paper, let the women off and headed to the men's shop to buy his new butler's outfit.

***

Shauna ran the tips of her fingers over the coloured cloths as if magic waited for her in the bright colours. Together they picked out reds and yellows with small patterns for the little girls' skirts and sleeveless blouses. The blues and greens with patterns were for the boys' wraparounds for their lower torsos. Shauna picked material for the women's saris in soft gauze-like cottons and slightly heavier cotton for the blouses.

The bill is rather high, but Donald has never complained about the way I spend money, so I hope this little project—well, big project—will please him too. He said I could start a school, but how can I teach children to have self-confidence if they look like ragamuffins? Dirk can tell us how long to cut the lengths of cloth for the boys' wraparounds and Shauna can practice hemming them for a start with her sewing lessons. Then I'll show her how to make the girls' clothes and the saris. While she is busy with those, Dirk and I will start the butler lessons. They are really very good with their lessons. How well my projects are going! Yes, everything will be fine until the rains come.

***

The next day Bella opened her front door to the sharp knocking of Hildebrand Leppard and her friend Faye, the two women with whom she'd had lunch.

"How nice of you to call," Bella said and invited them in for afternoon tea. As soon as Shauna left the tray of tea things and disappeared back into the kitchen, Hildebrand started the conversation.

"My dear Isabella," said Hildebrand with her head tipped back a bit while she gazed through her round spectacles down her nose with her sights aimed at Bella's eyes. "It is all over town that you plan to teach that woman who brought the tea how to sew."

"Yes, you are right, Hildebrand. I have a sewing machine and I sew, so why should I not pass this ability on to Shauna?" Bella answered with an I-dare-you-to-say-another-word-on-this-topic look as she stared into the woman's ice blue eyes.

Hildebrand twitched her shoulders and pursed her lips with disapproval, but Faye wanted to speak her piece as well.

"We tried to warn you once before, Isabella, that there are things you just do not do when you are a colonial overseas." *Ha, she's been practising that line.*

Bella smiled. "And what would those things be, Faye?" Bella baited her.

133

"You know very well what I am talking about," snapped Faye.

"Not really. Please explain yourself," Bella said. *She plainly does not want to put her thoughts into words. The very idea that they can retain their lifestyle by keeping the servants ignorant is deplorable. I shall see how long I can make the two of them squirm.*

Faye forgot the lines she had practiced and said, "You can sew?" Then, to cover her slip, she added grandly, "Just what was your station in England, my dear?" Hildebrand sat forward in her chair to better hear this next gem of information that she could present to the grapevine.

Bella ignored the question.

"Yes, that is what I said, Faye—I sew. I just finished sewing all the drapes that you see in these rooms and I sew my own gowns, for nothing in the shops fits me."

"Well!" huffed Hildebrand, "I order my clothes from Paris to have the latest fashion. And my shoes and lingerie too," she added, to make her wardrobe more elegant.

"How nice," said Bella, in a condoning fashion. "If either of you ever need anything altered or mended, I will be happy to help you out."

Hildebrand jumped to her feet. "Well, I never!" she barked.

Faye copied Hildebrand. "The very idea . . ." She did not finish the sentence.

"Must you leave so soon, my dears?" questioned Bella in a voice sweet as honey. "We have hardly had a visit at all. I haven't answered your question yet, Faye, about my station in life before I came to Surinam as Donald's wife."

The two visitors had tramped halfway to the front door but turned in unison on the balls of their feet to hear what Bella might divulge.

"My father owns a shipping company and warehouses in Plymouth. I loved my nanny and the house servants. I watched them at their work and increased my knowledge from books. Ultimately, I learned how to do a great many things." Bella ended with a smile. From the looks on their faces, the answer did not please either of the women.

Without another word, the two women, with the door still swinging on its hinges, clattered down the front steps and climbed into

Hildebrand's carriage. *I doubt the grapevine will be fed the truth about my proper upbringing.*

***

English, Dutch and geography lessons continued. Pillows were added to the chairs and potted plants were introduced into Moorcroft. Wednesdays came and went with lessons devoured by the people at Ernte. The women and children looked handsome in their new clothes and came to class with shiny faces and clean hands. Bella's projects were coming to an end, yet the sun continued to shine. On hazy days when the weather did not smite them like a blast furnace, Bella rode Mischief with Eve, Ange and Marie through the many little pathways that led off various plantation roads.

Despite Donald's absence, life has been very pleasant, except that no one has come knocking on my door since the day Hildebrand and Faye paid me that visit. The rains must come soon. Surely, Donald is on his way home. And Aunt Kate . . . why has she not written to me? I dropped my letter at the post office ten weeks ago. I do hope nothing is wrong with her or my family. In case the letter went astray, perhaps I should write her again and plead with her to answer the questions I proposed to her. Enough wondering, Bella, it is stout time and Shauna is waiting for you beside the padded loveseat.

***

The next day Dirk came to the scullery door. "I picked up the mail, Shauna. Mrs. McD received two letters! One has an English stamp and the other has a Paramaribo postmark. Do you know where she is?"

Dirk found Mrs. McD in the near-empty upstairs room that Donald called "the room that needs a billiard table." When he entered, she turned, saw the letters in his hand and ran to get them. Once seated at her bedroom vanity, she opened the letter from England.

Aunt Kate—I'd know her handwriting anywhere. Oh my goodness, she took my request so seriously that she went to the Bishop and he asked all of the churches in his diocese to contribute whatever they could. What is this folded piece of paper? A bank note for three hundred pounds to help the

Ernte community! She wants the men to have new clothes too. Why, I didn't even ask for that!

Bella turned Aunt Kate's letter over for a postscript written on the back of the page. It read: "Surprise! When this letter arrives you will also receive a letter from the SS *Balfour*, advising you to pick up the two shipments I sent you. Love, Aunt Kate."

Bella ripped open the second letter. "Please be advised that Pier One in Paramaribo has two shipments registered to you and ready for claiming."

"Dirk, harness Mischief to the trap! We must go down to the docks."

***

"The shipments won't fit into your trap, Ma'am," said the warehouse supervisor as he led her into the cool building. "You'll need a big wagon. There are carts out on the street waiting for business. I can call one for you, if you wish."

***

At Moorcroft, the driver and Dirk tumbled the boxes onto the grass in the back garden. The man took his pay and left. With a hammer, Dirk clawed one board from the five-foot square wooden box. Bella, Dirk and Shauna all took turns peering through the hole, but all they could see were the sides of a variety of brown paper parcels.

"This is all meant for Ernte," said Bella. "Don't open it any more or we'll have loose things to cart out to the plantation." Dirk and Shauna stood mystified.

"I asked Aunt Kate if she could collect toys, books and clothes from the people in her church. I also asked for a sand point, complete with a pump, and gave her directions to send it to me at my expense. It goes out to Ernte too." *There's no invoice. The people of the church must have collected enough money to buy it and ship it with three hundred pounds left over. My, oh my, I never expected such generosity.*" Tears of gratitude welled in Bella's eyes. "Dirk, you must hire a cart again. Tomorrow is Wednesday and we are taking this with us to Ernte. And bring the spade, hammer and saw. With the boards and nails from the boxes we'll make a platform for the pump."

"What is a pump, Mrs. McD?" asked Shauna.

"It's a way to get clean water. The metal poles in this box make a pipe-like object called a 'sand point.' With a hand pump attached to it, a person can pump up water found below the water level of the soil. From now on the people of Ernte will not have to go to the river with pails," finished Bella.

***

At Ernte, after the classes, Dirk broke open the first big box. Wumi and Asha unwrapped the brown paper packages and the students lined up like firefighters passing buckets of water to a fire, only they were passing things from the big box in the cart to the parlour of the plantation house: storybooks, toys, clothes, shoes and art materials. Squeals of delight and little jigs by dancing feet couldn't help but display the wonder and pleasure of the students. "Later, the gifts will be distributed," Bella told Wumi.

Dirk moved the cart to an area of grass behind the plantation manor.

"Will the stronger students unload the metal items in this other box and place them beside the cart, please?" Bella called in Dutch. The students had learned sufficient Dutch to understand her.

With Bella reading the directions, Dirk sank the spade into the grass and laid bare the sandy soil beneath. One five-foot pipe section had a sharp point on it that shielded a fine metal sieve-like area.

Bella stood in her wide-brimmed "plantation" hat, directing the work. The students, both women and children, crowded in to see what would happen next. With a sledgehammer he found in the box, Dirk started the sharp five-foot length of pipe into the ground. With a wrench to make the joint tight, he attached a coupling and a second pipe, then pounded it down after the first.

"It states here, Dirk, that if the sand point becomes difficult to pound into the ground, to use the wrench and rotate the pipe every now and then to free the point from gravel that might be hindering the point's progress." Dirk rotated the pipe. Sweat poured down his face in the noonday sun. Asha went into the house and returned with a pail of water and a towel.

"Here, Dirk. Wet the towel and cool your brow."

Everyone watched as the old beaches of the river allowed the pipe to descend into the ground.

"Chimi," called Dirk, "when I get the pipe end closer to the ground, you pound on it. You're a big fellow. Pound the sledgehammer straight down or you might bend the pipe." Chimi hammered, and then everyone wanted a turn, until the five pipes had been attached and the last pipe stuck up one foot above the ground.

"We did it!" called out Dirk. Everyone cheered.

"But what is it for?" they asked in unison.

"You'll see after lunch." said Dirk. "You have all learned to use a hammer and saw. We need to build a wooden platform three feet square, and on top of that we will put a pump."

***

Everyone came back after lunch. Older boys and girls measured, sawed and hammered under Dirk's direction as he translated Bella's requirements.

With the platform in place, Dirk attached the last pump fitting to the pipe in the ground. He pumped the handle once or twice and then stood back.

"Mrs. McD," called Dirk, "you pump now and see what happens."

Bella climbed onto the low platform and pumped once, twice, and then added several more quick strokes of the pump handle. *Is it not going to lift water after all this work under such hot conditions and curious eyes? Perhaps I had better let Dirk try.*

Bella gave the handle a few more jerks up and down. Suddenly water gushed forth and soaked her shoes and the hem of her dress. Heads bent forward to better understand the magic that they watched. Mouths dropped open in silence and then a cheer went up.

"Water! Water!" they hollered. "Mrs. McD has brought us clean water with her magic pumping stick."

"That's right, my friends. There will be plenty for everyone because the river makes the underground soil hold water. Tomorrow, Wumi will teach you how to care for your new magic pumping stick and how to store its clean water in your homes."

***

Two days later it rained. On the third day, the sun shone again. *Dear Lord, I never thought I would pray for rain to fall every day, but if it means Donald's return, please have it rain until the heavens run dry. I need to hear Cobus's hooves on our gravel carriageway and the sound of Donald's "Halo" as he rounds the corner into the back garden. I need him. That's all I know. I just need my Donald.*

***

At stout time Bella sank onto the loveseat and rested her head against the soft blue cushions. Rain washed across the windows, obliterating any view of the garden. Even the familiar taste of the stout did not interest her. Then she heard Dirk's yipping and she rushed to the window. There she beheld a very wet Donald standing on tiptoe to offer her a kiss through the windowpane.

14

SHUNNED

"**B**ella, my love!" shouted Donald from the scullery. "I have come with the rains just as I promised I would."

Bella rushed from the parlour, became airborne in Donald's powerful arms and cuddled against his sodden bosom. His stained pith helmet flipped from his head and rattled on the tiles, capsized by the intensity of their kisses. Shauna turned towards the sink to give them some privacy. Donald freed one arm to gather in Bella's legs and skirt. As he whisked her off to their bedroom, he called:

"I've been wet a long time, Shauna. I must get into a warm tub of water." Shauna drained rain water into the bathtub from the cistern at the side of the house. When she heard Mr. McD's slippers slapping down the stairs, she added two pots of boiling water to the tub. She waited. After a while the slippers climbed the stairs again. Later, the McDs appeared at the foot of the stairs and crossed into the parlour.

"Is this the same house I left, Bella?" asked Donald. "It's absolutely charming. You have a marvelous way with colours. We must have a party to celebrate this transformation." Shauna brought Donald a glass of hot rum, lemon and honey. "Come, Bella, bring your stout and sit on my lap. What do you think of having the colonials in?"

"It is a lovely idea, Donald, but the only ones who will come are my five friends and their husbands. Everyone else has shunned me all summer because the grapevine cast me as a seamstress before I married you, even though the perpetrators knew the truth about my family's position in Plymouth."

"Why would people act that way?"

"Because, Donald, I've broken their colonial rules. They know I've taught my servant to sew, helped Shauna and Dirk paint Moorcroft and started a school at Ernte." Bella mimicked in a superior tone. "One does not work alongside the servants!" She continued, "The old time colonials want to hold on to their lofty way of life by keeping the servants and poor people ignorant." Bella paused to control her voice. "Because that is not my belief, they disapprove of me." Barely audible through her sobs, she smothered her face in Donald's shoulder and cried, "People hate me for being Christian. I'm sorry if I have ruined your social standing in Paramaribo."

"Hush, hush, dear Bella. The colonials do not mean one cockroach to me. Your love and my dreams for upriver on the Corentyne are all that matters in my life. Dry your eyes and listen to me, my Rosebud. I did not find the mine, but panning for gold made us very rich this season. Here, look at the size of this nugget!"

Despite her tears, Bella broke out laughing. "I hope you brought home a saddlebag full of nuggets, for I have been spending all of your money. When you are rested, we must go to Ernte for you to see what I have been doing to keep from being lonely. Shauna, Dirk and I have travelled by trap to the plantation every Wednesday since you left, and Wumi teaches them on the other five days of the week. I hope you'll be pleased with what we have achieved." After another hug and kisses Bella went on.

"I have more bad news. To be ready for painting the house, I handed the bank manager a letter and asked him to forward it to your Dutch landlord. In the letter I told the owner that the house was in need of painting and I offered to organize the work if he would pay for the paint and labour when I presented the bills to the bank."

"It looks elegant in white and blue, so what is the problem, Bella?"

Bella collected herself with a few deep breaths in order to go on.

"I was so sure that I had made an offer he would not refuse that I went ahead with the work as soon as the dry weather came. I bought the paint and Shauna, Dirk and I painted the outside of the house. Just last week, I finally received a letter from him saying that he did not want the house painted. He planned to sell it to a friend and that we would have to move. Move, Donald!" Bella cried out, "We have been evicted!" Again, tears flowed down Bella's cheeks as she blurted in sobs, "You have paid for all of the improvements, Donald, and now we must leave!"

"I'm sorry all your work will be lost to us, my Rosebud." *Oooh, his serious voice, trying to calm me; I must listen.* "Maybe with my rich gold returns we'll buy a house of our own—a bigger house, one that is already decorated. We will worry about the house when we receive a proper notice."

Donald is right. One must not cry over material losses. The things and people that I truly love in Moorcroft can move with us: Shauna and Dirk and the horses. Stop blubbering, Bella; tonight is Donald's homecoming and it must be joyous. I hear Shauna scurrying about the kitchen preparing something special for dinner.

***

Tropical storms lashed at the palm trees, a forewarning that the rains would return in earnest. On Wednesday, rain or no rain, Bella insisted that she go to the plantation one more time before the steady downpours. In a rented covered carriage, Donald, Bella and their two servants left for Ernte early in the morning with Bella's usual basket of goodies.

***

Someone working in the fields of Ernte must have seen them coming, for everyone stood clapping their hands to welcome Mr. McD back from the hills as the carriage pulled into the area behind the plantation house. The families called out "Halo" and then sang them a song of welcome in Dutch.

Donald marvelled at the change in his workers and their families—the smiling faces, their vigour and the cleanliness of their clothes. Then he noticed the pump.

"My dear," he said to Bella in a voice for all to hear, "you have caused this community to become happy, healthy people. What you have done here should happen for everyone in Paramaribo."

***

Every day, with the garden awash, Bella sewed, worked on her embroidery or wrote letters while Donald pored over his mining maps and made plans for the next dry month after Christmas.

***

"The Governor's Ball is next week, Bella. Wear your most charming gown with pearls in your hair and a rose tucked under them."

While Donald continued with his business during the week, Bella designed and sewed herself a new gown in midnight blue Liberty silk, known to reflect highlights as a dancer moved across the floor. Unlike the tight bodice of the day, the slim gown Bella fashioned hung with a slight looseness from the shoulders and nipped in at the waist with a wide satin ribbon to form a huge bow where others would be wearing heavy, hot straw-filled bustles. The neckline came low enough to expose Bella's creamy collarbones and lovely neck. Bella modelled the dress for Shauna.

"Mrs. McD, the gown is beautiful, but won't the women think that the neckline is too daring? Won't they criticize the bow instead of a bustle?"

"You wait and see, Shauna. There is a designer named William Morris who is influencing London and Paris fashions with this style of cooler gown. Aunt Kate told me about him in one of her letters. Look, my pearl necklace fits around my waist. Remind me to buy five burgundy roses and some white satin ribbon."

***

Dirk drove the McD's to the governor's mansion, and in the fashion of the day, lined up with the other carriages to deliver his master and mistress to the front door of the building.

"Mr. and Mrs. Donald Macdonald," the announcer called out as Bella and Donald entered the ballroom. The women turned to stare but then faced away to make their disapproval of Bella obvious. The snub did not go unnoticed by Donald, nor did the waltz that the orchestra played as soft background music while people arrived. He bowed formally to his wife just inside the ballroom and whirled her onto the empty dance floor. With graceful movements, they danced solo around the open area, with the women staring at the "scandalous" neckline of Bella's gown and the men's eyes on her slim, contoured body. Donald timed their dancing with the music to be at the champagne table when the waltz ended. With glasses in hand, they moved among the other guests.

"Good evening, Mrs. Macdonald," said Hildebrand Leppard. She looked Bella's spectacular dress up and down like a cat with a mouse and said, "Did you sew it my dear? It certainly is a strange design."

"Hildebrand," said Bella as if they were old friends. "Have you never heard of William Morris, the designer whose work has overtaken the fashions in London and Paris?" Bella turned to show the three burgundy roses at her waist, a little to the right, just below the string of pearls. "Oh yes," Bella went on. "Mr. Morris's designs show plain necklines with the fashion statement in some other place on the outfit. This gown is the very latest fashion all over Europe." Bella smiled a friendly smile, gave a wave and turned away so that Hildebrand would see the rose at the back of her topknot. Donald stood by, amused at the counter play of the two women. Bella had won another round.

"So that's who muddied the grapevine," Donald said, quite sure he was right as they moved onto the dance floor in perfect unison.

***

Days of rain passed by with Bella and Donald enjoying each other's company or riding in the early morning sun with Eve and Olie or Rachel and Percy. Bella taught Shauna how to prepare for the marvelous dinner party they might have some day.

A letter arrived from Bella's mother in November. Bella read parts of it aloud to Donald during stout time. "Harry and Althea have a fine little son, born on September 11, 1888. The baby looks like his father. Althea and little William are both fine."

"William is my father's name," said Bella absently as she counted months on her fingers but said nothing. *Hmm, a November postmark. Christmas will soon be upon us. This will be our first one together. I wonder how Donald celebrates it. Shauna and Dirk might like to be with their families on Christmas Eve. We must make some plans.*

"Bella," said Donald at that very moment, "how would you like to go to Demerara and spend Christmas with Gabby if she will have us? The *Schooner Van Dam* leaves here on Friday, December the eighth, and should be in Demerara on the evening of the fifteenth. We'd return on the SS *Balfour* on the twenty-seventh. We wouldn't be home for the New Year's Eve Ball, but the steamer will have a fine party. Just think," he chuckled, "you could wear your new blue silk gown a second time without Hildebrand glaring at you."

Bella held her stout high in the air to salute the idea of Christmas with Gabby, and using her Cockney accent, she bawled out, "We c'n 'ave a party with our friends afore we leaves."

"Tha's right, Rosie," Donald feigned a drunken slur. "New Year's Eve with the boathan's'll be better anyway." With that, Bella swayed herself in drunken make-believe from the love seat to Donald's chair, plunked in his lap and gave him a sloppy kiss.

"I will make the reservations tomorrow, Bella, without consulting Gabby. If she has plans to be away, we can enjoy Demerara and visit with Simon Henker."

What a man! His plan sounds divine and I won't have to face being left off Hildebrand Leppard's Christmas guest list or mind not being invited to Faye's garden party.

***

The next day at five o'clock, instead of Shauna, Dirk arrived in his black pants, white shirt, bow tie and polished black shoes.

"What's this, Dirk?" said Donald in astonishment. "You look smashing in that outfit. Did Shauna just give you a short haircut?" he teased.

Shauna came into the parlour from the kitchen in her new sari. "Yes, I did, Mr. McD, as befits your new butler," said Shauna with a proud little cock of her head. "We wanted you to know that we're ready for the Christmas season."

"Come into the room, both of you," said Bella with her slender finger beckoning them. "We have made our Christmas plans. On Saturday, December second, we will have a dinner party for our friends, about ten couples. On Friday, December eighth, we are sailing to Demerara and we won't be back until a week after New Year's, depending on when the SS *Balfour* reaches Paramaribo."

Donald continued the conversation. "From the ninth of December to January fourth, you may both go home and visit your families. Dirk, take the trap and drop Shauna with her people before going on to your family. You must return every day to look after Cobus and keep the house free of cockroaches." Shauna and Dirk stood dumfounded. Donald added, "Dirk, teach Shauna how to ride Mischief and drive the trap if she would like to learn, and Shauna, I'm sure my wife would not mind if you chose to use her sewing machine."

With sparkling eyes, they said in unison, "Yes, Sir. Thank you, Sir and Ma'am," followed by Shauna's little curtsey and Dirk's formal nod of appreciation.

***

The following weeks brought sweet scents of Christmas baking, green garlands of tropical evergreens, potted poinsettias and bowls of candies and nuts being prepared for their dinner party. *I think I will buy a new khaki helmet for Donald's jungle trips and wrap it in palm fronds with a pink bow. Now, what should we get for Dirk and Shauna?*

***

Sam Morgan from the icehouse and his wife, Blanche, were the first to arrive for the Christmas party that Bella and Donald had planned for their friends.

"Welcome to our home. We haven't met, but I am Donald, Bella's husband."

A second knock on the door brought Stella from the flower stand in the market and her husband, Henry. Donald greeted them in the same way. The two couples were friends and found it easy to chat in the parlour. Connie and Ed arrived with Marie and Hamish at the same moment as Rachel and Percy Aston with their in-between neighbours, whom Bella and Donald had never met but invited anyway.

"Pleased to meet you, Deirdre and Angus MacKay. I'm Donald Macdonald and this is my wife, Bella," he said as he ushered the Astons and MacKays to his wife's side.

Within minutes came Eve and Olie with Ange and Mitch, and close behind them came the carriage of Sarah and Edward Hargrave.

Dirk walked with self-confidence, silver tray in hand with drinks, while Shauna passed crab hors d'oeuvres and toasted mushroom logs. The men emptied the dishes of roasted nuts and Shauna refilled them. Bella and Donald passed among their guests, making sure that everyone had been introduced. The invitation had asked for informal dress and everyone felt at ease without bustles and cravats.

"What a lovely party," said Rachel. "No one in Paramaribo has ever held a party like this. I think Percy and I will change our style."

***

"Shauna and Dirk have served dinner," announced Donald after forty-five minutes for visiting. "Please pass through to the dining room, take a plate and serve yourself an early Christmas dinner. There are seats for everyone in the parlour. You will be eating with the plate on your lap." The guests lined up in a queue, ready to serve themselves.

Bella stood beside the queue and bowed her head. "We are thankful, dear Lord," said Bella so all might hear and bow their heads. "We are thankful, dear Lord, for Thy bounty and for congenial friends. Help us to serve Thee and to be helpful and at peace with everyone we meet. Amen."

Everyone intoned, "Amen."

"And dear Lord," Bella added with a laugh and her head unbowed, "Thank You for showing me where to buy the Bentwood chairs so all of our friends can be seated while they eat dinner."

"May we say 'Amen' to that too?" Percy called out to add to the merriment of all.

"That's right," Donald chirped. "After we paid for importing the turkey, those cheap chairs were all I could afford." Everyone laughed at this amusing couple they held as close friends.

"Right," added Bella in her Cockney accent. "We been eatin' oatmeal porridge fer a week ter pay fer 'em. But I found some extra guilders in me sock fer plumb puddin."

Donald moved over beside Bella, gave her a peck on the cheek and whispered, "For your diminutive size, my Rosebud, you have twice the fun and life in you than anyone here. Don't blame yourself for being snubbed."

***

Simon Henker and Gabby met the schooner when it docked in Demerara.

"You are finally here, after eight months!" Gabby exclaimed as she rushed down the dock and threw her arms around Bella. After hugs all around, they climbed into Simon's carriage and rode out to Sunningdale.

"It was nice of you to meet us with your carriage, Simon," said Donald when they all had drinks in Gabby's parlour. "How did you know to meet us?"

Simon paused, then said, "It wasn't hard. Ever since you two eloped, Gabby and I have been keeping company." He cleared his throat and added, "I think this would be a good time for presenting a wish of mine." With this, Simon kneeled in front of Gabby.

"Dearest Gabby, will you be my wife?"

With a look of total surprise, Gabby threw her arms around Simon. "Yes, oh yes, dear Simon. I do believe we saw something in each other's eyes that first night in your restaurant, and it is so fitting to have Bella and Donald here, the two who revitalized our lives."   Simon took Gabby's hand, placed a large diamond on the fourth finger and embraced her for ever so long.

"Donald, have we ever kissed for that long in public?" Bella teased.

"You are not public," joked Simon in his best serious tone. "You are our closest and dearest friends."

***

"We have two weeks to visit with each other," said Bella during dinner that evening at Sunningdale. "What things do we really want to do?"

"I don't care what we do earlier in the day," said Simon, "but we must have dinner at my restaurant before all the seats are reserved by my patrons 'til Christmas."

Gabby laughed. "Really, Simon, I should think you could squeeze the four of us in tomorrow and on Christmas Day as well." She added, "Sometime during the day I think we should go for a walk at Vlissengen Botanical Gardens and the Promenade Gardens. I hear that the poinsettias are very showy this year."

"Fine," said Bella, "but I must have a moment in the morning to go down to the stable and give Strawberry a Christmas kiss."

"Who gets kissed first, Strawberry or me?" asked Donald, feigning a pout.

"I'm not telling; you'll have to wait and see," said Bella with a deadpan face.

***

Over drinks they tried to plan their holidays. Everyone added to the list: Would the little boat at Simon's plantation hold four for a picnic or should they go up-river in a steam-powered boat to see the jungle?

"Let's stop making plans for now," said Donald. "Who knows when the rain will come to keep us at home enjoying cards and just visiting with each other or with friends?"

"Right," said Gabby, and she rose to serve dessert.

***

"The days have passed too quickly, Bella," said Gabby on Boxing Day. "Tomorrow is December the twenty-seventh and you will be boarding the SS *Balfour* for Paramaribo. I am truly going to miss the two of you."

"We'll be back for your wedding, Gabby," assured Bella. "Heavens, if you want a wedding like ours, we will check the governor's schedule and pick you a wedding date. The big tub, the hot and cold running water *and* the crapper are divine."

149

"Bella, you are such a tease," said Simon, "although the big tub sounds inviting."

"Whenever you set the date, my friends, we will be here," said Donald, "unless you elope to a bushman's camp in the jungle. I hear those bushmen practice voodoo."

"You two!" said Gabby. And they laughed and talked well into the evening.

***

"Here it is, January 4, 1889, Donald," said Bella when they finally arrived home from Demerara. "The New Year's Eve party on board ship felt like a second honeymoon—such fun! I'm glad we had a week on board to rest up before starting our search for a house." Donald did not look up. He turned the page of his newspaper and kept reading.

"Your landlord said we have to move, Donald. Pay attention to me!"

"He hasn't arrived in Paramaribo yet, my darling, and he hasn't evicted us. I'm sure we will find a house. Don't worry; I am watching the advertisements. I suspect you will hear about a house from your friends once you pass the word to the bridge club."

"The bridge club, Donald? They've likely blacklisted us all over town."

***

"Thank you for asking us to dinner, Marie," said Bella. "It's very thoughtful of you and Hamish to have us over just because you missed us at the New Year's Eve Ball."

"What a lovely big home," said Donald, "and right on Heerenstraat, almost next door to the governor's mansion. I'm sure it has a history. You must tell us over dinner."

"We don't know that much about it," said Marie. "It is obviously of Victorian design, but the British left about 1670 when the Dutch traded New York for Surinam." Marie paused. "Enough talk! Do come into the parlour for drinks before dinner."

***

On January eleventh, while sitting at her vanity writing a letter, Bella heard a knock on the front door. *That's odd; I'm not expecting anyone this morning. Ten a.m. I wonder who it is. A strong knock—makes me think it's a man.*

"Ma'am," Shauna called, "please come down to the front hall right away."

Shauna sounds afraid. Bella descended the stairs slowly to have time to study the man. *He has stepped into the hall without an invitation and closed the front door behind him. His bearing suggests that he considers himself quite important.*

"You wish to speak with me, Sir? I am Mrs. Macdonald. What is your name and business here with us?"

"I am your landlord. My name is Brink, Mr. Brink," the man said with a heavy Dutch accent. "You received my letter regarding the sale of this house, I presume? Is Mr. Macdonald here? I would rather speak with him."

Indeed. The man has no use for women in business. I will make him deal with me.

"Mr. Macdonald rode out to the plantation this morning. If you insist on giving your message only to my husband, then you must wait for his return," intoned Bella.

"Hmph," said Mr. Brink, as if speaking to an underling. "I plan on going upriver to my friend's plantation tomorrow. I have the boat hired."

"Then, Mr. Brink, you will miss him. My husband won't be available for two more days," Bella reported in a firm voice. "He is very busy at Reiche Ernte making improvements for the workers." *What did he expect, coming to our door without making an appointment? Does he think Donald sits around at home all day drinking rum?*

"Madam," said Mr. Brink, with his jowls shaking, "I have no other alternative but to present you with your eviction notice." He took an envelope from his pocket and handed it to Bella. To make the man uncomfortable, she broke the seal and started to read the letter very slowly rather than merely taking the missive and saying good day.

"It says here that we must be out of the house by January 31, 1889. That does not give us much time to look for a new home, and I believe you owe us money for the improvements we made."

"My dear lady," the man said in a loud, condescending manner, "I gave no instructions for any work on the house. Frankly, I don't see that it needs any work. The paint inside and outside looks acceptable." *How dare he call our paint work "acceptable"! Why, it is the finest looking house on the street.*

"Before you leave, Mr. Brink, you must tell me how to reach you after tomorrow," insisted Bella, tapping the letter on the palm of her hand.

"Leave me a note at the bank," the man growled. "I'll not have your lawyer trailing after me trying to change this letter of intent. Mr. Macdonald will find that two weeks is sufficient notice to repossess one's property in Paramaribo." The man turned, yanked the front door open and slammed it behind him, leaving Bella with the certainty that they would be moving.

15

CANDLEWICK

Bella slapped her newspaper onto the breakfast table to get her husband's attention. This had no effect, so she raised her voice. "It's January, Donald, one of our few dry months. We should be out riding with our friends, but here we sit reading newspaper advertisements with the hope of finding a house in ten days." Donald sighed.

Bella continued her tirade, "Near the first of the month you told me not to worry about Mr. Brink's first letter. You dismissed it by saying we hadn't received an eviction notice. Well, now we have. You said that finding a house wouldn't be that difficult. I knew the grapevine wouldn't give us any leads."

With deliberate moves, Donald folded his paper and placed it on the table. In a steady voice, he said, "Bella, stop going on so."

That serious voice of his. He is going to tell me not to worry. Bella continued with the countenance of a bulldog. *How can I help but worry? They don't allow horses to live with you in a hotel. Can he not see the problem?*

Donald continued, "One thing I can guarantee you, little Princess, is that we will not go to the plantation and live in that bug-infested house. I know you are frustrated. I am too, but I feel things will turn out all right. I have always been a lucky person."

"Not with finding your gold mine!" Bella snapped as she stormed out of the room.

***

In her efforts to organize the household for that fateful January day when they would be homeless, Bella and Shauna sorted through the rooms, discarding the unnecessary and setting aside those things that were to be saved. The sewing room presented the biggest problem. Completely distraught, Bella grabbed a box and threw in scraps of cloth, scissors, the bobbins and a jar of pins, followed by anything within reach.

"Mrs. McD," said Shauna, with a soft touch to her mistress's shoulder. "I think you should stop for tea."

***

Donald showed Mr. Brink's eviction notice and Brink's original letter to Angus McKay, their next door neighbour and a lawyer.

"I'm sorry, Donald, but Paramaribo has rather loose laws when it comes to real estate. It is plain to me that your landowner had a lawyer draw up this notice. Plus, he did warn you about having to move and you chose not to heed the warning. Also, you pay the rent on the first of every month by having the bank transfer the rental sum from your account to Brink's account. Legally, you have only paid to the end of January. I would say that you have no alternative but to move before he puts you out on the street, and don't expect a penny for any painting. Your Mr. Brink knows the law and is a hard man."

***

With five days left until the end of January, both Donald and Bella had nightmares, tossing and turning until they woke each other. Once awake, they could think of nothing pleasant or funny to say. They turned away from each other to cling to their own edge of the mattress, and there they waited for sleep or the dawn to overtake them.

Bella insisted that if Brink would not pay for the improvements then he would not get them. Unable to convince Bella otherwise, Donald agreed to have Dirk remove all of the brass supports and drapes and pack them in a box. The house looked a shambles.

My goodness. A knock on the front door. If it is that Brink fellow, I'll chase him off the premises with this black umbrella. Maybe it is Hildebrand and Faye. It would be just like them to come calling with the hope of scavenging tidbits of information to feed to the grapevine. I can hear them saying something spiteful like, "After teaching those brown-skinned people anything, why would you think a colonial would want to help you find a house?"

Bella, umbrella in hand, wiped at the sweat on her brow and yanked the door open. There stood quiet Marie, her sewing friend.

"Hello, Marie. Please excuse my abruptness. We must move out on January thirty-first and I am trying to be prepared. I'm quite busy. Do you need something?"

"No, I don't want anything," said Marie, "although a cup of tea and a little visit might be nice. Where have you located a house for rent?"

"We haven't. That's the trouble! In five days we'll be out on the street!"

"Bella, dear Bella. I didn't know," said Marie, inviting herself into the house. "I have been so busy myself that no one came calling to bring me up to date on the news."

Shauna served tea. Twenty minutes later, when Marie stood to leave, she said, "Bella, at cocktail time I am returning with Hamish. I think you and Donald need a break from carrying your worries without friends. I won't allow you to say no. Clear four seats in the parlour and be prepared for cocktails at five."

Marie is right. We've been ignoring our friends. I've been wearing old gowns for working with Shauna and my hair is in an ugly bun. Tonight I'll be Donald's charming princess, but how can I look happy when I'm not? Bella chastised herself. *You mustn't be short with Donald. He is your companion and your love. Go to the mirror and practice smiling while you dress for cocktails.*

***

Bella took the hairpins from the bun and brushed her black hair until it shone. *Back home in Plymouth when I wore my hair this way, it hung to my shoulders like a wig of straight black thread. Now I see soft waves. I've never noticed them before—soft waves like my sister's hair. Now, which would Donald prefer, a young temptress or an adult Dresden doll?* Bella braided her hair into a topknot held by two turquoise combs, dressed in her burgundy gown and placed the pearl necklace around her neck. Donald came home and stepped into the front hall just as Bella floated down the stairs. For some unrecognizable reason, she felt happier than she had in weeks.

"Bella, how beautiful you are this evening. Have you found us a house?"

"No, Donald. It means that I dearly love you and I would live in a haystack with you if the cows would share it with us. Have you been house hunting?"

"I went to all the men with whom I have had business to see if any of them knew of a house, but they had nothing to offer. You are right. I should be more concerned but it isn't in my nature to worry. I'll wash up and be down in a few minutes."

As Donald climbed the stairs, Bella called after him. "Wax your red moustache into a smile, Donald. The Stevensons are coming for cocktails at five."

***

Donald and Bella waited in the parlour for their grandfather clock to strike five bells. Within minutes the knock came. When Donald started to rise, he heard footsteps in the front hall. Dirk answered the door and ushered the guests into the parlour.

"Mr. and Mrs. Stevenson, Sir and Ma'am," said Dirk most formally, then added in a make-believe whisper, "Did I say it right?" His eyes danced with merriment. "Shauna dared me to say that." Everyone laughed, including Shauna in the kitchen. "What would you care to drink?" Dirk asked, the perfect butler once again, and left to fill their orders.

"I just can't wait to tell you a secret," said Maria. "Hamish will tell you—it is his secret, but don't put our news on the grapevine."

"We've been transferred. You may buy our house if you wish," said Hamish.

Bella's mouth dropped open. Donald moved to the edge of his chair, elbows on his knees and said, "Did I hear you correctly? You're leaving Paramaribo?"

"Yes," said Hamish. "Remember, my company doesn't want anyone to know until February the fifteenth. Do you think you can talk your owner into letting you stay for an extra month? We'll be gone by then."

"The price is quite high," said Marie, "perhaps more than you had in mind."

"And the paddock is for one horse only," added Hamish. "I understand you need one for a mare and another for your stallion."

"That's not a problem, Hamish," said Bella like a frog licking in a fly. "We'll just dismantle the paddock we built and take the lumber with us. My friends, you have saved us from the arrogant colonials in this city. They will shoot sparks when they learn who has your elegant home. I promise we will be very good to it." With sincere words of thanks, Donald rose and shook hands with Hamish and Marie.

Bella set her chin as protruding and determined as Napoleon's and said, "I can intimidate people by my small size and big voice. Like a flea in a business man's beard, I will make Brink give us the extra month by saying that if he doesn't I will continue to return his house to the disgusting stained tan walls he allowed for the past ten years." Bella turned to Marie. "The rose paint is water-based calcimine, and fresh. It would wash off with a good scrubbing. Brink will know I'd do it in a minute."

***

The Macdonald family moved into Candlewick during the rainy months. Social evenings with friends and happy times filled their days. On the mornings when the sun hung longer in the sky prior to the coming dry season, Bella and Donald often went riding alone or with friends.

***

One day Donald and Bella rode along a creek bed where steaming jungle offered Bella glimpses of the conditions Donald faced when he prospected for gold. The foliage at the edge of the water formed a solid wall of green. A myriad of insects clicked away like the sound of a million grandfather clocks out of unison. From the dead limb of a tree a large blue and yellow parrot cocked its head and screeched at them. Despite all of nature's interruptions, an odd tranquility emanated from the depths of the jungle.

"This is so beautiful, Donald. Is this what it's like on the Corentyne River?"

"I suppose so, Princess, but we are relatively safe on this little creek. It is near to Paramaribo and I am with you and carrying a gun. Up the Corentyne, I dismount if I need to examine an outcropping. That is when I get to know the jungle first hand."

"There are not many weeks left before you leave again, my sweet. These past few months have been so filled with settling into Candlewick, enjoying friends and our trip to Demerara for Gabby and Simon's wedding that I have not noticed the days flying by."

Donald slowed, sidled his horse up to Bella's horse and reached to hold her hand. "I am glad we moved to Candlewick. I never realized the restraints of Moorcroft until I enjoyed our friends in the new house. Owning it outright is worth those extra gold nuggets it cost us."

"Well, Donald, do pan for extra nuggets if you must, but do it quickly so that you can come home with the rains. Ordering gowns from Paris and having an upstairs maid as well as Shauna in the kitchen is really very nice, my dear, but expensive. I hope you find your gold mine soon so we can afford this paradise."

Donald laughed, then switched to his serious voice. "I hope so too. Those men with whom I had lunch that day seemed to know far too much about my trips up the Corentyne. If I am to retain the area that interests me the most, I may have to lease the parcel where I hope to stake the gold mine by paying the government an expensive annual fee. While other prospectors think I have insufficient money to pay for the lease they seem happy just to spy on me. However, if they were to think

I have the money to buy the lease, they might run to the government and take out a lease before I do and attempt to find the gold mine themselves. Retaining rights with a lease is very expensive. I can't afford to take more than one year to find the mother lode within the area I lease. Now you understand why I am being so careful."

Donald did not end with joking nor urge his horse to outrun mine. He is serious about the cost; I hope we haven't over-extended ourselves with the bigger house and the extra maid. Then there is the new project I hope to start for the dry months if Aunt Kate's diocese favours the proposal that I have in mind for their overseas mission work. I can see by his expressionless face that he knows I have thoughts running around in my head. I must say something before he suspects that he has worried me about finances.

Bella reined in Mischief. "We have come a long way, Donald. Do you not think the horses might be tired of picking their way around rocks at the edge of this creek?"

"Mischief, maybe, but not Cobus," Donald replied. "Cobus does this sort of riding all summer while I test sites with a little panning. Perhaps you are right, though. We should return home before the sun heats the jungle and raises a fog or the rain comes early and soaks us."

***

Again, a mule brayed in the back yard. Donald's khaki riding outfit with heavy boots and the new pith helmet were laid out for the morning. The candlelight dinner for Mr. McD's send-off came to an end. The Macdonalds slipped upstairs to their bedroom with the last of the champagne and two glasses.

***

With breakfast over, Bella waited at the back door in her white gown while Donald sheathed the rifle in its scabbard and returned to her for a last hug and kiss.

"Reiche Ernte in your search for gold, my love. Rich harvest in the hills," she called and added, "Be careful while hanging out with the sloths."

Donald nudged Cobus forward. "Sloths indeed, my Rosebud. I ended your story by finding a gold mine. If I find a sloth colony, I will certainly hang out with them." He waved, then started down the carriageway, and soon the mule's tail disappeared from view.

He is gone again. Eve and my other friends will keep me busy, but they can't cure the loneliness. Only I can do that by attempting to achieve projects that are useful, and that does not include playing bridge with the grapevine ladies. I'll start a project tomorrow. Somehow, today, I feel tired.

***

Shauna and Dirk arrived at the dining room table for their English lesson shortly after Donald's departure.

"I have a new Charles Dickens novel for you to read to me. The title is *Oliver Twist*. It's the story of a young boy's life as he tries to rise out of poverty. Take turns reading to improve your diction. We'll look at Donald's English newspaper to know what's going on in the world. After that I'll give the new maid, Briya, her first lesson."

***

Bella spent the next month finishing little projects around the house: letters to her parents and Gabby and Simon, plans for Dirk to improve the garden and sewing a few cushions to add colour to the pale-yellow sitting room.

One morning Bella refused breakfast. She felt poorly—sick to her stomach—yet she hadn't eaten anything that would bother her. After a few days of this she visited Eve and asked if there were any strange illnesses in Paramaribo.

"Bella," said Eve in a serious tone, "from your description of the illness, could you be pregnant? Donald left a little over three months ago and I am sure you did not send him on his way without pleasant memories. Have you missed a menstrual period?"

Bella clapped her hands together in excitement. "Do you really think that is what is wrong? I don't keep a record of those days." Bella counted months on her fingers. "By the time Donald comes home in two months, I will be showing. I must prepare a new wardrobe, quickly."

Bella counted the months on her fingers again. "I suppose I should see a doctor and prepare for next May."

Eve promised to keep Bella's secret until Bella's tummy made the announcement by itself via the grapevine. With the right design of gown, full at the waist, they hoped Donald would be the first to know upon his return, not counting servants.

***

The next week, in Bella's trap, Eve drove Bella to the doctor's office. The office smelled of disinfectant and medications. The chairs were too high for Bella. While awaiting her turn in the muggy room, the more she tried to hold her feet from swinging, the greater the apprehension she felt.

"Mrs. Macdonald," the doctor said after making up a chart with the history of her health and a short examination. "I have good news and bad news. The good news is that at the moment you are in perfect health and, I suspect, pregnant. I can see in your eyes that this pleases you. The bad news is that your history of rickets not only gives you bowed legs and a pigeon breast, it also gives you an unusual shape to your pelvic girdle. It is long and narrow. You may have pain carrying a baby to full term and very often child-birth is difficult." The longer he spoke, the more dejected Bella became. "Cheer up, little lady. Think of the baby's great future. Come and see me if you have any bleeding or unusual pain. There are medical ways to assist your pregnancy and the birth of the little one."

Eve rushed to Bella when she left the doctor's cubicle. "What did he say? Am I right?" Bella said little. Once at home, she told Eve the whole story about her rickets. When Bella lifted her skirt, Eve could not believe the extent of the deformity.

"Never mind the rickets, Bella," said Eve. "Together, you and I and your servants will look after anything that distresses you. We will make the months go by quickly until Donald returns. His love will see you through this."

***

The hot, dry weeks of September to mid-October did not pass quickly. Bella counted every day. Shauna stood by and made sure that Bella drank milk with every meal. Dirk drove the trap for shopping and he and Shauna carried every parcel. Eve came over in the mornings and the two went for a quiet stroll to keep up Bella's strength.

"We must be doing something right," said Bella to Eve. "The books say that I should feel like I am glowing and I do. I don't know what the last few months or giving birth will feel like, but right now I have no pain and the morning sickness has passed."

***

The rains came and Donald did not return with the first big downpour. By mid-November Bella lost her compassionate nature. She complained if the flowers on the table seemed wilted, if her Melba toast sagged in the humidity or if her full-skirted gowns seemed too cumbersome. In the quiet of her bedroom she bowed her head.

Dear Lord, please watch over Donald and bring him safely home. I am so miserable without him that I fear I am miserable to the servants. Please reduce the pain I try to hide and give this little child, whom I carry, good health and a world of love. Amen.

***

Rain beat upon the house. Lightning lit up the black sky and thunder crashed about the heavens. Briya closed the windows. She offered to make Bella a cup of cocoa. Shauna suggested that she could read *Oliver Twist* to help pass the evening, but Bella refused the offers and stayed curled up on the love seat, staring at the rain coursing down the window.

Donald will not come home tonight. No ship would risk coming up the Surinam River in this storm. Perhaps I am unwell and should go to bed. I keep seeing shadows in the window. There it is again. A lantern out there. Perhaps Dirk is checking on Mischief—but it looks like a face—a face at the window and there's tapping noises. Why, it is Donald! It is Donald waiting for me to come and give him a kiss through the glass.

"Donald, my love, are you alright?" Bella shouted all the way down the back hallway to Donald. "Why do you always come home drenched with rain?" At that moment she fell into his arms and swooned in a faint.

"Shauna, come quickly!" Donald shouted. "Bella has fainted!" He carried her to the love seat and laid her head on a pillow. His wet clothing dripped everywhere he moved as he fetched a cold wet cloth for her brow and threw off his gun in the scullery. While he loosened the waistband of her skirt, Bella roused. She smiled up at him.

"Donald, would you like to have a boy or a girl? You are going to be a father about the end of April or the beginning of May."

"Lay quietly, my little Rosebud. You've had a bad turn. You're talking nonsense."

"Not at all, Donald. I have been carrying your baby since the day you left."

"A baby, Bella? Me—a father?"

"That's right, Donald. As you said yourself, things sometimes happen." Bella straightened around on the love seat and patted the other cushion for Donald to sit, but he did not sit. Instead, he strutted around the room talking to himself.

"Fatherhood? How can that happen so fast? Just a few months in the jungle, and when I return, there's to be a wee bairn. We made love the night before I left town and now my Rosebud is carrying my son—ah, my child." Donald clasped his hands behind his back to assume the pose of a proud father and smiled down at Bella.

"I'll be back to sit with you as soon as I get out of these wet clothes."

16

THE BAIRNS

Bella heard Donald's slippers on the stairs. Her gaze followed him into the parlour and watched as he eased himself into the rocking chair as if still trying to comprehend the news that he was to be a father. Shauna came in with a hot rum toddy to follow his bath.

"Donald," started Bella in her soft voice, "there are important things you should know, so please listen carefully. Dr. DeVeer says that I am in good health at the moment."

"But?" asked Donald. "I know you are about to say 'but.' You always use a soft, determined voice when you have troublesome news."

"I do?" Bella's eyes widened. *I wonder if he knows that he has a serious voice.*

Bella recovered from this fleeting thought and went on. "Rickets, Donald. My past with rickets poses problems. It may be hard for me to carry the baby full term. Because of the rickets I have narrow hips as well as a pigeon breast. If I do manage to carry the baby, my narrow hips will make it painful to give birth." To emphasize her words, Bella smoothed the rose fabric of her full skirt over her tummy. Donald looked up and waited for her to go on.

"I suppose the good news is that the doctor says there are ways to spread the hips at the time of the birth."

Alarmed, Donald rocked forward, his hands palm up. "What have we done, Bella? I can't bear the thought of you in pain. What do we do now?"

"We will do nothing, my sweet, but carry on, prepare a nursery and choose a name for a boy and a girl. God will watch over me." Bella's face lit up with the glow of her pregnancy. "Donald, are you happy with this turn of events? I hope it's a boy with red hair just like yours."

Donald crossed over from the rocking chair to the love seat to be near Bella. "And if it is a girl," he said, "she must be just like her mother. We will be wonderful parents, my love." He pressed his fingers to his forehead in thought. "The word 'appreciate' seems such an understatement, but I appreciate your delight with having a baby despite the torture Dr. DeVeer says you will endure over the next few months."

"Only Eve and our servants know," said Bella patting her tummy, "for I have been wearing gowns that hide this little pumpkin." Donald caressed her belly with his strong left hand as his right arm encircled her shoulders. Bella started to chuckle.

"I have sewn a slim pale blue silk maternity dress for the New Year's Eve Ball. Our little one will show nicely by then, don't you think? The Ball will be our coming out party." Bella laughed with pleasure at the thought of surprising the women. She wondered who would be counting months on their fingers. *How many will know that he didn't leave until early August? Such busybodies. Have they nothing better to do?*

"Donald, would you like me to make you a pale blue cravat to match my dress, or would you rather wear a pink one to show your preference?" and she laughed again as she pictured the scene of their grand entrance at the New Year's Eve Ball.

***

The next morning Bella led Donald across the hall to a bedroom door that Bella suspected Donald had never opened. She swung the door wide and stood aside.

"Bella, this room is a nursery! And it's furnished. Did Marie and Hamish leave us this furniture? Look at the lovely carving on the cradle. And the soft tones of pink, white and blue—you can't even guess if it was decorated for a girl or boy." Donald brushed his palms together as if he had readied the nursery all by himself.

"Now all we have to do is pick names for this baby," he chirped.

***

November moved on to early December, with poinsettias blooming in the garden.

"What plans shall we make for Christmas?" Bella asked Donald during one of their early morning walks. "Should I write to Gabby and ask them to come to Paramaribo?"

"I suppose we must write to them sometime before Christmas, Bella, but don't you think that would be too much for your wee frame?" They continued with their walk, the question unanswered.

Donald was first to interrupt the sounds of the parakeets and jacobins high in the trees. "I must send Dirk for the mail before it starts to rain today. We haven't been to the post office for a week."

***

Dirk brought the mail in on a tray at lunchtime. Bella seized the letter from Demerara. She knew the handwriting and wanted to know Gabby's news.

"The letter seems very short and hurried, Donald." Bella read for a moment. "Simon's father is terminally ill. She says they are leaving for Holland the day of writing this letter and will stay until mid-January." Bella let the letter fall to the table and waited for Donald's reaction. *Why is he smiling?*

"Bella, my bulging Dresden doll, would you like to spend Christmas week at the New Palace Hotel? The governor travels to Amsterdam for the holidays. I'm sure our room will be available." Donald winked one eye and Bella thought of the big tub.

"How interesting!" Bella smiled. "That would be a lovely way to spend the holidays. Shall I tell our friends we are travelling so we can just disappear for a few days? Shauna, Dirk and Briya will like the chance to go home. We must tell them to return now and then to whisk the cockroaches into submission and be back for the New Year's Eve Ball."

"Yes, my Rosebud, we'll dress in pale blue and announce to the guests at the Ball that we are going to have a baby."

With pride, Bella glanced at her tummy. "The grapevine will likely report that I am having twins."

***

Church bells rang in the New Year. Donald was sure that 1890 would be the year he would find his gold mine. He kissed Bella goodbye as usual, then he and Cobus spent the dry month of January in the jungle. The rains and Donald returned in four weeks. By March, Bella found walking more painful. She ate like a humming bird because her body felt so bloated. The doctor suggested crème de menthe liqueur in hot water to ease her indigestion, claiming it tasted better than baking soda.

***

One evening after a game of cards, Donald followed Bella up to bed with the lamp in his hand. Carefully, he unbuttoned her shoes, helped to slide the nightgown over her head and tucked her into bed. She seemed troubled and said little. Donald blew out the lamp and gazed through the window at the stars before he stole in beside her.

Suddenly, in the dark a cocky voice cut the silence. "Well, my prince, have you decided to call him Ezekiel or Obadiah, from the Old Testament?"

Donald rolled onto his shoulder and rubbed her belly through the nightgown. He rejoined her question with a quick, "I thought we had chosen Matthew, Mark, Luke or John, from the New Testament. They are all popular names these days."

"Come now, Donald, we have had lots of time to think of names and you are never serious about it." Even in the dark, from the soft steady tone of her voice Donald knew she had a stern look on her countenance.

"Actually, Bella, I have given the name some thought. What do you think of Peter for his first name, after my brother Peter?"

"Peter? Peter." Bella spoke into the darkness. "If I agree to Peter then you must give him your second name, Alexander."

Donald put his lips to Bella's tummy and called softly. "Hello in there, Peter Alexander Macdonald, this is your father speaking. Are you awake?" After no reply, Donald returned his head to the pillow and asked, "What names do you have in mind for a girl? Faith, Hope or Charity?"

"All three might be necessary, Donald, but I've been thinking of Katherine, after my Aunt Kate. And the baby must have a second name. With only the one name, Isabella, I've always felt that my parents didn't love me enough to think up a second name."

"Is that what's been worrying you this evening, Rosebud? I noticed that you were quieter than usual. How would you like Isabel instead of Isabella?"

"You down there," called Bella from the pillow, "Are you Peter Alexander or Katherine Isabel?" Donald feigned a gurgle, as if in answer to Bella's question, and they settled into a peaceful sleep.

***

Dr. DeVeer leaned across the desk to command Bella's attention. "Mrs. Macdonald, the second week of April has passed and finally your baby seems to be lowering his head into the pelvic channel. Now we must listen for the heartbeat regularly. I want you to come into the hospital until the baby is born. As I told you several months ago, I can help you with the birth once we are sure the baby is in the proper position. I feel that day is very soon. If the pain is frightful, I can give you drugs for it when you need them."

Bella closed her eyes tight to relieve the pain and said nothing. Dr DeVeer's upright chair tortured her. *If only I could stretch out.* The thought of giving birth made her cringe. Her eyes lifted from gazing at the slender fingers clutched in her lap, focused on one wall of the doctor's office painted in sickly white, swept across the red mahogany desk and finally rose up to take in Dr. DeVeer's concerned face. *Giving birth to this child can't cause more pain than the pain I have endured these past two months. If having the baby stops the pressure, then I will agree to anything. Dear God, let me survive.*

"You mean that there's no time to waste?" said a stoic Bella. The doctor nodded his head. Before he could speak, Bella slipped from her chair, ready to leave. "I'll pack and have Donald bring me back this afternoon." *After that he can give the English and Dutch lessons and organize the servants and I'll no longer have to force myself to look strong. It will be heavenly to be off my feet with nurses to care for me.*

***

Dr. DeVeer stood outside Bella's hospital room door talking to the nursing supervisor. "Isabella Macdonald has been with us for three weeks. Despite the pain she must surely be enduring, does she never cry or ask for pain killers?"

"No. Perhaps a whimper at night when the light breezes of evening fail to waft across her brow," said the nurse. "She is made of iron. Others would be howling. She insists on wearing her black silk robe covered with chrysanthemums for her husband's daily arrival and that I comb her hair to wave softly around her face . . ."

The nurse trailed off when interrupted by the doctor.

"Her time has come. I must do something. I told her long ago that I could help surgically to allow the baby to pass, but I hoped the day would never come. Symphysiotomy is risky and cutting the pubic symphysis could cripple her. We studied the operation at medical school but I have never performed one."

"The pubic symphysis, doctor? I'm unsure of your meaning," said the nurse.

"With her narrow hip bone structure from rickets, the head of the baby will not engage properly. I must cut through the muscle wall and snip the ligament that joins the pelvic girdle at the front so that the hips can open and allow the baby to pass. After the birth, I will mend the pelvic girdle, but the union may never grow strong again. She may always have trouble walking. There will be a lot of bleeding and we will have to guard against infection. You will assist me with the operation."

The nurse nodded with each of the doctor's comments. Dr. DeVeer straightened with resolution. "She is three weeks overdue and her hips are not spreading. I cannot let her or the baby die. Tell her that on May the fifth I shall perform the surgery to release the baby. She should tell her husband today in case they have any questions for tomorrow, and the following day they will become parents."

***

"Don't come until evening, my prince. I might scream during delivery and you should not hear that," said Bella the next day when Donald arrived in his white jodhpurs and jacket. Bella carried right on in a jocular fashion. "It would spoil our times together in bed if you feared the consequences." Donald paced a circuit of the room, bewildered at his inability to be as calm as Bella. He settled himself beside the bed. Bella continued.

"The surgery is quite simple, Donald. Dr. DeVeer tells me he will cut through the ligament that joins the pubic bones so that the pelvis may spread apart. After the baby is born, he says that in time the union of the bones will become as one again."

***

Donald returned to Candlewick. Alone and worried, he could not bear the empty house and found himself returning to the paddocks. He stroked Mischief when she came to him, then went over to saddle Cobus. They were a team in the jungle when he had worries. Together, they rode along the riverfront until late into the evening under the watch of a waning moon and a multitude of stars surrounding the Southern Cross. The following day he sat in his rocking chair with the newspaper unread in his lap, picked at his meals and waited for the moment when he should return to the hospital.

***

The nurses smiled as he strode through the door with his eyes darting in all directions looking for some clue to his wife's well-being. A nurse in her stiff white uniform stood inside Bella's door holding a bundle.

Donald rushed into Bella's room, leaned over and kissed his precious wife. He winced at how tired and fragile she looked. Again, he kissed her wan smile.

"Mr. Macdonald," the nurse interrupted him. She put the bundle that she held into his arms, then folded back a white flannel blanket that shaded a little sleeping face.

"Our baby, Bella! Is it Peter or Katherine?"

"Peter—Peter Alexander Macdonald, my love. And he is bald. I'm sure the red hair will sprout tomorrow." With that, Bella forced a little chuckle. She had made her joke.

Donald sat in the hard bedside chair and held the wee one where Bella could share his gaze, but her eyelids were heavy and they slowly closed. His Rosebud had performed a miracle and had come through with her health and a fine baby boy. Donald dropped his head to offer a prayer, handed the baby to the nurse and tiptoed from the room.

***

Three months later, with Bella's recovery assured, Donald kissed his little son and left for the jungle. *Donald will return as he always has. I cannot afford to worry.*

Later that day, the mail brought a letter from Gabby explaining that Simon's father had passed away and settling the estate had taken longer than expected. *What? They are not returning! They plan to remain in Holland and sell his restaurant and small plantation to the man who is running them for him? How I will miss not having them near.*

***

The next month passed with Shauna and Briya minding the baby while Bella regained her energy. Worried about the health of Bella and his son, Donald surprised the household by returning from the jungle for a week in late August. He left with a promise to come home at the end of October.

***

Each day the big English pram carried young Peter over the gravel roads. Determined that her surgery should mend with strength, Bella insisted on the exercise every day with Shauna accompanying them until the rains came in late September.

True to his word, Donald returned in October. Again, roses adorned the dining room table instead of daisies. At six months, Peter, now using the big crib, practiced trying to pull himself up inside its boundaries.

***

"For heaven's sake, Donald!" Bella came rushing into the garden from the house. "A child of seven months does not ride a horse. Lift him down."

"You sewed him the jodhpurs, Rosebud. His strong little back took to Cobus quite nicely. If he can't ride a pony yet, I'll give him a rocking horse for Christmas."

"Fine, Donald, and I shall give him a little brother."

Donald wheeled, his face convulsed with laughing. "Having Peter was a miracle, Bella. Why would you joke about producing another miracle?"

Donald tucked Peter safely into the crook of his arm, offered Bella his other hand and the little family walked across the lawn towards the house. Near the back entrance, Bella pulled them to a halt and began speaking in her soft steady voice.

"I need to tell you something, Donald. This is the third time I have missed my monthly period. Is it possible that I could be pregnant again? We did more than hold hands last August when you were still at home."

"My God, Bella. One doesn't get pregnant while they are nursing!" Donald counted months. "Possibly eleven months between births. No, it can't be."

Bella continued in her soft voice. "They say that nursing mothers can't get pregnant, but perhaps I have proved them wrong. If I am pregnant, I intend to carry the baby."

"At what risk, Bella? You nearly bled to death last time. What about the pain you endured? You can't go through another pregnancy. Please, Rosebud, listen to reason!"

"Now, Donald, we are not yet sure if I am pregnant. Calm down. And don't be concerned about the pain. As I managed before, I can manage again. God will see to the future." With dusk filtering over their shoulders, they entered the scullery door.

***

In the parlour after dinner, young Peter sat on his blanket on the floor. His strong back made him look like a little Buddha in the soft glow of their paraffin lamps. Bella sat back from their play with the baby.

"What about Christmas? We can't go to Demerara and visit with Gabby and Simon anymore, and I can't walk into the New Year's Eve Ball in a maternity gown again. You would never live it down, virile fellow that you are."

".Do the servants know yet?"

"No, my love, but when we are sure, I think we must tell them. Being pregnant again so soon may make it harder for me—or perhaps it will be easier. Either way, Peter is getting heavier and I should not carry him with my weakened hips."

Conversation ceased when Shauna entered to fetch Peter for bedtime.

***

One week later, Bella had her first bout of morning sickness.

"Donald, in two days Shauna will change the calendar cards to read December the first. We must tell the servants today before dinner when they are all here in the house. They need time to make their Christmas plans too."

When Dirk brought in the tray with Mr. McD's gin, Donald asked him to have the girls come to the parlour for an announcement.

Donald cleared his throat to start his speech. Suddenly aware of the magnitude of what he was about to tell the servants, he changed his message to: "Right after Christmas, we are going to the New Palace Hotel for a few days preceding the New Year's Eve Ball. Plan to take the horse and trap to visit your families on days before Christmas, but one of you must be here to care for Peter while we are away. We'll drop in every afternoon to see you. Um, ah, Dirk, teach Briya to drive the trap this year." He paused to clear his throat again and half-blurted, "Of more importance, we wish to tell you that, hrrm, that Mrs. Macdonald is going to have another baby." Flustered by his own words, he sank into his rocking chair.

Dirk looked at Mr. McD and gave the hint of a smirk. Shauna rushed to her mistress and hugged her, ready to be the nursemaid all over again. Briya stood quietly in awe, with her mouth open as if transposed into a curious creature of the jungle.

17

THE PROJECT

One day a knock came to the front door and Shauna answered. Bella heard voices but paid no attention.

"Mrs. McD," whispered Shauna at the bedroom door, "Dr. DeVeer is in the parlour. Did you invite him for tea? He walked right in as if you were expecting him."

Bella dropped her pen, closed the note pad and rose from her vanity. *How could I forget Dr. DeVeer's appointment to check the children's health? I must finish that letter before Donald comes home and reads it. He doesn't mind my little projects but I have no doubt that he will think like Eve will think—that the project is enormous for someone with two young children— but I have recovered well since Gordon's birth, and two-year-old Peter is no problem at all with Shauna and Briya to help me.*

"Yes, Shauna. Please bring Peter and Gordon to the parlour and have Briya serve tea."

***

"You have two fine sons, Mrs. Macdonald," said Dr. DeVeer, munching on the last cookie. He put his stethoscope into his black bag. "Gordon certainly has his father's red hair, and quite a crop of it for a one-year-old. I've checked Peter too, and they are both in excellent health. And how about you, Mrs. Macdonald? With your history of rickets, having a child in the first place counts as a miracle. Having two healthy children eleven months apart will certainly be reported in my record book for the Medical Association. You are truly amazing. Tell me, have you healed? Your colour is good."

"Why, yes, Doctor. Donald and I have been riding this past month and I am full of energy. After your expert care, how could I be otherwise? Do come for tea again sometime, any time you wish," Bella added while accompanying the doctor to the door.

***

As the rains ceased, the garden of Candlewick burst forth in colour. Passers-by often stopped to admire the pink bougainvillaea climbing the posts of the front veranda. In the same way, at breakfast, Bella watched those who passed her dining room window. Now, with her view of Heerenstrat, she saw both the wealthy going to dine at the hotel and the poor who disappeared around the far corner of the hotel. *There must be a lane back there. I wonder if those poorly dressed souls are scavenging for old clothes or broken furniture.* More and more, through the window, Bella noticed the poor and thought of the houses that she had passed in the slums of Paramaribo on "horse hunting day." *Why does the government not help these people who are forced to pick through the rubbish of others to survive?*

Bella finished her tea and rose from the table still thinking of the poor. *I wonder if Aunt Kate ever received my letter about having the churchwomen organize missionary work here. Aunt Kate would have answered me; the letter must have gone astray. I'll write again.*

***

Bella and Donald's breakfast always came early at Candlewick. The oncoming heat of the day made rising early a necessity. Again, Bella saw the poor passing the window when she took her place at the table. Now, a carriage with guests pulled up at the hotel. Bella turned and spoke towards the newspaper that Donald held in his hands.

"Donald, before you go off prospecting again will you teach me how to drive our new carriage?"

"No, Bella. It is too heavy for you to handle. If you wish to go out alone or with Shauna or Briya, take the trap. Dirk will drive you in the carriage any time you wish to take the children." After a moment Donald put down his paper. "Why would you want to use the carriage, Bella? Are you up to your old tricks?" He recognized the sparkle that came into her eyes when she had plans brewing in her head. Deciding it was better not to know, he said, "I'm off to the bank, then the club for lunch. I'll be back for stout time."

"I wrote to my family and Aunt Kate. Post my letters please; they are on the hall table. And Donald, ask Dirk to have Mischief in harness for ten o'clock. Eve and I are taking the trap into town. I've arranged for Shauna to watch the children."

***

"Where are we going, Bella?" asked Eve. "You're so mysterious this morning. And why did you ask me to wear plain clothes and leave my jewellery at home?"

"You'll see when we get there, Eve. In the meantime, we are merely having a nice morning ride." Bella guided the trap past the New Palace Hotel, then took a right turn and another one.

"Why have you come back here, Bella, with the hotel's dustbins and rotting leftovers?" Bella did not answer immediately. She wanted to be away from the area as quickly as possible in case Donald spotted them in the shabby lane. Mischief strained ahead with Bella's urging and soon the trap had left the downtown business area. Free to pay less attention to Mischief, Bella finally answered Eve's question.

"Most of Paramaribo's poor, the ones that have no job, exist by hunting the back alleys for things they can use or eat. I see them pass my window every morning. I've watched the poor go behind the hotel so often I wanted to see with my own eyes why they went there."

The red gravel road changed to a mixture of gravel and clay, then finally just clay. The farther they travelled from town, the more dilapidated the buildings became. The river's flood plain, between the green of the jungle on their right and growth at the river's bank on their left, housed more than a hundred unpainted squatters' huts put together with boards and tarpaper. An old lady, sitting on a chair with three legs, watched little children playing at her feet. Another woman draped ragged clothes over a rope that served as her clothesline. Bella concentrated on hurrying Mischief along so it would appear that they had somewhere to go and just happened to be passing through.

"Bella, you brought me this way to see Paramaribo's slums, didn't you? What are you thinking of now?"

"I am thinking that I'll turn around and go home before the morning sun gives Mischief a sunburn. Before we have lunch, we'll sit in the shade of the back garden, watch the children play and consider our good fortune. That's what I am thinking."

Eve guessed Bella had more than that on her mind, but she dutifully took in everything they passed. She noticed the area around the pump where spilled water turned the clay into muck, a breeding ground for germs. Many of the houses had a small enclosure at the back with chickens scratching at the dirt through their own faeces. The odour from outhouses drifted on the air. People who stood aside to let the trap pass were barefoot, but still they waved and smiled.

"Do they expect us to give them a few guilders, Bella?" whispered Eve.

"No, that sets us above them. Just wave and smile in a kindly fashion."

The trap wheels started to click over gravel. Green plants grew in gardens of modest painted houses. Cheap eateries served Indian curry. Slowly the buildings increased in value and good repair until Mischief turned onto Heerenstrat that would lead them to Candlewick.

Dirk took care of Mischief and the trap. The women sat in canvas lawn chairs with iced tea. Shauna brought Peter and Gordon to them. After hugs and kisses, the children entertained each other with Briya watching their safety from a distance.

"I've been guessing why we took that ride today, Bella, looking at the slums all the way out and back again and guessing. Now tell me why we went."

"You must come out to Reiche Ernte on Wednesday, Eve, and see the wonderful changes wrought by a little education and some help to make ends meet. I'm not popular with some of the colonial women in the city because I taught the people on the plantation how to speak and write Sranan and Dutch and understand good hygiene." Bella paused to sip her drink. "My Aunt Kate in Cornwall had her parish donate clothing and toys to the families on the plantation. I have written her and asked if the church would consider helping the poor of Paramaribo as their missionary work for this next year. If she says yes and they collect an even bigger shipment of used items, I will suggest that they pass on the missionary plan to another parish for the next year and so on. Do you think we can organize some means of handing out any clothes or toys that arrive?"

"Who do you mean by 'we,' Bella? That would be an enormous task."

Gordon came to sit on Bella's lap and Peter could be heard jabbering in his Dutch baby talk with Briya until he followed her into the house.

"I suppose, Eve, by having you see the slums for yourself, I hoped you would help me form a plan to help these people. Don't tell anyone that I've written to Aunt Kate until I've heard from her. Aunt Kate's answer will determine my project for the months when Donald is away. I see that Shauna has come to the door, Eve. We'll go in for lunch."

***

Ginger brayed in the back garden. Donald and Dirk readied the packsacks that the mule would carry into the jungle. Once again, Donald laid out the khaki jodhpurs and stained riding boots. Tomorrow he would leave for the hills above the Corentyne River. Bella knew that Donald must follow his dream. *In the morning I'll wear my new white gown and pretend not to notice his holstered revolver. I will stand at the back door with the children and let them watch their father stow the rifle in its scabbard. Donald needs to see me smiling when he thinks of home, so I will be smiling. May God protect him in the jungle and the children here with me.*

***

In the morning Shauna presented the children in their good clothes and the family enjoyed breakfast together. When they gathered at the back door in the early morning light, shrill children's laughter spoke only of happiness. Donald sat young Peter in the saddle for a moment while he held Gordon up to pat the nose of Cobus. Dirk, Shauna and Briya called their good wishes and Bella and Donald embraced in a final farewell. Cobus, with the mule trailing behind, carried Donald to the corner of the house and then they were gone. Briya took the children into the garden to play and Bella retired to her bedroom for a moment alone. Shortly, she roused her head, dabbed at her tear stained face and looked into the mirror. *Look to the future, Bella. You have a project to plan in case you hear from Aunt Kate, but first you promised to take Eve to Ernte.*

***

Early the following morning, the carriage rolled out of the driveway at a slow pace. Not only did Mischief disagree with the purchase of the new carriage, she let it be known that she thought five adults and two children were a few too many. Peter climbed up between Dirk and Briya on the driver's seat and Eve, Bella and Shauna sat inside with Gordon, who made a game of switching laps between Bella and Shauna.

Once the carriage wheels rolled along the clay road of the countryside, Mischief recognized that they were off to Ernte and moved along in what seemed to be a livelier frame of mind. Parrots winged overhead and snakes poked their heads out of the wispy grass at the side of the road.

"The next plantation is Reiche Ernte, Eve. We'll leave our big sun hats in the carriage until it's time for the picnic. The grounds near the plantation house are well shaded with palms and wild banana trees."

When the carriage rolled to a stop at the back of the house, all the women and children came running to see the newest addition to the family. The older children considered the carriage to be the new addition and shouted to Dirk for a ride. The women gave Eve and Bella their slight curtsy, then held up their hands to hold Gordon.

"Father is out with the workers, Mrs. McD," said Wumi. "He didn't know you were coming or he would have had everyone here. Would you like to hear our newest song?" After Bella introduced Eve to each lady, followed by a handshake, the two women were offered chairs for the children's performance.

"Wumi, you must show off your classroom to my guest. After that, Eve, we can visit the water pump and I'll ask if one of the mothers would like to show you her home."

***

Noon and picnic time came far too soon for everyone. Dirk lifted down the picnic basket for Mrs. McD and carried it to the riverbank. Shauna, Briya and he had a second basket for lunch with Asha and Wumi. From her vantage point by the river, Bella could see the rose garden where she and Donald would have had lunch, but she did not share that with her friend. Under Bella's care, Peter dabbled his bare feet at the water's edge and laughed at the splash of the seed pods that he threw into the river.

With lunch over, they began the ride home. Briya and Shauna put on their big sun hats and sat on the driver's seat with Dirk. Peter fell asleep with his head in his mother's lap and Gordon soon nodded off, curled up in Eve's arms.

"Bella, you've done the right thing by bringing education and good hygiene to Ernte. Do you think we'll ever manage to help the poor families of Paramaribo?"

"I hope so. When I hear Kate's decision, I'll work on a plan to distribute the clothes. We can't do it all."

***

Early morning light at the bedroom window woke Bella. *What is to happen to my project? I must start making a plan to hand the things out. Where will I store things while waiting for the contents to be handed out? They will mildew in our humidity if left outside. What am I to do?*

Bella finished dressing and went downstairs for breakfast. The drapes were drawn against the heat that the eastern sun forced into every cranny. The room crowded in on her. Even the smell of freshly brewed tea did not lighten Bella's step. *My days alone during the dry spell will be void of purpose if I cannot help the poor.* Feeling shattered, Bella took her seat. With unseeing eyes, she placed the napkin on her lap. She raised her view to include the familiar plate, and then she saw the envelope!

Leaning against a glass of orange juice stood a letter—a letter from the Port Authority. *Dirk must have gone to the Post Office early.* Adrenalin shot through Bella's body. *What if the letter announces a shipment to be claimed? I haven't heard from Kate that she's sending one. I have no plans to receive such a shipment!*

"Good morning, Mrs. McD." Dirk bounced into the dining room, apparently quite pleased with himself. "I knew you were waiting for an important letter, so I stood at the wicket, ready for the moment the post office opened. I'll take you down to the port right now, before the morning heat becomes unbearable, if you wish."

***

Dirk swung the trap alongside the loading dock next to the warehouse and helped Bella up the steep steps leading to the Port Authority office.

"Come along, Dirk. Perhaps someone has shipped me something we can carry home in the trap." Bella entered the office and showed the clerk her letter.

"I'm glad you have come along so promptly, Mrs. Macdonald. Your crates are taking up space that we need for outgoing shipments. They must be removed by noon. Shall I call for two of the large wagons waiting outside in the lot?"

Two wagonloads of crates! What can I say? I suppose we can store them in Cobus's stall for the moment. At least it isn't the rainy season. How have I managed to place myself in such a predicament?

"Yes, that will be fine. Two wagons, you say? My, oh my! The wagons can follow the trap. Head for home, Dirk."

The trap and two wagons climbed the rise heading away from the port. Bella felt she owed Dirk an explanation about Aunt Kate's second shipment.

"Dirk, do you remember the crates my Aunt Kate sent for Reiche Ernte? Don't laugh, but I thought that I might be able to help the poor who live in the slums of Paramaribo. I never dreamed that Kate would send so much so soon. What am I to do with these crates of clothes and toys?"

18

INVISIBLE CHRISTIANS

Still harnessed to the trap, Mischief stood in the back garden of Candlewick, clear of the driveway so the two heavy wagons could pass her on their way to Cobus's stall. Bella stepped from the trap to supervise the unloading of the crates. Dirk dropped the reins and ran to assist the wagon men. Mischief, uneasy with no driver and unused to the loud voices of the men, moved towards her stall. The right trap wheel engaged the edge of the flowerbed and the trap became entangled in a flowering red ginger bush. With a whiny, Mischief kicked out with her back legs to free herself. Amid the noise of scraping crates and grunting labourers, Bella heard her mare. She lifted her skirts and ran to grab the dangling reins from under the thrashing horse's hooves. Without losing a moment, she released the trap and led Mischief into her stall with quiet words to calm her before she removed the horse's harness. Dirk broke her concentration.

"Mrs. McD, the men are waiting to be paid."

She turned to see the two wagon men standing with their mouths gaping.

"Where did she learn to release a trap and remove the harness?" said one man in Sranan.

Bella recognized the question that had popped out of his mouth. In passable Sranan, she said, "I learned in Demerara, for there was no one else to do the job." Bella paid the men, speaking in Dutch, and finally, in English she asked Dirk to free the trap from the flowerbed.

***

"It's been a long day for you, Mrs. McD," said Shauna after a very late lunch. "I'll look after the children; you rest."

After dining alone, Bella sank into Donald's rocking chair, grateful that Shauna had taken the children. She rocked herself gently. *What am I to do? I'll never empty those crates before things mildew. Kate's letter telling me of the church's intentions so I would have delivery plans in place must have gone astray. What to do, what to do . . .*

She sat staring across the room with vapid eyes. *What am I doing here in Donald's rocking chair? I seldom sit here. My legs can't even reach the floor. Oh Donald, what have I done?* Slowly her head lowered to rest in her upturned hands while her shoulders shook with quiet sobbing. Briya turned the lamp low and left Bella with her tears, rocking slowly, very slowly.

***

In the morning Bella rose with smiles for everyone, although her face bore an ashen pallor. She ate breakfast with the children, but as soon as Briya took them into the garden she entered the parlour to stare at the empty rocking chair, her brow furrowed with the burden that the crates had placed upon her. *I need your guidance, Donald. Dear God, tell me what I must do to help the poor receive these things.* Her fingers twisted, flesh on flesh. Dirk stepped into the room.

"Mrs. McD, would you like to come with me for a trap ride?"

Bella could think of nothing better than fresh air and solitude to give her time to think in the face of so much trouble. Dirk guided Mischief away from town towards a jungle area foreign to Bella. They travelled in silence except for the chink, chink, chink of the harness and the buzz of insects in the jungle. They pondered their own thoughts until Dirk spoke.

"Mrs. McD, I'm taking you to meet my mother, Rani, and my girlfriend, Rinku. I think the four of us should sit under the palms and discuss your crates. Last evening, without your permission, I rode Mischief out here after I glanced through the window and saw how distressed you looked, crying there in the Master's chair."

"You rode out here at night, Dirk? Why, you might have been attacked!"

"Never mind the danger, Mrs. McD. I had to go. I think my folks can help."

The dear boy—I should scold him for putting Mischief in danger but I shan't scold him for such a courageous act. She smiled at Dirk for her answer and the trap jogged on.

Here and there, narrow clay roads led off the main track, pale against the shade of the jungle. Houses clustered together under the bright sun in small areas of open plain. Dirk pulled on Mischief's reins beside a neat hut. A middle-aged woman, with arms open wide, rushed from the house to welcome them. Her skirts were fresh. Dark hair, framing the coffee-coloured face, gleamed in the sunlight. *Dirk has taught them everything he's learned from Donald. That pretty girl behind Rani must be Dirk's friend, Rinku.*

After introductions, they were seated on crude benches nestled in the shade beside the house and Rani served warm lemonade. Dirk's face became serious. Speaking in Dutch, the two women and Bella followed his words easily.

"Mrs. McD, with a name like Dirk, I have a Dutchman among my forefathers. We are all Christians in my family. The big churches don't greet us with open arms, but that's fine with us. We would rather practice Christianity in our own way."

Bella's back straightened. Her eyes popped open with this revelation. "Where is your church? Who is your preacher? Why have I not heard of this church?"

Dirk's mother bubbled with laughter. "We have no preacher, nor any church. We hold our Sunday meetings under the palms. We sing, pray, read the Bible and give thanks for what the Lord has provided us. Together, we open our picnic baskets for the noon meal."

Rinku said very little but her eyes told Bella that this sweet young woman loved Dirk.

Dirk took up the conversation. "Mr. Morgan, at the Ice Company, owns an old warehouse where he keeps his big wagons. If he'll let you use the warehouse, my mother and Rinku will ask our brothers and sisters in the church to sort the gifts and distribute them. Would you want that?"

Bella felt as though a weight had lifted from her shoulders. She looked at Rani and Rinku. Their eyes, glistening with excitement, were riveted on her face, watching for her lips to speak or her head to nod or show in any way that she liked the offer of their help. Without a word, Bella jumped from the bench and gave Rani a hug. She grabbed for Dirk's hand and squeezed while her other arm encircled Rinku.

"My dear invisible Christians! Thank you, Lord, for answering my prayers. You and your friends will be doing a great service for your people. As soon as we have a plan with Morgan's Ice Company, Dirk will bring you word and we'll start delivering the gifts."

"No, Bella, my people will start the delivery; you have already done enough. If you speak to Mr. Morgan and six of your friends to loan us their carriages and drivers for an early morning start, Mother, Rinku and I will organize our people to hand out the gifts. The poor of Paramaribo will open their doors to my people more easily than to you, don't you see?"

"You're right, Dirk," said Bella. "I'm sure to have six carriages available through my friends. I'll speak to them and visit Mr. Morgan. Remember, Dirk, your brothers and sisters and the drivers must all choose two items for each member of their family. Take along some tools to break down the crates so you can throw the boards out along the way. The people need them to mend their homes."

***

Bella rose early to see her carriage, with Dirk and Shauna, leave Candlewick on the morning designated for delivering things to the poor. Her ideas for helping Paramaribo's needy had not worked according to her original plan, but she knew that Dirk's people, speaking Sranan, could approach the poor far better than she or her friends could. By lunch Dirk and Shauna were home again.

"Mrs. McD!" cried Dirk. "Wherever we stopped we were greeted with smiling faces. On our return route we threw toys out along the way, and the boards. The children were dancing with pleasure and the people lined the road and dipped their heads with thanks for this wonderful event that you and your friends caused to happen."

Shauna stood grinning, ready to speak. "Mrs. McD, I believe you are the only colonist who cares about the poor. I thank you for all the happiness you spread among them today."

***

Warm days, garden parties and children's outings continued on into the summer. Bella enjoyed Peter and Gordon, her friends and the exotic lifestyle of Surinam. She missed Donald but she knew the rains would return, and with them her loved one would come to smile his sassy grin through the windowpane while his red moustache dripped with water. Donald had spent enough summers in the jungle that she did not worry as much as she had that first year. *I am so blessed. Thank you, God. Life in Paramaribo is like paradise for our household. I'm glad Father sent me to South America.*

***

One August day Bella felt restless. Riding Mischief with friends, parties, visiting Reiche Ernte, writing letters, the garden and the children were all enjoyable, but she needed a useful project to fill her time. She fussed for a week before a thought came to mind as she finished a geography lesson with the servants.

"Dirk and Shauna, I feel your sisters and brothers are more Christian than my own church. Is there anything I can do for them?"

"Not really," said Shauna. "We are happy with the Lord and He seems happy with us."

Dirk's face broke into a grin. He blushed. "I know of one thing that might give you something to think about, Mrs. McD. Would you and Mr. McD come to my wedding? I asked Rinku if she would be my wife last Sunday and she said yes!"

"That's wonderful news, Dirk! Of course we'll come. When will it be?"

"Whenever Mr. McD returns, Ma'am. I wouldn't go ahead without him."

Bella blurted, "But where will you live? You won't leave Candlewick, will you?" Deep pink suffused Dirk's olive skin.

"I have no right to ask until Mr. McD comes home, but I wondered if Rinku could live with me in my quarters out back. They are better than I could build for us."

Bella clapped her hands with pleasure. "Just what I needed, a new project! Do you think Rinku would like Shauna and I to teach her to sew so she can decorate your quarters to your liking?" Dirk and Shauna could not contain the width of their smiles.

"Dirk, fetch Rinku in the trap for lunch next Saturday. I'd like Shauna to show her our modern kitchen and plumbing, and I'll start her English lessons."

***

The rains did come and Donald returned to continue the pleasure of being with his wife and children. On a wooden garden swing with two benches facing inwards, he and Bella swung in the moonlight on rainless nights. One evening, Donald stopped the swing and changed to his serious voice.

"Bella, please come upstairs; I have something to show you." When they were in the confines of their bedroom, his stern voice continued. "I do not trust the bank employees to keep information about my bank account private. I feel that other prospectors know about my annual deposits of gold nuggets and are just waiting to learn if I panned enough gold for the lease. As long as they know I haven't enough money for the lease, they are content to spy on me for better and better information. Times were not easy in the jungle this past year. On several occasions I felt as if I were being watched—not in a threatening way, but more as if binoculars were trained on me."

Donald took a turn around the room and started again. "No one but the bank should know the size of my bank account, yet other prospectors clap me on the shoulder as if we were friends and with teasing words ask, 'Did you find your gold mine this year?' as if it is a joke, but I think they are prying. For that reason, I deposited a smaller number of nuggets at the bank, to put them off, and hid most of the gold here in the house under a loose floorboard. The board is under the bed. No one will find it, but I thought you should know. I have hidden my maps there too. Here, I'll show you the board." Donald pushed the bed aside.

"If you have so many nuggets," Bella teased, "why don't you give me a few to keep in a bottle in the kitchen cupboard? They would be as safe there as the ones hidden under the bed."

"Safe from the servants, my dear, but what about thieves?"

**

The next day Shauna came to Bella with a small bottle.

"I found this bottle on a kitchen shelf, Mrs.D. It's half full of gold nuggets. I've not seen it before and I thought I should give it to you."

Bella remembered her teasing words and smiled to herself. "Shauna, I suspect Mr. McD wants to keep that bottle of nuggets exactly where you found it. I think he wants to leave those nuggets for household use in case we ever need them."

**

One soft sunny day the family—including the children, Shauna and Briya—put on their finest clothes and travelled to Dirk's home for his wedding. Donald drove the carriage with Peter sitting beside his daddy. The women and Gordon rode safely inside.

"Remember to bring your lunch," Dirk called when leaving Candlewick with the trap and Mischief on the day before his wedding.

Music from an odd assortment of instruments filled the air as the carriage arrived at the cluster of huts. Traditional Indian and African rites mixed with Christianity produced a distinctive Creole wedding ceremony. The festive occasion brought singing and the swirl of colourful skirts in the shade of the palms. Every member of the church came to enjoy the party and waved Dirk and Rinku goodbye when the newlyweds headed off in the trap. The wedding guests left for siesta time when the picnic baskets were empty. After hugs for Rani and her family, the Macdonald household left to return to Candlewick.

***

Two more happy years passed with the family and servants visiting Reich Ernte and Bella and Donald riding with their close friends or going on outings with the children. In the evenings Donald often worked over his hand-made maps of the jungle and the hills above, trying desperately to pinpoint where his elusive gold mine might be. Each fall, he returned with more nuggets than the year before, so he knew the mother lode must be somewhere on one of his maps. If only he could find the mine, he knew his life—and stability for his family—would be complete.

The rainy months passed so quickly with work, parties and elegant living that Bella hardly noticed her calendar cards turn to July. Donald, as in the past, left for the jungle as soon as the rain stopped, and the house became quiet, except for the laughter of the children. Then one month Bella found the heat oppressive for some reason. She declined when Eve suggested they go riding.

"Excuse me, Mrs. McD," Shauna said from the kitchen door. "You seem troubled. Is something wrong?"

"I believe so," Bella answered simply. "Please ask Dirk to prepare the carriage. I must go to see Dr. DeVeer. I believe I am pregnant."

***

For a month Bella kept to her bed, and then one afternoon it happened. Alone, with the servants downstairs, Bella found herself screaming in pain, sucking for breath and exploding with pressure as a stillborn baby girl arrived on bloodied sheets. Shauna came running in an instant.

"Briya!" cried Shauna, "Bring all the sheets from the linen closet. We must staunch the bleeding." Within minutes, Dirk readied the carriage while Shauna wrapped her mistress and the baby in the clean sheets. Bella felt Dirk's arms under her shoulders and knees. She awoke in the hospital with Dr. DeVeer standing at the foot of the bed.

"You gave us quite a scare, Mrs. Macdonald. I have stopped the bleeding. You are worn out. You may go home in a week, but you must rest in bed at home for a month."

"A girl!" wailed Bella. "I lost my baby girl because my weak pelvis could not contain the tiny fetus?"

The doctor slowly nodded his head. "Its small size allowed it to just slip out through the birth canal," said Dr. DeVeer.

Bella held her hands over her face and sobbed. *Why didn't I drink my milk!* From deep within she thought she heard Aunt Kate's voice. *Bella, you mustn't languor with guilt. You have two healthy sons who need a mother!*

***

On her first day back home Dirk appeared at the bedroom door. "Mrs. McD, you have a letter from the port." Bella ripped open the letter.

"Six more crates, Dirk!" Bella dropped her head to the pillow, closed her eyes and sighed. Dirk roused her.

"Mrs. McD," he said, "if there are more crates, my brothers and sisters will distribute the gifts just as we did before with the help of Mr. Morgan and your friends' carriages." Tears of gratitude came to Bella's eyes. Dirk patted her coverlet and left the room.

***

With the month of bed rest over, Bella's strength returned a little at a time. Sunshine lifted the pallor from her cheeks and playing with the children in the garden raised her spirits.

The rains came and Donald returned to hear of Bella's ordeal. Their first night together, before Donald blew out the lamp, Bella spoke in her distinctive soft voice.

"The doctor says we must be very careful with our timing, Donald. He says I cannot go through another pregnancy. My poor pelvic muscles were stretched to ripping with the stillbirth. Oh Donald," she began to cry, "our little girl did not survive and now I dare not have more children." Through tears, she whimpered, "No more giddy love with abandon." Donald held her tight and whispered comforting words until Bella sobbed herself to sleep.

19

GOLD MINE

At breakfast the morning after Donald learned of his stillborn daughter, Bella sat, eyes unfocused, her mind drifting. *I must think of my blessings. Peter and Gordon are fine little boys and I have my health. We have a wonderful life and loyal servants.* Bella hung her head. *God did not intend that baby to live—no Bella, don't think of that! Look to the future like Aunt Kate told you to do. Aunt Kate? I must write and thank her and the church for the crates of gifts. And my parents—must I tell them what's happened?*

Donald put the morning newspaper aside and reached for Bella's hand that lay inert on the breakfast table as she stared into space.

"Bella, don't dwell on unhappy thoughts. We will remember our loss but we must not let it sway the future. We have each other, our little boys and a bountiful life for which to be thankful. From the look of the sky, the sun is trying to shine this morning; perhaps it won't rain until this afternoon. If you feel up to it, I wondered if you'd like to go riding. I thought we could walk the horses to Ernte for a moment together in our rose arbour."

***

The morning breeze blew as cool as mornings ever started in Surinam. Parrots screeched, snakes curled where the sun warmed the ground and little animals scurried away as the horses trotted along. The sounds of nature that once made Bella cringe now seemed music to her ears, but Donald's lack of conversation touched her senses.

"Donald, I think you have something to discuss while we ride. I feel you wanted to get away from everyone to talk with me alone. What's troubling you?"

"How intuitive you are, my Rosebud. Yes, I do have something to discuss with you." Bella rode quietly, allowing Donald to carry on with what he wanted to say.

"Like the previous dry season, I had to be very careful of my movements in the jungle, or at least I sensed that I should be careful. I never saw anyone but I felt I was being watched. Not close and threatening—more like spying on me. Perhaps I am just nervous because I am so close to realizing my dream."

"What happens now?" asked Bella in her soft tone. "Do you just wait for the next dry season and claim your prize?"

"I need your help to make a decision, Bella. Before I stake the mine, I must lease the area where I want to actually test the rocks. The government charges a rather handsome sum for an annual lease. With a lease your claim is safe, by law, until you get to town and register the area you staked. I think I have been safe this far from someone stealing my area because whoever is watching knows that I haven't sufficient savings in the bank to pay for the lease yet."

"Very foxy of you, Donald. That is the reason your gold is hidden beneath the loose floorboard under the bed. Have you enough to pay for the lease?"

They cantered on a few paces before Donald answered.

"Yes, but I don't want to use everything I've saved. I have you and the boys to think of now. I could write to my brother Peter in Trinidad and offer him a half interest in the mine if he pays half the cost of the lease. He has made a great deal of money managing that sugar refinery and plantation and I'm quite sure he'll invest in the venture. Bella, should I include him to protect half of our savings for the family?"

His heart is set on having a lease, yet he's still concerned about the welfare of the boys and me—such a dear. Why should I say otherwise? Finding a gold mine is his life's dream. We want for nothing and still he puts us first.

"Of course, Donald, if that is what you want to do. Write to Peter." With that she urged Mischief into a gallop and sped away full of happiness, her black hair streaming in the wind. Taken by surprise, Donald and Cobus raced to catch up.

***

The routine of the rainy season again took over their lives. Donald gave the boys riding lessons when the sun shone, and the relaxed pace of life each evening brought them to stout time, a few moments with the children and a quiet evening for reading, cards or a visit with friends.

Bella often saw Donald at his writing desk and assumed he had written to his brother about investing in the gold mine. He never mentioned it again. They attended the Governor's Ball, followed by Christmas with children's parties, parties with friends and the New Year's Eve Ball. As usual, Hildebrand and Faye inspected Bella's gown and sniffed their noses in the air as they turned away, not recognizing that Bella's gown came from Paris. *Seven years and those two have not changed their ways. I must allow the grapevine to know that I ordered my gown from Paris the same as they did. Eve understands. I'll ask her to spread the news.*

Donald, too, had ordered a new outfit, but his came from Scotland. For the New Year's Eve Ball he arrived in a kilt with full Scottish regalia and looked magnificent in the forest green and navy blue tartan set with the thin red stripes of the Macdonald clan. It flared when he and Bella waltzed to the strains of the "Merry Widow Waltz." Bella could not believe the magic of that night and often fell asleep still floating around the ballroom in the arms of her precious husband.

***

One evening in March before dinner, Donald pulled a document from his pocket and waved it in the air.

"Bella, I have the lease. It had to be registered by the end of the month, so now it is done." His eyes shone in the lamplight. His face, wreathed in smiles, glowed with an inner happiness. Bella coyly stole across the floor from her loveseat and fitted herself into his lap so they could be happy together. That evening, the table held a bouquet of burgundy roses and two white candles. Shauna did not know why Mr. McD bought roses to be placed on the table, but she lit the candles and turned down the lamp before she called them to dinner. She only knew they ate dinner and stole off upstairs to their bedroom.

***

Come, Bella. It is time to get on with the rainy season. These last few showers will soon be gone. Dirk will be busy again if Aunt Kate's diocese sends another shipment of clothing. Gordon and Peter's birthdays need planning.

On April thirtieth under a glorious soft sun, the Macdonald garden came alive with guests. Children ran everywhere. They played kiddies' games while parents visited. Donald led Mischief around her paddock while the children screamed to be next. All hushed when the birthday cake arrived and Peter and Gordon blew out the candles.

***

By June the sun shone down on the garden every day. The wet ground steamed under its hot rays and caused the nights to be humid. The flowers and the flowering shrubs lifted their heads to the sun to create an enchanting tropical garden for Bella and her family. She knew the dry season, despite all of its pleasures, would bring loneliness after evening meals, but over the years she had found ways to fill the void.

That year before June finished, Ginger the mule waited in the back garden. Donald's rifle and revolver were cleaned and waiting in the scullery, then the bush boots and khaki outfit appeared on his bedroom chair.

"Donald," cried Bella, "it's not the end of July. Why is your jungle gear out?"

"I have planned the date a month earlier than usual to escape any eyes that might be watching for me." With this news, the following morning Bella donned her newest white gown for Donald's departure, to be his Dresden doll.

In the early morning light, Bella stood at the back door with Peter and Gordon waving goodbye to their daddy. Her lips moved. *God's speed to you, Donald.* She noticed the white knuckles of her clasped hands and pried them apart to fling one hand into the air in a loving wave while she forced a smile to brighten her face.

"Reiche Ernte, my love," she called along with squeals from the children.

With a wave that touched the edge of his pith helmet, Donald once again disappeared from sight around the corner of the house, with Ginger trailing behind. *The Schooner Van Dam, then New Nickerie and a paddleboat up the Corentyne River to the jungle, all a month early with a gold mine as his reward. He'll be so happy.*

Bella gathered her skirts and returned to the dining room to finish breakfast with the boys. *Tomorrow I will start on my projects, but today I will enjoy my children, the sun and my life in paradise.*

For the next few weeks Bella and Dirk worked on the flower gardens. She introduced Briya to sewing, wrote letters and embroidered in the evening.

***

"Mrs. McD! Come quickly." *Is that Dirk's voice calling me? Why, it's an hour after sundown; whatever can be the trouble? A light in the garden— Dirk is running with a lantern.* "Mrs. McD, it's Cobus and Ginger," Dirk shouted, "and Mr. McD! You must come. He's not well." Bella jumped from the loveseat. *Mr. McD? Did he say Donald has returned?*

Bella's brightly coloured spools spewed across the floor and her needlework flew from her lap when she started for the scullery door. Feet clattered down the servants' stairwell. Shauna appeared with a lamp and the two burst through the back entry. Bella saw the outline of a man slumped forward in the saddle. His feet dangled behind empty stirrups. The reins hung loose from the horse's head.

"Donald! What has happened to Donald?" cried Bella. Dirk and Shauna caught him as he leaned sideways to dismount.

"I came home, Bella." Donald's voice trailed off. His eyes opened again. "My dearest Rosebud—I came home—as I always promised—I would." His inert figure flopped to the grass at Bella's feet.

"Donald, dear Donald!" She placed her hand on his cheek. "Goodness, he's burning up with fever! Shauna, fetch a pail of cold water and four linen napkins. Dirk, we must get him to the hospital at once. Harness Mischief to the carriage. Briya, lead Ginger and Cobus to his paddock. If you can, take off their saddles, give them feed and water and rub them down."

Dirk returned with the wooden door from the tack shack. He placed it in the carriage across the seats. Together, Dirk and Shauna managed to drag and lift Mr. McD into the carriage. Shauna and Bella sat on either seat beside Donald, with the pail of cold water at their feet so they could dip the napkins and cool his brow and chest.

"Wash your hands thoroughly, Briya, and stay with the children. Dirk, I know it's farther, but we must take Donald to the military hospital. They will know the best thing to do. With his jaundiced complexion, I fear Donald has yellow fever."

***

Mischief tossed her head as she strained to pull the carriage with speed through the dark streets that were strange to her. The rattle of the carriage wheels and the cooling cloths brought more words from Donald's lips.

"Mosquitoes—went too soon—oh Bella, I love you," then he lapsed again until the orderlies roused him when trying to get him onto a stretcher.

"Bella?" His hand groped in the darkness. "Are you with me?" She took his soiled hand and held it to her cheek.

"Always, my love. I will always be with you."

The military doctor came immediately. "Mrs. Macdonald, your husband is very ill, but we'll talk about that in the morning. Now, I want you all to go home, wash yourselves with soap tonight and launder your clothes in the morning. Young man, scrub down the carriage inside and out and clean all his gear. We must take no chances with infection. There may be other germs at work here."

***

Bella returned to the hospital the next day.

"Mr. Macdonald has the jungle strain of the virus for yellow fever, Ma'am," said the doctor. "The mosquitoes must have swarmed him in the jungle. Their sting is particularly virulent this season. I am amazed that he managed to hold together long enough to get home. Surely his horse brought him from the docks, for his high fever would not have allowed him to know the way."

Bella spent every day at the hospital. She placed burgundy roses on his white bedside table to soften the white of the walls, the white of his painted metal bed and the white of the dress that she wore for him. The sun burned behind the heavy window blind. Nurses changed successive cold damp sheets to reduce Donald's fever. Some days Donald heaved black vomit, despite appearing to be in a coma. The doctor explained that the virus had now spread throughout his system. "The mucosa of his stomach is perforated. The black vomit is dead blood. Don't bring the children to see their father this way. It's better they remember him as their loving, playful Daddy."

"Remember him? You speak as if he is already dead. Just yesterday you said his fever had lessened. What are you telling me, Doctor? Is Donald going to die?"

"He shows the symptoms of the less fortunate, my dear. If he recovers, we all will have seen a miracle. He is becoming more jaundiced every day and his kidney and liver functions have succumbed to the virus. The fever will abate and then he will shake with chills. He may awaken, he may not. I will ask the matron to make you a settling cup of tea. I'm sorry that I have to give you such frightful news."

***

At sundown, Dirk arrived to find Mrs. McD staring into her lap and very pale. He could tell she had been given bad news and gently escorted her to the carriage.

"We must come back at sunrise, Dirk. I must be here in case Donald awakens," were the only words that passed between them. The next day, convulsed with shivers, Donald lay under blankets. Bella took his hand.

"Is that you, Bella?" His eyelids half rose and tried to focus. "Read— letter."

"Yes, Donald, I am here by your side." She squeezed his hand, but there was no response. "Matron, when my carriage driver arrives, tell him that I am not going home tonight. My husband may regain consciousness again and I must be here."

The shivers changed to violent spasms. Bella stayed at Donald's bedside for forty-eight agonizing hours as she watched Donald's body writhe. Each day Dirk brought his mistress a half-pint of stout to give her energy while she waited for another lucid moment with Donald. On the morning of June 25, 1895, without again regaining recognition of his Dresden doll, Donald Macdonald lay still in the bed.

"Your vigil is over, Mrs. Macdonald." The doctor reached to unclasp Bella's hand from that of her husband. "He is at peace now. I have summoned a carriage to take you home. Wash carefully and get some rest. My staff will make arrangements with the undertaker to come for his remains. By law, his casket will be buried tomorrow in the cemetery. I will send word for the Anglican priest to call on you this evening. God be with you."

***

Through the grapevine of the servants, word spread among the colonials by the afternoon. Eve came over to Candlewick. Driven, as if in shock, Bella dictated letters for her to write to the plantation owner, her parents and Gabby. Throughout this, she kept the children playing at her feet, answering their need for a hug and a kiss after her many days of absence. At stout time she gathered the two of them on each side of her and told them that their daddy would not come to rock in his favourite chair anymore because he had died in the jungle.

"You may both climb into it and rock it for him if you wish."

***

After the children were in bed, Bella's close friends dropped by with flowers, stayed a few minutes and left as another couple arrived. The minister and undertaker came to make plans.

Once they left, Bella cried herself to sleep. *It is all so sudden. Tomorrow, my little sons will stand beside me in their white suits and black cravats. No matter what anyone thinks, I shall wear white, not black—because Donald would have wanted it that way—and he shall have red roses on his casket. Dirk and his wife, Rinku, Briya and my Shauna will don their best saris, ride with the boys and me in the carriage and stand with me at the graveside, for they are his family too.*

***

And so it came to pass that Donald Macdonald received the blessing at the graveside in Rust Cemetery. Every colonist, Ken O'Reilly and his family, and Rani with the brothers and sisters of their church, stood in a circle around the freshly dug plot as the undertaker had his men lower the casket with ropes. Like a waxen statue, Bella shook a few hands until Dirk offered to take her home.

She turned one last time towards her love. "Please, God, let him guide me and send his love from the hereafter to sustain me," and with this short prayer, she turned away from the open grave.

20

THE FUTURE

The day after Donald's funeral, with a pallor like plaster, Bella rocked slowly in her husband's rocking chair. Her hands moved with fingers entwining and releasing. No matter how hard she told herself that she was having a nightmare, the more she realized what had caused Donald's death. The facts played over and over in her mind.

He feared that other miners might spy on his movements. To elude them while he staked his gold mine, he returned to the jungle too early—before the dry season reduced the threat from mosquito bites. Yellow fever killed him because he took an unforgiving risk. The children will grow up not knowing their father. My life must change, for widows never remain in the colonies— Gabby did, but that was different. Her friends wanted her to teach their children but ignored her when they planned social occasions.

Shauna checked on Bella from time to time but did not interrupt her rocking.

With no training at anything, I certainly can't work here. That Hildebrand would fill the grapevine with untruths. No, I must leave. Bella continued to rock.

If I must leave Paramaribo, I dare not return to Plymouth and poor health. I must go where people with good breeding and no training are allowed a free hand to make a living. I shall go to America. Yes, dear Aunt Kate, it seems you taught me a lesson for life, for here I am, thinking of the future. But still she rocked and consoled her aching heart until Eve came to call.

"Bella, you must not concern yourself with the gossip that is travelling on the colonists' grapevine. It reports that someone saw Donald on his horse in a drunken stupor while returning home after a late night game of poker. Whoever saw Donald riding home that night, slumped in the saddle, concluded that he must have fallen off and broken his neck. Those of us who love you and know the truth will do our best to reverse the story. I am so sorry that some of the colonists need gossip to fuel their idle ways."

"I have no time to think of rumours now, Eve. Leave me to rock here in Donald's chair, for he and I are planning the future for our children."

***

In the following days, Bella forced herself to appear strong. She played with the children, drank afternoon tea with friends who dropped by, attended to small household matters and ate light meals, all with a fuzzy recollection of the passing days.

"Mrs. McD." It was Shauna's voice. "I hate to trouble you, but Dirk needs money to buy feed for the horses and we need things from the market."

Bella looked for money in her purse. It held only a few coins. "I'll go to the bank with Dirk and then you'll have money."

***

"Mrs. Macdonald," said the banker, "how can I give you money when your account is just about empty? You have paid many bills these past weeks."

"Very well, I'll bring you some gold nuggets to replenish the account."

***

Once at home, Bella rushed to her bedroom and tried to push aside the heavy Georgian bed and overhead frame. When it would not budge, she kicked aside the little steps and, despite her silken gown, crawled under the bed to get at the removable floorboard. In the darkness her hand groped the hole for a box or bottle, but it encountered nothing except a piece of paper, a letter.

Is this what Donald was trying to tell me when he spoke the words "read letter"? She took the letter to the window and immediately recognized the handwriting of her brother-in-law, Peter. She read the date: April 1, 1895.

> "Dear Brother Donald,
>
> So you think you have found your gold mine and wish me to join you financially in the venture. Offering me half of the mine for half of the cost of the lease is very generous, but the figure you mention is outrageously high. I have considered my answer carefully these past months and I am sorry if the delay in sending this reply has inconvenienced your plans.
>
> You have always been a dreamer, Donald, a man that assumes all things will work out. I am not like that. I have no way to compare your plans to lease and stake your mine to anything else going on in that region. I know nothing about mines except that your search has eluded you for years. I cannot assume that your dreams of finding a gold mine are anything more than dreams. For this reason I am not going to join you in your venture. Find another partner or fund it all yourself."

Bella's hands tightened on the letter. She half swooned and rotated to sit on the edge of the bed. Tears began to wash across her cheeks. *Peter's letter is dated April first but Donald got the lease in March.* With quivering hands she reread the letter. *Peter called Donald a dreamer and refused to put money into the venture. Oh, dear God, what has Donald done? Surely, he didn't use the money he'd put away for the family!*

Bella struggled under the bed once more. Her hand dipped into the dark hole beneath the floorboards but her fingers felt only the rough laths and shards of plaster that formed the ceiling below.

"The little jar of gold nuggets in the kitchen—that is all the money I have," came silently from her lips." *I must take most of the nuggets to the bank so he won't know my circumstances. The future, Bella . . .* but she couldn't finish the sentence.

The next day, Bella gathered the servants in the dining room. With the children swinging on her black skirts or peeking around Dirk's work pants, Bella began: "My dear employees, I have frightful news. I find that I am penniless. Misfortune used all of our funds in Donald's search for gold. I must leave Paramaribo and live where I can make a living, and for that I have chosen America, in the city of Boston."

In mute disbelief, one by one, Bella's servants learned of their misfortune.

"Dirk, you and Rinku may continue to live in your quarters until I leave Paramaribo. Dirk, I want you to have Cobus and the carriage. Use them to earn a living or find work, perhaps with Mr. Morgan at the Ice Company. In return for remaining here at Candlewick, I expect you two to continue to care for Mischief and the garden.

"Briya, I can no longer pay you. With your skill in English, I am sure you will find a position in business or in a good home. I suggest that you pack your things and return to live with your family until you are earning an income."

"Shauna, you have a fine education, with skills in sewing and teaching. I will leave you the sewing machine. You should apply to be a teacher when the city starts to educate the poor. Will you stay until I settle my affairs and move?"

The servants' heads barely nodded when she finished addressing each of them. No more words were spoken, yet they felt dismissed and left the room. Bella fell into the corner of her loveseat and sobbed. *Such sudden changes for them, the poor dears.*

***

For Bella, except for minutes spent with the boys, the house became a solemn tomb for either work or resting. One by one, she went through the papers in Donald's desk, saving aside those documents that must go with her to Boston: the boys' birth certificates—one in English, one in Dutch, just like her wedding certificates. She set aside the deed to her beloved Candlewick and bundled together certain letters of importance regarding the sugar plantation. *Will Ken O'Reily become the new plantation manager? I must write the owner again and tell him Donald's expressed wish. So many business letters to write! It takes all of my energy. I must stop and go into the garden for tea.*

The next day, she found the document leasing the mining property that Donald hoped would produce gold. She read, "If not renewed annually, the property reverts back to the colony and the crown." Bella read on; she could not even inherit the lease. All their savings were lost. She crossed her arms on the desk and rested her head on them. She did not feel well. *Grief has robbed me of endurance.* "Bella," the voice from deep within cried out, *"things will look better tomorrow. Now go to your room and rest."*

***

Bella's feelings of defeat were so great that she did not hear Shauna's footsteps on the stairs or as she passed the open bedroom door on her way to the linen cupboard.

"Mrs. McD," said Shauna at the door, "are you not feeling well?"

"I'm sure I'm fine, Shauna. Tea time should refresh me," but the restful moments in the garden did not help. *Perhaps all those days visiting Donald in hospital have given me an illness. I must see the doctor to protect the household.*

***

"Mrs. Macdonald," started Dr. DeVeer, "I have run extensive tests and only one came back positive. You are pregnant." *The lease. Donald was so happy to have that lease that we cerebrated with roses and candlelight and making love . . .*

Dr. DeVeer paused while Bella recovered her composure. "I would say that you made love in late March at an inappropriate time. Bella, I begged you to be careful. You are at great risk. We'll have to watch this pregnancy very carefully or you will lose the baby like the last one." Bella hung her head, not knowing if she was pleased or concerned. *Dr. DeVeer is still talking. I must listen.*

"You may not lift anything, not even the children. As with the others, you must come into hospital before the baby turns or we might lose you as well as the baby."

Back at Candlewick, Bella summoned Shauna, and Rinku, in Dirk's absence.

"I am pregnant again. The baby will arrive in December. The doctor says I am at great risk. To protect my health, my life, I will do nothing about the move now." She faltered for a moment and added, "I cannot leave the boys without a mother."

"Mrs. McD," said Shauna, with a firm voice. "That is not going to happen. I am going to stay with you and the children even when you go to Boston. I suspect you don't know that Mr. McD saved me from being killed by the man who was raping me. He grappled with him, carried me to this house for protection that night and watched at the window with his gun in case my attacker came pounding on the door in drunken belligerence. After that attack, I vowed to always serve him and never marry, certainly never have sex. You have taught me about the outside world and I wish to see it. Now, with the baby coming, I want to go with you even more. You will need me to care for the children while you are at work, and I will see America."

"Oh, my dear, sweet Shauna, such a secret to keep in your bosom! What you said about needing you when I am working is true. If you are willing to leave your family, I will be very happy to have your company and support." And she gave Shauna a first hug.

***

By August, Bella's queasiness lessened. She missed riding with her friends but substituted short walks with the children. Some days she wandered about the house looking at the many things that could not go with her to Boston. Many times she checked her bank account and wondered how she would manage to survive until the baby reached six months of age and old enough to travel. *The den furniture—I could sell that now. Briya's bedroom furniture and the things in the guest bedroom can go too, and the living room does not need all those chairs. Later I can sell the dining room furniture. We'll make do with those cheap Bentwood chairs and the Parsons table from the front hall.* She looked around the room. *Donald's rocking chair—how can I part with it? All the heavy mahogany furniture must be sold; why not bit by bit when I need the money?* She looked at the clock. *I'll join the children for tea time.*

***

Dirk continued to collect the mail on his way home from work at the Ice Company. One day he brought two letters, one from Aberdeen and one from Plymouth. Bella opened the one from Aberdeen first, quite sure that the beautiful Scottish handwriting came from one of Donald's brothers whom she'd never met.

It's from George. My goodness, he is coming to see me and offering to be my husband and take care of the children and me. He's on the high seas right now! Poor dear, such a harsh custom, to expect unmarried brothers to marry a brother's widow. How dutiful of him, but marriage must come with love and I doubt that I will ever love anyone as I loved Donald. If George is about to arrive, I must tell Mrs. Condron that she may not have the guest bed until after his visit. Two weeks—he will arrive in two weeks. I hope nothing happens to put me in the hospital before then. Bella took the silver letter opener to the letter from home.

She stopped to check the signature at the end of the letter. *From Althea, and quite short. My goodness, her husband, Harry, the banker, signed it too. Whatever does it say?*

"Dearest Bella,

We have sad news. Father passed away last week with a heart attack. Constance came from Reading for the funeral but did not stay long. She is pregnant with her fifth child and had to return because her mother-in-law would only stay with the children for two days. Wallace could not get away from his job on the River Thames.

Mother is very upset about finances. Harry tells her that she'll be fine when she sells the business but she won't listen.

The stress of this past week and her fussing is hard on her blood pressure. I will write again when I have more news.

Harry and I, John and Jane are fine.

Love, Althea and Harry

Tears brimmed in Bella's eyes then overflowed down her cheeks. *Father's gone! I never saw him again after they waved goodbye in Plymouth.* Bella raised her eyes towards heaven. *I hope you know how much I adored you, Father. Dear Donald, give him my love, for I am sure you are together, watching over me.* And she sat at her vanity, sobbing to herself until roused by the sound of Shauna with the children in the nursery.

***

Dirk took time off from work at the Ice Company to meet George at the docks. Bella watched as her brother-in-law stepped from the carriage. George, four years her senior, looked like Donald, complete with red hair and moustache but without the height and athletic figure. *He's thirty-eight and has never married. Will he like children? Does he ride horses? Has he the ability to love?*

"You're here, George!" Bella threw her arms around him. "Do take off your jacket. The tropics are far too humid to be wearing that suit. Come into the garden and have a gin and quinine water." She led him through the diminished elegance of her home to the garden, where he met the children and Shauna.

***

George stayed one week. Bella did her best to entertain him by having Shauna drive him out to the sugar plantation and around town in the trap.

I wonder what he thinks of my pregnancy or if his thoughts about marriage have changed? He hasn't once mentioned either.

Over dinner without the children the night before George planned to leave, Bella found her soft voice and said, "George, thank you for your offer to marry me. I know that bachelor brothers are expected to marry their brother's widow. It is done in the old country, but I have changed since I left home. I am free of socially dictated traditions. I plan on going to Boston to start my own business and support my children. I know I have servants here, but I don't care if I work in a factory as long as I have the freedom to be me." George did not raise his eyes from the table to meet hers, so Bella continued.

"You have your own life to live and I am sure that it does not include moving to America. Find your own true love and live the life you wish to live."

Bella tried to judge George's reaction to the words she had spoken— *disappointed, no, relieved? Clearly, he merely wanted to do the right thing.*

"You are a very strong woman, Bella. I thank you for your candour. Perhaps the money I deposited in your bank account that day when I walked into town will help you start your business." The next morning they hugged and the carriage whisked him away.

***

Seven weeks after news of Bella's father's death, another letter came from Althea.

> Dearest Bella,
>
> It seems that all I have for you is sad news. Mother's stress made her blood pressure soar and she died of a heart attack two days ago. I am still trying to plan the funeral so this letter must be short. Her last words were of you.
>
> Constance and Wallace, with our approval, have decided to move into the family house in Plymouth and run father's business, as it hasn't sold.
>
> Dear Bella, I see no way to spare you from more sad news. The ship in which George took passage for his return trip foundered at sea and all were lost. I don't have any other news of the sinking but when I do I shall write again.
>
> As for Mother, she was so very unhappy and so lost after father died that I think she wanted to be with him in heaven.
>
> May God be with you, Bella, as you cope in your own difficult days.
>
> Love, Althea.

My stepmother and George gone too! Bella fainted and found herself in the hospital when she awakened.

***

On the sixteenth of December, 1895, after Bella had been two months in hospital, with the doctor's help young Stewart James came into the world ten days early. Each time Dr. DeVeer assisted Bella to have another child, her pelvis took longer to heal, but with Shauna to care for Peter, Gordon, the baby and her, the months passed until Bella felt strong enough to rise from her bed and begin planning their move to America.

***

"Mrs. McD, Dirk has brought you a letter from England," said Shauna one day.

From Aunt Kate. I do hope nothing is wrong. It isn't a very thick letter. Bella slipped it open.

Dearest Bella,

By the time you receive this letter I will be at sea on my way to Surinam. I have always wanted to visit you, meet my nephews and see the good works of the church. Life in the tropics sounds so grand. Flora is coming with me.

With the tragic passing of Donald and the happy birth of your third son, I feel I must come in case you decide to leave Paramaribo. We'll visit more when I arrive in Surinam. Check for the next arrival of the SS *Balfour*.

Love, Aunt Kate

There is no one else that I would rather see, but I won't be able to entertain her any better than I entertained poor George. Oh my, Mrs. Condron took the furniture from the guest bedroom after George left. Perhaps Eve has beds she can loan me for Aunt Kate and Flora. George's gift of money has been a godsend but I mustn't use too much of it. There will be passage to Boston, shipping charges and living expenses until we get settled.

***

Dirk brought news that Kate and Flora would arrive May tenth. *The rainy season! I won't be able to show her Paramaribo in the trap. How can I make it a joyous occasion with four deaths to mourn and still too weak to hold my third son? My paradise has evaporated. I wonder how long they'll stay—I must stop these negative thoughts.*

Aunt Kate and Flora arrived in a May downpour. After meeting her great nephews and Shauna, completing a tour of Candlewick and viewing the drenched garden from the study window, the three women returned to the sitting room for tea.

"Bella," said Aunt Kate, "you might as well know that I plan to stay until you are established in America. Your plan to leave here next month is sheer lunacy. Your health is in question and the rocking of the ocean is no place for a six-month-old baby."

"I will have Shauna with me, Aunt Kate," argued Bella. "The trade winds are at their best for the run up to Boston. We would arrive before hurricane season. I must make the break from Candlewick this year and spend my few resources in America."

This discussion turned up at breakfast, dinner and supper, in the market, on the road to Ernte and in the poor neighbourhoods of Paramaribo, where the houses were painted and the children greeted Bella's trap with big smiles and happy waves.

"Bella, if you must leave, then you must, but why not take just Peter to America and have him attend school while you work. Flora and I will stay here with Gordon and Stewart until you are settled in a home and prepared for their arrival. Shauna knows how to care for Candlewick. Now that we are here, I wish you would consider my proposal."

"Aunt Kate, I trust you more than anyone, but what if something happened? I couldn't bear separation from any of my three boys."

Bella's mind whirled with possibilities whether she faced the day or night. *Dr. DeVeer already finds that I am doing too much to let my pelvic bones heal, but who else can close up my house? I must sell it to have money to live. Maybe Aunt Kate could manage for a few months until I send for them, but how can I leave two of my bairns behind? No, no! Dear Donald, are you listening? Show me what I must do.*

I know Peter should be in school at age six. Mr. Morgan says I must enroll Peter in Agassiz School near Harvard in Cambridge. He says it is one of the first and finest grammar schools in America. I know fashion; maybe I could sell clothes in a shop. If Shauna is in America with me, then I will have my treadle sewing machine. Perhaps I can sew for a living. And Mischief, dear, gentle Mischief? Who will rub her down and love her as I do? The sky is growing light. Another day is here. Did I not sleep at all last night?

***

Again, after breakfast, Bella assembled her shrinking household: the children, Aunt Kate, Flora and Shauna.

"I have listened to many good advisers and have made my plan. Thank you, Aunt Kate and Flora; I will take up your offer to stay at Candlewick with Shauna, Gordon and Stewart. Peter and I will sail for Boston in July. We will travel quite lightly and find a place in Cambridge, and I will send for you as soon as I can."

Kate and Shauna made no comment. Bella moved to the loveseat; the children clambered across her lap and back to the floor. Bella continued.

"The grapevine will attend to finding buyers for items to be sold as things at Candlewick are no longer needed. Mr. McKay, our lawyer friend on Dominiestraat, will look after the sale of Candlewick and I'll give my beloved Mischief and the trap to Wumi to help with the school she has started along the plantation road."

***

Days included goodbye teas, a visit to Ernte and a carriage ride to see Rani and a nearby house that Dirk and Rinku had built.

By the time the dry season came, Bella had marked the few pieces of furniture that she loved and wished to have packed for America. Hildebrand wanted to buy Candlewick, but her husband said he couldn't afford it. *I can imagine her pique with that disclosure. The new doctor plans to rent until he can buy the house and he's asked for Briya's services. I'm so tired. Will I hold together on board the ship?*

***

Three days before they were to leave for Boston, Dirk brought a wagon from the Ice Company and moved Bella's trunk to the docks.

The following day, Flora and Kate insisted that they should walk over to the hotel at five o'clock—the same place Bella drank stout on her first day in Paramaribo. To Bella's surprise, her five friends and their husbands were waiting for her, along with a waiter ready to serve thirteen pints of stout. *What dear friends. I will miss them.*

***

The next morning, Peter and Gordon wished each other goodbye without truly understanding what was happening. Bella choked back tears as she said her goodbyes. Dirk and Rinku arrived with the carriage to take Bella and Peter through early fog down through the streets of Paramaribo to the ship, never to return.

Candlewick belongs in my memories, thought Bella as the familiar sound of the carriage wheels ground down the gravel carriageway leading away from the house. *The garden is beautiful but I'll not look back, for today is the first day of the future.*

***

"Look, Gordon!" cried Aunt Kate. "Your mother sent us a letter from the ship. She must have given it to the captain to drop off in America when a crew member went ashore for provisions."

From the look on Gordon's face, his five-year-old mind doubted the possibility of mailing a letter from a ship and the word "provisions" meant nothing to him, but he snuggled up beside his Great Aunt Kate on the loveseat anyway.

> Dear Kate,
> At first the sea lay like a turquoise mirror, but of course the sails hung limp and we made little headway. Now the sails are full, rain or shine, and the waves roll the ship at will. When it is rough, I stay in bed because the rocking of the ship hurts my pelvic bones and I must have them well mended for Boston.

Peter feels the cold, as do I. He befriended the cook, no doubt because helping him in the kitchen is one way for his tropical little body to stay warm. And guess what I discovered! The cook is Manfred Kolb, the German cook who signed our wedding certificate on the *Van Dam*. He treats Peter like he is a reincarnation of Donald, a little fellow who can do no wrong.

Such a transformation in Peter from child to little man! I am quite sure he is ready for school. Each day he spends an hour with me studying English. I will be glad when we reach Boston. It should be fall there and quite comfortable.

Give a hug to Gordon and Stewart from me and tell Shauna, Rinku and Dirk that they are constantly in my memories.

Love to you, Kate and Flora, with my sincere gratitude, Bella.

21

AMERICA 1896

"Mother, are we going to stay in this dirty room?" asked Peter. "There are bugs on the floor and stains on the walls. Shauna didn't allow bugs on our floors at Candlewick. I would rather go home than stay here."

Seated on the one wooden chair, Bella pulled Peter onto her lap. "Sh-sh-sh, my little one," said Bella, rocking Peter in her arms. "Let me hold you tight and things will seem better. It's been a long day for a six-year-old—and for his mother." Bella's voice trailed off. *Think positively, Bella. Give your son a boost of courage.* Bella carried Peter to the bed. "I'm sure America will look much better in the morning. Did you like the fog horns last night as the ship made its way into harbour?"

"Yes, they sounded like home. Will Gordon come to play with me tomorrow?"

"No, Gordon is at Candlewick with Aunt Kate. Tomorrow, we'll find a nice hotel in Boston. I am sure that this is not Boston yet." *We must be down by the docks in a poor district, but night shadows were growing and my legs could go no further.* Bella continued in a soothing voice, "Tuck the blanket under your chin and close your eyes. Go to sleep, my little parakeet. We won't have to wait in that long line to register as immigrants ever again," but Peter was already asleep.

Bella walked to the grimy window, knowing that the northern skies would not display a myriad of stars or the Southern Cross. *October 16, 1896. I am now an immigrant in America; that is all I am here, an immigrant with no status who must work with her hands for pay if the children are to have a future.*

"Dear God," floated from Bella's lips, "protect me and my family and take the pain from my hips. Amen." Silent tears seeped through her thick black lashes.

Now I must rest, before my bones disintegrate. She gently moved her son from the centre of the bed and laid her head on the dark pillow beside him. *Bella, the future is near. Grasp it and plan to never sail again. The sun will rise in the morning, just as Donald always promised.* In minutes Bella was asleep.

***

Daylight glared through the dirty window. Bella roused and pushed the washhouse-grey bedclothes from her face. *Tomorrow! It's already here! I must get up and dress before Peter awakens and sees me in my petticoat.*

The grey morning light exposed seeds of rat droppings on unswept floorboards. From the bathroom down the hall, the smell of stale urine creeping under the door brought Bella to her senses. *Surely there will be a carriage in the street that will rescue us from this rat-infested hole. How could I have had such bad judgement? Weariness is no excuse. I must cope. No matter what America throws my way, I must cope.* She roused Peter and they hurried down to the street to hail a passing carriage.

"Driver, please take me to the best hotel in Boston," Bella said, with no hint as to why a lady would stay the night near the docks. The driver raised his eyebrows, threw her portmanteaux onto the back of his open carriage and helped her mount the high step with Peter quick to scramble in beside her.

Fitchburg Railroad Docks, Bella read on a sign. *Why, we haven't even left the docks. Drunken sailors rent that room for heaven knows what! We likely used the same sheets!* She winced. The carriage rumbled forward on worn cobblestones.

"Peter, have you ever seen such a long bridge? The sign says 'Warren Bridge.' I'm sure it leads to Boston." Bella pointed to the far shore. "Look, Peter, it goes right across the bay." Peter nodded and continued to stare at everything with wonderment.

"Why are there so many buildings, Mother?"

"Because this is a city, Peter, a big city, but even I didn't expect this many buildings! They're all the way to the horizon." She paused. "I don't see any trees."

Streets clogged with carriages, carts, horses and pedestrians impeded their progress. Buildings of all sizes, lining the streets, reflected the grey of an overcast sky in their windows. *Dear Donald, I asked for the best hotel in Boston, just the way you would have done, but what if I can't afford it? I wonder how he interpreted my instructions.*

"We're here, lady," said the carriage driver. "The Rexford Hotel, a classy place just like you asked for. Advertises nice clean rooms for transients—seventy-five cents a night, or three dollars and up if you stay the week. You'll like it. Has hot and cold running water, steam heat and a toilet down the hall. Lots of my customers come here off the ships. It's at the corner of Bullfinch and Bowdoin Streets, if you plan to go out." He put the oversized suitcase on the sidewalk and offered Bella his hand while she climbed down the big step. "Tell them Elmer brought you." Once paid, the carriage disappeared.

You are here Bella, in Boston—another first day of the future. Will the sun shine on us here amid all these smoke-darkened buildings? With Peter's help, she dragged the heavy portmanteaux into the hotel and booked the cheapest room the hotel offered: three dollars for one week. *From the wear on the faded brown carpet, this isn't the best hotel in Boston, but it smells clean.*

Bella purchased a newspaper and registered at the desk. She took Peter's hand and they entered the dining room for breakfast. The foyer clock chimed once for ten-thirty a.m. Bella ordered eggs, toast, preserves and tea, with extra toast for Peter to make up for the lack of supper the night before. In the same way as she had seen Donald check the ads,

Bella took out a pencil and began circling ones that offered possible employment. She roused when she felt the presence of a person standing behind her. *The hotel desk clerk. What does he want?*

"Pardon me, Ma'am, but you're the same as most of my customers. I can tell when folks are straight off the boat because their clothing is different. I came over to see if you were reading the employment section of the newspaper. Because I heard you speaking Dutch with the boy, maybe I can help." Bella cocked her head, questioning.

"My sister works at the courthouse and they need an interpreter for drunken Dutch sailors that land in jail overnight, at least that's how she put it. The courthouse isn't far, just on Pemberton Square a couple of blocks away."

"Really? A Dutch interpreter, you say? Why, I never included my fluent Dutch among the possibilities of finding work."

Work! Mentally, she gagged on the word. *Smile, Bella.* "Thank you, Sir. My son and I will follow your directions to the courthouse right away." *I wonder if the courthouse will give me work before Peter is enrolled in school. I have booked here for a week to feel settled. Perhaps by then I'll have found a house.*

"Ma'am, you won't find the courthouse open," said the clerk. "Actually, you won't find much of anything open on Sunday except the churches. I'll have the kitchen prepare a box lunch that you can eat while you ride around on streetcars if you haven't some place special that you want to see." The desk clerk left and returned a few minutes later. "Here's a sketch of the streets leading to Tremont Station, where you'll find the streetcars." *Everyone is so helpful. Does exhaustion show on my face?*

In the elevator Bella continued her musings. *I wonder why the clerk suggested riding streetcars. Maybe that is what folks without carriages do.*

***

With Bella's short curved legs the height of the streetcar steps confounded her, but with tugging on the handrails she and Peter climbed aboard the streetcar destined for the town of Cambridge and Harvard University, according to the sign. After ten minutes, the big downtown buildings gave way to shops. Small houses lined the side streets. From her quick glance as they passed, Bella noticed paint peeling around the windows and junk abandoned near the front steps. Twelve minutes down the line, she saw rows of neat attached housing. As the streetcar bumped along its tracks, Bella dreamed of Harvard and the town of Cambridge, the place where Mr. Morgan of the Ice Company said she must go—Harvard, the unknown entity around which she had planned her future.

"Lots of people are riding with us," said Peter. "Why doesn't Paramaribo have carriages this long, and where is the horse?"

"It's an electric streetcar, Peter. Last year, a team of horses would have drawn this carriage down the street. Mr. Morgan told me that as soon as electric streetcars were invented Boston switched to them. He said Boston is the most modern city in America. Surely, we won't be jiggled much farther."

They climbed off at Harvard Square and marvelled at the brilliant colours of the trees—reds, oranges, yellows and greens. *Leaves in Plymouth turn brown in the fall. In Paramaribo they're always green. Are America's leaves coloured like this all year?*

"Mother, why are there trees on that side of the street and only buildings over there?" said Peter, pointing to big old trees spreading their wide crowns to cause pockets of shadow and sun over long green lawns.

"Those trees and lawns must be the grounds of Harvard University, Peter, and the buildings on the other side of the street must be the town of Cambridge. This is the very place Mr. Morgan said we must find. We have come to the end of our long journey!"

"Then why don't I see a house?" said Peter, looking up at his mother.

From Harvard Square they walked towards the buildings. Peter scratched at his ear, trying to understand his mother's pleasure with this place they did not know.

"Look, Peter, a church with a tall spire."

"Christ Church," Bella read on the sign. "Let's eat our lunch on that bench on the church grounds and then find Agassiz School."

Her eyes followed the many pedestrians as they climbed from the streetcars and turned down a street a few blocks away. After their box lunch, curious, they ambled along with the stream of sightseers that headed down Holyoak Street.

"An ice cream parlour, Peter. You deserve a treat." They found a seat and enjoyed the creamy cold dessert spooned into a dish, then returned to Harvard Square and stopped at the newspaper stand to ask for directions.

"Agassiz School? It's not far," answered the clerk. "Just keep going up Massachusetts Avenue for six blocks or so until you get to Sacramento Street; turn right and you can't miss the school as you walk east along that street."

"Mother, I'm cold. The ice cream made me cold. May we go home now?" *Poor Peter. In this northern latitude his body noticed the cold when the sun started to drop.*

"Perhaps we have done enough for one day, Peter. Tomorrow I'll buy each of us a sweater and then go to the courthouse for that job before coming out here. Let's cross to the other tracks and return to the hotel."

***

"We did it, Peter—well, half of it! We found the streetcar line to Cambridge and Harvard University." She hugged and kissed her son for being such a good, if not a puzzled, little boy. Next, she pulled an orange and a bottle of stout from her grip and sat down to play cards with him. *I wonder how much the courthouse job pays.* She paused to look at her cards. "My ace takes that." She scooped up the cards and made a new play.

I know, Peter, that you don't understand what I'm saying, but I have to talk to someone and maybe you'll hear happiness in my voice. Dear God, I am tired.

"Mother, are you paying attention? My king takes that."

"Sorry, Peter. I was thinking that tonight I must write your brother Gordon and Aunt Kate to tell them that we have arrived safely. Shall I tell them you are winning at cards?" *So many things to think about— writing Althea and Constance, money, finding work, a place to live, our trunk at the dock.* "Aha, Peter, I win that one. After this game we must freshen ourselves and go down to dinner." *I wonder how many dinners I can afford before I find work?* And she played her last card.

***

Dressed in a simple black gown with a white lace collar, Bella and Peter set out for the courthouse. *My funds won't keep us in a hotel after the end of the week and the dock master won't hold my trunk for more than that.* They entered the solemn building.

"You will have to leave the boy out there in the foyer while you apply for the job," the woman at a desk said in a cold, unemotional manner. Bella braced, unsure of parting with her son for even a minute. She turned her large diamond ring into the palm of her hand and went in to be interviewed by the judge.

"You have excellent credentials, Mrs. Macdonald, but the cells are cleared of overnight drunks at seven a.m. What do you propose to do with your son at that early hour of the morning? He can't sit in the foyer every day. If you solve that problem, come back again and I'll reconsider your application if the job is still open. Good day."

Bella's face whitened as she left the interview. *My son! I cannot consider buying a house, for who will watch to see that Peter is safely home from school? I must use a boarding house where the proprietor is at home all day so that Peter will have adult care before and after school. Oh my, this does change things. The boarding house proprietor must be a loving woman. Is there such a landlady? Will there ever be a boarding house with someone as nice as Gabby? What will I tell Peter? Nothing, I suppose, not yet. We must go out to Cambridge and find that school—find a boarding house near it so Peter can walk home for lunch—pay the landlady extra. However will I manage? Smile, Bella. Tell Peter that you are going out to Cambridge to see his school!* They walked the three blocks to Tremont Station, where all the streetcar lines meet in the centre of Boston.

***

"Look out the window, Peter, some shops. I didn't notice them when we passed this way yesterday. Perhaps this is where we can buy our sweaters." Bella's short stature made it difficult to reach the overhead cord to signal that they wanted off.

"This looks like a street in England, Peter." She waved her hand. "The meat shop, the fresh produce market, a hardware and there it is, the one we are looking for, a dry goods shop." Peter chose a thick heather-green pullover and Bella chose a black cardigan. *Boylston Street—about half way between Boston and Cambridge—I will have to remember that, for it seems to be a very nice neighbourhood of shops—not old and stuffy like the bookstore in Cambridge.*

***

At the end of the line, despite the October chill in the air, Peter and Bella sat on the church bench and ate their box lunch before they walked farther along Massachusetts Avenue and east on Sacramento. After a long block past plain row housing, they saw a two-story brick building clad with ivy. Handsome grey stone windowsills made the building look very important. The sign plainly named it "Agassiz Grammar School." *I have arrived at the end of my search, the heart of the neighbourhood where I wish to educate my children. Here they will go to school with the children of professors and other learned people and in turn seek education for themselves. Thanks be to God.*

"Peter, come, we must go into the school and register you in Grade One. The school term started in September, but I'm sure they'll take you. Now remember, speak English, not Dutch, if the registrar asks you any questions. Perhaps the registrar can suggest a place where we might rent a room to live until we send for the family."

Inside, they found a small office with a black lady deliberating over papers. She looked up with a warm smile and welcomed them.

"Hello, young man. Would you like to come to our school?"

Peter returned the smile and said, "Yes, Ma'am."

Bella filled out the papers and asked about a place to stay until they were settled.

***

"The registrar suggested a boarding house around the corner, Peter, so that's where we'll go next."

They climbed the front steps of the grey clapboard house. Bella's knock brought a middle-aged dumpling of a woman with straw-coloured hair.

"This is Crescent Street Boarding House alright, Missus, but my rooms are filled with university students. Yer not goin' t' find anything this close t' Harvard so late in the term. I'm sorry, but I just can't take ye." Bella turned and led Peter away from the lady's porch. With drooping shoulders, she reached the sidewalk and turned towards Massachusetts Avenue and the long walk back to Harvard Square.

"Hey, Missus," came a call from the porch that Bella had just left. "It's Agassiz School ye want, isn't it? Yer not goin' t' find anything close for yer wee 'un. Ye seem like a nice person and yer boy is behaved, so if ye have a bed, maybe ye could sleep in my basement until a room comes free. Perhaps by Christmas one of my students will quit or find another place t' live with his buddies. It's not much of an offer but I'm bettin' ye have t' work. Yer little fella could come home fer lunch and I'd watch him after school, if ye paid me extra."

"Did you hear that, Peter? Maybe we have a place to live." Bella wheeled around and, without looking at the basement, paid the first week's rent in advance and made plans with the new landlady, Mrs. O'Grady, to accept their trunk from the docks.

"Where might I buy two single cots and linens for them, including delivery?" Bella enquired before departing.

***

With more spring in her step, Bella and Peter left Sacramento Street knowing that by the end of the week Peter would be in school and they would have a roof over their heads. *I must go to the courthouse tomorrow and hope the pay is high enough to afford my rent. Surely, no one has applied for the job today. It must be mine.*

"Let's go into the fruit store before we buy the beds, Peter. What would you like to have for tea: an apple, a plum, an apricot?"

"What is an apple, Mother?"

"I can see that you have a lot to learn, my son, and learning it in English won't be the biggest chore." She shook her head in bewilderment. *There is just so much that's new to both of us. Tonight I must thread my diamond ring through my long chain and hide it inside my shirtwaist. Working girls don't own diamonds.*

The next day Bella secured the job at the courthouse from 6:45 a.m. until 3:00 in the afternoon. *I hope the streetcar runs that early in the morning. Lead on, Donald, my love; you are doing a fine job.*

In the next three days Bella and Peter bought more warm clothing, for the dampness chilled their bodies through and through. The coloured leaves had blown away and the mornings were darker, but Bella rose at the same early time to march through her plans in preparation for moving from the Rexford Hotel to Cambridge.

***

I must make my voice sound nonchalant about our dreadful living conditions. This is not how I expected to live, but I have no choice except to pay a landlady to care for Peter. He is such a stalwart little man.

"There we are, Peter. The concrete walls of Mrs. O'Grady's basement look a little better painted pale-yellow. With a cloth over the trunk we have a table, and the apple boxes that the fruit man gave us will serve as bedside cabinets. We can move in tomorrow. Which bed do you want?" Peter sat with his chin cupped in his hands, elbows on knees, idly swinging one foot at the edge of the bed where he sat.

"Is this our home, Mother? I liked Candlewick better and I miss Gordon and Stewart and Shau . . ." and his little shoulders shuddered as he burst into tears.

Bella rushed to his side. "Me too, Peter." and they rocked and sobbed together.

22

JUST A
WORKING GIRL

Monday morning, in the dark, Bella's streetcar rattled its way into Boston at six-fifteen a.m. People in plain garb sat shoulder to shoulder, their heads nodding. The jolt of the streetcar at Tremont Station caused a multitude to disembark and push their way between others as they sought to change streetcars or walk to their place of work. The sting of cold air swirling around Bella's head brought clarity to her mind as she walked the few blocks to the courthouse and the oak panelled foyer.

Bella forced a cheery "Good morning" when the office clerk arrived.

"Mrs. Macdonald, isn't it? Come with me." The clerk had no smile and spoke in a terse manner. *Get used to it, Bella; she's talking down to you with that superior fashion. You're a working girl now and the job pays. Just keep smiling.*

"Here's the closet for your coat. In a moment I'll explain our morning routine," said the woman. The sign on her desk read "Maria Ferelli." *Italian and no doubt very competent. I wonder if any of the Dutch drunks will recognize me.*

After checking a paper left in the middle of her desk, the clerk lifted her head, focused on Bella and spoke. "A Dutch brigantine is in port and most of the crew slept here last night. They are a troublesome lot. The judge will see them at seven in his chambers across the hall." The woman's eyes slid down Bella's small frame and immaculate grooming then refocused on Bella's face.

"You're not used to the drunks that land in jail, are you, my dear?" *My dear is it—saccharine-sweet and condescending. The landlady is abrupt too, but kindly; she'll have Peter off to school on time. I should be there for him on his first day. How awful for him.*

"Come, Mrs. Macdonald. Sit in this front pew. No other interpreter is needed today. When the judge calls for you, stand and approach the bench."

The judge arrived in flowing black robes. From his perch atop the high oak bench he, too, looked Bella up and down, then rested back in his leather chair while he rustled documents with more flicks of his eyes in Bella's direction.

I may be small, but I have a commanding voice—English, Dutch, French and Sranan. Whether because of my size, my beauty or my gentle voice, the sailors will quietly pay their fines and leave.

***

After coffee in a back room, Bella asked Miss Ferelli what was expected of her for the rest of the day.

"Nothing, there's no court case today. Go home until tomorrow morning," came the blunt answer from the clerk. "Was that not clear to you?"

Bella collected her coat and found herself walking into Tremont Station as if in a daze. Her courthouse work would never pay the bills, but she had agreed to the job for one year. She stumbled onto the Harvard streetcar, paid her ticket and found a seat.

It is plain that I need another job! The streetcar joggled on with Bella lost in thought. *But what? Sewing? A gown shop? How would I get started? Maybe an expensive shop needs a sales clerk. I'll try that tomorrow. Today, I'll walk home with Peter and hear about his first day of school.* Bella shook her head in self-loathing. *What kind of a mother am I to let my child go alone to school on his first day? Dear God, forgive me.*

Harvard Square appeared as if out of nowhere. Bella, after spending the morning in their basement room, walked over to Agassiz School at noon. The children burst from the doorway, skipping along with a little roughhousing. Peter left last with his head down. He kicked at a pebble then heard his mother's voice.

"Surprise! I wasn't needed at work this morning so I came back to walk home with you. What happened? You look unhappy?" Peter did not answer until they turned the corner and were away from any others. Then he started in Dutch.

"They laughed at my English. They're all Irish kids and they sneered at the name Macdonald and asked 'what kind of a Scot speaks Dutch?' What's a Scot, Mother?"

Bella put her arm around his shoulders as they walked home for lunch and explained how one's name describes one's background, only in his case the assumption didn't work very well. "Macdonald, your father's name, is Scottish, so you are a Scot. Americans can be Irish and Scottish, English, Italian, African, or anything else. It doesn't matter here in America, for everyone is equal."

"It didn't feel that way." They entered the house and went to the basement.

"Don't worry, Peter. Your English will improve."

***

Again in the dark, on her second day of work, Bella walked the lonely route to Harvard Square. The single light on the front of the wooden streetcar announced its approach. When a woman sat beside her, Bella ventured to ask her where she might find the better shops in Boston.

"Ha! What would I be doin' with fine gowns now? It's more like I'd be scrubbin' the floor in a shop like that!" and she turned her head to look out an opposite window to end the conversation. Bella spoke again with a hint of an Irish accent.

"That's just it. I thought 't would be nicer scrubbin' floors in a salon than in a factory, don't ye know. I might have a warm coat from the old country, but I'm new to America and I need a job. If ye can name the street with fashion shops, please tell me."

"Ye think you're a lady do ye? Well, la-de-da. Take yourself off to Fowley's Fashions on Newbury Street and see how fast ye find the back door." The lady paused. "Sorry, Missus. I should'na spoke like that. I'm just tired. May luck be with ye," and she rose to leave the streetcar. Bella was glad that her new overcoat covered the gracious gown she had chosen for her next effort to find a better job.

So that's what's happening to Peter. He isn't one of them so he is not accepted. We must work on his English. My accent from Plymouth is close to the Boston accent, so that is what Peter will learn—cultured English, not Irish street slang.

After work at the courthouse, Bella examined the signs posted on the Tremont Station walls. One advertisement showed shops on "The Alley" off Massachusetts Avenue. *That's the very line I use to go to Cambridge, just what I'm looking for.*

As usual, the streetcar jiggled along through the grey stone buildings of downtown Boston. *What street did the conductor just call? The Alley? I must pull the cord and get off* and she willed herself to wobble to the door before she missed the stop.

Bella started down The Alley, looking for gowns in the shop windows. A cold wind swirled off the pavement. Its icy tentacles grasped at her ankles. *The sign on the next street over reads "Newbury Street," the one that the Irish lady mentioned. I'll go to Fowley's Fashions. Whether it is you, God, or Donald leading me doesn't matter. I thank you both and pray that you stand with me when I ask Fowley's Fashions for a job.*

As Bella entered Fowley's Fashions, an overzealous saleslady pounced upon her, spewing her practised sales dissertation. While the sales lady opened her hand to point out their table of patterns and gowns ready for their patrons, Bella observed how a quality fashion shop took care of its customers. The elegant room held a tall mirror outside a change room, a small table for business and a display of fabrics. *Obviously, they don't need a saleslady. I wonder if they have a sewing room through that door at the back with someone who can fit a gown to the vagaries of the human body. I could do that.*

With more insistence, Bella repeated, "I'm looking for a job."

"You're looking for work! I mistook you for a customer." The sales lady lifted her eyes from examining Bella's gown. "You must see Madame LeBeau, the manageress of the shop. Come this way."

Perhaps the Madame would like me to speak a little French. Yes, Bella, put your coat over your arm to expose your dress. That should prove you know elegant fashion.

Madame LeBeau finally raised her large head to scrutinise Bella.

"My clerk tells me you want work as a seamstress. Can you sew?"

So curt! The answer is yes, but I wanted to be more than just a back-room seamstress. Whatever did that clerk say to Madame LeBeau? To answer, Bella said, "Yes," and showed her dressmaking ability in the gown she wore.

Madame LeBeau's thick figure circled Bella.

Bella watched for any agreeable sign from the woman. *Now is my opportunity to speak a little French and tell about William Morris and his fashions.* She tried.

"Mrs. Macdonald, French is not used in America." At that moment Bella realized that Madame LeBeau used an assumed name. The Madame continued: "The only opening that I have is as an apprentice. If you work at that for two years, you'll earn your journeyman's ticket as a qualified seamstress. Until then, the pay is limited."

It sounds like I'll need the ticket to open a shop of my own. If I accept, even with two jobs, we must live on a pittance for two years. How will I bring my family together? Bella's eyes misted with the turmoil of her thoughts.

***

Again, Bella arrived home in time to meet Peter, this time at four o'clock. A button had been torn from his coat and he had a deep red bruise on his cheek. With eyes cast at the sidewalk, he came to the corner where she waited.

"Can you teach me how to fight, Mother?" he asked. "There must be some way to beat a bigger kid."

Feeling her son's desperation, Bella said, "No, Peter. I've never had to fight, but we can go to the library and find a book that will show us how." With Peter, she turned her tired feet to retrace her steps towards Massachusetts Avenue.

***

"See the picture, Peter. That's how you make a fist. Clench your hands. Put your feet apart for balance." Peter widened his stance and assumed the position of the boxer in the picture. "It says if you want to hit with the right hand, have the left foot forward and your weight on the back foot until you make the hit." In the middle of their basement room, Peter swung at the air with one fist to try out his mother's instructions. "Keep your elbows and forearms in close to protect your ribs and make your fists protect your chin. Raise your hands more, Peter." Bella read on: "When you hit, swing upwards at the chin. Oh, my, this does sound dangerous. Can't you meet nicer boys?"

"I guess so, but if I can bloody this guy's nose, then I think they'll leave me alone. He's bigger than me but I'm strong and fast." *How do little boys know such things?*

"Not *guy's* nose, Peter," Bella corrected. "Say *boy's* or *fellow's* nose. The word 'guy' is slang. You must learn the difference between proper English and slang."

Peter took a few more swipes at the air.

"Get washed up for supper, Peter, and afterwards I'll have a fight with you. At least my size makes me a good practice partner. After that, I'll tell you my news."

***

"That's enough, Peter. You have pummelled me for half an hour; I must sit for awhile. Here, I'll prop your mattress against the concrete wall and you can try dancing your feet around in front of it. Imagine landing punches where they'll do the most good—an uppercut to the chin and square on the nose—if it bleeds, all the better. *My goodness! Did I say that? Donald, are you showing me how to raise boys?*

"Now for my news, Peter. Today I found a job as an apprentice seamstress with the finest gown maker in Boston. It seems she didn't like my Parisian French any more than the boys at school like your English.

231

Apprentices don't earn much money, but when I finish, I will be fit to start my own shop." Peter asked what "apprentice" meant.

"Apprentice means learning a trade. I start tomorrow after I finish at the courthouse. I won't be home until six. After school, you can read the book on boxing."

The meaning of apprentice still eluded Peter, but his English improved with reading the books that he borrowed from the library every week.

Combining Mrs. O'Grady's good cooking and the exercises that went with the book on fighting, Peter grew as if overnight, but his mother didn't notice. With Christmas approaching, Bella worked overtime each evening. Peter watched in silence as she came home to cold dinners, exhausted. Every evening Bella accepted the plate and took it to their damp basement room and sat on the edge of her bed with her head in her hands. *Dear God, help me to be grateful for the overtime pay. Without it, I couldn't pay Mrs. O'Grady's overtime sitting charges. And galoshes—the snow will fall any day—and Christmas—Peter wants an atlas or a dictionary and I must buy gifts to send to Candlewick. Bella, you must stop worrying; it might make you ill. Already, you have lost weight! Eat your dinner.* Bella sighed a long sigh and nibbled at her dinner. *The small amount of money I brought from Surinam must carry me for two years. At least Peter is receiving a good education at Agassiz School.*

"Peter, come and play cards with me," said Bella and promptly dozed off.

***

Again, the same as all the mornings before, Bella set off to help her Dutch drunks.

It's finally 1897 and the rush for New Year's Eve gowns is over. I'll be home in time to meet Peter after school. She waited on the corner.

Look at that, two boys are fighting and other boys have made a ring around them to bait them on. Listen to them! Why can't they be politicians and flail each other with useless words instead of fists? Bella crossed the street and hurried towards the group of children. *Good, the group is breaking up. At least they didn't fight very long.*

From out of the gang of scurrying boys came Peter with a smile on his face.

"I bloodied his nose today, Mother. Maybe that will end his months of bullying."

"Months? He's been at you since school started? Why didn't you tell me, Peter? I could have spoken to the principal."

"That doesn't work. They just beat up on you somewhere else away from school."

"What language, Peter—'beat up on you'—really!"

"Oh yeah? Well, now you don't have to worry 'bout me 'cause I'm the best fighter in Grade One. When Gordon comes, I'll teach him to fight." Peter punched at the air. "I have other news, Mother. I found a new friend, Timmy; he likes books too."

***

"Mrs. Macdonald, come into the kitchen," called Mrs. O'Grady when Bella and Peter came in the door. "I have good news. I booted that good-fer-nothin' Mike out of the big room. He never paid his rent on time. Now ye can move upstairs."

Can I afford it and save for a business too? Smile, surely something will work out. You can't keep living in the basement forever. You must move before Peter gives up hope of ever having a home or seeing his brothers again.

"Wonderful, Mrs. O'Grady. How much is the rent?" She heard the price. *Dear God, but what can I do? Eat away at my capital, that's what. Peter looks ecstatic.*

They moved upstairs when the Christmas holidays started. *At least this main-floor room, with the smell of Mrs. O'Grady's baking wafting down the hall, will make it seem more like Christmas.*

***

Snow came, rain came and more snow while Bella continued her trek back and forth to Harvard Square. Finally, spring breezes warmed the air. Daffodils sprung up in the gardens at Harvard. Red and yellow tulips brightened Sacramento Street, but even with the coming of spring she plodded her way home, exhausted.

One day, Bella picked up her mail from the hall table and went to their room.

"Mother, why are you wearing that long apron? Only maids wear those," Peter asked when his mother removed her coat. *Oh my. I forgot to leave my apron at work. I wonder if it showed under my coat on the streetcar. If someone saw it, they'll start to tease Peter again. But truth is truth.*

"I'm wearing the apron because I forgot to take it off at work. In a way, Peter, I am a maid."

Peter looked at the floor. "So it's true what they say at school."

Oh, the poor boy! "I'm not a cleaning lady, Peter. I sew gowns as an apprentice seamstress, remember? Someday I hope to have my own shop, but first I must learn the sewing trade, and before that, I must find a house to rent near here that's big enough for your brothers and Shauna." *Perhaps changing the subject will raise his spirits.*

The mention of family still at Candlewick made Peter turn away. *Were those tears I saw brimming in his eyes? What a staunch little man.* She glanced at the letter she had thrown on the bed. The cancel mark on the stamp showed Aberdeen, Scotland.

"Dear Bella,

I hope you and little Peter are doing well in Cambridge. My brother Peter tells me that your Aunt Kate stayed on in Paramaribo to care for Gordon, Stewart and Candlewick. He says that they are anxious to be with you, so I hope that will happen soon. This letter is to tell you that I am planning a trip to Boston in the middle of May with the hope of visiting you. I understand that Cambridge is quite close to Boston, so perhaps you and Peter can meet me at the docks and we'll go home in your carriage. . .

Bella flipped to the end of the letter. It came from her brother-in-law William.

What kind of stories has Kate been telling Donald's brother Peter? Then again, maybe it's what I am not telling them that has caused the problem. Well, for better or worse, a second brother-in-law is coming to visit me and then there will be no secrets. Once William has visited, he will surely tell his brother Peter how much grief came to our family because his letter, with his refusal to be part of Donald's gold mine venture, came too late. If that letter had come on time, perhaps Donald would not have gone to the jungle early and died of yellow fever. Bella paused and shook her head. *No, I must not torment myself with those thoughts again. Little Peter and I are fine—not rich, but fine, and somehow, someday, I will send for Gordon, Stewart and Shauna.* She looked around their simple room: pale blue walls, blue drapes past their time, two cots covered with colourful afghans she had knit, a wooden chair, apple crates and a trunk. *How will I tell William that he must sleep at a hotel or here on the floor?*

She cried out in a happy voice: "Peter, Uncle William is visiting in May. He wants us to meet him at the docks."

***

"Look, Mother, a steamship! He didn't come on a sailing ship like we did. How will you recognize him if you've never met him?"

"I'm not sure, Peter. Perhaps he will recognize us—a short lady with a young boy—or perhaps, if he looks like your father, we'll know him. He may even have red hair like your father and Gordon. Let's watch; the passengers are coming down the gangplank."

Peter hung his head. "It's getting harder and harder to remember Father, so I hope Uncle William looks like him to help me remember." They waited.

"What do you think, Peter? Is that him?" A man moved their way.

"Bella and young Peter? I am William Macdonald." Their meeting took place with handshakes and very little emotion. After William collected his suitcase, Bella knew the moment had arrived when William would start to know the truth about her life.

"William," said Bella, "in your letter you mentioned a carriage ride home. That will be very expensive. I use the streetcar. Perhaps we should take a carriage to Tremont Station and go on to Cambridge by streetcar."

"Nonsense! We'll take a carriage to your home."

Bella stood as tall as she could and squared her shoulders for the beginning of squashing any presumptions that William might have.

"I don't have a home. I live in a boarding house because that is the best way to care for Peter while I work."

Bella heaved a sigh of relief. The truth was out. Dampness showed in her eyes.

"Now, now, Bella—caring for Peter, is it? There is no shame in how you live. I will find a hotel and we can still have a visit." They took the streetcar.

William is listening but not understanding that we are not rich.

At Harvard Square, William ordered a carriage to ride the distance to Mrs. O'Grady's boarding house. Peter's Uncle William spoke only to Bella.

Peter finally piped up: "That's my school, Uncle William, Agassiz Grammar School. See, it says so on that sign." William nodded with no words of acknowledgement to Peter. At the boarding house, without coming in, he announced that he would be back at five o'clock to take them to supper at whatever hotel the carriage driver recommended.

Five o'clock—my stout time. Does he know I drink stout both at home and in public? William might be embarrassed—Donald wasn't. Poor little Peter, struggling so hard to speak perfect English and trying to show he could read his school sign and William didn't even notice. I wonder if Peter realizes that William looks like his father? So undemonstrative, that William.

***

"Peter, put on your Sunday clothes. We must look our best for your uncle."

Bella braided her topknot and applied the pearls as she had done many times for Donald.

"Mother, you look beautiful. I don't remember that burgundy gown."

"I haven't worn it recently, Peter. You look smart in your school blazer."

At five, William returned to take them to dinner.

"William, did Donald ever tell you that our first date came when he found a saloon where I could enjoy my half-pint of stout?" Nothing changed on William's square countenance. *An emotionless Scot with no sense of humour. Donald must have been the exception. I'll have it with dinner.* In minutes, they climbed into the carriage that still waited at the door.

***

On Sunday, Bella showed William and Peter where she worked as a seamstress. With a gracious—or curious—invitation from Mrs. O'Grady that came earlier in the day, they returned to the boarding house to eat supper with the landlady.

***

"Tomorrow, William, I must go to work at six-fifteen or lose my job translating for drunken Dutch sailors who land in jail. I do the seamstress work after that. I'll be home at six. *Poor man, I have shown him that I am a woman of resilience—struggling, but determined. If he came with any thought of doing his duty by asking for my hand in marriage, according to the old school, he'll have gained my secrets but not a wife.*"

***

The next night, William chose to have supper at the Harvard University dining room. From past experience, Bella became the charming woman that Donald had loved, and young Peter became a perfect little gentleman quite used to his parent's fancy functions. *I wonder if William thought Peter or I would gawk at the crystal chandeliers or burnished oak paneling.* After Bella ordered stout, the waiter served dinner.

"You are a sly one, Bella. You've guessed that I came to visit for the same reason as George visited you. Poor George, of course you knew we lost him at sea."

"Yes," replied Bella. "My sister wrote and told me that the authorities thought the ship disappeared in a place called the Bermuda Triangle. I'm sure you miss him."

"Don't you see, Bella? We don't know if you agreed to marry him or not." With no quick comment from Bella, William, unused to such personal conversations, leapt into a new subject. "Why are you in such desperate straits, Bella?"

This time she answered. "I had no choice, William. My childhood rickets and pneumonia makes it impossible for me to go back to the fog and rain of England. As for work in Paramaribo, what job is open to widowed colonials? They can't do menial jobs there like I can here. I'm poor because Donald had written to your brother Peter and asked if he wanted to share in the gold mine venture, but Peter's letter arrived too late to meet the deadline for securing a lease the government required for prospecting. Donald took the risk of using all our savings to buy the lease on his own and I lost that when he died from yellow fever. Ask Peter if you want to know more of this venture. I've had to manage on very few resources in order to leave Aunt Kate and the boys with any money at all. America offers everyone a chance for equality and work." William said nothing until the waiter finished serving dessert.

"This means then, that even if you would marry me, you would not wish to live in Scotland where I earn my living. Am I right?"

Some proposal! Dry as a cotton ball. He just doesn't understand America and the freedoms that people enjoy here. Tradition is a terrible mantle. It's good that there are no more bachelor brothers feeling duty-bound to save me.

"William, as I told George, I have changed from when I lived in England. I am now a woman of independence." Bella spoke with her soft compelling voice: "You must choose someone you love, not marry me out of tradition."

Poor little Peter, he has never heard adults speak of such matters. His head goes back and forth each time the conversation switches between William and me. His eyes are about to pop out. What a cruel way for him to learn that he will never again enjoy his home in Paramaribo. William has lost his tongue. I must say something.

"My goal is to educate my sons in the shadow of Harvard University and I plan to achieve it by opening my own shop and sewing fine gowns for the professors' wives."

"Own your own business? Women don't start bu . . ." William didn't finish the sentence. Instead, he said: "Very well, Bella. Your candid reply has answered all my questions. At least let me leave some money in your bank account so you can afford to bring your family to Cambridge. I have means and I would like to do that."

As if by magic, Bella produced a small hanky from her sleeve and dabbed at her eyes with gratefulness. *The man has a heart after all. How generous of him.*

"Don't cry, Mother. Uncle William said something nice," young Peter implored.

"Yes, Peter, he did. I am crying because I'm happy. Thank you, William." Bella stepped around the corner of the table and gave William an explosive hug and kiss in front of all whom wished to notice. "Your kindness will unite my family. God bless you." William lifted his linen napkin and wiped beads of perspiration from his astonished face.

"Peter, you and I must find a house to rent soon or we'll miss the good sailing weather for those back at Candlewick. Won't it be wonderful to be together again?"

The next day, his mission completed, William took the train to New York.

23

A NEW
BEGINNING

One day, over the usual breakfast of oatmeal porridge, the brusque Mrs. O'Grady decided to chat. "Mrs. Macdonald, I have never seen ye so radiant. What has caused this transformation? I trust ye're well."

"Yesterday," started Bella, "when Peter came home from the last day of school, he saw a 'For Sale' sign on the lawn of 49 ½ Sacramento Street. You know, the row housing a block east from Agassiz School? I visited there last evening and at this moment I am overcome with joy because I will now be able to have my family together again."

"Ye're telling me that ye plan t' move. That's all very nice, but how can ye work and care for three boys at the same time?" *Such blunt questions—as if it's any of her business—but then, it is her business. I'm her highest paying tenant.*

"I won't move right away; with summer coming, caring for Peter does pose a problem. The family won't arrive from South America until September. When my Aunt Kate brings the children, their nanny will be with them." Bella paused and casually bit off a corner of her dry toast. *Yes, "Nanny" has more position than maid does; Shauna will be known as the children's nanny here in America.*

"Mrs. O'Grady, may we live here all summer with Peter under your care? After we move in September, would you have him for lunch and after school until I get home?" *A full summer's rent and extra for Peter should please her, yet her face discloses nothing.*

"Mrs. Macdonald, my first name is Bertie and I believe yours is Bella. Please call me Bertie. May I call you Bella? I think ye have a fine plan except fer one thing." *I never expected that! We are now officially friends. What's the problem? Why is life always putting roadblocks in my way?*

"I've seen how tired ye are when ye come home late. In the fall, make yer own breakfasts, but t'would be best if ye stay here for supper when ye come fer the lad."

"Mrs. O'Grady—Bertie—what a gem you are! That will be wonderful." Bella jumped from her chair and threw her arms around the landlady's square body.

"And Peter," added Bertie, "ye can sit in my parlour in the overstuffed chair and read yer books until yer mamma comes home."

What a woman. Beneath her crusty exterior she's as warm as St. Paddy himself.

***

"Peter," said Bella early in September. "The family will arrive next Friday if the winds hold steady. I'm going to rent a hotel suite for our first night together. You can miss Friday's school and play with Gordon at the hotel. This time I'll get the best hotel in town, not a dump by the docks." Bella winked at Peter.

Peter examined his shoelaces with no hint of amusement in his demeanor. Bella suspected that Peter remembered their first night in America like an unwanted nightmare.

"Just imagine, Peter, you, Gordon and Stewart together again! We have waited so long for this day . . ." She finished the sentence in her thoughts—*I have waited so long I am afraid to count on the ship's arrival. After a year of not seeing two of my boys . . . dear God, don't let anything happen to them now.*

Peter spoke with caution. "Should I speak Dutch or English?"

"Both, I suppose," laughed Bella. "With Aunt Flora and Aunt Kate speaking English at Candlewick this past year, I imagine Gordon's English will have already improved, and who knows what Stewart will say at two years of age under Shauna's care. Perhaps Sranan." Despite her efforts to lighten the moment, Peter remained silent.

***

Fog horns blew and a cold wind sheeted across Boston Harbour to the dock where Bella and Peter waited for the *Charles L. Mitchell* to discharge its passengers.

"Look, Mother," said Peter, showing some spirit, "they came on a two-masted schooner just like we did. I hope the ship didn't toss the furniture around."

"I'm sure they will be fine, Peter—cold, but fine. I've already hired a carriage to stand by for us. Here come the first passengers down the gangplank."

Bella and Peter, pushed by the crowd, found themselves crushed against the restraining rope. Bella's eyes searched for three ladies with two little boys.

"Aunt Kate and Flora are tourists," explained Bella, just for the sake of talking to mask her sense of foreboding. "Shauna and your brothers will have to be registered as immigrants. It will take a while, but I'm sure Kate will stay with them." They waited.   "Look!" cried Peter, pointing. "There they are at the top of the gangplank."

The disembarking passengers moved at the pace of a tortoise, all searching the crowd for the face of a loved one.

"Here they come, Mother, but they're not looking this way."

Bella shouted, "Hello! We're over here! Over here!" but her voice failed to carry above the commotion. "Oh dear, I'm too short for them to see me and they can't hear me. Quick, Peter, run to them! The dock police aren't watching. Slip under the rope and guide them this way. We mustn't lose them now." Soon a group of hugging women and jumping little boys raised a chorus of happy squealing.

Thank you, dear Lord, oh, thank you! And Donald, as you can see, we are united again and we will be fine. Bella roused herself from her moment of prayer and breathed an audible sigh of relief. With the smaller suitcases, they broke away from the throngs of weary people. Bella led them towards their waiting carriage, and after what seemed like a long ride, the lights of the hotel welcomed the newcomers to America. The foyer offered warmth, delicious aromas and a feeling of great splendour. The metal-cage elevator captivated Gordon and Shauna. After settling into their rooms, they went down for dinner.

***

"Tomorrow, I must go to work," said Bella at bedtime after happy hours of talking. "I'll return at lunchtime. Aunt Kate, please take everyone down for breakfast, and if you and Flora wish to go shopping, the stores are only a block away. Shauna, I suggest you stay in the hotel room with the children because they are so excited they might run off in different directions and get lost if you venture out. I'll have lunch sent up for all of us when I arrive about twelve-thirty."

***

"I'm back, children. Did you have a nice time with Shauna?" called Bella when she returned at noon.

"Yes, Mother," piped up Gordon. "We played hide and seek until Shauna stopped that game because Peter tried to hide on the closet shelf and fell."

"That's not so, Gordon. We stopped the game because you climbed on the bidet and got scared when it flushed with your feet stuck in the hole."

Shauna chuckled. "Stewart slept with contentment all day, quite happy to be off that ship, but the boys are little boys. They need to run and be outside."

"And so they will be. After lunch they can play on the quiet streets of Cambridge." Bella enacted noises from the streetcar as she trotted around where the boys were playing in the centre of the carpet. "Rattle, rattle, ding, ding, ding, get out of way, a streetcar's coming through." The boys giggled and Shauna smiled with memories of the old days.

Aunt Kate arrived with sweaters and coats for Shauna and the boys. "It's a coat, Gordon," she explained. "We wear winter coats in England too. Now tell me about your new house, Bella. Yes, Gordon, you may have a sandwich."

"It isn't new but it's ours as long as I cover the rent," Bella started. "The fellow and his wife, Mr. and Mrs. Uvari, wanted to sell the house with much of its furniture and travel west to find a homestead. I didn't have enough money to buy the house plus save money for starting a business, so I convinced them to rent it to me in case they decided to return. Now, no more details," she wagged a finger. "That way it will be a surprise. We can have the dock master send your baggage and the crates on Monday."

***

"It's lovely, Mrs. McD," cried Shauna as she came through the front door of 49 ½ Sacramento Street. "It's just like Dominiestraat, with three rooms upstairs and a hall running beside the living room and dining room all the way from the front door to the kitchen. It even has pale-pink paint on the walls."

"You missed something, Shauna," teased Bella. "We have a crapper, called a toilet in America, and we have hot and cold running water. It isn't fancy, but there are no bugs and the hardwood floors shine. I'm sure you and I can make it look like a real home. We have a basement too," said Bella, "but basements aren't very interesting, are they, Peter?" Bella looked around for Peter. "Now where did Peter and Gordon go?"

"Outside, Mrs. McD—chasing up and down the street. I have my eyes on them."

***

At Sunday dinner Bella called for hush. "Gordon, tomorrow, you and Aunt Kate will go to school with Peter. I'll be at work, so Aunt Kate will register you in Grade One. Bella bit her lip. *That makes me an inadequate mother for the second time, but I must complete my apprenticeship.*

On Monday, with Bella at work and the two older boys in school, the crates and baggage arrived. The wagon men dropped everything on the small plot of grass that served as a front lawn. Kate and Shauna carried in the luggage but couldn't open the crates.

"May I help you with those nails?" came a voice from next door. "I'm your neighbour, Doug Wray." Soon the crates were open and Bella's Parsons table and Bentwood chairs graced the dining room. Shauna found space in the kitchen cupboards for plates and silverware, and Kate and Flora carried children's clothes and toys up to the master bedroom, now to serve as the boys' room, according to Bella's wishes. Home from school at lunch, Peter cheered when he saw his father's heavy rocking chair in the living room across from the Uvaris' blue sofa and overstuffed chair. By the time Bella arrived home at six, everything had found a home and a young man named Doug Wray sat beside four bottles of stout in the parlour while the three little boys, with their lemonades, sat on the floor around the rocking chair.

"This must be Bella!" Doug exclaimed as Bella came through the front door. "I'm your half duplex neighbour, Doug Wray. If you ever need any help, just ring my bell, number forty-nine. If not me, one of the other fellows should be ready to lend a hand."

"You four are students at Harvard, are you?" asked Bella.

"Yes, all farm boys taking medicine," Doug replied.

"He came over this morning," said Aunt Kate. "He opened the crates for us and helped with the furniture." Bella saw eight place settings at the table. *Good, I wanted Shauna to be part of the family and sit with us. The eighth place must be for Doug.*

***

Flora and Aunt Kate sailed for England two weeks later, their long vigil over. Back home from the docks, Bella sat motionless in Donald's chair. *At last I have my family and Shauna all together in one house, thanks to Aunt Kate and Flora, George and William.* Bella's gaze moved to the front window to look out at the stars. *Donald, we will be fine. George's money sustained us until now. The money from Candlewick and my two jobs will pay the rent and keep us. The bulk of William's money is in the bank earning interest. Just you watch, some day I will own a house and have my own shop.*

"Are you unwell, Mrs. McD? You are so quiet, just sitting there gazing at space."

"No, Shauna, I'm fine. Perhaps tired, but perfectly well and ever so happy. It has taken over a year to gather you all under one roof—much longer than I realized it would take—but now we are ready to start a new beginning."

***

After supper one evening, with the boys in bed, Bella mentioned Stewart's second birthday coming soon on December thirteenth.

"If you can afford it, Mrs. McD, I know just the thing—a big wagon like Tim's! With a wagon, Stewart and I can walk into town for groceries. If he's tired, he can ride. Both Stewart and I could use a wagon."

On December the thirteenth, with Stewart climbing on the laps of the boys from next door and Bella in the rocking chair, Gordon and Peter pulled a large red wagon into the room and screamed, "Happy Birthday, Stewart!" Stewart had no idea what Happy Birthday meant but immediately took possession of the wagon and ordered his brothers with "Go!" Everyone took turns pulling him around the house. Shauna finally stopped the procession by placing a birthday cake, burning two candles, on the Parsons table. At that moment Bella felt they had turned an invisible corner towards stability in their lives.

***

Following Christmas, the winds were sharp and snow hampered Bella's 6:15 trek to Harvard Square. *This trip gets harder every day, but I need the money.* She entered the courthouse.

"You are late, Mrs. Macdonald. At least the judge thinks so," scolded Maria. "He's in a nasty mood, so don't rile him by taking too long with each drunk," *Humph! I'm early by five minutes. Why can't she call me Bella and be Maria to me. It's as if there's a barrier of position between us—and the way she insists on referring to them as drunks is uncivil. They are men and in America we're supposed to be equal.* Bella entered the judge's chambers.

"At last you're here, Mrs. Macdonald! Bring in the three prisoners," the judge intoned. The men were led in the side door. The first two men paid their small fines and stepped into the foyer to await their sailing comrade.

"Kolb," said the judge. Bella gasped. "The police report says that you were the ringleader in last night's brawl. Five nights in jail and twice the fine. We'll teach you foreigners to behave in Boston." The man, Kolb, turned beseeching eyes towards Bella and wagged his head sideways.

"Your honour," said Bella, "Mr. Kolb wishes to have me interpret his plea."

"Kolb is a German name. Let him speak to me in German!" *The judge is in a foul mood, and he's right. Why doesn't Manfred use his German? I'll ask him.*

In Dutch, Bella inquired and the man answered in broken sailor's Dutch.

"You recognize me, ya? I Manfred Kolb, cook on de *Van Dam* when you got married, de vun who make vedding cake an' sign marriage paper. I de vun who played wit' Peter when you come to America. I no fighting las' night." Manfred stood twisting his wool hat and shifting his weight from foot to foot.

"De boys were so drunk dey couldn' stan' up," he went on. "One ob dem lurch towards bar and dis man took it as good excuse to swing fist, but my friend didn' swing back. I was tryin' to get de friends out ob der when de police come. Ve said ve didn' fight, but de police lock us up. I didn' speak to de judge in German 'cause my German's bad like my Dutch. When I saw you, I t'ought maybe you help me wit de judge."

"You've had long enough, Mrs. Macdonald, what is this man's complaint?"

Bella decided against telling the judge that she knew the man. She told his story and added, "Judge, I think five days punishment is uncalled for. His ship sails tomorrow and with five days of incarceration he will miss it. Working as a ship's cook is his life's work. He has nobody but his friends on board that ship."

"Who are you, Mrs. Macdonald, to tell me how to administer the law?" the judge blasted at her. "You are merely an interpreter in this court, not an advocate."

"Then, Judge," said Bella standing on her tiptoes beside the docket, "What if I was not staff? Then could I be an advocate and speak for this man?"

This ruffled the judge; he shouted, "And how can you do that?"

"Judge, at this moment I resign my position as interpreter. My contract to remain with you for one year lapsed months ago. I have no reason to stay, but I do have good reason to report this court as uncaring and unfair to the men who pass through here every morning." Bella took a step closer for perfect eye contact with the judge. "I'm sorry if your taverns are too loosely managed to keep men on liberty from imbibing too much, but this man, Mr. Kolb, is innocent. If you keep him here, I will go to the newspapers. Good day to you, Judge."

"Maria," said Bella, just to use Maria's first name to establish equality that one time, "I will return on Saturday morning for my pay envelope." The three sailors were waiting on the steps of the Court House to thank Bella.

"Come fellows," she said, "No more Samuel Adams for you, even if it is Boston's finest beer. Go to your ship and stay there until it sails." They went their separate ways, the sailors to the *Van Dam* and Bella, towards Fowley's Fashions. As she kicked through the snow towards Fowley's she felt a new happiness. *I never realized how much I detested that loathsome judge and his brand of justice.*

All day Bella tipped the treadle back and forth, urging her legs to go faster and struggling to make her fingers sew as if twice as nimble. *What have I done? Will I be able to make up the lost pay by completing work faster? Work, Bella. Make the cloth obey your fingers; cut a perfect slit, stitch an elegant buttonhole. Will my pay cover the rent? I mustn't keep nibbling away at the Candlewick money if I ever hope to have a shop.*

***

"You look pale, Mrs. McD," said Shauna that evening. "What is troubling you? The boys are fine." Bella steadied her voice.

"I gave notice at the courthouse today. I quit. Perhaps that is what makes me pale. True, I had words with the judge about his uncaring justice, but he deserved it and I'm glad to be free of that job. When I walked to Fowley's after I'd quit, I realized that leaving at 6:15 in the morning and returning at 6:15 at night had become too much." Bella paused and then went on. "All day, I sewed as fast as my fingers would go to make up for the lost courthouse wages. Now I just realized something else. All year I've been doing finishing work at Fowley's. From the dress I wore that first day, Madam LeBeau knew I could sew and recognized my desperation for a job. She hired me as an apprentice so she could use me for cheap labour until I earned my qualifications as a seamstress. I'm stuck for nine more months." When Shauna stood speechless, Bella tried to soften the situation.

"Don't worry, Shauna. I'm sure I can make up the difference in income by completing more piecework every day. I'll be able to see the boys in the morning and evening."

***

Months passed while Bella continued her frantic pace, with completed items nearly making up the difference in income. At first, each month Bella regularly deposited her month's rent in the Uvaris' bank account, but work at Fowley's slowed during the summer. To help with the rent money Bella countered by planting a large vegetable garden to augment their grocery bills. Every evening, after sewing all day, she weeded the garden. On the weekends, she harvested, followed by canning. In August, she preserved fruit and made jam. With fall, new fashions slowed her pace while work rose to a peak. Bella pumped her machine faster. For more income, Bella let it be known that she sewed gowns. Immediately, Bertie wanted a gown.

"I'll show you the styles for spring, Bertie. You buy the material and findings and pay me for my labour." Shauna and Bella set up a sewing corner in the basement.

Bertie's flattering gown roused her neighbour's interest. She knocked on Bella's door and insisted on haggling over the cost of labour.

"I refuse to lower my price, Shauna, even if she is Bertie's friend."

Bella stamped her foot. "If I allow an unreasonably low price for labour, how will I be poised to attract trade as a quality seamstress when I open my own shop?" *Why do I feel this cross? In two weeks I'll have my journeyman's ticket, ready to start my own business.*

The next day Bella stepped into the warmth of her home, ripped off her tam, woodenly stretched out an arm to hang her coat on the peg, swayed and slammed her shoulder against the door jam. Dizziness overtook her and she collapsed into Donald's rocking chair. She regained her composure, accepted the stout from Shauna and sat with the children playing around her. *The house is too hot!*

"Can't you play with less clatter?" she snapped at Gordon. "Peter, take him upstairs and read to him. Do whatever it takes to keep yourselves quiet and take Stewart too. He keeps climbing on me. I'm tired. I can't stand your noise." Startled by their mother's sharp command, the children disappeared. Shauna came from the kitchen.

"What is it, Mrs. McD? I've never heard you so short with the children. Are you sure you're not ill?"

"Nonsense, Shauna, I'm just tired. The coming of winter chills my bones and makes me feel down." Shauna crossed the floor and deliberately held her hand to Bella's forehead.

"Your head feels too clammy. I've been watching you this past week and you've hardly touched your meals. Stand up. No, don't give me that look. Stand up and let me feel the waistband of your gown." Bella stood and slipped her own hands between her blouse and skirt. The waistband hung an inch too low on her hips.

"Oh my, Shauna, I've lost quite a bit of weight!" Bella sank back into Donald's chair. Fear flashed across her face.

"I'm quite sure you are ill, Mrs. McD. I'm calling the doctor. Tomorrow morning you are not going to work. Overwork is one thing, but pneumonia is life threatening. Now get yourself into bed. I'll feed the boys and get them to bed."

"My dearest Shauna, you remind me of Gabby and her stern teacher's voice. Do you remember how you ordered me around when I lost my third baby and again when Stewart came? I do believe you saved my life both times. For now, I'll do as you say."

"Close your door until the doctor comes. If you get hungry, you'll find a little brass bell at your bedside." Bella looked up with a questioning look. "Yes, the bell you used at your dinner table in Paramaribo to summon me from the kitchen. I found it when we were unpacking. Ring if you need me."

Some inconceivable time later as she tossed in bed, Bella heard a knock on the front door. Soon the light on the bedroom ceiling flashed on and the doctor stood over her, peering down her throat, in her eyes and into her ears. Constantly, he asked questions as he thumped his fingers outstretched over her back and stomach. Bella's paper-white face, dry and dehydrated, blended with the pillow.

"From what Shauna has told me," said the doctor, "I believe you are thoroughly exhausted, Mrs. Macdonald, stressed to the breaking point. Your chest is clear for now but the rims of your eyes are very pale. I suspect you're low in iron; eat eggs and liver. I'll listen to your chest again tomorrow. If you don't start immediate bed rest, with your history of lung disorders your tiny lungs may not stay clear." Bella looked away in dismay.

The doctor continued. "Now that it's winter here in the northern states, you're not getting any sunshine. Northerners all take cod liver oil." The doctor finished packing his bag and turned again to Bella.

"Shauna tells me that you don't like milk. The taste of milk has changed since you drank raw milk in England. I will instruct Shauna how to pasteurise and chill it. Drink a glass a day and eat the pudding that she makes for you. I'll bring some cod liver oil. Your children need it too. With your past health problems you must take my advice—bed rest until I say you may get up, and no work until you are thoroughly well again. Goodnight"

Bella's head slumped deeper into the pillow. *The children need a mother even if I never buy a nice house. Please, Lord, save me from pneumonia.*

The next morning the boys went off to school while Bella slept. By ten a.m. she roused and insisted she must phone Fowley's Fashions to explain her absence. For safety, Shauna preceded Bella down the stairs and afterward struggled to drag her mistress up the stairs and back into bed.

"What did Madame LeBeau say, Mrs. McD?"

"She ordered me to return immediately. When I told her that the doctor said working would kill me, her demeanour changed and she said to come back as soon as possible."

***

The day passed with times of worry about missing work and her pay envelope, followed by the sleep of the dead. Bella roused to an unusually quiet house.

"Where are the children, Shauna?" Bella screamed at her closed door. "What have you done with my children?" Shauna came running.

"Peter is learning to bake cookies and Gordon and Stewart are colouring. We are being quiet so you can rest."

"I don't like resting. Hang a calendar by my bed, Shauna. Have I slept all day?"

"Yes, Mrs. McD, you've slept for two days."

The children came to say goodnight. Stewart waved and blew Bella a kiss.

"Don't look so solemn, Peter. Smile for me," said Bella. "I'll be better soon."

Gordon brought his freckled countenance and knot of red hair up close to his mother's pale face resting on the pillow. "I'm whispering, Mother, to show you that I can be quiet. I'm sorry if my noise made you sick."

24

FRUSTRATION

From her bed, Bella heard a shovel scraping on the pavement below.

It must have snowed. Who's clearing my sidewalk? I can't stand being treated like an invalid. Bella clanked the brass bell until Shauna appeared at her bedside.

"Shauna, my wallpaper is driving me to distraction." Bella puckered her eyebrows. "Those disgusting little violets keep changing position. What day is it?"

"November thirtieth. You've been quite ill. Try not to upset yourself, Mrs. McD. The boys and I are fine."

Bella's head flopped back onto the pillow and she lapsed into sleep.

A weak winter sun shone through Bella's window later in the day when Bella rang for Shauna again.

"Shauna, if it is morning, why is the sun shining in my window?"

"You only had a nap, Mrs. McD; it's the afternoon. While you were sleeping the postman brought you a letter from England." Shauna opened the envelope and Bella sat up to read her mail for the first time in many weeks.

"Goodness, Shauna! Flora wants to immigrate to America. She has her passage and will be arriving just before Christmas. Wherever will she sleep?"

"Your illness makes you edgy, Mrs. McD. Don't worry; with the boys using the beds that the Uvaris left, we still have your old cots. She can use one of them."

"I must be up and about when she arrives. There are things to do."

"Say what you will, Mrs. McD, but you are not getting out of bed until the doctor says you can. If you do, you will find that you have no energy. Now settle yourself. The boys and I will manage. Kiss your mother, Stewart, and we'll go and make supper."

***

The following week, the doctor came. Bella objected when he allowed her only two hours a day to be dressed and downstairs with the children for supper.

"Mrs. Macdonald," Dr. Durham implored, "you have very little choice but to do as I say. The weather could freeze your lungs in a moment. Be happy that you are showing signs of improvement. Don't even think of returning to work until the days are warmer. Your health had a complete breakdown and depression loomed. Days passed that you can't even remember. Believe me when I say 'you must rest.' That is what you must do to regain your health. I'll be by in a month."

Again Bella felt the loneliness of her room, the frustration of having so little time with the boys, the disappointment of not completing her apprenticeship on time and the annoyance of the dancing violets. She remembered her childhood and prayed that she had not pushed her body too far. Bella turned on her side and pulled the covers to her chin. A single tear trickled from the corner of her eye, threaded its way across her temple and soaked into her dark hair.

A month! He's not returning for a month—just two hours a day! Mothers are supposed to be strong. I cannot fail my family. Why, a month from now will be Christmas and before that is Stewart's third birthday! Where will I find the money? George's money vanished long ago when I used it for our passage to America, and now William's gift dwindles while I laze around in bed. Donald, where are you when I need you? Bella positioned her head on the pillow to gaze out the window at layers of grey overcast sky. *A colourless sky—why can't the sun cheer me? Where are the stars that Donald followed to guide him in the jungle? Oh Donald, I need you. I feel so detached from my family. I'm failing them.*

Somehow the greyness beyond the windowpane attracted her attention. With clouds so close, she wanted to push them away to see what lay beyond them; she wanted to know if the sun would ever shine again. *Are you pushing the clouds against my window, Donald? Are you telling me that with blind faith things will improve? Dear God, the change must come soon. I have three little boys to protect and nourish.*

When a second tear squeezed from her eye, Aunt Kate's voice from within forced itself to be heard. *While you lie in bed, Bella, you could always make plans for the future.*

"I'll try," Bella mumbled. *What should we get Stuart for his birthday? Perhaps a book for the birthday and a blue wooden truck for Christmas. Shauna could use material for a warm gown, but the two older boys—what will please them at Christmas?*

Bella lay still for a few minutes. Suddenly, she realized that the violets were no longer changing position. Her inner thoughts started again. *I'm feeling more positive. If I can't get out of bed, I must keep my brain active planning for the future.*

***

The following afternoon, with Shauna's help, Bella dressed to be ready for the boys' arrival after school. Later, they cuddled close to her on the blue sofa while she read them a story by Louisa May Alcott entitled *Little Men.*

Peter interrupted. "Nat Blake, the boy in that story, makes music on a violin. What's a violin, Mother?"

Bella recalled the violin played at her wedding and did her best to describe it. She promised that the library could answer his question.

***

When the boys and Bella were tucked into bed, Shauna came to Bella.

"I have a question, Mrs. McD. Why is it that when I go to the boys' room to help Stewart into bed, Gordon's mattress is always propped against the wall?"

For the first time in many weeks, Bella laughed. "They are practicing boxing, Shauna, so they can defend themselves if someone wants to fight at school. Long ago, Peter said he would teach Gordon how to fight when he came from Surinam. I guess he's tired of being Gordon's punching bag." Bella chuckled again and her face lit up. "That's it, a perfect idea. I'll get them each a set of boxing gloves for Christmas."

***

When the doctor came a month later, just a week before Christmas, he allowed Bella to dress for the day and do light work around the house.

"You may not go back to work or walk in the snow or rain," he emphasized.

***

Shauna travelled alone to the docks to meet Flora. Bella kissed her boys goodnight and saw them into bed. She covered herself with an afghan and waited on the sofa for Shauna's return with Flora. *I am so embarrassed that she's found me unwell. What will she think? She mustn't learn of my financial straits. No matter the cost, she is family and welcome.* Then came the bump of a suitcase on the outside landing.

Before Bella could rise, Gordon and Stewart flew from their bedroom and hugged the aunt they knew so well. Peter dutifully pecked her on the cheek.

"Dear Flora, you are welcome to share what we have," said Bella. "You'll sleep on the sofa until you and Shauna can bring a cot from the basement."

***

Flora's trunk arrived the next day. Rather than crowd Shauna, Flora chose to place the cot in the dining room with her things in the Uvaris' sideboard. To look less like a bed in the dining room, she covered the blankets with the afghan, as bright as Jacob's coat of many colours.

***

Just as Stewart's birthday had come and gone, so did the simple Christmas dinner along with Bella's savings—a bit more every day. Sitting around doing very little while winter railed against the windows palled upon Bella's need for activity. Needlework held her interest only a short while. *At least Flora found work as a saleslady in that shoe shop. 1899, a New Year. We must invite the boys next door to come over.*

Doug arrived the next day. "Come and look out the window, Peter."

"A bicycle, Doug? Whose is that?" asked Peter.

"I found my old bike in the barn," said Doug. "It isn't shiny and new, but I serviced it and it works well. I thought it might help when you run errands for your mother and Shauna. Ride it for the sake of speed and wind in your hair, and share it with Gordon." The two boys gave Doug a solid round of hugs.

***

The next week, Bertie came to visit with cookies for Bella's boys. "You're getting around more, Bella. Do ye think ye could make me a gown for May? I must go to my brother's second wedding and I want to look slimmer. I'm thinking if my brother can marry again, then I should be on the lookout for an eligible man at the wedding."

"Perhaps a project is just what I need, Bertie. I'll have Doug and Desmond carry the sewing machine up to my room, where it's warm, and sew a little at a time."

The sewing project kept Bella busy enough to fill her idle time, but Shauna only allowed Bella to work a few hours a day and the work didn't bring in the much needed income. *It's nice to make a few dollars, but it will never replace my investments. I've gained a few pounds. Why doesn't the doctor notice that instead of the weather?* Bella examined her eyes in the mirror. *I do believe my iron is improving; the skin is pink in there. Doctor Durham comes tomorrow. He must release me from this dreadful existence.*

***

257

"You are doing nicely, my dear," said the doctor, "but I said *warm* weather. When the daffodils bloom at Harvard, you may go back to work from ten a.m. until three, with an hour's rest at lunch. Give this note to your employer with my instructions."

Rest where? There's nowhere at Fowley's, unless maybe the hotel foyer at the corner. That means dressing decently—perhaps my old slim green gown. Dear God, it is March. Please help the daffodils pop their heads through the ground soon.

***

In mid-March the daffodils began to display their yellow blossoms in the gardens of Harvard. Bella phoned Fowley's with the good news of her return. She enjoyed the warm sun pouring in the window as the streetcar carried her back to work. Madame LeBeau focused her actions and words towards work without idle chatter. By noon, Bella couldn't wait to lounge on the hotel sofa. By three, she dragged herself onto the streetcar to return home, exhausted.

Why am I so tired? I wonder how long it will take me to do a full day's work. While the streetcar jiggled its way to Harvard Square, Bella tried to figure how long she'd have to work to recoup the income from five months away from work. *What am I thinking? Lost hours, even minutes, can never be recovered. I'll never recover those hours, never have a shop and a house.*

Bella alighted from the car and started the long walk home. *Yes. Why is the word "yes" running through my mind? It must be because I saw those daffodils nodding their heads up and down. Perhaps "yes" means that my dream of owning a shop will remain alive. I will work as much as I can and enjoy the summer with the boys. Perhaps, when my apprenticeship concludes, Madame LeBeau will increase the amount she puts in my pay envelope.*

Bella arrived home before Peter. Next, his friend Tim and then Gordon came tumbling in the door. With Stewart playing at her feet, Peter told about the 99% he received in grammar and how Cassie poured perfume in Gordon's hair. *I wonder if she got a black eye for that. I'll soon know if her mother telephones me to complain.*

"The kids call me Carrots instead of Gordon," came Gordon's claim to fame for the day. "Everyone's got a nickname and I'm the only kid at school with red hair—red the same as Father's, isn't it? *Poor little fellow, he's forgetting his father's thick red hair and mustache. I must hang a tinted picture of him in the hall so they will see him every day.*

Tulips followed the daffodils and then came the lilacs, and on doctor's orders, Bella still worked only four hours a day. On Friday, May 2, Madame LeBeau asked Bella to come to her office before she left at three o'clock. *How strange. What does she want with me that she couldn't say out on the work floor?* Perplexed, Bella collected her coat and went into the manageress's office. She stood in front of Madame's oak desk and waited. In her usual superior manner, Madame LeBeau finally raised her head to address Bella.

"Mrs. Macdonald, I have determined that, in the last six weeks of part time work, you have completed sufficient hours to account for the two weeks of your apprenticeship program that you lacked when you took ill. Here is your diploma as a qualified seamstress." Madame LeBeau then handed Bella a four-by-six-inch rectangle of paper that read:

The State of Massachusetts
On the Recommendation of the Management of Fowley's
Fashions Recognizes

ISABELLA MACDONALD

Qualified Seamstress
Having completed the required apprenticeship program
of two years May 2, 1899

Mr. Quincy Fowley   Madame F. LeBeau
Owner   Manageress

"Thank you, Madame LeBeau. How good of you to follow my progress so completely. This is the best news I've had all wint—"

Madame LeBeau interrupted any further words from Bella.

"Mrs. Macdonald, you must realize that, when you are not at work, I have an idle sewing machine. While you were away, naturally, I enrolled another young woman into the apprenticeship program to work on that machine. In the last six weeks, to have a machine available for you, I kept her busy in the design and cutting rooms, but now I need the sewing machine for her. You are a fine seamstress but you are no longer needed at Fowley's Fashions. Your employment here is terminated as of today. Good afternoon." Madame LeBeau ceased eye contact with Bella to read papers on her desk. Stunned, Bella fell back a step in disbelief. *I have my seamstress qualifications but no work as a seamstress! Where is the pleasure I should feel when I've waited so long for this day? I should be happy but I'm terrified. Who will hire a seamstress for only four hours a day?*

In a daze, Bella reached Boylston Street and Massachusetts Avenue. She climbed aboard the streetcar, sat alone and watched her fingers entwine and release. *I can't start my own shop working just four hours a day and I've used my investment money to live these past months.* Thoughts of doom and bankruptcy raced through Bella's head until she saw the flowers at Harvard Square. *Harvard already? How did the trip home pass so quickly? I must tell Shauna and the boys that I am out of work, but first I think I will sit on the church bench across from Harvard and force myself to enjoy the beauty of spring.*

Sitting allowed Bella's thoughts to spin in circles as she gazed ahead in a blank stare. *The flowers know that the sun will shine tomorrow. God, please let the sun shine on me. As for now, I must recognize the freedom of choice this turn of events gives me. I can spend more time with the boys and use my savings however I wish—or must. Sooner or later, things will improve. And just think, I am free of this dreadful long ride to work. Be happy, Bella. This freedom is your fastest road to health.*

Bella walked the six blocks to Sacramento Street amid the green of grass and trees as if the street had taken on new colour. *I'm going to tell the children and Shauna that we must plant the garden again and be very thrifty about everything. Dear God, help me to be a happy soul with everyone I meet, especially the children. My troubles are not of their making. They must play and be happy. I will worry about work in due course, but tomorrow we'll celebrate Peter's ninth birthday and Gordon's eighth with a*

joint birthday party. Tomorrow it will be me, not Doug, who'll buy the boys'
presents.

Bella mounted the front steps and gaped in awe as the door swished
open to reveal Shauna in her new gown. In response to Shauna's elegance
and happy grin, Bella reached up to give Shauna a hug, and their pleasure
went with them into the house.

"Somehow, Shauna, I feel happier than I have in years, which is
strange because I must tell you that Fowley's fired me today. I have no
job and at this moment I don't care. Just think, tomorrow morning I'll
be free to buy a baseball bat for Peter and a ball for Gordon and wrap
their gifts in bright paper. After cake, I'll go across to the field with my
boys and their friends and learn to play baseball. Oh, yes," added Bella,
holding up a rectangle of paper. "Madame LeBeau presented me with
my Qualified Seamstress ticket just before she let me go."

"It's a bit early, Mrs. McD, but I think we should have stout time
and I will join you with a glass of iced tea to celebrate finishing your
apprenticeship, or losing your job—whichever you wish." Shauna's new
gown swished into the kitchen while Bella laughed at the audacity of
their pleasure.

25

THE FARRAGUT BUILDING

"Shauna," said Bella after she saw Peter and Gordon off to school, "I think Dr. Durham is over-cautious. I will give him two more weeks of not overdoing and then I'll set my own pace. On May twentieth I'll be a middle-aged woman of thirty-six years and not as delicate as he thinks I am."

Shauna continued to clear breakfast dishes from the table as she listened.

"Come in here, Shauna, and sit while I tell you what I have in mind. I need someone to talk to." Shauna returned to the dining room and dutifully took a seat.

"Plainly, I need work," started Bella. "Would you not agree that folks who take the risk of owning their own business make more money than folks who work for someone?" Shauna nodded and Bella continued. "That means that as long as I have faith in my ability to attract customers, I should start my own business. I believe I have a flare for style that will attract customers. I've scrimped until now to keep savings to start a shop, and I believe that day has arrived even though I've used much of the savings. The grapevine can make or break me, but I feel it will work in my favour. I'll ask Flora to work with me and have you at home to run the household. What do you think, Shauna?"

"Mrs. McD, I'm not used to having big thoughts like that. Where would you have the shop?"

"That's my second problem. If I want to appear capable, I must have a shop down by Fowley's Fashions, an upper class area where the customers would expect me to be. My goal is to open a shop by this September. It will take that long to find a shop, advertise and design styles of my own." Shauna listened but did nothing except bob her head for the rest of Bella's ideas.

"Instead of resting these next two weeks, I plan to determine my budget and prices. We'll sell hats too. Ladies might buy hats at first and graduate to buying gowns." She paused. "Perhaps I'll have a cup of tea with a little milk. I'll just sit here quietly, as ordered by the doctor, and work until noon on finances, and then I'll go outside and tend the garden." Bella sat at the Parsons table with a stack of paper. Sometimes she wrote numbers on the white page, sometimes she pulled a fresh page and sketched a gown with a hint of colour from crayons, and sometimes she gazed into space while Shauna moved quietly around, straightening the house with Stewart padding behind her.

"Mrs. McD," asked Shauna one time when Bella looked up as they passed, "if you plan to be in the garden after lunch, could Stewart stay with you? I'd like to visit the streets in town where I've not been."

"Yes, of course, Shauna; you deserve a break. Take the afternoon off. When I finish weeding," said Bella with mischievous eyes, "I'm trotting over to Bertie's to find out if she caught a man at the wedding."

By May, not a weed blemished the rows of vegetables and Bella glowed with a tan unseen since leaving Paramaribo. With Bella attending to scraped knees and torn clothing, her family life bloomed. On her vanity, whether the pages showed new styles, budgets or advertising, the piles of paper grew thicker with each improved plan.

"Dr. Durham has had enough time to cure me, Shauna. Tomorrow I am going down to The Alley and Newbury Street, where Fowley's Fashions flaunts its ads. I'd go today but the school is having their musical program this afternoon. Can you imagine, in three years, I've never attended a concert? You'll come too, won't you?"

***

At two o'clock Bella, Stewart and Shauna left for Agassiz Grammar School. They passed the homes in their row housing, all painted clapboard with various coloured doors.

A woman from the end unit closest to the school descended her front steps, turned ahead of Bella and walked towards the school. Bella hurried to draw near.

"Good afternoon," said Bella, with a courteous tip of her head as she and the lady entered the double school doors together. "My name is Bella Macdonald. I believe you live in the same row of houses as I do." Kathleen Anderson introduced herself and together they climbed the stairs to the assembly room on the second floor and sat in the middle row of chairs set out for the concert. Bella introduced Shauna as her friend from South America, and soon conversation divulged the names of their children. *Cassie? That's the name of Gordon's tormentor. So this is Cassie's mother. She didn't ask about Donald. It seems that the grapevine has established that I am a single mother, but do they know that I am a widow?*

Kathleen called over another neighbour to sit with them, and bit by bit, Bella met several of her neighbours before the concert began.

At two-thirty the students filed into the other end of the room to make a large horseshoe backdrop to outline a stage. The children stood three rows deep, with the youngest grades in the front. A dark-skinned lady stepped forward to address the guests.

"Who's she, Kathleen? I met her two years ago when I enrolled Peter."

"Don't you know?" came the question. "She's Maria Baldwin, our Head Master. She's well known and respected around Cambridge for her work with coloured people."

"Really? I must meet her again," Bella whispered as they were addressed.

"Welcome, parents and friends. Please stand for 'The Star Spangled

Banner.'" The piano sounded a strong introduction, but Bella did not know the words.

Next, the little ones in Grades One and Two stepped forward and sang "Incy Wincy Spider" and "Where is John?" Peter bent his arms and flapped his elbows with great exuberance for the line about the old grey goose, and somehow Cassie managed to stand beside glum-faced Gordon. After this, the middle grades put on a tumbling act and line dancing and the senior students presented their choir. As the harmonic chords faded, everyone clapped and shouted "Bravo! Well Done!" *Peter's face lit up when he sang; I wonder if he likes music.*

That evening, Bella readied her list of interests for her business foray into town the following morning.

***

The streetcar jolted as much as ever. She chose to alight at Boylston Street, the same major intersection where Peter and she stopped for sweaters that fall day when they first arrived. Just as she remembered it from 1896, the meat shop, flower shop, newsstand and the dry goods store still flourished near the Boylston streetcar stop. Bella walked on to Newbury Street. There she entered a fabric shop and bought yardage for three new gowns to be worn in the shop she would open. On all of Newbury Street she couldn't find a single vacant shop to rent. *Too close to Fowley's anyway. I should return to those little shops on Massachusetts Avenue.*

Before she came to the shops she passed a building with a sign announcing the grand opening of Inman's Furniture in August. Out of curiosity, Bella looked upwards to read the name emblazoned on the building's centre stone. "Farragut Building," she read. She noticed that a tobacconist's shop filled a corner suite of the building. *What's that little white sign on the window?* She read: "Tobacconist moved to 132 The Alley." *What? Nobody's renting that shop?*

***

As the streetcar bumped home, Bella's mind weighed many thoughts about her plans for a shop. *The tobacconist's place is small but possibly encompasses all the room I need if we just display hats and cards showing designs for gowns with the fitting room in back. Short store hours would suit my customers and the boys' routines. I'll need a small carriage and horse to carry things to the shop. We have a stable. I wonder if the Farragut Building has stables. Tomorrow, I'll look up the Farragut Building and inquire about that shop. What do you think, Donald? Am I ready to invest in a shop of my own?*

***

Bella swished into the house with a flourish, and for reasons unknown to the boys, hugged each one of them before settling herself in the rocking chair, ready for their evening visit. When Shauna arrived, Bella held up her hand to make an announcement.

"Boys, your mother is ready to start a business. Soon we will have a carriage and horse. We'll have a new dining room table big enough to seat the boys from next door and for cutting fabric for gowns. Just give me a few days and I am sure I will have it all arranged. Now, sit together across from me on the sofa and sing your school songs again for Flora. Stewart, come up here on Mother's lap." *A few days, I said. It'll be more like months, but to catch the Christmas trade I must give myself a deadline of September first and here it is already near the end of June. It is time to put the capital I still have to work. Donald, are you listening to the boys' singing or my thoughts? I know I have less money than I had planned to have, but somehow I'll cut corners and succeed.*

"Lovely, boys. I didn't know you could sing. Do you like singing, Peter?"

"Yes, Mother, but I think I'd like violin-ing better, like the boy in *Little Men*."

"Have you been thinking of that story all this time? Why didn't you tell me?"

"I didn't know until I saw a violin last month in the Harvard museum. The man played it for me and the instrument sang more beautifully than I could ever sing."

"Then you shall have a violin and lessons if that is what you'd like. *I may not have the money, but I must do this while he's young.* "And you, Gordon, would you like to play an instrument?"

"I'd rather play with frogs," came his answer.

***

The next day Bella phoned the office of Mr. Farragut and left a message for him to call her. All week she sewed on her three new gowns, draping the latest materials into fashion statements.

Doug dropped by to invite them to the farm to meet his parents. "My parents want all of you to come for dinner," he told Bella. "Our wagon is big enough for Shauna, Flora and you and me to ride up front while the boys have their first hayride out back."

***

The next Sunday when the wagon reached the farmland outside of Cambridge, the sun shone on green fields, birds sang in the sky and the boys tossed in the hay. When Doug's wagon ceased its rumbling, they beheld a white, boxy two-story farmhouse. The lot, surrounded by a windbreak of ash trees, included a big red barn and a farmyard out behind. In front of the house, on the curved path, stood a handsome carriage. *Other guests must be here.* Doug's parents came out to the wagon to greet them and introductions were made all around.

"Do you like that carriage over there?" asked Doug. "Nice, don't you think?"

Bella stepped over to the carriage. *Not too big, not too small— handsome and light enough for a smaller horse to pull—covered too.* "It's very nice, Doug, black trim on burgundy. Who owns it? Do you have other guests?"

"You can own it if you like, Bella. It's my surprise. It belongs to Father but he has a new carriage and wishes to sell this one. He'll sell the mare for it too, if you're interested."

Immediately, the children were climbing on and in the carriage, while Bella clasped her hands under her chin with delight.

"It's perfect, Doug." Bella turned to Mr. Wray. "If I could drive it with the horse, I would know in a minute what I thought of it. Shauna, too; we are both very capable horsewomen and carriage drivers. What price are you asking?"

"Come in for dinner first and then talk about the carriage," suggested Mrs. Wray. "Men! Always more interested in their horses than mealtime." They entered the house.

"Come, Bella, sit here, and please call us Carrie and Charles."

At a large table next to the kitchen window, the nine of them sat down to a dinner of roast chicken, dressing and garden vegetables in a mix of carrots, beans and peas. In a bowl, steaming gravy waited to be ladled over whipped potatoes.

"Doug, will you ask the blessing, please?" asked his father.

His blessing is not a rhyme or something that comes as repetition day after day. He started out, "Dear God" and then spoke of their friendship with us, the Macdonalds, as if we are a blessing in their lives. Everything he says seems so perfect for one who communes directly with God. It reminds me of Shauna and Dirk's people and their open church beliefs—so much better than the blessings in my church.

"Just a bit of chicken, Charles. I'm not very big, you know," Bella said when Charles started to fill plates with Carrie adding the vegetables at her end of the table.

Conversations jumped from topic to topic so quickly it became a game to follow them during dinner.

"Charles isn't really a farmer, he's a country doctor and Doug plans to follow in his father's footsteps if he doesn't get carried away with yearnings for the wilderness of Canada."

"Pass the gravy, please."

"You're opening a new shop for gowns? I must tell my friends"

"The mare is eight years old."

"You're a seamstress too, are you, Flora?"

"Your rose garden is lovely."

"May I have a drumstick and pick it up in my fingers?"

"The carriage is relatively new, but I need a larger one."

"Doug, your grace made me think of the brethren of Shauna's church in Surinam."

Doug turned to Shauna. "It seems our religions are similar. If you wish, I can pick you up on my way to the meeting next Sunday."

The afternoon allowed the children to see all of the animals and meet the Wrays' farmhand, Jed, who looked after the farming aspect of the property. In front of the barn, a gravelled area formed a working space for hitching the draft horses. Jed brought forth Muffet, their small mare. The children shrieked with pleasure.

"Buy her Mother, buy her. Has she a saddle?" Each boy rode the mare. Then Bella asked Jed for a boost with his cupped hands, threw one leg over the saddle and dashed off on a run up to the house and back again to show Muffet that she was a horse-woman. They harnessed Muffet to the carriage. She flattened her ears when she heard Bella's "Ggk Ggk" but quickly eased to her new driver and pulled the carriage in a lady-like circle around the lot while the family cheered. Charles Wray's generous price suited Bella's limited budget, and after profuse thanks from the children and adults, the family drove home in their new carriage.

***

The following day, Monday, the phone rang. *At last, a call from Mr. Farragut. I'll have to meet him face to face so he recognizes that I am a businesswoman. If he doesn't think women should be in business, then in me he will find a challenge. Rather than have him clean up the shop, I'll talk him into a lower rent. He likely wouldn't have the work done well enough to suit a ladies' gown shop anyway.*

"Yes, Mr. Farragut, 10 a.m. in your office. I will be there."

At 9:55 Bella, dressed in one of her dazzling new gowns, brought her elegant carriage to a halt at the Farragut Building, and despite her wobbly legs, climbed the narrow staircase to the second-floor office.

"Mr. Farragut?" started Bella the moment his secretary opened the man's office door. He nodded. As she stepped farther into the room, her eyes took in the stale cream-painted walls, the disarray of papers on the old desk and the man sitting behind it with a preponderance of flesh above the belt. Without waiting, Bella continued in a pleasant lively voice. "Good morning, Mr. Farragut. I'm Bella Macdonald," and she stepped forward to offer her hand in a most charming-yet-business-like manner.

"Do have a seat, Mrs. Macdonald. You came to talk about the tobacconist's shop. You know it's in a prize location and in demand."

So you say, but if it is in demand why didn't the Furniture Company want it? I shall put it to him. "I'm sure it is, Sir. Shall we go and look at it right now?"

"Perhaps tomorrow, Ma'am. The owner of the shop left things behind and I haven't had them removed yet."

"Really? Is it so bad that a prospective renter couldn't discern the possibilities the area represents? Surely I am capable of making that decision. Let us go down to the shop. I am here now and I may not be here tomorrow."

Slowly, Mr. Farragut rose from his swivel chair with a furrowed brow above his deep-set eyes. He said nothing but led the way to the street entrance of the shop and fitted the brass key into the lock. The stench hit their nostrils.

What was this man selling besides tobacco? It smells like very bad quality stout. Mr. Farragut wouldn't expect me to know about stout, but this stuff would poison a Billy goat. They must have dropped a case of beer and not washed the floor.

"Mr. Farragut, you realize that your renter sold bootleg liquor, do you? You must. That's why you tried to put me off from coming in today. Foul liquid soaked into this floor and is now growing bacteria. Am I right?"

"You have been quicker to determine the problem than me, Mrs. Macdonald. Do you wish to leave now?"

"Certainly not—I haven't seen what's behind this reception area." Bella circled past Mr. Farragut and headed through the doorway at the rear of the room. "Look here; the sewer is stopped up with mould. It will take a great deal to reclaim this place." With no words coming from the owner, Bella headed for the back door, motioned for Mr. Farragut to open it with his key and stepped into the back lane. Immediately two figures appeared, as if from nowhere, looking to make a quick purchase.

"How long have you known that the tobacconist had a second business?" Mr. Farragut shrugged his shoulders. "Now, Sir, I wish to go back to your office."

Purposefully, Bella followed without conversation until Mr. Farragut sat in his chair. She stood at the edge of his desk, her eyes even with Mr. Farragut's eyes.

"That shop is a disgrace, Sir, and you have let it get worse by inattention. How do you intend to clean the tobacco stench and bacterial growth out of there?"

"You were the one who wanted to see it," came his contrary reply.

"That does not answer my question." Using her soft sweet voice in contrast to the stronger direct way she had started, Bella asked, "If I had come tomorrow as you suggested, would it have been clean?" The man shook his head as if baffled by this little bit of dynamite holding him pinned like a fly to flypaper.

"What is it you want of me, Mrs. Macdonald?"

Bella changed the subject. "I want to know where you stable your horse and carriage in the winter. It must be an indoor area big enough for that black and burgundy carriage that you saw at the curb before entering the shop."

"You drove the carriage here alone?"

Bella smiled and continued to charm the man with her voice and intense green eyes. "Yes, I am a proficient driver and attend my own horse. If one is to be in business, one must be self-reliant."

"Right. Then a stall will be provided, but I doubt that you want the shop."

"Quite the opposite, Mr. Farragut. I want the months of July and August rent free during restoration. For half the rent you mentioned on the phone, I will take the shop starting September first for a two-year lease, damned as it is with its disgusting stench. For this rent, including the stable, I will be responsible for returning it to respectability." *Look at his eyes pop out with pleasure. I do believe he has no idea how to clean the place and thinks I am out of my mind. His greed makes him think that two years of half rent is a bargain while I fight with the mould.* By the time Bella finished her dealings with Mr. Farragut and held the key in her hand, only one hour had passed.

***

Bella drove the carriage to the docks and looked for a Dutch steamship. *The Van der Veldt*, she spied. *That might do.* She mounted the gangplank and shouted a cheery "Halo!" and in Dutch called out, "I would like a word with the man on watch." A rough sea dog climbed down from the aft deck and melted in front of the beautiful diminutive woman who had dared to come aboard the domain of a man's world.

"May I help you?" he said politely in Dutch, with a demeanor scarcely remembered from his days as a youth. Bella continued in the language of the ship's crew.

"Do you use steam from your boiler to clean the engine room?" asked Bella. "I would like to take steam to a foul smelling room and need to know how that would best be done." The seaman told her the name of the officer to see at the Boston Naval Shipyards and pointed out the direction to go. *I imagine he thinks I'm crazy and in need of humouring. It's noon; I wonder how long it will take me to follow that fellow's route in this heavy traffic?*

***

Later that day, Bella directed Muffet into her paddock, removed her harness and rubbed her down. Shauna met Bella as she entered the back door.

"You've been gone the whole day, Mrs. McD. What have you been up to? I see that old twinkle in your eyes."

"I have rented a filthy, ideal shop—ideal because of its location and filthy because the former renter sold tobacco and bootleg liquor. Tomorrow two workers from the naval shipyards will rip off the cupboards and steam-clean the shop from its front threshold to its back door, from its front window to the drunks hanging around in the alley." Bella washed her hands at the bathroom sink while she continued her story. "The place stinks of old beer and bacteria, but the brick walls and tin ceiling will peel clean under high-pressure steam. They promised to steam the floorboards until they turn white. Tonight I will dream about the best way to decorate when the steamed interior has completely dried." *And tomorrow I will determine if I have overstepped my budget.*

"Now I'll tell the boys my good news."

26

HOPE, FAITH
AND CHARITY

"Tim," said Bella to Peter's friend, "do your parents know of a violin teacher?"

"I'll ask my mom, Mrs. Macdonald. She knows about things like that from her bridge group. The bridge club ladies know everything. They knew that Peter's father died of yellow fever even before Peter told me." *That's nice they know I'm not a divorcee. I'm short of money for lessons, but I promised Peter, so I must try.*

***

Again Bella went to the Naval Yards in search of two workers in need of extra cash—workers who knew how to paint the hulls of ships. She found two fellows willing to do the job she had in mind and made plans to meet them the next day at eight in the morning, 124 Massachusetts Avenue. Next, she went down the street from her shop to the hardware store and bought gallons of white oil-based paint, wide brushes, turpentine and a tall ladder. The hardware clerk carried her purchases to her shop. *That's good enough for tonight. Now back home to continue planning for tomorrow.*

***

At seven-thirty a.m., Bella headed down to her shop with a pail, a quantity of rags, a variety of tools, three glasses, a gallon jug of water and two baseball-sized rocks. The early August morning glowed with promise. Traffic snarled some intersections but soon Bella's carriage stood in front of her shop.

"Hello, Patrick and Sancho; you're right on time. I want you to start at the ceiling and paint every square inch of this place with white paint. I believe the combination of the steam cleaning, paint and linoleum glue will cure the shop of any previous odours. There's a pail for turpentine, two rocks to prop the doors open and water if you get thirsty. If the paint odour gets too strong, go outside and fan the doors."

After a little more chatter, Bella left the men to their painting and drove to the *Cambridge Chronicle* to place an ad in the paper with the intention to sell the cupboards that the steamers had ripped off the walls. *The cash might buy the paint, and a buyer will furnish a means to be rid of the unwanted cupboards. It is getting close to noon and those men will be hungry.* At a delicatessen she made up a box with four large buns, a pound of sliced meat, a chunk of cheese, two apples and a large slab of cake. She returned to her shop to find one man perched on the ladder painting the tin ceiling and the other one working along the bottom level of the brick walls.

"The work is going well, men. I think you should go outside and get some fresh air. Here's a box of lunch."

"Thanks, Mrs. Macdonald," said Patrick. "We didn't expect this. You know, Ma'am, everybody down at the port knows how you stuck up for that Dutch-German cook. Did you really quit to help him?" Bella nodded. "That judge is easier to get along with now." Patrick stood wagging his head in disbelief that this bit of a woman could cause such a change at the courthouse. "Come on, Sancho; let's go over to the park."

"Gracias, Senora."

"De nada," Bella answered with two of her few Spanish words.

While the men ate lunch, Bella determined the areas of the floor and walls for the entire shop. When the men returned, she left for a linoleum shop to choose a new floor covering for the day when the painters were through.

Much like she had done to christen Candlewick with its name, Bella made a forest green sign with white old English lettering to spell "Gowns." She ordered two new electric sewing machines, a stand-alone full-length mirror and two standing dress forms.

God, I'm tired. Is it blasphemous, God, to use your name as I just did? I suppose it is. Instead, I will say thank you God for providing Sunday as a day of rest. I will follow that practice as you have ordained. Tomorrow I will relax and play with the boys.

***

"Mrs. McD, I'm going to church again with Doug and his parents. Do you and the boys want to come? I'm sure you'd like the service. It starts at ten, then there's lunch and Bible reading for the adults while the children attend Sunday School. That might be enough time spent there for the boys, but there's an evening service after tea."

"I think I'd like that, Shauna, but I'll take my own carriage."

It's time the boys included God in their schooling, and sitting quietly in the presence of the Lord, for me, will be peaceful after the hectic days I've been living.

***

The Meeting Room held no décor except for the rows of pews facing an oak pulpit and an upright piano. With the assembled members, Bella prayed, listened to the gospel and sang hymns while the boys sat stoically beside her. A carved wooden bowl came to the boys, passed hand-to-hand down each row of people. Bella retrieved it from her sons, put in some coins, then passed it to the man next to her.

Stewart nudged Peter in the ribs and opened his fat little fist. "I got two monies; how many did you get?"

"Shh, children. No talking. We must stand now for the offering."

When the protective cloths were lifted from a table at the back of the room, potato salad, coleslaw, sliced turkey and sliced tomatoes appeared. Folks filled their plates and walked outside to sit on the grass surrounding the meeting hall.

"Such a lovely service, Carrie," said Bella to Mrs. Wray when Doug's family joined them. "I'm glad Shauna asked us to come."

"Charles and I always like to come in the summer when the weather is warm like this," said Carrie. "Have you heard that Doug will be leaving for Chicago to do his medical internship? We'll be sorry to lose him, but we always knew he would go his own way sooner or later." As if in response, Doug angled his head and lifted one shoulder.

***

"Hot or iced tea, Mrs. McD?' said Shauna another Sunday when they relaxed after pulling carrots. Either suited Bella, so iced tea arrived with cookies.

"Oh, my! That ice hurts my teeth," said Bella. "Now, I wonder why that is? Mind you, I haven't been to a dentist for some years. I wonder if Dr. Wray can suggest one. I'll have to go to one if that pain comes again."

While relaxing in the sun, Bella produced a pad of paper and a pencil.

"Shauna, help me list twenty neighbours' names. I plan to invite them to tea at the opening of my shop. Carrie Wray said she would invite her country friends to come, so that could be the next day, and Tim said his mother's bridge club would come. That makes three opening day teas. But how will I make tea without a stove? Yes, of course, we'll have iced tea and take it to the shop in the preserving kettle." Although questions were being asked, Bella answered them all herself and Shauna just listened.

"I want the whole family to enjoy the grand opening. The boys will not be in school, so they can serve the cookies and napkins." Bella pushed aside the paper.

"Come, Stewart, take Mother's hand and we'll walk to the school yard for a swing and call the boys while Shauna makes supper."

Only two weeks before September first—I wonder if I'll have the shop ready in time. Flora and I have painted the walls in the main room, but the flooring company laid the linoleum a week late and that put other things behind. I'll ask the boys next door to take the old Parsons table down to the shop. We don't need it here with the new dining room table, and it will make an elegant display table to hold my design cards and hats.

"Climb up on the swing, Stewart, and hang on tight while Mother pushes you high as the sky."

***

"Dinner time, boys, let's go home," Bella called across to Peter, Gordon and their friends. Bella saw some new faces in the group and met Geoff, Will, and Tom, all professors' sons. "Gordon, please catch up," Bella called back. "We're leaving now. Peter, who is Gordon walking with? They are just ambling along."

"That's Cassie. She cut her own hair and her mother covered it with a hat."

***

"Hello, Charles," said Bella on the phone the next day. "It's Bella. Could you suggest a good dentist? Both hot and cold hurt my teeth. What would you suggest I do?"

"Harvard's chief faculty is medicine, Bella. We have excellent dentists right here in Cambridge. I'll set up an appointment for you tomorrow, if you wish."

***

When the dentist heard about my history of rickets, he wagged his head. Now he says my lack of calcium all those early years has left me with very little enamel and strength to any of my teeth. Just the way he keeps peering into my mouth with that bright light makes me fearful. Why is he hammering each tooth with a mallet? Every tap hurts!

"Mrs. Macdonald, you have a serious problem. My recommendation is to have all of your teeth pulled, one by one, before they decay. If you wait, the gums will fill with poison and drag down your health. I suggest the sooner the better."

"Can't they wait until after Christmas? I'm about to open a new shop for fashionable gowns. I need the orders to reconcile the money I've invested."

"Very well, but you will have to put up with that aching tooth. It is a front tooth that's giving the pain. To pull it would be most obvious. If you stay away from hot and cold foods, perhaps you can wait until January, but then you must attend to them. If you have more pain, come immediately despite your concerns for the shop."

***

Luke warm tea and porridge started Bella's Saturday. After breakfast, with the boys romping beside her, they delivered the neighbourhood invitations for her grand opening. Shauna sensed something troubled Mrs. McD when she allowed her macaroni and cheese to cool at lunch. During the day, Tim took home sixteen invitations for his mother to give to the ladies of the bridge club. Doug and Desmond came to carry away the Parsons table and return with a new sewing machine. Bella gave Doug the invitations for his mother to distribute. After visiting with the family for an hour, Doug announced that he must say goodbye; Chicago awaited him. The children protested and clung to him.

"Enjoy Chicago," said Bella at the front door. "Look to the future and send me your address every time you move." She reached up and kissed the two boys goodbye. Squeals of goodbye resounded until Doug's carriage rounded the corner.

"Mrs. McD," Shauna started, as soon as the fellows left. "You let your stout get warm before you drank it. Your teeth are bothering you, aren't they? Don't damage your health by not attending to them. The shop could have opened next week."

"Shauna, my sweet Shauna. Yes, my teeth ache, but the opening couldn't wait. I saw the dentist and I must have them all removed, so I am trying to hold on until after the Christmas rush for gowns. I must generate income by opening now to pay my bills. Don't worry, the doctor has given me some Aspirin powder to take if the teeth ache too much."

***

On August thirtieth, a Wednesday evening, at supper, Bella invited the whole family to see the new shop that Flora and she had finished painting and decorating. With ceremony, Bella turned the brass key and in they trooped.

"White, burgundy and pale green—Donald's favourite colours among my gowns," said Bella. "I accepted his good judgement and surrounded myself with those colours."

"Oh Mrs. McD, it's beautiful! You told me this place reeked with bacteria and rotten beer! How did you produce such a lovely shop in six weeks?"

"With money and hard work, Shauna. Walk around and see everything."

Stewart wanted to know why the dressed-up dead lady in the window had a scarf on the stump of her neck instead of a head. Shauna ran her hand over the polished finish of the Parsons table that had come all the way from Candlewick. And there in the corner, she saw three of the old Bentwood chairs at a small table for business. Gordon and Peter made faces in the full-length mirror. Through the door they went to the fitting room as Bella turned on the lights, and on into the back room. Here they saw trays set with glasses for iced tea and twenty folding chairs ready for the next day. Under a bright light, on the inside wall the new sewing machine, with another Bentwood chair, looked ready for use.

"Tomorrow," Bella announced, "we'll celebrate our first Grand Opening, and I hope everyone goes home with plans to return and order a gown."

The next day, September first, Bella mixed a small dose of Aspirin powder with water, swallowed the bitter dose of painkiller and dressed for the first Grand Opening.

***

While Bella greeted the neighbours, Shauna ladled and Flora served iced tea. Gordon, with help and interference from Stewart, passed napkins, and Peter followed with the cookies. The two older boys remembered having guests at Candlewick and rose to the occasion as if being with ladies happened every day. The family followed the same plan for the second and third days of the openings, with every chair filled. The guests oohed and awed over every aspect of the shop and vowed to return closer to Christmas.

After three days of openings and liberal use of Aspirin powder, Bella felt the stress and symptoms of too much painkiller. She dragged herself to the breakfast table.

"Shauna, I'm so tired—will you drive me to the shop at ten and return for me at two so I don't have to fuss with Muffet in the stable? I must be there in case anyone comes to order a gown." Bella crossed her arms on the table in time to catch her head as it flopped forward. She brought it up again and asked, "Will you, Shauna? Will you take me down? I might have customers."

"Nonsense, Bella," said Flora. "Will you never slow down and accept a little help? You look so peaked. Let me go to the shop today and you stay here and rest. If folks come in, I'll have them call you on the telephone."

"I agree," said Shauna. "Your teeth are troubling you and you're not willing to concede one moment towards their care. Peter is at his violin lesson, Gordon is over at Cassie's and Stewart can come for the ride while I drop Flora at the shop. I'll even give her a lesson in driving the carriage. Rest on the sofa, Mrs. McD; that is what you must do."

Resigned to her weary state, Bella flopped onto the sofa. "I must admit my teeth are bothering me, but we must not lose any sales."

"Whether I sell any gowns or not, Bella," said Flora, "doesn't change the fact that today you must rest. The poison from your teeth is making you tired."

***

Two weeks after the shop opened, with Bella in attendance most days, she had five orders for gowns. Missing some back teeth and relying heavily on the doctor's Aspirin powder, Bella forced herself to visit exclusive material shops for fine Egyptian cottons, Persian linens, British woolens and silks from the Orient, according to the desires of her customers. She sat late at night tweaking each gown design to suit individual customers so that no two gowns would be the same.

***

"That front tooth is spreading too much poison, Mrs. Macdonald. The rest of your teeth must come out now!" said the dentist. Without teeth, to stop the bleeding Bella sucked on ice while she worked at home making the pattern pieces from which to cut the material. With Shauna's help to lift the bolts of cloth, and doses of Aspirin powder, Bella cut out the gowns. Flora sewed the pieces together and left the special sewing for Bella. *Will my jaws never heal? With poisons from the dentistry surging through my body, I can hardly focus on what I'm doing. Bills keep coming. Why is it so hot in here? I'm so tired.*

"Mrs. McD!"

Is that Shauna's voice?

"Mrs. McD, wake up!" cried Shauna. "Flora, come! I think Mrs. McD has fainted at the cutting table with her head on her arms." They worked to rouse her.

"Shauna? Is that you calling me?" said Bella's weak voice. Shauna helped Bella onto the sofa and ordered her to stay there until she could do without Aspirin powder.

Dear Shauna, she still wants to be my mama. Without the understanding and the charitable attitude of my customers, my business would be in ruins. Oh why didn't I drink my milk? Focus, Bella. Forget Sadie's milk. Bella fell behind in finishing the gowns as quickly as she had hoped, but she made enough money to pay the rent and fabric shops.

By November many more gowns were ordered for Christmas. Bella insisted on sewing late into the night, despite having a head that felt like a rotten pumpkin. Flora, under direction from Bella, improved her sewing skills. Business started to turn around about the same time as Bella's jaws began to heal.

On Christmas Eve Bella laid in bed looking at the stars through her window. Downstairs, ready for Christmas morning under the tree, she had a violin for Peter, a bicycle for Gordon and a tricycle for Stewart. Shauna and Flora chose material. *Good night, God. We'll have Christmas, even if I am in debt.*

Unable to fall asleep, Bella's thoughts turned to her beloved.

Donald, my darling, with my hope for success and faith that the sun will rise every morning, as you taught me, I believe my shop will succeed. The charity of my customers and my helpers, Flora and Shauna, including the goodness of your sons, has allowed me to weather the first few hectic months of business, although I would rather have accomplished this without need of a dentist. Good night, my dearest. Yes, I'm taking my cod liver oil, now let me go to sleep. I'll smile for you in three days when I receive my new dentures.

27

THE NEW CENTURY 1901

Sitting in the rocking chair following a year of successful business at her shop, Bella caressed the bottom of her stout glass and thought of all the trials and tribulations that had befallen the family since Donald's passing. *It's just six years ago that the bubble burst in my world. It's 1901. How did the years go by so quickly and where did 1900 go? Now, for the first time in America, we've had a year of peaceful existence and I have enough customers to pay the bills. Peter's eleven and as tall as me. He's happy practicing his violin and sketching pictures. Gordon won't pay attention to music, yet he'll work at anything that makes money. And then there's Stewart—I finally managed to enroll one of my sons on his first day of school.* Bella sipped her stout and rocked, totally pleased with her world.

Shauna is twenty-nine and runs the house better than I might. Flora must be thirty-four and still sleeps on the cot in the dining room. All things of the past have sorted themselves out. Donald, are you visiting with me? Your boys have grown up without servants and know how to take on jobs like gardening, shovelling snow and care of the horse and carriage. Are you proud of them? Be sure to come to the school's Christmas concert tonight. The boys have already gone on ahead and it seems strange to sit here rocking on my own, just reminiscing.

Knock, knock. *A knock on the front door—who can that be so late in the day? I'll go and see; Shauna's busy in the kitchen.*

Upon opening the door, a middle-aged man said, "Mrs. Macdonald, I presume. I am Ivan Jenkins with the Cambridge Real Estate Company. I have a letter from Mr. Uvari. He states that he wrote to you too. At any rate, he wants to sell his property—wants me to put this house on the market January 1, 1902, unless of course, you would like to buy it before that date."

"Mr. Jenkins, do step in," said Bella, displaying a bulldog-like countenance. "I've had no letter from the Uvaris. Can't this wait until after Christmas? If I am to receive a letter, it is incumbent on your company to wait until my letter arrives. I will be in touch before January first. Thank you for coming, and good day, Sir." Bella's words were quite plain and Ivan Jenkins retreated.

As Bella's hand lifted from the edge of the door, her brain fluxed with a torrent of thoughts. *I don't want to move. With it being only midyear at Harvard, there won't be any houses on the market except the cheaper ones near the industrial zone. I don't want to live there. Am I telling myself to buy this house? Does that mean another bank loan or mortgage when I felt so smug just a few minutes ago? Dear Donald, you don't have to help me on this question. Whether I want to or not, I must go to the bank tomorrow and see if I have enough credit to buy this house—in debt again.*

Bella, back in the rocking chair, rocked rhythmically—back and forth, back and forth—thinking over her new problem. Suddenly, she stood with a scowl of determination. *I refuse to have Ivan Jenkins spoil the holidays for my family. Christmas comes first!* And she stormed upstairs to get dressed for the school Christmas concert.

***

With Flora and Shauna, Bella called on Kathleen and Jack Anderson on their way to the concert. Up the stairs, the two families climbed to the assembly room on the second floor. Soon Bertie joined them.

"I may not have children in school, Bella" said Bertie, "but I had to come and hear Peter play his solo." Bella leaned towards Bertie to be sure of what she'd heard. Bertie's eyes opened wide and her mouth popped open. "Oh dear," she wailed, "I've let out Peter's secret! I talk too much. He's been practicing at my house." A hush came over the audience when the principal, Miss Baldwin, walked to the centre of the stage.

"Welcome, parents and friends. Tonight the children will sing Christmas music. Please join in after we have heard each class perform their number."

The older children stood back and the little ones parted to allow a boy to place a baby doll in a small manger before them. A girl knelt beside the manger and the boy, gazing down at the baby, stood opposite her. "Why, that's Stewart," Bella whispered to Shauna. "Silent night, holy night," came from the young voices. *How did he keep that a secret?* The manger disappeared and the grade four students came forth to dance old-fashioned dances. *Gordon's still dancing with Cassie, and look at them grin this year!*

"Grade Five offers us two solos before the children sing," announced Maria Baldwin. Sadie O'Flaherty played "Jingle Bells," everybody sang, and then Peter stepped forward with his violin. His eyes flashed over the audience. A big grin spread across his face as his eyes made contact with his mother smiling at him in sheer pleasure. The principal announced his name and Peter nodded to the pianist to begin the introduction. In long, strong strokes, the melody of "Lo, How a Rose E'er Blooming" floated over the room. Next, the Grade Five students sang with Peter playing. The third time, the Grade Sixes joined in with harmony. Everyone clapped. Peter bowed and slipped into a group of classmates. The senior choir led the audience with several carols. The evening closed with "Joy to the World," and the families passed through the doorway into a crisp winter's evening resplendent with stars.

The next day meant work for Bella and Flora with Christmas gowns to finish. From the kitchen table, Bella picked up the box lunch meant for the two of them, joined Flora at Muffet's enclosure and off they went to the shop. Bella's mind still whirled with Ivan Jenkins' revelation that the Uvaris wanted to sell the house.

Sacramento Street is a good place to live and the house is sound, but I hardly have years of experience behind my gown shop to prove how much I can pay on a mortgage. My heart says to buy the place no matter the cost, but my mind won't settle on a decision. Yes, I must see my banker today.

"You're very quiet, Bella," said Flora as she reined in Muffet at the Farragut stall.

"I suppose I am, Flora," said Bella. "Please mind the shop for a bit. Something has come up and I must walk over to the bank."

***

Bella sat opposite the bank manager with her account books on his desk. "Mr. Stallworthy, you asked me how I know that my shop will make the same amount of money next year. Well, Sir, I do not possess a crystal ball, so I don't know the answer to your question. However, if you look at my accounts you will see that, whether just before Christmas or springtime or in the off seasons, my clientele has risen steadily despite raising my prices." The banker flipped pages in Bella's books and muttered to himself.

He raised his head, and said: "Mrs. Macdonald, for mortgages, banks use a percentage table to determine the maximum you should be paying for shelter."

"Does that mean you are denying me a mortgage, Sir, or do you plan to offer me one?" Bella's quick cut to the question at hand without lady-like conversation made the banker lose eye contact with Bella. Finally, he lifted his gaze again.

"You are quite the business woman, Mrs. Macdonald, coming in here with your accounts and a determination not often found in ladies—hmff, hmff," he cleared his throat. "That is to say—hmff, hmff—what am I supposed to say? I've never dealt with a woman before. You do not fit bank requirements, yet you expect me to say yes." Mr. Stallworthy shuffled papers once more. Bella said nothing. Seconds passed. Finally, Mr. Stallworthy sat back in his chair, exasperation written across his face. "You may have the mortgage, but it might mean a tight reign on your household expenses to meet the payment every month. If you miss a payment, the bank will repossess the house. Is that clear? My bank superior will condemn my judgement if this mortgage goes sour."

"I have every confidence that my business will be more successful with each passing month, Mr. Stallworthy," said Bella. "I'll return when Mr. Jenkins and I have settled on the price of the property."

"Yes, yes, quite so," said the banker. "Good day, Mrs. Macdonald."

"And good day to you, Sir."

***

When Bella returned from the bank, she sewed industriously and allowed no time for conversation. *There's nothing for it but to wait for Mr. Uvari's letter. Ivan Jenkins can wait. I shan't tell anyone about this until after the holidays. Can you imagine bringing on this sort of business at Christmas? Flora is turning out the lights and coming with my coat! It's time to go home. I must put a smile on my face and think "Christmas!"*

"What would you like for Christmas, Flora? I've decided that I want a photograph of the three boys and me tinted professionally to hang in my room, and I'll send small copies to Aunt Kate and our sisters back in Plymouth."

"I'm not sure, Bella, but perhaps I'd like a new pair of daring shoes with pointed toes and higher heels. Even if I shop for it, the children will think the gift is a surprise."

"Peter needs a bicycle with a sprocket that works," said Bella, thinking out loud. "Gordon might like a fishing pole or a basket for his bike and Stewart might do well with a Meccano set or tools to take things apart, like Doug Wray's old bike."

"A fashionable hat, made right in the shop, would please Shauna," said Flora.

"And a basket of baking would be best for the boys next door," added Bella. "I plan to do everything possible to make this a grand Christmas."

***

"Family and friends," Bella started with her hand raised on high. "Tonight, as we bring in the New Year of 1902, 49½ Sacramento Street, Cambridge, belongs to the Macdonalds. I have just concluded the purchase contract with the former owners, Mr. and Mrs. Uvari, who are now successfully homesteading in Wyoming. This house is ours!" For an instant the room swayed in silence, then great commotion broke out with everybody hugging everybody.

"Does that mean we keep the furniture they left behind, Mother?" asked Peter.

"Yes, every stick of it, Peter, and you three will each keep your feather tickings."

Donald, I have a house! Thank you, Lord.

***

While riding his bicycle down Oxford Street to his violin lessons in the spring of 1902, Peter noted the daffodils blooming, the trees budding and the grass turning a brighter shade of green. The trip took him past the Harvard Museum of Natural History, where he often dropped in to look at the museum's collection of glass flowers.

"Mother," said Peter after one of his Tuesday trips. "You must come and meet my friend Leopold Blaschka. He is a glass blower from Bohemia who creates beautiful glass flowers. He's blown hundreds of perfect replicas of flowers that you would know and zillions of plants we've never heard of. Say you'll come next Tuesday on your way home from the shop. I'll be there after my lesson."

"I'll do that, Peter. I've often heard of the glass flowers, and now with the shop running so well, it's time I met your Mr. Blaschka. How nice of you to suggest I come.

"Gordon, what did you do today?"

"Geoff and I fished from some fellow's dock down by the Charles River, but the man chased us away before we caught anything. He kept saying we might fall in and the river's too high right now with spring run-off, so when's a guy s'posed ta fish?"

"Now, Gordon, we don't say 'guy,' or 's'posed ta.' In our family you will speak proper English. Try, 'When is a fellow supposed to fish?' Perhaps we can invite your friend Geoff out to the Wray farm next week on Saturday afternoon and you two can fish on their creek.

"Now it's your turn, Stewart. What is that you have in your hand?"

"It's your alarm clock, Mother." Stewart smiled the smile of accomplishment. "Today I took it apart and put it together again. See? The hands still go around."

"So I see, Stewart. Do you think it will wake us in time for church tomorrow?" Stewart grinned, Flora chuckled and Shauna served dinner.

***

"Welcome to our meeting, my brothers and sisters," said one of the men. "Shall we all bow our heads to give thanks to God for bringing us together in worship on this lovely spring morning?" More people spoke or read the Bible. Hymns were sung, and finally, lunch served out on the lawn came as a blessed relief for the boys.

"It's hot out here," said Stewart after a bit. "I'm going back into the Meeting House." His two brothers followed. "Let's see what's at the front of the room," said Stewart, skipping ahead. "I've never been up there." The boys followed Stewart down the centre aisle and found a chair, a lectern and a fancy basin with a lid. Gordon lifted the lid and found the basin full of water.

"Look," said Stewart. "I've found somebody's rubbers under this chair. I bet they'd float if we put just the soles on that water."

"Yup, they float," said Peter, "but I don't think that's what that dish is for."

"Boys!" came a shout at the door. "What are you doing with the baptismal font?" The boys saw a man striding down upon them. Quietly, they slipped the lid back on the bowl.

"Just looking at the Meeting House, Sir," Gordon spoke up politely. "We're here because we've never seen what it's like at this end of the room. Now that we've seen it, I suppose it's time for Sunday School. Let's go, fellows." As they left the room, Gordon said to Peter, "Mother should have heard me—I said 'suppose' and 'fellows' correctly."

***

With giving riding lessons on Muffet to the boys, the gardening and keeping score for the boys' baseball games, summer weekends came and went quickly. Bella's business flourished just enough to pay the high mortgage payments with little left over.

***

"Mrs. Macdonald," she was greeted by Derek from next door one summer morning. "The boys like baseball so much. May I take them down to see the Boston Americans play tomorrow? See, here in the newspaper it says they're playing on Saturday."

"How much does it cost?" asked Bella, fearing that the price of entrance might make the outing too expensive for her tight budget.

"Just the price of streetcar fares," Derek answered. "This isn't major league ball. The major leagues wouldn't recognize the teams that didn't have stadiums, so the teams left out of the National League formed the American League. The game is at the Huntington Avenue Grounds. The Grounds form a big play area and we sit on the grass in the outskirts of the ball diamond behind the fielders. Here, read my newspaper, it tells all about it in the Sports Section. I know how to get there."

"Please, can we go?" begged Peter. "Gordon and I will stick right close to Derek and not get lost, honest." *The boys are getting older and bound to venture farther afield. I should be glad that Derek will take them. I'll send them off with apples and cookies.*

***

Flora and Bella walked from Farragut's stable to the back door of Bella's shop.

"Flora, how can we increase the number of gowns and hats that we sell? We have times of the year that are slow, and with that big mortgage payment for the house I just never seem to keep ahead of the bills." Flora stopped in stride and gaped at Bella. "Yes, that's right," said Bella. "I borrowed money from the bank to buy the house. The Uvaris would have sold it out from under us. We would have been out on the street . . . but enough of that. I know the boys go down to the Charles River. They can't swim and I can't afford swimming lessons. How can I increase profits?"

"You're not losing money, Bella. Why change anything?"

I suppose she's right. Thank goodness Muffet can still pull the carriage. I haven't any money to cover a problem for her or the carriage. Times are tight all over the city. Like Flora says, have faith that the Christmas rush will solve any shortage of income.

28

RAISING BOYS

"Mother, have you seen those fancy new dormitories built for rich students?" Peter asked at their evening meal. "I've seen one of their clubs down on Holyoak St. It's called Hasty Pudding. Some name!"

"What about Claverly Hall?" cried Gordon.

"Is that one of those expensive residences on the Gold Coast?" asked Bella. "Folks call it that because you need a gold mine to afford living there."

"Really?" said Gordon. "Geoff's father is a professor with students living at Claverly Hall and they invited Geoff and his father to swim in Claverly's private pool. His father said he'd teach Geoff and the three of us to swim and it wouldn't cost anything. He wants us to know how to swim before we drown ourselves fishing in the Charles River. Can we go, Mother?"

"If you keep high grades," answered Bella, "of course you may learn to swim."

"Mother, after my violin lesson, I visited with Mr. Blaschka at his glass flowers museum and met Mr. Eliot, the President of Harvard. We talked about Gore Hall, the big library where I borrow books. He smiled when I said that I liked books."

***

"Shauna," said Bella after supper, "what is that racket in the basement?"

"Peter and Gordon are practicing wrestling," answered Shauna. "They want to build muscles. Gordon has a book upstairs about the Young Men's Christian Association of Boston. The book advocates that physical ability improves the mind and the understanding of religion. He told me that strength will either make him smarter than Peter at school or the religion part will make church less boring."

My poor boys, they really do need a man around. I must ask Derek over more often and suggest that he bring his friends now that they are returning from the Christmas holidays. I had little money to spend on Christmas, yet I should be able to afford having those boys over for dinner now and then. I'm sure 1903 will be a better year, despite the mortgage payments. Donald, are you with me? This is not the way I planned to have a business and a home—by being short of money all the time—but then again, these things don't happen overnight. Please save me from more problems, and God, please inspire more customers to come my way.

***

After the holidays one evening, Bella sat deep in thought.

Orders for gowns are slow. With spring coming there should be some way I can reach more customers. Flora wasn't right to suggest things were fine last fall. I know! I'll speak to some of my better customers about having a fashion show. Bella thought for a moment, then wrote down "Carrie Wray, Catherine Anderson, Bertie O'Grady, Flora and Shauna." *Perhaps Catherine, Carrie and Bertie each have a friend, which would make eight models. I'll offer to make them two outfits with the labour on the second outfit free if they will model their gowns in front of invited guests. I must find a hall with distinction.*

"Flora, Shauna, if I have a fashion show will you two model for me? I'll buy the material for two dresses each and you can sew them. What do you think?"

"Bella!" said Flora, "where do you get your ideas? I keep learning more and more from you."

***

"Good afternoon, Mr. Elliot." Bella smiled. "How nice of you to see me."

"Hello, Mrs. Macdonald. I believe I met your boy the other day—smart young man. Your note says you need a hall to entertain the professors' wives. That can be arranged. Just use Harvard's address. The mail room will sort them." *Hurrah, the finest room at Harvard and rent-free! Now I must visit the eight women.*

***

Three days later, Bella told Flora that the ladies had agreed to her plan.

"I'll be gone this afternoon, Flora," said Bella. "I want to visit the fabric shops to see what fabrics and colours will be fashionable this spring. I'll pick you up at closing time." *Once I see what the designers are showing for 1903, I can buy yardage for the gowns.*

Hmmm, I didn't realize Muffet is slowing down. I must drive her more often.

***

Good afternoon, ladies," Bella addressed the women assembled before her. "I would like to thank the President of Harvard, Mr. Eliot, for allowing me to hold this fashion show in your lounge. It may be February, but spring arrives in March, with many functions to attend in April and May, so February is a good time to view this year's fashions. Before the ladies walk among you to model their gowns, we will have tea."

From a little kitchenette, Shauna and Flora arrived with tea. Peter and Gordon served split baking powder biscuits topped with strawberry jam and clotted cream, and Stewart passed out paper napkins.

After a few more words from Bella, Carrie Wray sashayed forth and wound her way among the tables, allowing the guests to see all aspects of the gown. One by one, with Bella's commentary, the other ladies came from the back room to display their gowns and show the new spring colours. The ladies modelled a second time in light summer gowns. As the guests left, Bella handed each one a personal invitation to visit her shop in the Farragut building. *I hope the expense for this show brings customers.*

"The show went well, Flora. Do you think we'll have any orders?"

"Maybe by March," she answered. "In the meantime, we'll have to make hats."

***

"Mother?" asked Peter, holding up the newspaper. "The *Cambridge Chronicle* writes about 'The Boston Marathon.' What's a marathon? It seems to be very important."

"It's a footrace that's run on the third Friday of April," said Bella, "with a finish line at Copley Square in front of the Boston Library, near my shop."

"A foot race!" squealed Stewart. "I like foot races. Let's go—I can run really fast."

"No, Stewart, it's for men," said Bella. "Let me see. Why, April seventeenth is Patriot's Day in Massachusetts. There'll be no school and the shop will be closed. Yes, we could go. I've heard it is an exciting race. *And it will cost me nothing. I'll ask Derek to come with us so I have an adult quick enough to chase after Stewart. Perhaps I should be sewing spring orders, but I have to play with my children too. Where will I find the time to accomplish everything?*

***

Bella raised her voice. "The racers must be coming; the crowd is beginning to swarm the finish line!" Bella began to shout. "If we get separated in the crowd, Derek, stand on the corner of Boylston Street. Did you hear me, Shauna? Meet at Boylston Street in half an hour," Bella finished as the press of people swallowed her up.

"Peter!" cried Bella over the noise of the crowd, "Hold my hand; I'm afraid."

"I'm here, Mother, right behind you," shouted Peter. "Stand still and the crowd will pass us as they push to see the winners come in."

"I'm too short for this, Peter. We must get out of here before the crowd starts to disband and pushes me over going the other way. Break a path for me!"

***

"I rather enjoyed the excitement, Flora" said Bella back at home after the race. "In all my years, I've never been in a big crowd. The energy of the spectators reached such a pitch as the racers came across the finish line that I feared I would be trampled or knocked about the head with elbows. I was so afraid, boys, that I asked Peter to protect me and get me out of there. Poor boy, he didn't see any of the race."

"What would you like to try next time, Mother—turtle races?" asked Gordon.

"No, you tease, but watch the papers and maybe something else exciting will come along," said Bella. "Derek, you must stay for supper."

"Thanks, I will," said Derek. "We could always take you to baseball games. I know your boys want to go the same as last year."

Baseball. I'll let the boys go to the games with the fellows next door and just be boys together. Whatever it is that being boys together means, they'll learn. I have gowns to sew. It's uncomfortable having that big mortgage always on my mind.

***

That evening Bella gazed at the stars from her bedroom window as she often did. *I am wearing my engagement ring again, Donald. I couldn't wear it as an interpreter or apprentice; it didn't match my station in life. Now I'm building a fine shop and have many friends among the professors' wives. Are you listening, Donald, or are you hiding behind your newspaper pretending to read?*

At the shop the next day, Bella spoke up. "That finishes the spring gowns. I hope we get more summer orders. With more free time, I must invite Geoff's parents over for tea. The boys say that, thanks to them, they can swim. That's a relief with fishing season coming so soon."

***

Weeks later, Peter found his mother in the garden and grabbed her attention.

"See here in the paper, Mother, the biggest baseball game of the season is coming up. Maybe you had to miss the other games, but this one's really big. Our American League is playing the National League to see which league is the best. It's the first time for the two leagues to play each other and they're calling it the World Series! I bet October second, 1903, goes into baseball history. Come with us."

"That's right, Mother," chipped in Gordon. "The fellows next door won't mind having a girl with them." *So now my boys have noticed Derek's friends with dates and Gordon calls me a girl. Instead of having my hair twisted up, I'll wear it in soft waves so I'll fade into the crowd better. It's nice to have a young man in the boys' lives.*

***

Even on the streetcar to Huntington Avenue Grounds, Bella could feel the excitement growing, for everyone on the car held a blanket to sit on out beyond the fielders. The crowd swelled the closer they got to the grounds. Derek led the way from the streetcar by offering his arm to Bella.

"She looks pretty good with her hair down," whispered Gordon, "considering she's our mother. That's the first time I've seen that pale green gown."

"Quit ogling your own mother, Gordon," said Peter. "We've come here to watch baseball, not girls." Derek and his friends spread two blankets. Bella watched the crowd as much as she did the baseball diamond. *The crowd has started to chant. Someone threw out the ceremonial ball. Now everyone's cheering, with some spectators yelling for the Boston Americans and some for the National League's Pittsburgh Pirates. It's a good thing I read that newspaper article or I wouldn't understand a thing. The game has started. They're pitching, hitting and throwing. Should I ask the boys which team is Boston? Both teams use red, black and white in their jerseys. I know, I'll cheer for the team wearing red sox. I think that's right. The boys said that if the Boston Americans win, they'll have won the first World Series Pennant. That would be quite remarkable when they don't even have a stadium. This isn't anything like our schoolyard games.*

Peter's cheering for Cy Young, the Boston pitcher! Collins, Collins. Now, a cheer for Phillipe. Who's he? So many names and the boys know all of them. I guess I'll just soak in the electricity of the crowd. My bones are aching, sitting here on the ground for so long. What's happened? Everybody has jumped up—some are dancing around while others are grabbing their blankets.

"We won, Mrs. Macdonald!" shouted Derek above the noise. "The Boston Americans won the World Series against the Pittsburgh Pirates!"

"Come on, Mother," said Peter. "Let me help you up so you can cheer with us. Yea, the American League, we beat the snotty National League."

Well, I won't cheer with those words, but I can wave my hands and yell as good as the rest of them. "Yea, Americans!" shouted Bella.

***

"Bertie O'Grady wants you to call on her, Peter," said Shauna when Peter came in from school. "She said something about taking your new Box Brownie camera with you."

***

"Guess what, everybody," said Peter that same day, "Mrs. O'Grady's getting married on December the first! She asked me to be the official wedding photographer and ride in her carriage to the wedding at the Catholic Church."

"Who's she marrying?" asked Stewart.

"I didn't catch the name. I think it's a different fellow because I picked up on it sounding like a Dutch name this time—something like Weerstra. I'll need a suit."

From the tailor's. Every time I think I'm getting ahead, a new expense arises.

***

On the wedding day, Shauna, Flora, Bella and the two younger boys arrived at the church and took a seat halfway down the pews.

"This is some castle," whispered Gordon to Stewart. "Look at all those windows and statues. I wonder who pays for all of this. Their pope must be really rich."

Bella glanced around. *It's not much different from my old Church of England with all its gold trim and pomp. I wonder if it impresses God. Bertie won't care if the service is in Latin or English as long as she has her man.* The organ started and everybody stood. Peter slipped into the pew beside his mother.

"I might as well sit with you," said Peter. "I can't take pictures in this gloom."

"If the groom is from Holland, I must practice my Dutch with him before I forget too much. How's your Dutch, Peter?"

"Not very good. I haven't used it, except with Shauna. I'm an American now."

"Not really," Bella whispered. "You may be a landed immigrant, but you have two birth certificates, one for Britain in English and one for Holland, in Dutch. Shh, we must be quiet. The bride and groom are at the altar."

***

At the Wray farm while Gordon, Geoff and Stewart fished, Peter sat on a stump of wood in the pasture and drew a pencil sketch of the Wrays' big workhorse with its massive curved neck and solid legs. Below the sketch, he penciled in "The Bruce," then showed his picture to Jed, the farmhand.

"That's good, Peter. Why don't you enter it in the county fair next month?" Then Jed changed the subject. "Do you want to see the birth of a colt? She's out of season but about due. Our neighbour came ridin' over on his stallion, Brujo, and that's when we knew the mare was in heat. I tell you that stallion pounded after her, saddle and all. That's the way with males, they're always ready for a little sex, but the females— they can be shy."

Peter and Jed entered the barn and stopped with fingers hung over the gate to the mare's stall. Madge paced but paid them no attention. "Nope," said Jed. "I don't think we'll have any surprises t'day."

"I'm not sure I understand," said Peter. "How does a mare grow a baby?"

"You mean you don't know? Never lived on a farm?" questioned Jed. "Well, let's sit on the bench behind the barn and I'll explain it to you, just as if it were happ'nin', and maybe there's other things you'd like to know too."

***

A few weeks later, Shauna and Flora were obvious in their absence. Bella sat in her rocking chair as usual. Peter and Gordon trooped in and sat lounging on the sofa. Stewart took over the overstuffed chair. They waited for Bella to start the conversation.

"Boys, you are getting older and I believe I must talk to you about manhood." The boys smirked.

"We know about men's big penises, Mother," piped up Stewart. "When we swam at Claverly Hall in the nude, did they ever shrink when they hit the cold water." *Really!—and they never mentioned it to me. They didn't need those black knit swimsuits after all.*

Bella started again. "I'm sorry that your father is not here to discuss this subject with you," and Bella paused again and made a fresh start. "As is obvious, boys—well, men," she stammered, "are different from girls and women."

"Mother," said Peter. "If you are trying to tell us about sex, I already know all about it. When we were at Wrays' farm, Jed wanted to show me a mare about to foal. He and I sat outside the barn and I learned lots of things. Gordon and Stewart and I have talked it all over and we were wondering how we were going to tell *you* about sex."

"That's right, Mother," cut in Gordon. "Afterwards, Peter tried to take a book out of the medical library on sex, but we had to wait until someone else returned it. We have the book now, but it says the same things that Jed said."

"Yes, Mother," said Stewart. "I even saw Tina's cat have kittens the other day. The baby cats came out all wet and slickery and the mother cat licked them clean. If having babies is the same for humans as cats, did you lick us clean?"

"No, Stewart, but a nurse washed you clean," said Bella. *Here it is I who am worried about the subject, while they are curious and open. I wonder if I have answers for anything that they don't know. Perhaps they know more than I do, although I suspect they read the same book after I returned it.*

300

"I'm glad you compared Jed's information to a learned book, boys. Any time you have questions please come to me and we'll discuss whatever it is you wish to know. Perhaps this is a good time to tell you that you might have had a sister, had the child lived. The birth date would have fallen between yours, Gordon, and yours, Stewart. When a baby dies in the womb it is called a miscarriage, and I had that happen because my hips were too weak to support the baby. Have I explained that well enough?"

"If you had trouble, Mother, were we normal babies?" asked Peter.

"Yes, all three of you, thank the Lord. Your father worried so over my health. He loved his family, even though he never saw you, Stewart."

"I don't really like girls just now," ventured Gordon, "but they seem to like me. Does this sex thing mean I should get married first before I play around like animals do? Is that right?"

"Yes, Gordon. Your description of sex is rather graphic, but quite true. If you cause a girl, or a woman, to get pregnant and have a baby, then it is your duty to raise the child and that would be quite a responsibility. I would say that loving a woman and marrying her should come before having sex." *My goodness, is this me talking with my young sons? My step-mother never talked to me so openly. Perhaps Jed's yarn made this complicated subject easier to discuss. If they have no more questions, I see that Shauna put the brass bell on my side table.*

"If you like, one of you can ring this bell for Shauna to serve supper and we can talk about sex some other time when you have more questions."

29

BANK WARNING

At breakfast on New Year's Day, Flora came to the table with tear-stained eyes.

"My dear family, I have been trying to figure out how to tell you what I have decided, so here is my story. Once upon a time a young lady left home to see the world and years later, in 1904, she realized that she yearned for home. That lady is me. I plan to return to England and start my own business as Bella has taught me to do."

The family sat dumbfounded. Flora took a deep breath and continued. "I plan to sail as soon as I can find passage on a steamer. I'm sorry if I've spoiled New Year's Day, but I never could find the right time to tell you. I thought starting the New Year this way might be my only opportunity."

Bella broke the silence. "Dear Flora, I never realized you were pining for England. Of course you must go. Children, you must be happy for Flora. Now, give her a hug and we shall all finish breakfast." *However will I manage the springtime sales? What a blow to my business. I imagine she'll be gone by the middle of February. How I will miss her, but I must share her with my two sisters and Aunt Kate. Why did I not see this coming?*

***

Bella advertised for a seamstress in the *Cambridge Chronicle*, but those who answered the ad admitted that they couldn't sew or else they wanted a higher wage than Bella had paid Flora, considering the board and room she received. Unsure of her ability to do all the sewing, Bella hesitated with plans for her spring fashion show. *Some orders will come in. I will sew them and not advertise my fashions this year. If I find a seamstress, I can try to pick up some new orders. If I can't pay the mortgage, I'll take out a loan and pay it off as soon as I find a seamstress. Surely the bank will let me do that.*

***

"Mrs. McD," said Shauna one week after Flora had been taken to the docks with hugs and kisses. "Today's mail brought a letter for you from Paramaribo." Bella rushed to open the letter; she read it, then interpreted bits of it to Shauna.

"It's from Mr. McKay, our lawyer friend. He says he knows of a mulatto girl in Chicago and wonders if I can help her find work. I am to write to her in Dutch or Sranan and he gives the address. What do you think, Shauna? Can we take in this girl?"

Shauna smiled. Bella sensed that Shauna would like a friend who spoke her own language. Bella continued with her musings. "I rather like having our dining room back again without Flora's cot. Can we make a room in the basement? Does this house have an attic? When Peter comes in after school, I'll ask him to inspect that covered hole in the ceiling at the end of the upstairs hallway. Perhaps we can make an attic room up there."

***

"Guess what, Mother?" called Peter after he had lifted the hatch in the ceiling. "There's a storage room up here. It's not very big, but it has a little window." Peter held his kerosene lantern high and continued to call down new revelations to his mother at the foot of the ladder. "A cot would fit in here and our old apple boxes would fit through the hole. We could add pegs for hanging gowns. I think this is nicer than the basement." *Yes, Peter would think that. He had enough of basements back in 1896.*

Peter climbed down the ladder. "Just as I came to the hatch, I bumped my head on a light bulb hanging on a cord from the slanted ceiling, so there must be a light switch. If you called that an attic bedroom, how would a person get to it?"

"People had ladders to their lofts in the old country," said Bella. "There's time to build a ladder and paint the attic to make it look homey if this girl comes to us."

***

That evening Bella sat at her vanity with more thoughts about the girl from Chicago. *Maybe she could learn to sew while we improve her English. How I love my mulatto friends. Yes, I must write this person and Angus McKay too.*

***

After letters going back and forth, Jentje arrived from Chicago.

"Halo, Mrs. Macdonald," said Jentje when Bella met her train. Bella greeted her in Dutch and whisked her off to Sacramento Street to meet the family. Peter did his best to speak to her in Dutch, but the younger boys had trouble.

"My name in America is Jenny," Jentje tried in English.

"How good of you to use your English," said Bella. "You see, boys, it's difficult for people to remember foreign names so she uses the American version of her name, Jenny, and Jenny it will be."

Peter and Gordon carried her suitcase and cloth bag up to her room. She beamed with pleasure to discover she had a room of her own. The following week brought new abilities in cooking and cleaning while working side-by-side with Shauna.

***

With the cold and damp of snow and rain, nothing seemed very cheery as winter dragged on. The skies would not open to let sunshine into the streets. Day after day, the household blended the work-a-day rhythm of schoolwork, housework and sewing.

I miss Flora. She and I often visited together in the evening. Now Shauna enjoys Jenny's company while I am alone. The boys are the ones losing out on family fun. Donald, where is the solution? I need more time with the boys as they grow older, and yet, I must sew to make a living. How will I cope? I don't wish to become ill again.

***

"Mother!" cried Peter near the end of March. "This morning when I went out to groom and harness Muffet, she didn't say hello to me. She didn't whiny or turn her head. Come out and see. You know about horses."

Bella ran out to the stable, but the horse hardly acknowledged her.

"She has mucous coming from her nose, Peter. I don't like the way her head hangs down. I'll call the veterinary clinic. Put the horse blanket on her and stay with her."

I don't like what I see at all. The mucous suggests an infection. Poor Muffet is both ill and growing old. If she survives her illness, I doubt that she'll pull the carriage again, but I can't bear to tell the family that she has to be put down. The veterinarian's bill—can I even afford a doctor for Muffet? I must!

As Bella approached the house, there stood Stewart at the window with tears streaming down his cheeks.

"Would Muffet get better if I went out and hugged her?" he asked. "You help me by kissing it better. I could do that, Mother." Bella stopped to hug the forlorn little figure, then walked with her arm around Gordon's shoulder on her way to the phone.

"Don't worry, boys, I won't go to work today. I will stay and make sure that Muffet is cared for as soon as I can get the doctor here." *It's not just the infection; I can tell. I should have recognized that she pulled our carriage out of sheer loyalty.*

A horse cart arrived and took Muffet to the veterinarian's warm stable. For a week they had no word of improvement. Bella jostled to work on the streetcar and, overwhelmed with work, sewed late at the shop most days.

"Mother," said Peter one evening, with Gordon and Stewart standing behind him as if Peter had been appointed their spokesman. "Maybe

Muffet misses us and would improve if we went to see her. Please, Mother, figure out the streetcar transfers and take us on Saturday." Gordon kept his eyes wide open to keep the moisture from rolling down his cheeks, but it did not go unnoticed by Bella. Derek helped Bella to find the route, and on Saturday afternoon, Bella, Derek and the three boys set out for the veterinary clinic.

***

"Come in, Mrs. Macdonald," said the veterinarian. "Of course you may see Muffet," he said to the boys. "Somehow she caught an infection called 'strangles.' She has a very sore throat and her face is swollen and sensitive. Tell her you love her, but don't touch her or any part of the stable. Seriously, boys, keep your hands in your pockets; strangles is infectious." While the children moved into Muffet's stall, the veterinarian turned to Bella in the stable corridor. "She has a particularly virulent case of strangles, Mrs. Macdonald, and the infection is taking a great deal out of her. Did anyone introduce a new horse into your daytime stables at the Farragut building? Muffet might have caught the infection there from a feed bucket, any other equipment or a coughing horse that actually recovered from strangles and is a carrier. Most cases clear in three weeks, but Muffet is not responding well and I fear for her overall health in the future."

Muffet stood statue-like while the boys took turns talking to her. She blinked her eyes slowly, as if in appreciation of their kind voices.

"She's been here for three weeks," Peter said to the doctor. "I've been reading a book at the library on animal husbandry and illnesses. It says that horses tell you that they are suffering by their attitude. If Muffet is suffering, will you have to put her down?"

The question came so unexpectedly that Bella struggled for composure. *In his quiet way, Peter turned to books rather than worry me with the question that I feared to broach. For fourteen, he has maturity beyond his years.* She held her breath while waiting for the doctor's answer. There in the soft light of the stable, with the faces of her three boys turned up to face the doctor, they learned that he could not save their beloved horse. The three boys turned to their mother, clung to her, and sobbed.

Before the sobbing subsided, the veterinarian spoke softly to Bella. "Your horse is a work animal who cannot work. Say your goodbyes and help them to love a new horse."

"Boys," said the doctor in a kindly voice, "I am glad you came to say goodbye to Muffet. I am sure it eased her pain. Someday your mother will find another horse for you to love." The boys acknowledged the doctor's words and Bella, with her three boys huddled close to her and Derek trailing behind, walked out into the cold grey day.

***

Finally, April sunshine brought forth the daffodils and tulips along Sacramento Street. Bella attacked the sewing to assure herself of rent money at the Farragut Building. The boys seldom asked for anything because they sensed that money was scarce. With simplicity, the family celebrated Peter and Gordon's joint birthdays. The boys dug and planted the garden and Shauna taught Jenny more English and how to do housework.

Things are going well for Jenny but there's not much sparkle in our lives. I will certainly have to take out a bank loan to make up for the veterinarian's fees and to keep us in groceries. Hopefully, I'll be able to pay down the loan quickly with spring orders. How I wish I could afford a horse. I had good reason to hate the streetcar. Donald, where have I gone wrong? Everything fell apart just when I thought things were getting better before Flora left. I can see the stress our misfortune is causing the boys.

***

One June evening the streetcar stopped at Harvard Square and Bella walked the long blocks home in the last shadows of dusk.

"Mrs. McD," said Shauna. "Your return grows later every day. Please don't make yourself ill again. Let me help at the shop. Jenny should be able to care for the house."

"Don't worry about me, Shauna," said Bella. "I determined my limits and turned some orders away. Using the streetcar is much cheaper than owning a horse and the walk home is good for me. With summer vacation time soon upon us, I prefer you at home with the boys. Both the boys and I trust your every instinct as if you could read my mind." Bella's shoulders heaved with a long sigh. "Perhaps I will have you and Jenny do the canning this year without my help. Please make sure I have some dinner before I fall asleep in Donald's old rocking chair."

***

To Bella, it seemed only days before school started again, with Peter in his last year at Agassiz School. *He hasn't asked what happens next year. I can't afford a private school. His grades are high; maybe he'll win a scholarship. Jenny can cook and do housework, but she simply doesn't understand sewing.*

***

During fall baseball games Bella sewed so she might enjoy time with her boys after they came home from a game. Many nights the boys went to bed without their evening visit. This time, Bella herself noticed that her waistline allowed her skirt to drop an inch on her hips. *I'm losing weight. Why am I never hungry? Stress! The money saved by not having a horse helps, but there's no money for extras and I still struggle to meet the bills. Perhaps the bank will let me miss a payment and catch up next month.*

***

Riding to work each day on the swaying streetcar allowed Bella's thoughts to ramble, and this brought her fears to the fore. One day, like an automaton, she unlocked the front door of her shop. Just as she reached the workroom, the telephone rang. She startled! *Surely the bank hasn't noticed a missing mortgage payment on the first day of non-payment! Perhaps it is a customer.* Bella lifted the receiver.

"Mrs. Macdonald," the man's voice said, "I warned you about losing your home if you missed even one payment of your mortgage. My boss is adamant that I should seize your house. He's smug about never giving a mortgage to a woman. I assume you have overlooked the date. Please come immediately with the payment before he starts the paperwork for repossession." The caller hung up his receiver with a clang in Bella's ear.

Dazed, Bella braced her hands on the small telephone table where she stood.

Is that the bell on the front door tinkling? Someone has entered the reception room. Put on a smile, Bella; customers must see your usual friendliness. Perhaps Mrs. Storrar has come for her gown. If she pays the full amount, that plus the grocery money might make up the mortgage payment and give me a few more days to work things out.

"Hello, Mrs. Storrar," Bella greeted her customer with a smile and cheery voice. "Your gown is finished and waiting for you." *But has she the money?* "Why, thank you for such prompt payment. I'll have materials in for fall styles very soon. Goodbye."

Mrs. Storrar left the shop. Quickly, Bella emptied her wallet and the bottom of her purse, looking for spare coins. She added this to the money she held in her hand. *Just enough.*

Bella locked the shop and walked to the bank, paid her mortgage and apologized for missing the date. *Now what? I've come to the end. My shop is doomed.* With wooden fingers, she counted the number of gowns that she might manage to finish ahead of time in order to buy groceries and make the payment the following month.

Again the phone rang. This time Jenny blurted out her message in Dutch.

"Come home, Mrs. McD. Shauna's belly hurts. She's crying with the pain!"

Bella called the doctor and again locked the shop. Her purse held enough coins for streetcar fare, but she wouldn't be home for twenty minutes. *Shauna must be in trouble. In all the years I've known her, she has never cried. Her belly hurts? That's what Jenny said. What can the pain be? When I called the doctor, his nurse said that she would tell him to go quickly. What if he's slow? Poor Jenny won't know what to do.* Bella jumped from the streetcar at Harvard Square and dashed the six blocks to her home.

"I'm here, Shauna. I'm here!" Bella cried out as she burst in the front door. "Jenny, where is the doctor? I don't see his carriage. Has he taken Shauna to the hospital?"

Jenny ran down the stairs. "Doctor? No doctor has come."

"Where's Shauna—in her room?" demanded Bella as if calculating what must be done. "I'll phone the doctor again. He must come."

Bella could hear Shauna's moans and whimpers all the way to the dining room where she stood at the phone. "What? The doctor is out on a call and hasn't returned to receive my message yet? Maybe an hour or more? Well, send him as soon as you can."

I'll phone Dr. Wray. If he's home perhaps he can tell me what to do." She phoned Wrays' number. When Bella finished listening to Charles Wray, she left the receiver to swing on the line as she ran up the stairs to Shauna's room. A faded pallor spread across Shauna's face. Her eyes shone like black diamonds, telling of pain and fear.

"Mrs. McD," she murmured, "it hurts so much." She clasped her hands over her belly and curled back into a ball.

An intestinal problem like food poisoning? But if it were that, we would all be ill. Appendix? Perhaps it is her appendix.

"Shauna," asked Bella. "Can you point to the exact spot it hurts the most?" Shauna cupped her right hand over her right hip and dug the tips of her fingers into the flesh some two inches inside the hip bone. Bella raced down the stairs, her wobbly ankles scarcely able to keep from going over. "Charles, she pointed to her right side. Her appendix? You want me to call an ambulance and get her to the hospital immediately? You'll meet me there? Yes, Jenny can stay and look after the boys at lunch. Yes, I understand—the ambulance men are to carry her downstairs. She's not to walk or blow her nose. Thank you, oh thank you!" Bella called an ambulance and returned to sit by Shauna. She cooed with soft words of affection and caressed her forehead with a damp cloth to wipe away the perspiration that shone on her face.

Where is that doctor, or the ambulance? Bella's agony over the wasted minutes grew as Shauna's murmurs rose to pleas for help.

"Jenny," said Bella, "go out to the sidewalk and wave down the ambulance so they find the house quickly. Urge them to hurry!"

Shauna's pain subsided a little. The ambulance carriage arrived at the house before the doctor, and Bella, after instructions to Jenny, left with Shauna. *Shauna seems in less pain, but this carriage travels the speed of the ragman.* "Do hurry, men, please hurry."

***

"Charles, you're here!" Bella called out when they finally reached the hospital. "The other doctor never did come. Shauna seems to be in less pain than before."

"She is?" Dr. Wray almost shouted. "Orderlies, take this woman to the operating room immediately! I must leave you now, Bella. If Shauna's pain has lessened, it might be because her appendix has ruptured. That is very grave indeed. Phone that other doctor and cancel your call. I will attend Shauna."

Within seconds Bella found herself alone with busy nursing staff running in every direction while the hall doors swung aimlessly behind the departed Dr. Wray. She phoned the doctor, then sat alone on a hall bench—alone and frightened for her dear Shauna.

"Mrs. Macdonald?" asked a woman in white. "I believe you are waiting for news of Shauna Stuzer. Dr. Wray asked me to suggest that you go home and he will come by to see you later. Miss Stuzer's appendix ruptured and he is very busy with her in the operating room." *Ruptured! I must not keep the seriousness of this from the boys.*

At noon the boys came tumbling into the house but sensed immediately that something had happened to bring their mother home at lunch.

"Boys, Shauna has taken ill. Dr. Wray met me at the hospital and operated on her this morning. Please bow your heads. Dear Lord, we are gathered here to pray in your name. We know you are with us and will hear our prayers for Shauna, a beloved family member who loves you as your servant. Please guide the knowledge and hands of Dr. Wray as he cares for her. Give her strength to recover from the illness that befell her this morning. We ask your blessings on Shauna. In Jesus' name we pray. Amen."

"Mother," said Peter in a soft voice. "You are frightened for Shauna. I can hear it in your voice. What's happened?"

Gordon and Stewart said nothing as the three boys sat side-by-side on the edge of the sofa cushions, their hands still clasped in their laps from prayer.

"There is a small part of the intestine—intestine means your tummy, Stewart—that is much like a little sack. It is called your appendix," and she put her fingers on the right side of her abdomen half way between the navel and hipbone. "It has no real purpose but it fills with intestinal waste and empties again from time to time. Sometimes it doesn't empty. If it becomes plugged too full to stretch any more, the pain is intense. Shauna's pain came on very quickly. We rushed her to the hospital, but the appendix had burst. There is very little we can do but pray that the Lord will watch over her recovery."

The boys' eyes appealed for more information, so Bella continued.

"You're all very young to understand what I have said. Have you any questions?"

"Will she die?" asked Jenny from the kitchen. Before Bella could answer, Gordon spoke as if to answer Jenny's question.

"You don't need to explain Shauna's illness any further, Mother. We'll help Jenny and stay out of trouble so you don't have more worries." Peter nodded and turned his head away, trying to hide the moisture forming in his eyes.

"I'll be good," cried Stewart, dragging his fists through his tears.

"Thank you, boys. I need your support. Let's have lunch with Jenny."

30

A VISITOR
FROM THE PAST

"The doctor says we may go in to see Shauna, boys," said Bella. "She has a fever and is not well, so be gentle but cheerful. She has been asking for you."

The nurse left Shauna's bedside as Bella and her sons entered the room, but Bella could tell by the rustle of the woman's starched gown that she remained discreetly outside the partially closed door to Shauna's ward.

"Dear Peter, Gordon and Stewart," Shauna murmured. "How I longed to see you. Are you being good boys for your mother?" Each boy answered Shauna with a short phrase about school or play, and Shauna sank back on the pillow as if exhausted. Her eyes turned to Bella. "Mrs. McD, I love you as I loved Mr. McD. I don't ever want to leave you. Please pray for me." Tears welled in her eyes.

Bella kissed Shauna's fevered brow. "I know, dear Shauna, that only with your constant care of the boys and me have we managed to prosper in America. Sweet girl, rest and get well." Jenny moved forward to join the family standing around the white metal bed with its white coverlet.

"Jenny is here too, Shauna. She wishes to say 'hello' in Sranan and say a few words as is your custom." Bella translated the words the best her memory could remember Sranan. *She's saying that God watches over his flock and knows best how to care for them. What a thoughtful way to tell Shauna not to worry, for God is with her.*

Shauna smiled and stretched forth a hand to Jenny then looked again to the children as the nurse returned to the room, waving her hand to indicate that they must leave because Shauna appeared to be very tired.

"Before you go, boys, let me kiss you goodbye," Shauna pleaded. Bella lifted Stewart up to Shauna so he could reach her forehead with a kiss. Peter and Gordon followed with kisses and quiet goodbyes. Shauna closed her eyes.

"Shauna," said Bella, holding Shauna's hand and kissing her temple, "I will send the boys home with Jenny in a carriage and return to sit with you." Jenny, followed by the three boys, left the room, but the nurse put her hand on Bella's arm.

"Mrs. Macdonald, there is no need to stay. Shauna has just slipped away. Take your family home and come tomorrow morning to make arrangements for her remains."

Bella could not save herself. She burst out sobbing and rushed to her sons to hold them tight while the tears streamed down her face. Her shoulders heaved in uncontrollable sobbing. The nurse led them to a side room. The boys instinctively knew what had happened and together they wept for Shauna's passing.

***

Bella closed the shop for a week while she mourned and planned a memorial service at the Meeting Hall. She wrote to Shauna's family and told them of Shauna's untimely death and that she had sent Shauna's ashes back to be buried with her people.

***

During that week Bella spent many hours rocking in Donald's chair. One night after the family retired, she went to her room, turned off the light, and gazed out the window from her pillow. *I have lost Shauna, Muffet and much of my business; I must not allow the bank to take the house. Please, God, deliver me from my financial woes by sending me a seamstress. Donald, if you are out there with the stars, comfort me; show me the way as you have in the past. Lift up my spirits.* She finished by giving her problems over to God.

***

The following day the sun shone. It reminded her of the many times Donald had said, "Don't worry; the sun will rise in the morning." She left the rocking chair and strolled to Harvard Square, past the daffodils and through the university grounds.

She saw Quincy Street, where Peter took his violin lessons, and turned up Oxford Street. Suddenly, she realized that she heard the birds in the trees and saw little twigs budding, all backed by the radiant blue of the sky. *With my own misery, I've forgotten to recognize God's work. These beautiful plantings rise up again each spring and so must I. Kate and Shauna would be after me to plan for the future. My walk has brought me full circle to the other end of Sacramento Street. I'll begin planning now even before I reach home. First, I must advertise again for a seamstress. I'll advertise in the Boston newspapers and offer room and board. Surely someone will want to leave crowded Boston and come to Cambridge.*

For the first time, Bella admired the flowerbeds freshly dug at her front door. She poured herself an iced tea and sat in the back garden, surrounded by the work of her sons, where the parallel rows of the vegetable garden waited to sprout. *While I mourned, the boys took out their sorrow by digging and planting. Like them, I must move on, with Shauna in my heart. Before Shauna passed away, I thought about having her sew at home and how I hated riding that bone-rattling streetcar. It is I who should sew at home and be done with the Farragut building. I'll add French doors covered with sheers across the dining room arch and turn the living room into a reception parlour with the tall mirror in the corner of the parlour.* Bella's thoughts raced on. *A change room can be fashioned using screens. I'll attend to customers from ten a.m. until two. After that, the living room will be open for the family, with the furniture as it is. Why did I not think of this before?*

Bella rushed into the house for a paper and pencil to write down her ideas and the work that the ideas would demand. *Thank goodness I've passed the two-year contract with Farragut. I can terminate him at the end of the month.* The more Bella added to her plan, the more relaxed she felt. Bella soon found herself walking towards the kitchen to ask Jenny if she'd like to be the new housekeeper.

***

At the end of the month, the boys next door, using the Wrays' farm wagon, came to move all the fittings of Bella's shop to Sacramento Street.

"Mrs. Macdonald," said Derek, "I've taken down your sign reading 'Gowns.' What shall I do with it?" Emotionally drained with the knowledge that, in fact, she had lost her shop, as with other things that had to be removed from the building, Bella consigned it to the wagon with a lifeless wave of her hand. Under the burn of Mr. Farragut's beady eyes, she busied herself with locking the door and handing him the brass key. Bella climbed onto the high seat of the wagon to leave and, as with Sunningdale and Candlewick, she did not look back.

***

On Monday morning Bella painted a small card with the lettering "Gowns" and placed it in the front window. Derek's housemate, Jason, a farm-trained carpenter, installed the French doors and made the three-panelled screen.

Bella phoned the *Boston Evening Transcript,* the *Boston Globe* and the *Boston Herald* with her advertisement requesting a seamstress. *The bills will surely flow in. Think, Bella—how will you pay them?* She made a second sign advertising the horse stall in the back garden. She placed an advertisement in the *Cambridge Chronicle* announcing the opening of her shop: "Gowns, at 49½ Sacramento Street, hours 10 a.m. to 2 p.m." *I can do no more now except sew on the orders that I do have and wait for miracles to happen.*

***

Bella rushed from the upstairs sewing room to answer the incessant ringing of the phone.

"Hello, Mrs. Macdonald speaking."

"Bella," came a voice from the past. "It is I, your brother-in-law Peter. I am in Boston and I'd like you to come down to my hotel for dinner with me."

After ten years my brother-in-law shows up, just like that. Go to him! Donald would have come for me in a fine carriage. Years ago I hated Peter, my parsimonious brother-in-law, and now I am to go to him for dinner. Hard feelings drain away over time and one either forgives or forgets. With him, I'm not sure which applies—perhaps both. With my life in pandemonium, I suppose meeting him at his hotel is wiser than having him come here, at least for our first meeting. I wonder what he wants.

"Peter," Bella replied in a cheery voice. "You are the last person I expected to have call me. Do you mean supper this evening? Yes, I suppose I can do that. What time shall I arrive? Fine," and Bella replaced the receiver. *His hotel will require one transfer at Tremont Station. A fine way to travel when I must look stunning. I hope I don't get accosted in the underground.*

***

In her midnight-blue gown, Bella entered the hotel and spied her brother-in-law in the hotel foyer. A catch came in her throat—except for the red hair, he looked like Donald. *Be with me tonight, Donald, and keep me from haranguing about the past.*

"Good evening, Peter. I hope you are well." Peter closed his newspaper and jumped to his feet with a hug and peck on Bella's cheek. The maître d' seated them in a quiet corner of the dining room. *The chandeliers and polished brass light fixtures are as dear to me as when they were paraffin lamps in Surinam. How different life would be if I still had Donald. I wonder why Peter is here. Will he beat about the bush or tell me outright?*

"You are looking very grand, my dear Bella, contrary to stories that have come my way from your side of the family."

"I have no idea what you have heard," said Bella sweetly, "but I can tell you that riding the streetcar into town from Cambridge in my best gown would not have been my first choice for arrangements this evening. I had a horse and carriage but the horse died of strangles and I cannot afford another one. Does that titbit agree with your other stories?"

"Bella, I can sense frustration in your voice, so I will come directly to the point of why I am here." Bella sipped her stout and waited for Peter to continue.

"I read in *Argosy* that a gold mine is in operation above the Corentyne River where I believe Donald's claim would have been. I want to apologize for doubting his ability as a mining engineer." Bella nodded and sipped her stout, quite sure that her brother-in-law had not travelled to Boston just to give her that news.

"My actions years ago, I am told, have brought you hardship. Accordingly, I wish to give you the money that I should have given Donald years ago." Bella fluttered her delicate hand in protest. "No, Bella, hear me out. I am a man of means, and yet, perhaps self-centred. By refusing Donald ten years ago, I never dreamed of the adverse consequences it would have on you and my nephews, nor did I try to discover how you were faring. I have come to Boston to ask your forgiveness and be a guest in your home so that I might know your boys."

"Dear Peter," said Bella, "yes, I have struggled and, in fact, I am still struggling, but I forgave you years ago. Donald held no grudge against you when engulfed in his agonizing path to death, so why should I not do the same? I have a free bedroom at my home for the moment, as my servant of many years just passed away. My family members are in mourning. You are welcome to use the bedroom if you wish."

"Just as Donald always told me, Bella, you are charming but forthright. I shall be delighted to drive you home tonight in a carriage and stay if that is fine with you and your household." *Family is always welcome at my home. I wonder if Jenny has moved her things into Shauna's room. I can't imagine the boys' Uncle Peter sleeping on a cot in the attic, but perhaps that is where he will be.*

***

"Boys," said Bella the following morning as the boys bounced into the dining room. "I would like you to meet your Uncle Peter." The boys stopped in their tracks and stood ramrod straight. "Uncle Peter," Bella announced to her brother-in-law, "this is your name-sake, Peter. Gordon and Stewart, meet your Uncle Peter."

"Good morning, Sir," came the boys' respectful voices, in contrast to their plain clothing. The boys continued to stand erect as they offered their hands for this initial contact with a man they thought they might never meet.

Uncle Peter spent the day visiting colleagues at Harvard while the boys were in school and Bella sewed. At stout time, the family gathered.

"I meant what I said, Bella," said Uncle Peter before the boys assembled. "I went to the bank this morning and wrote off your mortgage and bank loan with the money I should have offered ten years ago. You are debt-free, with enough extra in your bank account to buy a new horse and buggy. When the boys arrive, I want to know all about your family and the boys' plans for further education."

***

Young Peter let his eyes drop to the floor when his uncle asked him what he planned for school after this, his final year at Agassiz Grammar School. Peter raised them again and looked his Uncle in the eye, as he had been taught to do.

"I have no plans, Sir. Further schooling costs money, so perhaps I will choose a trade and help mother regain her gown business."

"Before you consider that route, Peter, let me tell you about my son, your cousin William, known as Will," said Uncle Peter. "Despite earning his degree in Scotland as a civil engineer—one who knows the business of building railroads—Will abandoned that to fulfil his dream of owning land in Canada. He is homesteading in the province called Saskatchewan, and although the life is tough, he is very happy. From Leopold Blaschka I understand you have an interest in plants and farm animals. Is that right, Peter?"

"Yes, Sir," came young Peter's short answer, for he had never had such an adult conversation about the future.

"Think about it, Peter. You could join your Irish friends and work in the brick factory, but I suggest that at the end of the school year, you pack your bag and go to live with Will. You can earn your keep by helping him on his homestead and at the same time attend school for a level of education that will fit you to enter a university in Canada. Only private schools do this in America, but in this one thing Canada is ahead of America. In actual fact, you are a British citizen and Canada is part of the British Empire. You are only a landed immigrant in America, but in Canada, with your passport, you will be a citizen. Do you understand that I am urging you to follow your dream of higher education, not to take second best? Your mother has shown great stamina in managing her life. Now you must manage yours. Before I go, we'll talk about this again, young man."

Uncle Peter glanced towards the dining room. "I see that Jenny is ready to serve dinner. Gordon and Stewart, we'll have a man-to-man talk too, when I know you better. Now, let us go to the dining table and continue our conversations."

At the table after grace, Uncle Peter turned to his youngest nephew. "Stewart, your brothers have not mentioned my appearance, but I'm sure that their memories are racing, for I am very like your father except for my dark hair. If it helps you to know your father, think of me as if I had fiery red hair like Gordon's." This put everyone at ease and Jenny brought forth the vegetables and platter of meat before joining them at the table. *It must be difficult for Peter and Gordon to see their father's likeness in their uncle and hear the pleasant Scottish burr of his accent. Poor little Stewart, he won't have those latent memories.*

That evening Peter and Stewart performed on their musical instruments and Gordon gave a rambunctious recitation. Uncle Peter never once complained about his small cot in the attic, but he stayed only a week. For Peter's time with his uncle, they returned to the museum of glass flowers. Gordon discussed his various schemes to make money while he and his uncle fished in Wrays' brook. Stewart took him to meet Miss Baldwin and see his school.

"Miss Baldwin," said Uncle Peter at the principal's office doorway, "I have read about Agassiz Grammar School in the *London Times*. The school and you are famous in the Western Hemisphere. I am pleased the Macdonald boys attend your school. Your educational grounding will last them a lifetime."

"Did you really read about Miss Baldwin in the *London Times*?" asked Stewart on the way home.

"Yes, Stewart. Miss Baldwin is well known for her school and for her charitable acts towards the coloured people of Cambridge. Yes, indeed, she is quite a woman."

***

"Mother," said Stewart in private one day, "Uncle Peter seems to like us but he is so stiff and proper. Did he never learn to play games?"

"Perhaps not, Stewart. He was the eldest boy in a large family, and as a sugar plantation manager and refinery superintendent, he has always been in charge of other people. He doesn't know how to let others be his equal. Don't be afraid of him. He came to Boston just to meet you and your brothers and I am sure he is well pleased with the intelligence and proper decorum of you three."

***

At the end of his stay, Uncle Peter and Bella had dinner in the professors' dining room at Harvard.

"Bella," said Peter, "you have raised three fine sons. Donald would be proud of them and of you in meeting the challenges that life has thrown your way at every turn. I do believe my suggestion for young Peter is a good one. Working with Will on the farm will give him robust health and a view of the world less apparent here in this secluded community of Harvard's academia. I suspect that in three years of schooling in Canada he will pass the university requirements in the faculty of his choice. And, although this is a moot point, his further education until high school graduation will cost you nothing. High school is included with Will's taxes."

"But, Peter, the boy will only be fifteen years old come May twentieth!" cried Bella.

"That's old enough to leave home, my dear. If he went to learn a trade, he would leave. Whether in Canada or some American city, you will always have communication by the post office and the telegraph system." The waiter arrived with dinner.

"Now, take Gordon," went on Uncle Peter. "He's intelligent but he likes to work with people rather than books. I can't tell you what he will want to do in a year, but I can tell you that Canada is younger than America and because of this there are many more opportunities to gain work experience and then start your own company and have it grow. It might be wise for him to go north too."

"You have determined the boys' attributes well, Peter. Stewart likes books and no doubt, like young Peter, will choose university some day. I have always looked and worked towards the future, but life has given me so many bad turns that I don't allow myself to second-guess it."

"I must say, Bella, that I didn't believe the stories I heard from Flora when I returned to London. I just couldn't imagine that your life had been so difficult. Why did you not ask for my help?"

"Because, Peter, you would have turned me down—thought of me as a useless creature. Your brother allowed me to take my place among men as well as women, and I was not about to lose that freedom even though he passed on."

"Again, I apologize," said Peter. "When I first arrived that night over dinner in Boston, I apologized for doubting Donald's ability to find a gold mine, and this time I apologize for the fact that I might have doubted your abilities, as you have just said. The music is playing. Would you care to dance, just for your memories of Donald and for mine with my wife, Margaret?"

***

That night, once again at home, Bella wept for the days in Surinam and the many times Donald had held her gently as they crossed the dance floor, for Peter danced superbly too. The week ended and Uncle Peter continued on to New York, having left a male focus with the boys about their upcoming futures as mature men.

***

My brother-in-law is right. My boys know nothing of life except in this sheltered town of Cambridge. They don't even know much about Boston and less about New York. With the relief from debt that Peter has given me, I believe we should have a holiday. With Shauna's and Muffet's deaths following so close to one another, our minds are drowning in sadness. We'll go to New York when school finishes.

***

Bella went immediately to the front window and removed the two signs. *Instead of sewing I will go—what were Donald's words so long ago when we found Mischief in Paramaribo?—yes, I will go horse hunting.*

Bella sat down with the newspaper, circled ads for a suitable horse and proceeded to phone promising advertisements. Carrie Wray offered to come to town in her open trap and drive Bella to see horses.

"Even if we don't find a horse," said Carrie, "driving in the country will lift our spirits with the perfume of sweet hay and the sight of green sprouts spreading across the fields."

The two women set out on a fine day in mid-May to travel towards the Medford area. West Somerville, their first stop, resulted in failure. The ill-tempered beast listed in the newspaper shied, kicked and bit. They went over to Winter Hills and found a possible horse with some Arabian blood, but as Bella felt no chemistry with the animal, they decided to circle back through Somerville on their way home for the day.

"Look, Carrie!" cried Bella. "That farm sign says that it raises Arabians. Let's go in and ask them if any are for sale." From her many phone calls to advertisements, Bella knew the going prices. One in the pasture caught her eye—cinnamon coloured with a white blaze on her face. *If only they would sell her to me.* Bella and Carrie pulled up inside the farmyard and spoke to the man who came their way.

"That brown one with the blaze?" said the owner of the ranch. "He's a gelded stallion. My men are training him to pull light carriages and to wear a saddle. We don't sell them until they are fully trained." A man led the gelding into the yard. Bella accepted the tether and walked towards the animal. The horse stood still. He allowed Bella to stroke his neck and lift his lips to examine his teeth. "We call him Blaze," said the rancher, "because of the white stripe down the centre of his nose. He needs a couple of months more training. If you want a horse before then, I can show you some others."

"No, thank you. I rather like this horse and I don't need him until mid-July. I'm surprised with myself for considering a stallion. I've always owned mares."

"Gelded stallions sometimes bond with their family even better than a mare," said the rancher. They discussed price. Bella wanted to have a veterinarian check her choice of horse, but she knew in her heart that she had found a horse the boys could love.

***

On the last day of school Bella, Jenny and the boys dressed in their Sunday best to attend Peter's graduation. Both Peter and Gordon wore their new tailor-made black suits that they had chosen for this year's birthday gift, and after Bella's remodelling, Stewart looked fine in the old black family hand-me-down. The Grade Eight girls dazzled the spectators in their fancy gowns, while the boys looked handsome in their starched collars. Miss Baldwin introduced Mr. Charles Eliot, President of Harvard University, for an address, and a Presbyterian minister said a prayer. With Miss Jones at the piano, Miss Baldwin announced that they would sing "Onward Christian Soldiers," by Sir Arthur Sullivan. Everyone clapped when she announced the Valedictorian, Peter Alexander Macdonald. Peter spoke with confidence on behalf of his classmates and received a tumultuous round of applause. With beaming parents, the Grade Eight students went home clutching the rolled document that proclaimed their graduation from Agassiz Grammar School, Cambridge, Massachusetts.

***

"Now, children and Jenny," said Bella at home after the graduation exercises, "to start summer holidays I have planned a trip for us. We will travel by train to New York for a few days and see the sights. When we return, I have a surprise for you."

31

LIFE AFTER
UNCLE PETER'S VISIT

The train wheels rumbled softly through the black of night on the main line out of New York headed for Boston. Pinpoints of light could be seen as they passed farm homes and towns. The engine's dim "whoo-whoo" came as an eerie sound through the glass of the window. With Stuart and Gordon on either side of her, Jenny propped up the two sleeping boys and soon, like them, she allowed her head to nod. Across from them sat Bella and Peter, talking quietly in the subdued lighting of the coach.

"Mother, if I went to Canada, would I lose my immigrant's status in America?"

"No, I don't think so. You've been thinking of what your Uncle Peter said, haven't you, Peter? If you go to high school in Canada, you may very well choose a Canadian university. I've been looking into your uncle's words too, and Canada has some fine universities."

"Mother, if I went to Canada, would that bother you? Would you be lonely or fearful for me?"

Bella realized that she was rubbing the fingers of one hand over the other hand. She looked out the train window at the stars. *If the boy wishes to go, I must let him go. I have done what I set out to do in giving him a good start with his education; from now on he must be free to make up his own mind. That's right, isn't it, Donald? You will watch over him, won't you?*

"Perhaps," said Peter, when Bella didn't answer his question, "I shouldn't have asked right now when you're tired. I'm tired, but not sleepy. I know when we get back to Cambridge that I must start planning for next fall, and the first part of planning is to talk over possibilities with you. Would you rather go to sleep like Jenny?"

"Not if you'd like to talk, Peter, but first, perhaps I should tell you some things. Years ago your Uncle Peter didn't believe that your father had the ability to find a gold mine and refused to invest money in your father's business venture. In many ways, this lack of brotherly support proved deadly to your father, for he went into the jungle before the mosquito season ended and died of yellow fever. To survive as a widow, I had to earn a living and chose America as the best place to do that. Your Uncle Peter has now discovered that a gold mine, registered where your father thought it should be, has started operation. Because your uncle feels guilty about not trusting your father, he came to Cambridge to ask forgiveness and give me the money that he withheld years ago. I'm now debt free. I own our Sacramento home outright and I have money for my future. You do not have to work near Cambridge to support me."

Peter turned and hugged his mother. In faltering words he said, "Thanks for talking about Father. I don't remember him very well, but I must tell you that it was hard for me when Uncle Peter sat in Father's rocking chair and talked to me like Father would have if he were alive. Those words with Uncle Peter about my future seemed to be my first adult conversation, and this is my second one. Should I do what Uncle Peter suggested? Should I write Will to see if I'd be welcome at his homestead?"

"Oh yes, you'd be welcome—your cousin Will suggested the plan. I know that, before the harvest season comes, he expects a letter from us regarding your interest in the idea. He needs to know if he can count on your help in clearing the land." Bella looked at her watch. "It's getting very late, Peter. Snuggle down beside me and let the train lull you to sleep. We can talk about your future again tomorrow."

***

In the early grey light of morning, the train chuffed into Boston. The sleepy family straightened their clothes, took up their suitcases and made their way to Tremont Station.

From the streetcar at Harvard Square, Bella hired a carriage for the ride home.

***

"Mother," said Gordon when he went into the kitchen, "I think someone is using our horse stall."

"My goodness, children, how strange! Let's go out and look."

Stewart ran ahead and yanked the stable door open. "Mother, a cinnamon-coloured horse is in here!"

"She's nice," said Gordon. "I like that white stripe down her nose."

"He, Gordon," said Peter with a view of the back end of the horse. "That's a gelded stallion, not a mare."

"Do you think the owner will let us ride him?" asked Stewart. "He's sure pretty."

"Handsome, if it's boy," said Gordon, "and handsome he is."

"Who do you think owns him?" asked Peter.

Bella gathered the boys around her. "Remember I said that when we returned from New York I had a surprise for you? This is it! Boys, meet Blaze, your new horse."

"Really, Mother?" said Peter. "Blaze is ours to ride and pull your carriage?"

"Yes," said Bella. "Blaze belongs to the three of you. You are all old enough to feed and water him, brush him, clean his hooves and exercise him. Someone will have to take him riding every day, now that he won't be used for the carriage as much. He will come to love us in equal proportion to the love and care that we show him. It's up to you boys to make him our family pet. Now, everyone in for breakfast before we try on his saddle. I will ride him first; I need to know how he reacts in traffic."

***

"Mother," called Peter, "a young fellow just delivered a telegram addressed to Master Peter Macdonald. Should I open it?"

"Of course," laughed Bella from the sewing room. "You are Master Macdonald, aren't you?" Peter's fingers fumbled until he stretched the yellow page before his eyes.

"It's from Cousin Will," Peter called up the stairwell to his mother. "He says he'll bring his wagon into Regina to meet the train." Bella came down to the living room to share Peter's excitement. "Mother, am I doing the right thing?"

Bella sat on the sofa and patted the seat beside her as an invitation for Peter to sit with her. "The right thing?" she questioned. "Do you mean the right thing for your career, financially or socially?"

"I haven't thought of it that way," said Peter, suddenly appearing too immature to face the changes he contemplated.

"Then I will answer for you, and you can decide if you like my answers," said Bella. Jenny set the tea tray on the serving table with two teacups instead of lemonade for Peter. "First, young man, how do you take your tea—with cream and one or two lumps of sugar?" Bella continued, "When you are on your own the hostess will ask you that, so do have your first cup of tea, Peter, and determine the answer. Peter nodded and gingerly accepted the cup and saucer that his mother passed to him.

"Now, for answers to your questions. Regarding Canada for your career? Most certainly. You're interested in plants and animals, and living on a farm is the best way to study them. You need qualifications to attend university, and you'll simply continue attending school, as you have here, until you meet Canadian University entrance standards. I would say going to Canada fulfils your career goal very well." Peter nodded.

"Next, let's talk about finances. Further schooling, called 'high school' in Canada, will cost you nothing at Will's because school is included in his taxes, which is not the case here in America. In Canada, you'll be working for your keep and, I might add, not eating my groceries. Financially, going to Saskatchewan is good for both of us."

"Now comes the question of are you prepared socially. That means are you adult enough to go off on your own at fifteen. I believe you are,

Peter, when it comes to making wise decisions. However, there will be times that you'll feel very alone. Can you manage that? When I sailed away to British Guiana at twenty-four, I had a terrible time. Some call it depression. Take your violin and play it often, play it for others, read books, meet people, write letters, phone home, learn new things and you will manage."

"I think you are telling me to go to Cousin Will's farm, but won't you miss me?" *The poor boy needs the same assurance I needed when I wondered if my family was glad to be rid of me. What can I say to assure him of my love, of our love?*

"Of course we'll miss you, but life must go on, and if that means enjoying each other through letters, then that is the price your siblings and I must pay. As your mother, I must learn to let you feel your wings and fly the nest. You are a good, honest, intelligent, healthy young man; just work to stay that way and come home to visit us every year." By the time she finished, her voice started to crack and she burst into tears. "Yes, Peter, we will miss you." She put her arms around him and cried on his shoulder.

***

Within the week, the family took Peter to the train bound for Montreal, where he would begin the long ride across Ontario, Manitoba and half of Saskatchewan on Canada's new Canadian Pacific Railway.

"I'll be fine, Mother," said Peter, with a perceptible hitch in his voice. "You'll see." He swallowed hard and managed, "I'll write," and gave her a long hug.

Gordon and Stewart shuffled their feet with their eyes downcast, looking at the station platform. Bella gathered one on each side of her, hugged them at the shoulders and softly consoled them: "Yes, boys are allowed to cry." Their sobs began. Bella could no longer contain her tears. With final hugs and tears, Peter's train chuffed out of the station and the distraught little family returned to their carriage for the lonely ride home.

***

"You have mail today, Mrs. McD," called Jenny from the bottom of the stairs. Bella rushed to the living room, hoping to find a letter from Peter. All she had heard in three weeks came in a short telegram that said, "Cousin Will met me at train stop I am fine stop Peter." *The dear boy did the best he could with a limit of ten words per telegram, but why is it taking so long for him to write?*

Bella accepted the letter from Jenny. It bore an American stamp, not a Canadian one. She looked at the cancellation mark across the stamp. "Boston? Who in Boston would be writing me?" She slipped Donald's letter opener under the envelope flap to find a single piece of common paper, and read:

> To Mrs. Macdonald,
> My name is Mary Thomson. I read your advertisement for a seamstress who could board at your house. If I come to your home, will you see me?
> Yours truly, Mary Thomson.

"My goodness, Jenny, after all this time someone has answered my advertisement. The woman's letter is reasonably well written. The handwriting reminds me of Donald's writing and that of all his Scottish relatives. With a name like Thomson, she might be Scottish. With no return address for an answer, I wonder when she will turn up—perhaps by September first. I suppose we'll have to wait until the doorbell rings."

***

On the last Saturday of August, Bella and the boys drove out to Wrays' farm. Jed saddled two horses, one for Stewart and one for himself, while Gordon unhitched the carriage and saddled Blaze. Gordon tied a picnic lunch behind his saddle and the three headed down a trail that lead across the farm and out into the country. Bella's eyes watched the threesome disappear across the meadow. *I wonder if Peter has a horse to ride.* To escape the talons of the hot sun, Bella and the Wrays went inside to enjoy a cold-plate lunch.

On Sunday, Stewart and Gordon skipped the afternoon portion of church and went to a Boston Red Sox baseball game with two new Harvard students living next door. Gordon's chest puffed out with the thought of showing the students how to get there instead of the students taking him. *I must say, he's fulfilling the role of eldest child in the home quite well.*

On Monday at ten o'clock, the doorbell rang and Jenny called for Bella to leave her sewing. Upon descending the stairs, Bella could see that Jenny had invited someone into the parlour, a Creole woman the same as Jenny. Bella wondered who it might be. With Bella's entrance into the parlour, the woman dipped her head as Shauna used to do and thrust forth her hand.

"Good morning, Mrs. Macdonald. I am Mary Thomson, the seamstress. I wrote you a letter saying that I would be calling."

"How do you do, Mary. Please be seated." The two women sat and Jenny left for the kitchen. Bella spoke first.

"From your name and handwriting, Mary, I thought you'd be a Scottish woman. Forgive me if I looked surprised."

"I am Scottish, Ma'am. I was born in Scotland of Scottish parents, although my mother's mother came from India and we lived in Demerara in my childhood. My parents moved to Detroit two years ago, when I was twenty-one. I worked at sewing straight seams on factory electric machines." Bella nodded and Mary went on. "I didn't like the factory and Detroit, so when my friend came to be married in Boston, I came too."

"How did you come to see my advertisement? I placed it some time ago."

"During a day job the lady gave me some old newspapers to protect the table while I cleaned silverware. I happened to notice your ad and I saved it. I would so like to be with a family, Missus," said Mary, who then confided that she missed her family who had come to America but later returned to Scotland. In an apologetic voice, Mary added that her mother had much whiter skin than she had. *It sounds like they left her behind rather than have a dark-skinned daughter in their home. I wonder if Mary felt dumped, just as I wondered if my family was happy to be rid of me.*

Mary looked at the attic room with pleasure showing on her face. Soon Bella realized that, by her tone of voice, she had hired a seamstress and boarder, whether the young woman could sew or not, because her heart went out to the Scot with mulatto skin.

"When can you start, Mary?" asked Bella.

"If you wish, Ma'am, I can start right now. I left my suitcase on the front steps."

"Then bring it in, Mary, and settle yourself in your room until lunch, and then we will see how well you sew." Bella called. "Jenny, come and meet Mary, our new seamstress—and Mary, do as Jenny does. Call me Mrs. McD."

***

At lunch Gordon and Stewart, pleased to have a replacement for Aunt Flora—including the olive face like Shauna's and Scottish burr to her voice like Uncle Peter's—kept Mary busy with conversation. They both wanted to introduce Mary to Blaze, only to discover that Mary knew nothing about horses and carriages.

"Well then, Mary," said Gordon, "I will teach you. I am the best horseman in the family. You will be driving about town in our carriage in no time."

"I'll show you how to sit in the saddle," offered Stewart. "Today is my day to exercise Blaze."

Bella insisted that Mary take half an hour each day to go with either Gordon or Stewart to learn how to hitch Blaze to the carriage or saddle and ride him.

"Mother," said Gordon at dinner, "I like explaining things to people. It's fun thinking up and organizing ways to teach Mary to ride. What does that mean I should do when I finish school? I wouldn't want to be a teacher in a school. They don't make enough money."

Bella sipped her tea and finally answered.

"Gordon, I'm not sure how to answer you. For one thing, this is one of the first times you have been dead serious with your question. I suspect that you are a natural salesman, but how a person gets started in such a career is usually by chance—being at the right place at the right time. I advise finishing school and thinking about it when next summer comes." *Next year is so soon to lose a second son. Why doesn't Peter write?*

"Oh yes," piped up Mary. "School is most important. I only had home schooling in Demerara before we came to America, and then I had to earn wages as a nanny for an elderly lady and later work in that factory. You must stay in school."

***

Another week passed and still no letter from Peter. Bella looked at the wristwatch that Donald had given her. *I can't waste my time worrying. Mary needs training and I have orders to fill. The mailman comes in two hours. Maybe then there'll be word.*

***

"Mrs. McD! Mrs. McD," came Jenny's shriek of excitement. "The mailman brought you two letters. With shaking fingers, too excited to use the letter opener, Bella ripped at the envelope addressed to the family and started to read aloud.

> Dear Mother, Gordon, Stewart, and all those who hear my news.
> First off, I'm fine. Will is a swell fellow and we are good friends."

Bella read on silently to herself with short comments taken from the letter—"He had no trouble with his British birth certificate. Canada is huge with forests and lakes. He ran out of money and food and arrived hungry but safely. I'll leave the letter on the hall table for everyone to read.

Bella took the other letter to her room to read in private. In her bedroom rocking chair, she sat by the window with the tips of a hanky showing out the side of the hand that held the letter.

Dearest Mother,

I really am fine. I would be lying if I said that I don't miss my family. The train ride gave me hours to think—to think of the future and of the past. I convinced myself that I am doing the right thing as long as I don't consider what you called 'the emotional cost.' I love you and my brothers so very much.

I went walking up and down the coaches to take my mind off our parting. I saw people who reminded me of you and me as immigrants to America. Neither you nor I ever spoke of those days, but I remember them as if they were burned into my mind. I didn't have any answers until that day over dinner at Harvard, when you and Uncle William spoke of our move to America from Paramaribo. How did you manage to keep going? I may need that kind of courage until I'm a little older and used to being on my own. I'm glad I have my violin. Cousin Will has a tiny pump organ and he and I play together. That's when my eyes are damp, but he's looking at the keys and doesn't notice. Maybe his eyes are moist too.

We make a good team. By the time the crop is in I'll either have a broken back or I'll be strong as a horse. I rather expect the latter. Mother, don't worry about me. The two of us, you and me, we'll just look to the future together.

Love, Peter

P.S. This letter is just for you. I'll write again soon.

32

GOWNS

"Indeed, Mary," said Bella to the new seamstress, "you can sew a very straight seam and you're so fast and nimble with the electric machine that I can't keep up to you." *Mary's working hard at Gordon's riding lessons and at her reading with Stewart. In Mary, I have a gem. Jenny performs her domestic duties well enough, but why does grocery shopping take her so long?*

***

With Mary sewing in the dining room and Bella sewing in her bedroom, the household soon struggled for space. Business flowed in the front door, and without rent for the Farragut Building or payments on the house mortgage, Bella watched her savings account grow. She noticed, too, that her customers wore more rings and arrived in handsome carriages with drivers.

"Two ladies that I've never seen before are coming up the walk," called Jenny. "Quick, Mary, close the French doors so they can't see the sewing in the dining room. Mrs. McD must be doing something right to attract all these customers."

Bella came downstairs with Jenny's commotion.

"Do come in, ladies," said Bella with her lively velvet voice. "I'm Bella Macdonald. I don't believe we've met before." Within minutes, Jenny arrived with coffee while Bella offered the ladies her artistic hand-drawn cards showing suggested patterns.

"You have come to order dresses for Christmas a little on the late side, but I know of material in the shades you wish to have. Let me see if I can still buy it. Here is my card. Please phone in three days. If I can buy the goods, you must come in for measurements," said Bella as she accompanied them to the door.

What am I doing taking orders so close to Christmas? I'm so busy sewing that I have no time to think. That's what I'm doing, isn't it—sewing to keep my mind off Peter's well-being? With all of that farm work, he writes that he's grown two inches and lost ten pounds, yet he says they eat well with lots of chicken, eggs and vegetables. Why does the postman pass me by for a month and then bring three letters at once? I hate the waiting.

She stopped with her hand on her forehead. *If I keep at this pace, I will make myself ill again. I must make changes.*

Donald's rocking chair slowed its rocking after the departure of one of the new customers. *Donald, are you signalling me to slow down with your rocking chair?* Bella looked at her watch. *Eleven forty-five. The boys will soon be in for lunch. Today I will be ready for their arrival. I haven't given them much time lately.* Bella opened the French doors to make the living room available during lunch and returned to the rocking chair.

We have more business than we can handle. We're all working too hard. Change! I must change something, but what? She pressed her hands together like a padre in thought. Bella rocked as the minutes ticked away. *Change—obviously time off is the answer, and if I take time away from sewing then I must give the girls time off. I could match the stores in Cambridge and close for Wednesday and Saturday afternoon plus Sundays, but I must not get behind.* She rocked and pondered the thoughts forming in her mind. As the boys rushed in the back door, her thoughts crystalized. *Yes, Wednesday and Saturday afternoons for the girls, and I'll take Saturday and Sunday to be with my boys. That might work.*

***

At five o'clock, Bella quit her machine and went down to the living room. The boys weren't there, but then, lately she had not arrived on time either. When the boys finally trooped in, Bella asked Mary and Jenny to sit with them in the living room.

"What are your plans for the weekend, boys?" asked Bella.

Gordon answered first: "Not much. What's there to do on a winter weekend except homework and church on Sunday?" Stewart agreed. The girls said nothing.

"That's it?" said Bella. "The cold weather has put an end to baseball and your friends are all busy with their parents? I'm making some changes. From now on, the girls will have an afternoon off during the week plus Saturday afternoon and Sundays off. I'll take all of Saturday and Sunday off so I can be free to plan things as a family."

With this pronouncement, Stewart jumped up, shouting "Hooray!" He tripped over Gordon's foot movement and landed, arms akimbo and facedown, in Mary's lap.

"Don't hug Mary, dummy, hug Mother," teased Gordon. "She's the one who'll take you to see the model train at the convention hall."

Mary and Jenny ran over and kissed Bella on the forehead.

Jenny, with a sweet smile on her face, said, "I know of a place where people gather to dance. I've watched from the doorway when I've been grocery shopping. I can follow their steps. Maybe that's where I'll go." Mary kept her ideas to herself.

***

Meeting with the family regained its "five o'clock sharp" routine. Oddly enough, Bella and Mary accomplished the schedule for sewing despite the time off.

As the days passed, Bella watched for the mailman from her upstairs window. Gathers, little tucks and hems were all completed with one eye on the sidewalk below. *The mailman's coming up our walk. Dear God, let him have a letter from Peter.*

"Gather around, boys. Come, girls. I have two letters to read from Peter."

Dear Mother, Gordon and Stewart, Mary, Jenny and Blaze,

We are having Indian summer right now. On the prairies, the first killing frost comes at the end of August or early in September. It came, and after that we've had perfect warm days to finish up haying and getting things ready for winter. I'LL BE HOME FOR CHRISTMAS! Will says that he has to stay with the livestock and chickens. 'Livestock' means our Ox, Aries. He's no ram but he does have horns. Then there's the milk cow, Margarita. That's Daisy in Spanish, and there's a bunch of chickens, just called dinner.

I had a toothache, so Will had me ride the ox bareback into Regina to see a dentist. It felt like he used a hatchet, but my jaw's all healed and the toothache is gone. He says that I'll grow a wisdom tooth in that space when I'm older.

I've just finished making porridge for breakfast, and after we eat, Will and I are digging potatoes to store in the dugout under the house.

Bye for now, Love, Peter

"There are two letters today," said Bella as she reached for the other envelope. "Here, Gordon, you read it." Gordon began:

Hello again my family,

School has started. It's a good thing that I have heavy work boots. I walk a gravel trail that's as straight as a hoe handle except where it crosses a little creek. I first saw the schoolhouse nestled in a fenced grassy yard when I breasted a low rise about a mile from Will's shack. Some kids were putting their horses in a stable at the back of the yard next to two outhouses. The white clapboard school has four rooms with four teachers. I know I'm going to like it because there's a library and lots of maps. There are eight boys and seven girls in our room. Wendy shares a desk with me. She has hair the colour of Blaze's mane.

The school has a baseball team and I'm on it. Do my hard hands and strong muscles ever make a difference in how fast I can pitch the ball! Will lets me use his man-sized baseball glove. Kids practice ball at school every recess.

After school Will and I are going to can some crab apples we bought at the market. Then there's homework at the dining room table until the daylight fails or doing something after that when we light the kerosene lamp. If we still have any energy, we play a little music together.

Until next time, Love, Peter

***

Stewart spoke up first. "It doesn't sound like he has a blue sofa like ours. He's always sitting on chairs at the table. I'd get tired of sitting on wooden chairs all the time."

"Naw, Stewart," said Gordon. "Forget chairs. You missed his important phrase about Wendy, with the strawberry blond hair, sitting beside him all day."

"Ya?" said Stewart. "What if she has a horsy face to go with the horse's mane?"

"Gordon and Stewart," said Bella, looking over the top of her glasses. "We speak good English in this house and that does not include 'Naw' and 'Ya.'"

"Yes, Mother," said Stewart. "If I don't say those words, may we go to see the Lionel trains on Saturday? The models have shiny painted coaches that whiz around on miniature metal tracks. The kids at school talk about it all the time."

"Yes, dear, we'll hitch Blaze to the carriage and we'll go," said Bella. "If Mary and Jenny wish, they can come along too."

***

Customers arrived and gowns were sewn. The grapevine carried Bella's name for miles around. Her small house could hardly handle the trade. *I cannot disturb the family any more than I have. Even though Peter's gone, we just don't have enough room. My salon is hardly worthy of the prices I could charge if my shop were more attractive. Enough! I must plan a joyous Christmas to welcome Peter and the boys from next door.*

***

Belching grey smoke, the train chugged into the station. Peter jumped off and flew into the arms of his mother. He cuffed his brothers on the shoulders to greet them. Bella stood back and stared. "Peter, you're filling out just like your father! Look how tall you've grown!"

"It's the fresh air, hard work and good food that's done it. You should come, Gordon. It's a good life. Now that the creek has frozen over, the kids ice skate at recess."

***

In a few days, with crepe paper streamers in red and green stretched from one corner of the ceiling to another, spruce boughs over the doors and the smell of Christmas baking, the family felt prepared for the festive season. On Christmas Eve, after church, Peter and his mother finally had a chance to talk, sitting together on the blue sofa.

"School is going well, Mother. Will seems to like having me around, so I'll stay for grades nine, ten and eleven."

Bella let Peter do all the talking while she sat in awe of her eldest son, now a young man. *Agassiz Grammar School taught him well. I'm glad I knew it existed. Donald, are you proud of your eldest son? I am. From his enthusiasm, it sounds like his Saskatchewan school is doing a good job. He's certainly happy there.*

"It's late. Tomorrow is Christmas, with gifts to open. We must go to bed."

***

In the morning, when she heard the boys thumping down the stairs to the living room, Bella finished the last twist of her braided topknot and applied the pearls around it, then floated down the stairs in her new gown.

"Mother, I've never seen you so radiant!" burst out Peter. Gordon and Stewart rushed to kiss her. Jenny and Mary stood and clapped.

"Thank you. I'm glad my Christmas gown pleases you. Let's open the gifts."

One by one, the pile of gifts dwindled as tissue wrappings filled the floor and squeals of delight filled the air. The happy voices and smiling faces continued through a Christmas dinner of roast beef and plum pudding, followed by singing carols.

On her way to bed that night, Bella stopped by her bedroom window and looked out at the crisp winter evening. She raised her eyes to the stars. *Nearly the end of 1905 and I'm finally debt free and a successful businesswoman. I give thanks, Oh Lord, for having Shauna and Donald in my life. They helped me at every turn. Although they have gone on, their good judgement still guides me. I must not forget the generosity of Donald's three brothers, for without the funds they gave me I would have failed. Amen.*

***

"Stewart," Peter asked a few days later. "It's your day to exercise Blaze. Do you mind if I take him for a ride around my favourite haunts?"

Peter trotted down to Harvard Yard and then went up Oxford on his old route home from violin lessons. The sun shone and Blaze cantered along at ease with his rider, so Peter extended the ride. He turned the opposite way along Sacramento out to Massachusetts Avenue, crossed it and turned right onto Hudson, then right again onto Bowdoin. He realized that he didn't know this side of Massachusetts Avenue very well so decided to find his way home. At their gathering before dinner he told of his ride.

"The other side of Massachusetts Avenue is fancier than our side, Mother. I saw the biggest old half-duplex up for sale. A bay window filled the front corner, another bay window bulged out on the side of the house and windows dotted the third floor. I don't remember the name of the street but I could find it again if anyone wants to see it."

"A winter sale?" said Bella. "I doubt that that will work while Harvard's winter semester is in session. Who would want to move in the winter?"

Next, Gordon spoke up. "Geoff has invited us to go swimming if we want. The students are home for the holidays and Claverly is deserted. I suggested tomorrow. Is anyone interested?" This caught the boys' attention until Jenny announced supper.

Hmmm. A large house, Peter says. I shall offer to take the boys over to swimming and then follow the route Peter described. I'm curious about a house for sale in the winter. It's silly of me to be curious. The last thing I need is a mortgage over my head again, yet I need more space.

***

The next day Bella entered the offices of the Cambridge Real Estate Company.

"I'd like to speak to Ivan Jenkins, please. Tell him that Isabella Macdonald wishes to see him."

"Good afternoon, Mrs. Macdonald," started Mr. Jenkins. "Is your business that urgent? In two days it's the New Year."

"Yes, Sir, it is as urgent as the Christmas that you wanted to sell 49 ½ Sacramento Street out from under me. As it happens, that turn of events has served me well. Now, I have a prospect for you to work on immediately." Ivan offered Bella a seat and listened.

"There is a house for sale on Hurlbut Street, on the west side of Massachusetts Avenue. I want to know all about it: when it was built, why it's for sale and the condition it's in. I want to know who's selling it and if you think the house offers value for the price. Next, I wish you to compare my house on Sacramento Street to the market and ascertain its present day value. My interest in these houses is between you and I. If news comes back to me on the grapevine, you will lose my business. I'll call you tomorrow to hear what you have found out. Good afternoon, Mr. Jenkins."

***

At two o'clock the next day, from her room with the door closed, Bella rang Ivan Jenkins. After a lengthy conversation she sat in her chair and mulled over the real estate agent's report. *6 Hurlbut Street—built in 1888—eighteen years old—being sold by a bank and in need of modernising. It's large—a parlour and a sitting room on the main floor—that's one for the shop and one for a family parlour. The second floor has five chambers— two for sewing rooms and a bedroom each for Gordon, Stewart and me. My goodness, another four rooms in the attic! Mary and Jenny can have a floor to themselves with their own staircase at the back hall. With a nicer shop I could attract upper class clientele and my prices could rise to match their wealth.*

***

On New Year's Eve Jenny found candles to place on the table with their best tablecloth. Mary helped her in the kitchen and together they served a regal dinner of roast turkey, mashed potatoes, gravy, carrots and boiled cabbage. For dessert, the girls brought forth red jelly with thick cream and varieties of Christmas baking.

"As always," said Stewart, "after eight, our family concert will begin. Please be prepared."

***

As usual, Stewart took his place in the archway between the living room and dining room and called upon himself to lead off the concert. His banjo strings twanged as he sang in a fine boy's tenor voice. Gordon recited all eleven verses of "The Day is Done" in a clear, melodious voice. Peter showed a picture he'd drawn of the homestead. He spoke of the early sunrises that climbed over the fields to warm the days followed by sunsets in yellow, scarlet and orange. He delighted in the sweet smell of hay mixed with the body sweat of the animals. He spoke of the rooster, crowing at dawn, that sharpened his desire to rise and join the peace of the fields, and how his body revelled in his new-found strength and how his brain attacked whatever problem he encountered with a will to succeed at solving it.

Jenny came forth and hummed while she danced a clog dance, and Mary recited "The Mouse" by Robbie Burns.

Everyone clapped and waited while Bella rose to offer her entertainment.

Bella took her place in the archway. "What I have to say concerns us all. I am thinking about going into debt again." She paused. Every eye became riveted on her face. "Don't look so concerned. I have seen the big duplex on Hurlbut Street that Peter discovered for me and I believe the move is worth the risk. We need more space for my growing family and more room for my business. Now I open the floor to discussion and hot cocoa."

33

NO. 6
HURLBUT STREET

"Mr. Jenkins," said Bella, "your client, the bank that's selling this house, must lower the price. The whole place smells like dirty clothes because the bank neglected to clean the house after they repossessed it. Removing odours is difficult and it needs redecorating. I don't intend to haggle over the price. Bring me the bank's best offer. I'm sure they want to be done with paying the taxes and checking on it. If the price isn't considerably lower, I won't buy it or sell my Sacramento Street home." *Two homes—that should make him want the sale!*

***

"Well done, Mr. Jenkins. That is a much more agreeable price," said Bella when Mr. Jenkins came to her house. "I will phone you after I've spoken to my banker."

***

"I know that you'll have your financial records all ready for me, Mrs. Macdonald," said Mr. Stallworthy, "and I know you make beautiful clothes. My wife buys your gowns and her appearance has improved immensely."

"Now who is trying to butter up whom, Sir?" replied Bella. "It sounds to me as if you are trying to prepare me for a letdown. I have gone over my figures very carefully and I do have room for making mortgage payments to afford that house. Just read my report. Lower your eyes to the paper and read. That is all it takes." The banker shook his head as if to escape from Bella's ability to turn a phrase. When his eyes reached the bottom of the report, he did not raise his head.

"What seems to be the problem?" said Bella. "Do your superiors still have difficulty doing business with women? You must get over it if that is the case, for more and more women will involve themselves in business. Forget your superiors. You saw my books. Now, what about allowing me to sign those papers?"

With a sigh, Mr. Stallworthy sank back in his office chair, and without saying a word, pushed the mortgage papers across his desk towards Bella. She, in turn, read every word and determined where to sign.

"Thank you, Mr. Stallworthy. I'm sure that your superiors won't regret your decision to do business with a woman. When my salon is ready, I will host an opening cocktail party and you and Mrs. Stallworthy will be on the guest list." With that, Bella put the mortgage papers in her bag, gave a nod of her head and left. *I do believe that he's finally accepted me as a businesswoman, not just someone of the female gender.*

***

"Now, Mr. Jenkins, we must conclude the arrangements to sell 49 ½ Sacramento Street."

"No problem, Ma'am. I have three clients looking for just such a place."

"In that case, Ivan—may I call you Ivan? Call me Bella. In that case, show it to the richest client first, and to the price you suggested to me add an amount equal to your fee."

Ivan Jenkins completed the paperwork without a word.

***

In early January, with the move in view, Bella surprised Jenny and Mary with her zeal for home decorating. As if using a crystal ball, once Bella had conjured in her mind the effect she wished to portray in her salon, colours popped into her head and fabrics for drapes collected on her vanity. Following the exact tones she desired, Bella purchased paint. The next day she appeared in her old paint pants with a scarf over her hair.

"Mrs. McD," cried Mary, "you're much too delicate to paint your salon. I've never painted anything but I'm willing to learn. Let me help."

"Thank you, Mary. That's very kind of you but I'm not that delicate, even if my hair is starting to turn grey. Find a pair of Peter's old pants. They are much more comfortable for the job. With any luck we'll be able to open my new salon by the end of the month and pay off the mortgage with the orders that flood in. If we're successful, I may have to hire a third seamstress. That means you'll be sewing much fancier parts of the gowns. You are ready for it, don't you think?"

***

Every morning Mary and Bella drove to Hurlbut Street to continue their redecorating spree, and each night the carriage trundled home with two weary women. Bella searched the hall table for a letter from Peter, but the mailman only brought bills.

By the last week of January, Bella had an announcement to make.

"After supper, boys and Jenny, I'll take you to Hurlbut Street to see what Mary and I have accomplished. You remember how dirty and worn the place looked when you unloaded the paint for me? Well, you won't recognize the front entry and parlour now."

***

"Mother, you installed brass outdoor lamps at the front door," raved Gordon as they climbed the front steps of No. 6 Hurlbut Street. They entered the front vestibule. The walls were cream with white woodwork.

"What's this on the wall?" asked Jenny as she tested the wall surface with her index finger. "It looks like cream-coloured linen."

"It is linen," replied Bella. "Mary and I applied wallpaper glue and stretched the cloth into it. The ivory-toned linen sets off the white of the woodwork. I believe the new décor by 1910 will show white on white. We'll see the end of dark colours."

They stepped into the parlour and immediately felt the glamour of the salon. The staircase banister shone in white enamel, as did all the woodwork. The parlour walls had ivory wallpaper with a small gold motif to match the white fireplace and its polished brass fire screen.

The family walked around the salon, looking at the lavish decor. The ivory sofa held grey-blue side cushions to match the carpet. Gold figurines graced the white side tables and mantel. White drapes and sheers hung in the bay window. One corner of the room held the long mirror while an opposite corner had three adjoined screens to form the change area.

"It looks very grand, Mother," said Gordon. "I'll be afraid to sit on anything except maybe those two side chairs upholstered in grey-blue."

"Where did you find the gold statues, Mother?" cried Stewart.

"I simply went to the second-hand shops and when I found a suitable statue, I painted it gold. I did the same thing for the gold picture frames and the lamp. We recovered second-hand furniture. It's amazing what hard work and imagination can produce."

The family started towards the door to the rest of the house.

"You mustn't look at the other rooms," warned Bella. "We haven't had time to finish them yet. Only the kitchen and lower bathroom are painted in case the guests see that far into the house. In February Mary and I will paint more rooms, and with the help of the boys next door and the Wrays' big wagon, we'll move in before March the first."

***

"Come in, Mr. and Mrs. Stallworthy," said Bella. "I'm sure you'll find other guests whom you know—perhaps Dr. and Mrs. Charles Eliot, President of Harvard, or Leopold Blaschka, standing just to his right." Bella continued to welcome the guests while Jenny and Mary, in elegant saris, moved among the guests with trays holding mint juleps. Gordon and Stewart, wearing their black suits, served mushroom logs, olives and small squares of Melba toast with pimento cream cheese sprinkled with chopped parsley.

Carrie and Charles Wray arrived with a carriage full of Bella's customers from the rural area, and the old neighbours of Sacramento Street arrived in their finery.

With the room radiating a colourful collage of gowns accented by the men's dark suits, Bella gathered the attention of her guests. She welcomed them to her new salon and proclaimed it officially open by placing a blue and white card in the window that read: "Gowns – Open from 10 a.m. until 2 p.m. on weekdays."

***

With her grand opening and advertising, Bella had no shortage of customers and soon she and Mary needed their room-painting days for sewing. *So much paperwork. I'll have to turn that old-fashioned china room that opens onto the hall into an office. A typewriter! That's what I need, with a white desk. I shall look as grand as Madame LeBeau at Fowley's Fashions. I wonder if the Examining Board of Massachusetts would grant me the right to train seamstresses.* Then the voice from deep within said, *Finish sewing that waistband, Bella. It is time for your visit with the boys.*

"How do you find the walk to school, Gordon?" asked Bella when everyone had assembled before dinner.

"Fine, Mother," laughed Gordon. "A few steps further than before will make me hardier and ready for Cousin Will's homestead in Canada. Peter seems to think he made a good decision. During high school I'll read the newspapers to see what's going on in Canada, and after I graduate, I'll learn some business and then start my own."

"That's what you did, Mother," piped up Stewart. "You learned about sewing by apprenticing and then started a business."

"Yes, Mother," added Gordon, "you're good at starting businesses. Why don't we all go to Canada now? We're British subjects."

My, the boys are growing older, with ideas of their own milling around in their minds. It sounds like I will lose my second son at the end of this year, yet he doesn't want the family split between Canada and America. He may have a point, but I will not move until Stewart finishes at Agassiz School, for that's what gave Peter such a good start. I should have heard from him by now. It's so hard not to worry when I get no letter!

***

"Mrs. McD, the mailman just brought a letter from Peter," squealed Jenny as she ran up the front stairs to the sewing rooms. Bella grasped the letter and ripped it open.

Dear Mother, and Family,

Cambridge doesn't know snow! Just after I arrived home from my Christmas holidays, it started to snow—pretty soft flakes at first that melted on my tongue. Will kept looking to the northwest, watching the sky. He insisted that I stay home from school, and by noon, snow swirled everywhere. Can you imagine? Just by looking at the sky, Will knew to keep me home.

The weatherman meted out a ten-day blizzard with howling winds that blew the snow into great drifts that nearly buried the shack, barn and outhouse. Snow, pushed by the wind, streaked across the flat land so you couldn't see in front of you. Will called it a "whiteout." He went out with a long rope that he keeps under his bed and hooked one end of the rope to a huge spike imbedded in the shack. He tied the other end around his waist before he wandered out into the blizzard to tend to the animals. I worried when he didn't return. After two hours his grey form appeared through the blowing snow as he worked his way, hand-over-hand, along the rope that now held fast to a spike in the barn wall.

Across his shoulders he brought a second rope from the barn and dropped it at my feet. He told me that it was my turn to find the spike on the outhouse. Without those ropes we would have been in trouble. We spent two weeks indoors, mostly reading his books by kerosene light. We had lots of food. The chickens furnished meat and the dugout had vegetables.

One morning I awoke with a start because the house seemed so quiet. The wind had stopped howling! My window showed nothing but packed snow, so I rushed to the cabin door. Snow banks marked the only two humps in the yard: the barn and the outhouse. Blue sky met a flat white horizon as far as you could see. We shovelled for hours, making paths to the barn, the outhouse and the road that passes nearby. We had to shovel the shack roof too. Will said the weight of the snow might break it down. This isn't meant to scare you, Mother. We were fine the whole time, and seeing what nature could do excited me. I'm really going to study my cloud book. If you know how to read the sky, it tells you everything in advance of what might happen with weather on the prairies.

Our neighbour should pass by with his team of horses and sleigh and Will plans to go to town with him for sugar, tea, flour and kerosene. School starts tomorrow. At school, to celebrate the end of a blizzard the kids always hold a pie social, so I'll be baking pie tonight. At the social there's dancing. I must close and address the envelope; Will's putting on his coat to hike out to the road.

Love, Peter

I never thought of a blizzard. This letter should teach me to stop worrying about Peter. He is a man now and I must let go of him. Next, it will be Gordon, and then, Stewart. What will I do then? Take care of my business, I suppose.

***

Spring arrived with a flood of orders. Katy O'Rourke, with no training, came on staff. She lived at home in East Cambridge and rode her bicycle to work. Often, in the evenings, Bella opened her salon to charitable groups who wished to hold meetings or for Miss Baldwin's classes for coloured people. Bella kept her weekends for the boys, paid the redecorating debt and worked on the new mortgage.

***

"You've grown taller, Gordon," said Bella one evening before dinner. "We must lengthen your suit for your graduation." Stewart sat up, looking hopeful "No, Stewart, no suit this year. The old one is not worn out."

"We dug the flower gardens, Mother," offered Gordon. "This place has lots of perennials. Buy us some flower seeds and we'll make it the finest garden on the street."

"And an old lawnmower," added Stewart. "I'll fix it and we'll mow the lawn."

"I'll add mower to my list, Stewart. Come with me on Saturday and pick it out."

Mary spoke. "Could you buy more bobbins, Mrs. McD? We lose time changing the colour of thread on them all the time."

***

"Don't the graduating girls look lovely in their spring gowns?" Bella whispered to Mary when the graduating class took its place in the assembly room at Agassiz School.

"They should, Mrs. McD; we sewed half of those gowns. Look, the boys are wearing flowers in the button-holes of their suits!"

Bella thought for a moment, then whispered, "Perhaps, as soon as someone realized that suits had a useless button-hole, another person decided it should be used for something. The frothy white flower they're wearing on the lapel is the Arbutus, the State Flower of Massachusetts." The crowd hushed. "Here comes Miss Baldwin to introduce the graduation program. What a wonderful educator she is!"

As with previous years, the graduands were introduced with applause and Dr. Charles Eliot, President of Harvard, spoke. The audience stirred with anticipation when Miss Baldwin stood to announce the valedictorian's name.

"We will now hear from our valedictorian, Master Gordon Macdonald." Gordon took the podium and spoke of hard work and wisdom and all of the usual things, but he salted his speech politely with talk of girls and sewing one's seeds of youth, which made everyone laugh and clap loudly when he finished.

Cries of "Well done!" rose above the clapping. Bella sat back and proudly accepted her son as the outstanding person that he was. *He will do well because he can make people laugh and make them feel at ease. He's determined to go to Canada. Somehow, I believe he will be too busy making money to bother with university.*

***

By early July Gordon left to join his brother near Regina. The train chuffed out of the station, heading north, with Gordon hanging out the train window and the whole family shouting goodbye until the curve of the tracks pulled Gordon from view.

That evening Bella looked out her bedroom window at the stars. *Dear God, I have committed two of my sons to your care. Please watch over them until we can be united again. Donald, you had no chance to be with your sons as they grew to be young men, but they know you in their hearts and I am sure they will live as you would have them live: with a zeal for life, prudence, endearment, and integrity. I know that I will lose them all sooner or later, and then what?*

With this, she burst into tears, ran to her bed and buried her face in her pillow.

34

THE BLUE BOOK

"Mother, I need boxing shorts," said Stewart at the start of the fall term. "I can use the boys' old gloves, but everyone at the club has special shorts and a white singlet."

"Boxing Club?" asked Bella. "When did you join a boxing club?"

"Today," answered Stewart. "With my brothers away, I need boxing partners. I'll learn the Marquess of Queensberry Rules," he offered. "I might become the top boxer for my age in Cambridge. I know because, if I tried, I could beat up everyone at school."

"So you say, young man," Bella responded. "What if you meet some tough fellow from East Cambridge where the Irish live? They are excellent boxers too."

"Please, Mother, just sew me some shorts and let me try."

"Very well, Stewart. A couple of bloody noses are fine. Just remember to keep your hands high and elbows in, so your opponent doesn't break your nose."

"How do you know so much about boxing?" cried Stewart.

"Did Peter never tell you that I was his original punching bag while we learned to box from a library book?" Bella stood, took the pose of a boxer and swung a left hook.

***

"Mary," said Bella one morning, "help me make a list of fifteen clients to model in a fashion show. You may be one of them—Jenny and Katy too, for that matter."

"A fashion show, Mrs. McD?" said Mary. "Why a fashion show? We have more customers than we can handle now."

"The fashion show will raise money for a group in town that helps poor children. A charity fashion show will raise their image and gain them support. I'll be out this afternoon booking a hall at the university. Don't worry, Mary. I've done this before."

***

"Mother," an excited Stewart said before dinner, "tomorrow at seven p.m., parents may watch us fight in a boxing tournament at the club. Will you come?"

Bella shuddered at the thought of some big lout walloping her son, but she swallowed and said, "Why, of course, Stewart. Just tell me when you need to leave and we'll go there in the carriage." *At least I'll know more about this club.*

***

Stewart left Bella to seat herself in one of the folding chairs set up for the parents while he went to join his club mates. The place looked fresh enough, with its apple-green walls and ceiling fan to suck away the body odour. The boys, dressed for their fights, came from a back room and sat on the other side of the raised boxing ring. In the first fight two boys, ten and under, jabbed at each other. Everyone clapped when the referee held up both boys' arms.

"Fight Two: Twelve and under," shouted the referee. Stewart, eleven, jumped into the ring with a bulldog countenance while he loosened his shoulder muscles as if he had some. *Oh dear, is this the sweet child I raised?* Stewart's opponent climbed into the ring wearing a sneer and a green satin kimono. Bella's fingers entwined anxiously when she saw the size of him.

"In this corner," shouted the referee, "wearing blue shorts, we have Stewart Macdonald of the Cambridge Boxing Club." Stewart sallied forth, holding up a gloved hand. Bella clapped and screamed with the crowd.

"And in this corner, wearing green shorts, is Sean McGuinty from the Irish Boxing Club in East Cambridge." Sean's club mates cheered while the Irish fighter shrugged off his robe. Bella closed her eyes. She wasn't sure if she could watch.

"Round One," shouted the referee. Sean swaggered forth to pound Stewart, but Stewart danced like a firefly and caught the boy on the side of the cheek with a right jab. With his teeth gritted, the bigger boy lunged for a quick kill. Stewart looked just like the boxer on his pamphlet, eyes focused with his gloves up, weaving and bobbing so artfully that his opponent's gloves flew through the air while Stewart managed to plant a blow to the body and a double to the chin.

"Round Two," intoned the referee. Now and then, Stewart caught a jab on a shoulder, but usually this gave him an opening for an even more solid punch to the boy's ribs. By this time the lace handkerchief that Bella held had ripped at the corner.

"Round Three." The bell sounded. The Irish fighter's eyes blazed with anger as he pounded towards Stewart. *That's right, Stewart! Stay light on your feet and dance away before Sean's blows can land.* "Yeah, Stewart!" *Flit in to bust him one in the ribs. Sooner or later he'll drop his guard and you'll connect with his nose or chin.* The bell rang. The boys joined the referee in the centre of the ring. Bella noticed a small trickle of blood on Sean's upper lip. *Oh my goodness, my Stewart bloodied Sean's nose! Are they supposed to fight that hard? What if it were the other way around?*

"By counting points," shouted the referee, "the winner is Stewart Macdonald." The referee held Stewart's gloved hand high. Bella sank back in her chair with a sigh of relief. At nine p.m. the fights were over and a jubilant Stewart talked all the way home.

"Mother, I won because I've trained myself to have elastic in my legs. He thought he could flatten me in one punch but he couldn't catch me!"

"You bloodied his nose at the end. Did you know that?" asked Bella.

"I did? Good for me—he deserved it. He didn't follow the rules of boxing."

"Stewart, must I attend more of your fights? I shredded my hankie twisting it around my fingers worrying with each punch that fellow threw. It would be better if you asked one of the boys from Sacramento Street to go with you. If some boy downed you, I fear I'd rush into the ring and catch him one right on the chin with my bare fist." They attended to Blaze and went into the house.

"You should have been a boy, Mother. You have the right attitude. Goodnight."

***

"Mary," said Bella while they were sewing, "tomorrow, at lunch, I've been asked to speak to the Chamber of Commerce about women in business. I want to sound like a businesswoman, not a women's rights crusader. That's it—I'll speak to them about how to run a successful business, for business is business, whether it's managed by a man or a woman." Again, Bella felt the need to will her fingers to work faster at her sewing to account for time lost at speaking engagements.

***

Christmas came and the house flooded with the energy that having three boys together produces. The orders for Christmas gowns staggered the three seamstresses, but all the gowns were finished on time. The Boxing Day trip to Wrays' farm and New Year's Eve with the family's performances were the same as ever, except Jenny went dancing with her beau.

After the excitement of the evening, Bella dreaded the sleepless night that would follow while her brain reworked too many questions: *Is this our last Christmas together? I'm forty-five—getting older—getting grey—I must restyle my hair, short and curled as is the fashion. Is my business finally a success? I still have a mortgage. Have I achieved raising my boys to the high standard I set when I arrived in America? So many questions. I must go to sleep. I must, I must.*

***

The day came for the fashion show. By eight o'clock, with every table filled, the guests rustled with anticipation as the lights dimmed and a spotlight fell on Bella.

"Good evening, ladies and gentlemen," she began. "Welcome to our evening of fashion. I hope you continue to reach out to the less advantaged children of Cambridge by volunteering your time to the work of this charity." Bella paused to allow for applause.

"I am Bella Macdonald, of a salon known as 'Gowns.' In a few minutes, volunteers—fifteen women of your community—will model gowns from my spring collection. Miss Jones, the music instructor at Agassiz Grammar School, will provide accompaniment for the models while I explain the fabrics and styles of each gown." Bella nodded a bow and her spotlight faded.

The pianist gave a flourish of notes, lights came on so that all would see the models with their colourful gowns and Bella started her commentary.

"First, we have Mary Thomson, wearing a slim-line burnt-orange gown with a flared skirt and a sash that ties in the back." Mary gave a delicate turn to show off the back of the gown and continued on around the room between the tables. The fashion show continued, with the pleasure of the audience growing as each model received more applause. An hour and a half later, the fifteen ladies took their final bow. Each guest received a small card that bore the name of the charity and who to contact.

***

Back home, Bella decided on tea and some of Jenny's cookies. "Well done, girls, and thank you. You both made lovely models, and if I might say in a kindly way, the poor children of this city come in many skin tones and I thought the two of you sent a message of self respect to those who might not know people with mulatto-toned skin. In many ways, I thought you two were the whole show. I haven't felt this happy since I found clothes for the poor of Paramaribo. Goodnight, ladies. I'm bone tired."

***

Bella's name became known around Cambridge. Women said hello and men tipped their hats—people she didn't even know. The brothers at church asked her to lead the service. Mrs. Stallworthy reported at one of her dress fittings that her husband had been promoted. Mr. Farragut rented her old shop to a florist, and the manageress hadn't changed a single colour in Bella's décor.

What do you think, Donald? Has your family found success? Next year Peter will enter university. Gordon is planning his future and Stewart will start his last year at Agassiz School. You have no idea how focused Stewart can be. In that he is much like you, my dear. Goodnight.

***

"Mrs. McD," Jenny called from the hall. "You have a letter from Cambridge."

"Really? Whatever do they want? I've paid the taxes." Sitting in Donald's rocking chair, she slit the envelope and removed a gilt-edged card. It read:

Isabella Macdonald and Partner
Are cordially invited
To the Annual Dinner of the Cambridge Chamber of Commerce
7:00 p.m., March 28, 1908
The Ballroom, Harvard University
RSVP   Black Tie Attire

"Jenny!" cried Bella. "Come and see the fancy invitation I've received. It says, 'Isabella Macdonald and Partner.' I'll have Stewart attend with me. Now, why would the Chamber of Commerce invite me to their annual dinner?" Jenny came, examined the card and remained as bewildered as Bella.

"Stewart," called Bella after dinner. "Come down to the dining room. I want to retrain your elastic legs. We are going to waltz and two-step at a party."

***

"Isabella and Stewart Macdonald," the Chamber of Commerce Secretary announced as Bella and Stewart entered the ballroom. A gentleman, whom Bella did not know, welcomed them and asked Bella to join his group in conversation.

Bella watched Stewart observe the whole scene. Crystal chandeliers sprinkled light across the room that highlighted beautiful gowns and gentlemanly figures in black. Fresh flowers centred each table. From the expression on his face, everything together painted a scene of grandeur for his young eyes.

"Stewart," said Bella in a low voice, "you are looking at the trappings of education and good management. Someday, I am sure you will sit at a head table." Mr. McLeod, the man who had first welcomed them, invited Bella and Stewart to sit at his table near the front of the room.

The Master of Ceremonies rose to announce the first speaker—the mayor—to bring a short address. Next came a report on the economic health of Cambridge. Following his report, the president of the Chamber of Commerce rose.

"Guests, as you know, every year we recognize an outstanding person who has added his personal touch to Cambridge in business and charitable acts. This year, for the first time in Cambridge history, this distinction goes to a woman. Please recognize Bella Macdonald." Rapid applause and calls of "Hear, hear!" filled the ballroom. The president came to Bella's chair to escort her to the podium. Bella felt her feet walking. She knew her hands had come together and she wondered if a smile had taken over her whole face as she looked out over the guests who had risen from their chairs to pay homage to her. The president waited for the clapping to subside. Holding his hand open-faced towards Bella to present her, he said:

"This woman, less than five feet tall, not only started a flourishing business in our town, she did it despite the roadblocks that we men tried to put in her way because we thought that the business world belonged to men. Please recognize Bella Macdonald, the first woman to sign her name in the Blue Book of Cambridge. Only ten years ago, she came to this country as an immigrant and widow. She apprenticed as a seamstress, and with her journeyman status, opened the shop known simply as 'Gowns.' Her two older sons graduated at the head of their class at Agassiz Grammar School and her youngest son, Stewart, who accompanies his mother this evening, appears to be following in his brothers' footsteps." *How does he know all these details?*

A spotlight picked out Stewart at his table. He rose, nodded his head in appreciation of his brief moment in the evening's events and sat down, with pride in his mother painted across his face.

The president ended his speech with: "Bella Macdonald, please sign our Blue Book. The Cambridge Chamber of Commerce is honoured to have you live in our midst and support Cambridge in the many ways that you have."

To another round of applause, Bella signed the book, accepted a bouquet of roses, and blew "thank you" kisses in all directions.

***

Jenny and Mary waited up for Bella's return home.

"Did you find out why you were invited to the party, Mrs. McD?" squealed Jenny.

Bella tripped lightly into the house in disbelief of the event that had just occurred. She told them of the evening while Stewart added to the excitement of it in his version of events, and finally they all retired. In the morning Bella realized the whole truth of the evening's event when she came down to the salon and found her bouquet, a dozen burgundy roses, displayed in her crystal vase. *Can it be coincidence? A dozen burgundy roses as if my Donald had placed them there? No matter; I know he watches over me.*

Bella's calendar now held speaking engagements and work with charities as well as designing very expensive gowns for her customers. With less time to sew gowns herself, Bella had Mary take over the finer sewing after she designed the gowns. Katy learned the trade, but without Bella sewing full time the shop had to make changes. To reduce the number of customers and continue the incoming flow of revenue, Bella raised her prices, and still, the shop flourished. *1908—I believe I can call myself a success, despite clothing factories producing cheaper clothes.*

***

Letters continued to arrive from Peter or Gordon. Gordon's address appeared on the next letter.

Dear Family,

The crop is in and snow is accumulating on the ground. Peter and I are having a great time reading Cousin Will's leather-bound, gilt-edged classics from Scotland. We've fashioned a sled for the gang to go sliding down the creek bank. Gang?—that's girls and boys.

Two fellows at school have their own two-man band. They want a Master of Ceremonies who can talk to the crowd, tell a few jokes and sing. I can do the first two things. I'm not sure about the singing, but it's a job. I'll get a cut of the door money. See you at Christmas. Love, Gordon

***

The boys arrived four days before Christmas in a drizzling rain, and again the house was alive with Bella's big boys joking, laughing and helping where they could. As in the past, the holidays came and went. Bella could only grasp the moment but not hold on forever. *Last year I worried about it being our last Christmas, and here we've had another one, so I refuse to worry anymore.*

***

Winter turned into spring and business flourished. Various letters arrived, telling of the Valentine's Dance, hockey games, blizzards, spring planting and Cousin Will's new girlfriend. The next letter came from Gordon.

Dear Mother and Stewart,

We are beginning to feel more like Canadians. There's a real community spirit here. I'm writing with input from Peter because he's preparing for June exams. I will too, but we thought we should write.

I found a job for the summer painting the school. I plan to save all my earnings for when I'm a novice salesman. Peter saves every dime he makes helping out other farmers. He's studying to earn a scholarship.

This is Peter writing now. If there are scholarships out there to win, I might as well try for them. I love you both, but back to studying.

Gordon now. I've been doing a lot of thinking about my future. Life here on the homestead is great. When I finish school I'm going to stay in Canada. Life on the prairies has more challenges and that means more opportunities for me.

Will has a young lady named Jessie. She doesn't carry a conversation very well but she sure can cook. I'll finish Grade Ten this year and Peter finishes his last year. Grades 9, 10, and 11 are in one classroom. I'm smart enough to listen in on Peter's classes as well as my own. The principal said I could try the diploma exams a year ahead of time. If I pass the exams and get my diploma early, I'll stay until the crop's in. If I'm right, Will plans to marry Jessie by next fall. They don't need me around their love nest.

I've chosen Winnipeg for a place to find a job. I hope you like my plan.

Love, Gordon

Gordon sounds anxious to be on the road to riches as a salesman. One by one, they are slipping away. I'll write Gordon tomorrow with my blessing. In the meantime, I must enjoy the time I have with the son still with me.

"Stewart, with Jenny not here on her half-day off, I think the two of us should go out to dinner this evening," said Bella. "The salon is doing well and I feel like going to the hotel dining room tonight." Stewart smiled, and soon they were off in the carriage.

***

With Christmas coming, orders for gowns mounted and Bella had to attend to customers with measuring, suggesting styles and buying material.

"You mind the customers, Mary," called Bella. "I must go to the bank."

***

"Is Mr. Stallworthy here?" asked Bella at the Information Counter.

"Do you have an appointment?" inquired the teller.

"No, but I think Mr. Stallworthy will see me if he isn't busy."

Mr. Stallworthy strode happily from his back office. "Bella, how nice to see you. Do come into my office and chat."

"Thank you, Roger, I will. I'm here to personally make the last payment on my mortgage. *Now* do you think you made a good decision that day we arranged for it?"

Mr. Stallworthy gave one of his nervous chuckles. "Yes, my dear, it helped me earn the senior manager's back office, just as you predicted it would, and it helped to give you recognition from the Chamber of Commerce." Bella looked surprised at this comment. "I put forth your name, Bella. How else would they have known that much about you? Did it not occur to you that I might be the only one in town to know your past? Thanks to you, I'm now a strong supporter of women in business."

"That's very nice, Roger. Women deserve a chance to make good. Yes, I did wonder about the Chamber's source of information, but I never tried to guess where they found it. Thank you for that honour." After some additional small talk, Bella completed her business and returned home with the deed for Number 6 Hurlbut Street safely tucked into a brown envelope. *When I came to America I wanted education for my children, a successful way to support the family and a home. When Stewart graduates, I'll have accomplished my goal. People know me on the street. I feel at home in America.*

***

Over the year Bella often entertained, but on one evening only the family and close friends were invited. Stewart arranged the back garden with nine chairs and two folding tables nestled beside a colourful flower garden.

"Tonight, my friends, on this lovely August evening I am giving a garden party for those in my household plus the boys from Sacramento Street who, although the names change annually at their residence, have been with me from my first days in Cambridge. Tonight is a surprise dinner for Mary." Puzzled, Mary stared at Bella.

"Mary, my dear, I never told you that I had applied for recognition as an accredited business capable of training journeymen seamstresses. I registered you as an apprentice seamstress as soon as the accreditation came through two years ago, and tonight you have earned your Journeyman's diploma as a seamstress."

"Me?" Mary squealed. "I have my ticket as a seamstress? Mrs. McD, you are an angel! I never realized that some of the extra duties you gave me in the cutting room and working with customers had a secret purpose. This will surely change my future." With this response blurted out to all the neighbours, Mary ran to kiss Bella and Stewart brought forth a corsage for the neckline of Mary's gown.

***

As usual, Bella did the hand sewing while sitting in her rocking chair watching for the postman with letters from her boys, for Peter and Gordon would soon have the results from their high school exams. Two letters arrived.

> Dear Mother,
> I skipped Grade Ten exams and passed the Grade Eleven exams to earn my diploma. As soon as the fall work is done, I'm leaving for Winnipeg. The marks were average, but it will never be a problem because a high school diploma is a high school diploma. One size fits all, you might say. Will is marrying Jessie and she can feed the chickens and milk Margarita. Wish me luck. I'll write you from Winnipeg when I'm settled.
> Love, Gordon

Bella read Peter's letter.

Dear Mother and Stewart,

As you can see by the address on the envelope, I am settled in Roblin Hall, the campus residence of the Manitoba Agricultural College in Winnipeg. I'll be here for five years and will graduate in Agriculture. I'm not sure yet where that will lead me, Mother, but I want you to know that I'm determined to continue my education.

I've saved enough money, plus some scholarship money, to get through this first year. I'll have to work at something during Christmas, so I won't be home this year. I'll write again as soon as I can, but don't worry if I'm slow about it. Just know that I'm busy studying and I'm fine.

All my love, Peter

Bella rocked and thought of her two eldest boys. *I must consider them men now. To me, they will always be my boys, but they have moved on into the world. There's no stopping the passage of time. I'll just have to enjoy their letters and make life for Stewart as exciting as when his brothers lived at home. Cheer up, Bella, no sad thoughts; the future will be fine.*

35

FACING THE FUTURE

Before lunch Bella stood at the window and looked down at the gardens. The flowers had lost their brilliance and the mountain ash tree hung heavy with orange berries that splattered on the sidewalk.

"There are two letters from your brothers, Stewart," said Bella when he arrived home for lunch. Bella sat at the dining room table and started to read Peter's letter.

> Dear Mother,
>
> I felt like writing sooner than I expected. Writing feels like a little visit. The lads in my classes are swell fellows, but tossing a football around with them doesn't match the good times Gordon and I had on the homestead. University studies take more time than high school ever did. Assignments require a lot of reading, so that's my excuse if you don't get a letter for a while.
>
> My room in residence has a bed, desk and closet. It's small, but I'll manage—my feet dangle over the end of the cot. I'm six-foot-two now. That's taller than Father, isn't it? Gordon is

six-foot-even. Cousin Will married Jessie, and Gordon is in Winnipeg. I saw him yesterday at Eaton's. We're getting together for Thanksgiving at his place, a house where he rents a room and has a hot plate. He's going to be the cook.

Until next time, love, Peter

"Here, you read Gordon's letter," said Bella.
Stewart started to read:

Dear Family,

I'm now a man of fortune, free and easy. When Will announced his wedding date, I thanked him for having me and left. Winnipeg is the Hub City for the west, so that's where I went. The train arrived in the early morning with the sun shining like no other prairie sunrise. I climbed on the streetcar that ran along Main Street, just to see the city. It turned down Portage Avenue, the shopping district. On a big red brick building, I saw 'Eaton's' on a brass plaque. I pulled the cord and bolted for the door. Two hours later, suitcase still in hand, Eaton's opened and I found myself with a job—just like that! Feeling quite successful, I treated myself to an expensive bacon-and-eggs breakfast at the restaurant across the street, read an abandoned newspaper and looked every bit like a businessman in my black suit.

At the back of the *Winnipeg Free Press*, I found a list of rooming houses.

My address is on the envelope. Not bad for one day—a job and lodgings! I start   work tomorrow as a stock boy.

Mother, don't worry about me. I'm seventeen. I'm a man now. With money coming in, the only way I can go is up.

Love, Gordon

My babies are growing up so fast it makes me want to weep, but Stewart wouldn't understand. Bella blew her nose to collect the tears that rimmed her eyes. The next day, a letter arrived from Doug Wray. It read:

Dear Mrs. McD,

I promised to tell you if I moved. (See envelope.) We bought a house with big old trees on Arlington Street in Winnipeg. Can you imagine, Mrs. McD, I now have my own practice with 'Dr. Douglas Wray' on the door of my office.

I hope our paths cross again. If not, I'll see you when I visit my parents.

Love, Doug.

***

The horse cantered home from Wrays. *We've existed on letters from Gordon and Peter for four years. I'm so thankful they write to me. Peter works all his weekends and holidays to earn money for classes, and Gordon's been promoted to the sales floor, selling office equipment. Stewart starts Grade Eight, but why is he so quiet?*

"A penny for your thoughts, Stewart?" said Bella as Blaze trotted along the familiar road from Wrays' farm back into Cambridge. Riding in silence and enjoying the warm countryside in the final days of summer suited Bella, but she sensed that Stewart had something on his mind, for his eyes looked straight ahead as if unfocused.

"Pardon?" said Stewart, coming alive. "Did you speak, Mother?"

"Yes, I asked you what you had on your mind. Tomorrow's your first day back in class in your last year at Agassiz Grammar School. I thought that's what might have put you in another world as we trotted along."

They sat on the driver's bench on the outside of the carriage. Stewart leaned forward, elbows on his knees, with the reins draped softly between his fingers.

"I guess I wanted to drink in the whole scene before getting older makes everything change," said Stewart. "Peter and Gordon seemed to pass into manhood easily enough far away on Will's homestead. We only had their letters to guess their feelings that first year after graduation. What am I supposed to be feeling? I like my life here in Cambridge. In another few months, Christmas will come, the winter will pass and I'll graduate. And then what? I'm not interested in living on a farm."

"Your question, 'What am I supposed to be feeling?' is a good question, Stewart, and one that no one can answer for you. No matter how young or old you are, no one can feel what you are feeling, decipher your emotions or experience your surroundings for you. One thing, though—by the time graduation comes, you will be nearly a year older and you may have different thoughts by then. New opportunities might change your options."

Blaze rounded the corner that took them into the back garden of Number Six Hurlbut Street. Together, Bella and Stewart took care of Blaze and the carriage.

"If I go away to school, Mother, who is going to exercise Blaze every day?"

"Your head is full of concerns that no one your age should have to face, Stewart. Without a father, I suspect you are more worried about me than yourself. For that, there is an answer. People get older, and somehow, their age determines the changes that have to be made." They walked together towards the house. "Maybe you'll win a scholarship to a Cambridge Upper School, live at home and ride Blaze to school. If you live in residence, maybe I'll take in a university student with rent in the form of helping around the house, like caring for Blaze. Tonight you must forget these worries and think of the pleasure of being back with your friends and teachers."

***

"I did as you asked, Mother," reported Stewart after he finished exercising Blaze. "The four fellows at 49 Sacramento are delighted with your invitation to Thanksgiving dinner. The one I spoke to, Grant, is a post grad student from M.I.T. He's working on his thesis about building underground streetcar systems, and he often visits the field office of the underground railway being built out to Cambridge." The more Stewart talked about Grant's thesis, the more animated his face became. "Grant says he'll take me down there some Saturday." By this time, Stewart's eyes sparkled.

***

Again, Bella stood at the window and looked down at the gardens. Falling leaves furrowed along the edge of the sidewalk. An early frost had now killed the flowers. *The end of autumn—how I suffer when winter chills my bones with damp cold. The mailman is wearing a hat and jacket.* Bella rushed to the front door for the mail.

Fall brought new materials and styles. Mary practiced drawing gowns with Bella. They visited the warehouses for fabrics and findings that suited her designs. Katy took lessons at the cutting table from Mary. When fall brought the Christmas orders, Bella prepared a profit and loss statement to compare with the previous year's income.

True, the mortgage no longer drains away funds, but this house is bigger to heat and Mary's increase in salary as a journeyman seamstress and Jenny's small raise increased the overhead. Bella puzzled over the books a second time. *Fabrics cost more. Taxes are up. My charitable use of the salon must have cost more than I thought and the orders are down from last year. Perhaps my income is a bit lower, but not so low as to cause me worry.* Bella dropped her pen and sat back in the office chair. *Thanksgiving should add some merriment to the house. Maybe Jenny would like to invite her boyfriend.* Bella closed her account books and returned to the sewing rooms.

***

In her sitting room on Thanksgiving Sunday, Bella heard a knock on the back door. *Jenny's boyfriend. I can hear voices that sound like sweet nothings to me.*

Soon, Jenny, in her best gown, led a young man into the sitting room.

"Mrs. McD," said Jenny, showing her shy side, "I would like you to meet my boyfriend, Iszak Szabo. Iszak, meet Mrs. Macdonald, my employer. I met Izsak at the dance hall. He's from Hungary and he's learning to be a chef. He wants to help me prepare supper, but first may I show him my room?" Bella shook hands, smiled and answered with a nod. She listened as the two climbed the back staircase to the third floor.

I see love in their eyes. If she marries and moves to Winchester, what will I do without her? I suppose I could cook for Stewart, Mary and me. If our number keeps growing smaller, I'll be rambling around in this big house by myself. Today will be fine with turkey and nine for dinner, but what about tomorrow?

The university students arrived and introduced themselves.

"Stewart," called the new fellow, Grant, "I brought you a copy of a magazine I like called 'Popular Science.' It explains all the new things being invented these days and tells about assembly lines that build things faster and cheaper. You fellows are lucky to be in medicine; people will always need doctors." Conversation passed among them, and at six, Jenny and Iszak served dinner.

***

After the guests left, Bella sat alone in the salon. *This month's* Popular Science *magazine might tell me the future of the clothing industry. I suppose a worker could sit at an assembly line and sew sleeves into a garment all day and not know a wit about making gowns. If you allow your mind to expand and dream, I suppose anything is possible. Maybe my sales are lower because my old customers are buying assembly line clothing! No, that couldn't be. I'll check my customers list. Machines couldn't make the quality of clothing that we make.*

Bella turned out the lights and climbed the stairs to her bedroom. The door on Gordon's room stood ajar. Light from the hall fell across his empty bed. *Soon I will walk past two empty rooms. My mind says I must change with the times, but I cannot grasp what that change should be.* November winds beat against her bedroom window. Bella pulled the covers over her ears and begged the Lord to be allowed some sleep.

***

"Katy," said Bella, "the Christmas orders are finished. Here is your pay envelope for December. Go home for the holidays and return the second week in January."

"But Ma'am," said Katy, "you are paying me for weeks I have not worked."

"You worked long hours finishing the orders, Katy," said Bella. "Now, off you go and Merry Christmas." Bella sorted findings and put the covers on the sewing machines. Mary came from the cutting room after she tidied it for the Christmas break.

"Come downstairs to the sitting room and have coffee with me, Mary. There is something we should discuss."

Once settled with coffee and Christmas cake, Bella began.

"Quite simply, Mary, we must discuss the future. What if people do not place enough orders to keep the shop in business?" Mary gasped and Bella continued. "At Thanksgiving you heard Grant describe assembly line production. That could apply to clothing as well as cars and furniture. Already the factories have taken over the underwear business, bed linens and less expensive gowns. I see no reason why the factories won't put me out of business."

"Mrs. McD," cried Mary, "your customers are too loyal for that!"

"How can you be sure? Maybe I can carry on sewing a few gowns, but what about you? You have your journeyman's ticket for a dying art with your whole life ahead of you. Household sewing machines will become more popular and housewives will sew for their children. You did well teaching Katy. Have you ever thought about teaching housewives to sew?"

"No. I've not worried about the future since I came here."

"Well, Mary, we must think about the future before it overpowers us. Our business is shrinking. What if Iszak asks Jenny to marry him and she leaves? In two months I will award Katy her Journeyman seamstress ticket and she may leave to work closer to home. In June Stewart must continue his schooling elsewhere and he might leave. Something has to change but I'm not sure what. Mary, I want you to think about your future over the holidays. I understand you are going to Washington to visit your friend. Talk with her; she may have some ideas about possibilities in the big city as compared to this quiet academic town."

Together they sat sipping coffee and eating cake for a few minutes in silence.

"Pack your bags and leave early, Mary. You deserve a holiday. Jenny wants to go to Winchester to be with Iszak and my older boys are working. Maybe Stewart and I will take a vacation too. School holidays begin on Friday," Bella's eyes suddenly popped open. "Mary! Why don't the three of us take the train to Washington together? You can go to your friend's home and Stewart and I will see the nation's capital as tourists. Like I told Katy, come back the second week in January and then we'll see if we have any ideas about the future." Bella lowered her voice to denote confidence. "Here in Cambridge, these thoughts are just between the two of us. I don't want the grapevine to suggest that 'Gowns' is in financial difficulty, for business isn't that bad. It's just that the future always has the power to catch up with you if you don't pay attention to it."

***

Bella and Stewart returned home from Washington the day after New Year's Day. Bella saw Stewart off to his classes the following Monday and retreated to the sitting room. *This is how it will be—me alone, trailing around in this big house. If business gets worse, I will have to let Katy go as soon as she finishes her ticket, just like Fowley's Fashions dumped me. With only a few customers, Mary will have to go too.*

To fill the void, Bella busied herself in the kitchen. She hadn't cooked since her days in Demerara with Gabby at Sunningdale. Shopping at the green grocer's allowed her to remember the joy she once found working with food. *Why, I haven't forgotten how to cook after all these years. Stewart will be amazed that his mother can produce meals.* Bella felt so happy after her marketing that she entered a flower shop and bought a dozen burgundy roses. *I'm not sure why I am so happy, with all my worries about the shop, but I'm sure the reason will come to me soon.*

***

The Sunday before the second week in January, Jenny arrived back.

"Jenny!" exclaimed Bella. "You're wearing an engagement ring!" and she ran and hugged her pretty little maid. Bella continued in a happy voice. "When is the wedding?"

"Mrs. McD," Jenny's tears started, "I didn't want my news to come this way because the wedding means that I will leave here to live with Iszak." Bella consoled her until Jenny blubbered: "The wedding will be as soon as we find a place to live that we can afford. Iszak finishes his chef's course at Easter. In June we should have an income."

"That's lovely, Jenny," said Bella. "The girls and I will have time to sew you a wedding gown! I'm so excited, I could dance around in circles."

***

The following day, with Mary and Katy's arrival, Bella brought the girls together so Jenny could tell her news over a morning cup of coffee.

"Katy," said Bella, "ask Jenny what she might like for her wedding dress and two other gowns, then draw her some sketches with a little colour added. Mary, you and I will harness Blaze and go around to the fabric shops and see what materials are in for spring. If customers come while we are gone, Katy, you look after them." Mary winked at Bella. She knew Bella's reason to leave Katy in charge.

Tucked under a blanket in the carriage, Bella shuddered with the cold while Mary held the reins as Blaze clip-clopped over the frozen road.

"Mrs. McD," started Mary, "I have news to tell you too." She paused as if determining what to say. "Remember how you suggested that I should look to the future? Well, over the holidays I did just that. The school system in Washington includes Domestic Science and they are short of instructors. I've only come to collect my things and say goodbye, for they offered me a position that I couldn't refuse. Imagine, me being treated like a white person! I owe my success to you, Mrs. McD. I will be the headmistress of the Domestic Science courses, with two teachers under me."

"Oh my," said Bella. "I mean 'Oh my, isn't that wonderful news,' not, 'Oh my, what if I need you?' Stewart and I will miss you. We've become such good friends, you must call me Bella. I don't know why I didn't think of that years ago. Please send me your address, Mary; you are like family to me," blurted Bella amid a sudden onrush of tears.

"Hold me tight, Mary. I need a hug that will last forever." Mary reined in Blaze, and inside the carriage she cradled Bella until her tears stopped. "Dear Mary, we have worked so well together and visited so often over coffee or in the evenings. You are doing the right thing. You must look to your future, but oh, how I will miss you."

"There's more, Bella," said Mary, rolling her r as if it meant something special. "I met a very nice fellow at a party. He's a friend of my friend's household and I am sure to meet him again. We rather liked each other for the three weeks I stayed in Washington. I don't meet people my own age here. I'm sorry, but for the sake of my future, I must go."

***

Mary stayed for supper and left the following morning. Before Stewart left for school, he hugged her and asked her to visit often with her delightful Scottish brogue. *Poor boy, Mary's Scottish accent is all he has to connect himself, through his Uncles William and Peter, to his father. Even mothers can't guess at the emotional pain that their sons bear.* Bella sat in the salon alone after Mary insisted on taking the streetcar to the train station, where a train would take her to New York and Washington. *She's gone. While Jenny found a husband, Mary earned an education and found respect. In a way, apart from raising three boys, that is all I have done.*

Sitting there on the white fabric covering of the second-hand sofa and surrounded by fake gold statues, the burgundy roses held Bella's attention. *Why did I buy roses when I know money is going to get scarce? Donald, are you trying to give me a message? Do you know my future?*

"Mrs. McD," said Jenny, "are you unwell? You have been sitting here alone for some time. Have my wedding plans upset you?"

"No, Jenny, not in the least. You are looking to your future and that's the way it should be. I'm just thinking of mine here on Hurlbut Street." Bella helped herself to coffee in the kitchen and went into her office.

What did I just say to Jenny? I said, "my future here on Hurlbut Street." That's it! Why must I stay here? Assembly lines will cut my profitability in the near future. I've lost Mary, I'll lose Jenny in June and Katy will have her ticket in two months. I've never liked the damp cold in Cambridge's winter. I'm getting older and I shouldn't be harnessing Blaze on my own. The house is too large and it's worth a great deal of money. There are so many reasons to sell off and go. But where?

Bella leaned towards the bookcase and retrieved an atlas. She flipped pages until the map of the world showed the British Empire in pink. *I am yearning to be with my roots in the British Empire. Why did I not see my destiny before? There, in Canada, where it's pink! I shall go to Winnipeg with my sons and work at teaching Domestic Science just the same as Mary. Why should I grow ragged trying to hang on to my shop when I can see that, in time, it will fail because of new technology?* Bella closed the atlas with a snap, as if to punctuate her decision. *I shall teach sewing and grow old gracefully.*

Bella left her office, smelled the roses and went to see the sketches that Katy had drawn. *I must be sure she has her ticket before word leaks out that I plan to close the shop. We can handle any orders that come in before spring. With January and February being slow months, I can start clearing out the extras that have collected over fourteen years. I'll not go out like a candle—I will leave Cambridge in a blaze of success.*

With more spring in her step, Bella enter the family parlour and sat in Donald's rocking chair to commune with her thoughts. *I will unite my family on British soil. Dear Lord, thank you for leading me to a conclusion about my future. I've had to start my life over three times, through no fault of my own, and I can do it again! Hallelujah.*

***

On March first, Bella held a dinner party with surprise guests, Katy's parents, Maude and Patty O'Rourke. Iszak and Jenny catered.

"My friends, we are here tonight to honour Katy, who has completed her Journeyman's Diploma as a seamstress." Stewart stepped forth with the corsage and Katy gave kisses all around with a solid stream of excited giggling.

***

The following night before dinner, Bella assured herself of time alone with Stewart by suggesting that Jenny take her afternoon off.

"Stewart, you asked me about the future back in the summer," said Bella. "I believe that certain changes allow me to answer your question now. Would you like to move with me to Winnipeg, where you can complete high school, attend university and be with your brothers?"

Stewart jumped to his feet with a whoop of joy, then immediately sat down with a worried look. "But how could we do that? How would you manage?"

"I plan to ask the Winnipeg School Board to hire me as a domestic science teacher. If that fails, perhaps I can be a fashion consultant for Eaton's or continue my work as a seamstress."

"But what about your business and Jenny and Katy and Blaze?"

"Slow down, Stewart. You and your brothers are my life, not sewing gowns. I'll sell everything we don't need and crate the keepsakes for a house in Winnipeg. We will manage with income from my work and investments from the sale of this house. You will graduate in June, Jenny will marry in June and Katy will sew any orders we have and then go off to use her seamstress's ticket in any way she chooses. I'm sorry, but Blaze will have to find a new home."

"It will be good to see my brothers, Mother. Can I tell my friends?"

"Yes, I plan to phone Ivan Jenkins in the morning and put the house on the market for the end of July occupancy. We'll advertise Blaze later if the Wrays don't know of a loving home for him. Hopefully, we can keep him until near the end of July." With eyes shining, Stewart jumped up and hugged his mother. "Consider the move in whatever way your emotions take you, Stewart, and make any plans you wish with your friends. Just don't allow your grades to slip. You'll need them to get into high school in Winnipeg. Also, if Jenny wishes, and with your help, I would like to offer the salon for her wedding reception."

***

The days passed and the grapevine swamped Bella with phone calls. The house sold quickly. Stewart gave the valedictory address at school. Carriages collected the length of Hurlbut Street on the day of Jenny's wedding. Bella ordered the movers to come in late July to crate the beloved rocking chair, her crystal vase, a sewing machine and other treasures that they had collected over the years.

"What about Blaze, Mother?" sighed Stewart as he helped clean cupboards in the kitchen with his mother, Jenny and Iszak. "No one seems to want him."

"Don't say no one wants him, Stewart," said Iszak. "Jenny and I would, but . . . "

"Did I hear correctly, Iszak?" asked Bella. "Jenny and you could use Blaze?"

"Use him, we can, but use isn't the right word, Mrs. McD," said Iszak. "We love Blaze but we have no money to pay for him."

"Then you shall have him and the carriage as a wedding gift," cried Bella, hugging him. "You and Jenny will take us to the train station, then drive on to your home."

***

Before giving up Hurlbut Street, with Iszak and his friends catering, Bella held an open house for their friends to drop by—and the grapevine worked its miracles. Crowding into the salon came Stewart's friends and their parents, Miss Baldwin, professors and Leolpold Blashka, Wrays and their neighbours, everyone on Sacramento Street, the Stallworthys and those who had attended the Blue Book ceremony. They all came to say goodbye and wish them well. Again, the salon table held a dozen burgundy roses in the crystal vase.

36

NEW BEGINNINGS
YET AGAIN

Bella and Stewart said goodbye to Blaze, hugged Jenny and Izsac and boarded the train for Canada.

The customs man stamped my British passport. I'm a citizen here in Canada. With berths and a dining car, our trip to Winnipeg doesn't compare to Peter's trip west—poor boy, out of food and out of money—his first time away from home, sitting alone in an uncomfortable day coach. I wonder what Stewart is thinking while he stares at Lake Superior, shining and blue across to the horizon. He's likely wondering how the engine works.

"Mother," said Stewart breaking the silence, "tell me about the roses. Always a dozen and always dark red?"

"Stewart," Bella paused, in search of words for this surprise question. "The short answer is that the roses remind me of your father's love. On every important occasion he always gave me burgundy roses. It's my way to include him in my life."

Stewart smiled with his mother's answer. "What about the first bouquet? When did he give you that?"

"On our first date. Then came our wedding—your father had burgundy roses all over the *Schooner Van Dam*." Bella laughed and went on to tell Stewart the story of his father's masterful plans for the wedding, followed by many more stories of Paramaribo. Stewart had never heard of his parent's lavish life in Surinam nor of his own hectic sea voyage by ship to Boston. Telling stories filled the days and hours before the porter called, "Next stop, Winnipeg!"

***

Peter, Gordon and Doug Wray found each other in the lower level of the train station and stood together as the passengers, struggling with luggage, fumbled their way from the overhead train platform down the tiled staircase. The crowd, anxious to spot their loved ones, swarmed closer to the gate. Peter spotted his mother and hardly recognized the tall boy walking beside her.

"Mother, let me shield you from all these people," he shouted and led her to the back of the crowd where standing room had opened up. "Stewart, you've grown!" cried Peter with a slap on the back for his little brother.

After hugs and kisses, a Red Cap arrived with Bella's suitcases.

"I have trunks and crates as well," said Bella. "What address should I give for their delivery?"

Gordon shuffled his feet. "Not my place, Mother. I live in a rooming house."

Peter opened his hands in supplication. "Mother, in the past you always planned everything the way you wanted it. I thought you'd have this arranged too. I stayed on at the university residence with a job washing windows. You can't sleep at the men's dorm and I haven't two bucks in my pocket for a hotel room."

Bella's eyebrows pinched together; her lips compressed in a straight line.

Doug jumped into the awkward situation. "It's settled, then. You'll all come home with me and meet my wife, Mavis, and our two little ones." With downcast eyes, Bella nodded in agreement, took Doug's arm and paraded off, leaving her three sons to pick up the baggage and trail behind as if somehow her adult sons had failed their mother by not providing lodging. Doug led them to his new roadster. Bella took the front seat while her three tall boys crammed into the back.

With the joy of little children romping among them, they all enjoyed a fine evening remembering past years. *I mustn't be disappointed. Soon I'll have a house with a bedroom for each boy and the four of us will be a family again.*

As the evening closed, Gordon offered unwanted news. "I've changed jobs, Mother. I'm not with Eaton's any more. I have the franchise to sell Underwood typewriters in Southern Alberta and I'm leaving here on Monday. I'll write when I'm settled out west."

Even Peter's shy report that he had won the Lieutenant Governor's gold medal for being the top student in Agriculture for all of Manitoba did not stem Bella's disappointment at learning that Peter, too, would be gone by the third week of August. *It is my own fault. It never occurred to me that my older boys might not live here forever.*

***

Doug encouraged Bella and Stewart to stay as long as they wished, for their baby boy's crib could be moved in with them so Bella could sleep on a cot in with their little girl and Stewart could sleep in the basement on their other cot. *The basement! Is life repeating itself? Not if I can help it. I'll establish a home immediately, where the boys can come to visit, and I'll look out for myself as widows learn to do. The future, Bella; that is the important thing.*

***

During August Bella researched job opportunities that Winnipeg offered while she enjoyed Doug Wray's new home on Arlington Street. *What's holding you back, Bella?* said that voice from deep within. *You've started over before. You can do it again. Why are you stalling? You haven't gone for one interview.* Bella sat in the Wrays' overstuffed chair and looked at her fingers entwining and disengaging until she saw the mailman. Gordon's letter arrived from Alberta.

"Dear Mother and Stewart,
With Peter's new job as an instructor at the Claresholm School of Agriculture, I decided to find room and board in

Claresholm. I needed a car to travel from town to town with my stock of typewriters, so I took out a loan and bought one. Don't worry; selling typewriters has proven to be profitable. I often have to teach the stenographers how to type. Prairie girls are very pretty—but not as pretty as my sweet Clarice back in Winnipeg.

Address letters to me in care of my landlord, Mr. Marlborough Knight, Claresholm, Alberta, and I'll receive them with his mail.

Write me about your new house, Mother. I'll try to come for Christmas.

Love, Gordon

***

By the third week of August, Bella still lived with Doug's family. She felt alone. Stewart had found a near-by library and immersed himself in books to be out of the way. *Having the boys around me again will never happen—just a foolish dream. I will not be buying a house for us; it will be for me.* Bella stared out of the Wrays' living room windows.

I must stop dallying and secure a job if I am to teach Domestic Science. With a job, I'll buy a small house to suit me for the rest of my days. I must realize that the boys I reared are now men making their own way through life. Neither they nor I will ever understand what it is for a mother to let go of them. What was it that Peter said at the train station? "You always organized things before." Well, I can do it again. I may be forty-eight, but there are many good years left in me.

With these thoughts, Bella collected her documents, walked to North Main Street and climbed on the streetcar that would take her downtown to the School Board building. *I have been an immigrant searching for work before, and much as I detest begging for a job, being a teacher still has honour.*

***

The School Board secretary handed Bella a form to fill in. *He's a secretary? Why, he's hardly old enough to have stubble on his chin. He should learn not to let his eyes wander below an applicant's hemline.*

Before he could possibly have read her qualifications, he tossed her application on his desk and said that they were looking for new graduates.

"Really, Sir! Have you noticed that I am applying to be a Domestic Science teacher? In that line of work, teachers are rarely just out of college. Most women in college have never touched a sewing machine, yet I have held my qualifications for ten years. I am an acknowledged designer of fine gowns and knowledgeable in nutrition and cooking. Would you please look at your list again for Domestic Science teachers and send me in to be interviewed by your superior?"

On second glance, the man found several openings for Domestic Science teachers on the second page of his list. As Bella slipped into the Superintendent's office, she said to the secretary in a kindly voice, "I suggest, young man, that you keep your mind on your list rather than on ankles."

Of the three positions open, the School Board needed a teacher at the high school in the community where Doug Wray lived, so Bella chose that opening. *Now to buy a house nearby and get Stewart registered in high school.*

***

Peter's letter arrived.

> Dear Mother and Stewart,
>
> The first day I arrived in Claresholm, Gordon took me home to his boarding house for supper. Mr. and Mrs. Knight welcomed me at their front hall. In moments, their beautiful daughter, Eneta, floated down the adjacent stairs like a princess. After introductions, I regained my composure and we sat down for a fine meat and potatoes meal with fresh vegetables and apple pie.
>
> Downtown Claresholm has one main street with a few shops parallel to the railroad tracks. The Agricultural School is a little way out of town, so I'll try to find lodgings out that way. Tonight, I'm at the only hotel in town. Without streetlights, I

had forgotten how dark it gets when the sun goes down on the prairies. There are sure to be coyotes calling each other by the light of the moon. I'll finish this in the morning after I've been out to the school.

Luck is with me. They have a dormitory and a dining room out there. They say I must teach English to the Domestic Science students as well as Animal Husbandry and Horticulture, but that's fine—Eneta is taking Domestic Science.

Around the school are golden fields of grain with a backdrop of green hills and snow-capped mountains to the west; I see grandeur in every direction. I'll write again when I know the address and have more to say.

I suppose by now, Mother, you're settled in a house.

Love, Peter

Settled in a house, indeed! I didn't expect to find a shortage of houses near the high school! How long does the real estate man expect me to be patient! How can I be patient when the oak leaves have turned brown and blown across the lawn, soon to be replaced by snow?

***

In the silent house, with everyone out, Bella stood alone at the Wrays' living room window, her fingers entwining. Minutes passed, yet she seemed unable to move. *Nothing is going as planned. I can't stay with the Wrays forever. What to do. What to do! Christmas will soon be here and the boys might come. Three months, and we are still parked on the Wrays' doorstep. Three months, and Doug won't take a dime for rent while I teach and Stewart goes to his classes. I try to help Mavis about the house, but she is so efficient that I spend my spare time entertaining the two little ones.*

***

One evening the phone rang. Doug handed Bella the phone to hear, "I think I've found you a house, Mrs. Macdonald." The real estate salesman gave the address as 59 Athole Street, just three blocks from the school.

"It is not as big as you first wanted, but there are just the two of you so I thought I should include it in my search."

***

"Boys, you've come!" cried Bella when she answered her front door. "You are both so tall—stand down one step so I may hug you," cried Bella when Peter and Gordon arrived four days before Christmas. "I've just taken occupancy of the house and it isn't a home yet, but if I hire a truck perhaps you can bring all the crates and trunks from Wrays' basement and we'll unpack."

"Mother," laughed Peter, "you said you had a *little* house. This one has a screened front porch and an upstairs." They spilled into the front hall.

"It's much like the Sacramento Street house," marvelled Gordon as they circled through the living room arch to the dining room, the kitchen and again down the central hall to the front door. Stewart heard the arrival of his brothers and came down the stairs, two at a time, to land in a three-way bear hug. *It may not be for long, but I have my three boys united under my roof. Thank you, God.*

***

The rest of the day was spent bringing Bella's belongings from the Wrays' house. The second day, they worked until midnight unpacking dishes and bed linens, clothes and her few pieces of furniture.

"I've checked with Eaton's Department Store, boys," said Bella. "They'll deliver on the morning of Christmas Eve if we shop today. Come, let us go on a grand spending spree and perhaps on Christmas Eve we'll sleep in beds instead of on the floor."

On Christmas Day Bella cooked a turkey dinner for the first meal from her stove. Her two older sons stood in awe as they watched her command of the kitchen. They had no idea that she knew about anything but horses and business.

"Mother," questioned Peter, "you've always had a maid. When did you learn to be such a wonderful cook?"

"I learned in British Guiana from my landlady who told me that someday I might need to know everything about running a home.

385

Don't worry about me; I will survive as long as you boys keep writing to me."

***

Here I am, starting a new life again with school courses to plan, a new home requiring housework and no friends. Stewart hasn't mentioned friends either. He studies all the time and has become the school's top student. I must enhance our lives.

***

Three years later, Bella hung her coat in the closet and walked through her familiar front hall to the kitchen to make a cup of tea after classes. *The years have flown by. Little by little, I've made new friends and Stewart has become the centre of attention with his easy-going ways and banjo. Teaching Domestic Science suits me very well and my house is large enough for the boys to be together at Christmas. I must remember to invite Doug and Mavis to Stewart's high school graduation ceremonies.*

***

"I've registered for university, Mother," said Stewart in July. "I'll be studying engineering way out at the Fort Garry Campus, so I'll have to live in residence, but I'll come to see you on the weekends."

***

It's finally happened, as I knew some day it would. I'll live alone for the rest of my days, so I must make them eventful days. But how can I do that with the War raging in Europe and my three sons involved? Dear God, I pray that they return safely.

***

The third letter, this one from Stewart. They are all back. Next, I'm sure there will be three weddings for me to attend, and then where will they live? I'll just have to visit them.

***

"Mother," said Peter after their wedding ceremony. "Eneta and I are moving to Winnipeg! I've accepted a position with a rural magazine, so we'll see each other often."

***

Over the years the huge oak trees grew bigger. The Red River nearby froze over every fall and cracked with break-up in spring, but Bella did not mind the dry cold of winter on the prairies; at least she could bear it better than Cambridge's damp cold. On Sundays she took the streetcar to Elim Chapel, a Christian church on Portage Avenue. After church, she went on down the line to Peter's home for a visit.

***

"Peter," shouted Bella, as she came into his home one Sunday. "Look at this letter! After seventeen years of devoted service, the School Board has sent me a retirement notice. If I taught school successfully at age sixty-four; what strange malaise has come over me that says I'm incapable at sixty-five?"

"That's how employers are, Mother," explained Peter. "If it's their policy that employees retire at sixty-five, then you must retire."

Bella stamped her foot and muttered: "If they won't let me teach here, I'll move to Vancouver. I've started over before and I can start over again. There must be a girls' private school out there that doesn't endorse retirement at sixty-five. I will find it and apply with my years of teaching experience."

***

"Take care, Mother," said Peter as she boarded the train for Vancouver.

Bella's spirits were high as she alighted from the train and followed the station signage to the Hotel Vancouver. *Travel by train is quite delightful, with their grand hotels built at the railway stations. A newsstand. I'll need a map of Vancouver showing the streetcar system.* Once in her hotel room, she settled on the bed, with the telephone directory opened at Girls' Private Schools, and made a list of addresses to guide her search.

The following morning she set off by streetcar to look for work. Recognizing the huge dose of personality and flare for style that the trim little woman possessed, one private school hired her to teach Home Economics.

Now I must find accommodation! Granville Street has a streetcar that leaves the residential areas and goes right into town where the school is located. I'll look for a big home along Granville that's been divided into apartments. The old living room on the main floor should do very nicely. Bella bought a *Vancouver Sun* newspaper, circled ads that offered lodgings on Granville Street and found the perfect apartment.

***

Back in Winnipeg, Bella sorted her things, chose only what she needed for the bed-sitting room apartment she had rented and said goodbye to Winnipeg. Over the following years, she loved the school where she worked, the students and the change to milder weather.

On the last day of the school year in 1941, Bella cleared her desk for the summer. She packed her personal items and a picture of her sons in a small briefcase. As she fastened its clasp she noticed her hands. *My fingers are gnarled with hard work and the intricacies of sewing. By next term they will likely refuse to hold another needle. How many years have I worked here now? Thirteen years? For someone who was supposed to die at thirty, I've done quite well in seventy-eight years, but I think it's time to retire and enjoy what Vancouver has to offer—the heavenly winter, my snug apartment and the Granville streetcar line that can take me anywhere when I want to visit my friends, church or the arts. I am a lucky mother to have sons who write me letters.*

Sitting in the rocking chair in the sun of her bay window, she looked at her sons' picture on the side table and leafed through their latest letters. *Peter is the editor of the magazine now, and he's known across Canada for his thoughtful insightful editorials. Gordon's a director of a large marketing company and Stewart is the chief engineer of a huge lumber company. With summer coming, it's time I visited them all again, riding on those marvellous trains, sitting there in the comfort of the parlour car.*

***

Ten years later, Eneta rushed to Vancouver when Bella finally allowed that she could no longer live alone. Together they looked at elegant Seniors Residences.

"What a lovely place," said Bella. Eneta's hopes rose, then Bella finished her sentence: "But I couldn't live there. Those people are all waiting to die!"

"Then come and live with us, Bella," said Eneta. "With our sons grown up we have plenty of room, and your granddaughter will be delighted to hear your wonderful stories."

***

With this invitation, Bella moved back to Winnipeg, including the rocking chair and crystal vase. Here, under Eneta's care, Bella lived a pampered life—always dressed to her own high standards with her pure white hair coifed in style. Despite her growing frailty, she sat in the living room with smiles and pleasantries for everyone.

"Mrs. Macdonald," said a family friend, "I see you're reading a magazine."

"No, my dear," answered Bella. "I am much too old at eighty-nine to read magazines. I just look at the pictures to see how the styles are changing."

On Bella's last Christmas, the fiancé of her granddaughter lifted the sixty- pound woman in his arms to carry her to the dining room for Christmas dinner. She made him stop while passing through the archway into the dining room. There she crooned: "Mistletoe!" and pointed above her head. The young man gave her a loving kiss on the cheek. She pretended to shiver all over as she grinned with pleasure and said: "I've waited for that kiss all day and I didn't intend to miss the opportunity."

***

This tiny, courageous, powerful woman passed away in her sleep in 1953 at the age of ninety. Eneta, keeping watch, heard Bella's deep sigh as if she had enjoyed the chase—had done everything she'd set out to do— and was finally willing to let go of the future.

ABOUT THE AUTHOR

Lyn Thompson grew up in Winnipeg where her father, P.M. Abel, the editor of The Country Guide magazine, insisted that the family use proper English. With her B.Sc. in Human Ecology and a post-graduate in dietetics completed, she married petroleum engineer, Bill Thompson in 1953. They lived in most major oil towns and cities on the Canadian prairies and took their four young sons to Peru for three years. Later, she travelled with her husband during his transfers to England and the Middle East. They retired to Calgary where she continues to live as a widow.

She weaves the knowledge of sports, outdoor lore and volunteerism into her fiction and non-fiction. She served Girl Guides and Scouts Canada as a senior group leader for twenty-three years and in her lifetime held credentials as a swimming instructor, scuba diver, first-aider, camp director, and wilderness trainer. In all her junior and adult life she has been involved with serving, organizing, and managing volunteer committees for her community, including her years abroad. Sports included golf, downhill skiing, curling and horseback riding. She has spent over fifty years enjoying their family cottage and all it has to offer in outdoor life, boating, and family togetherness.

With many writing courses in her portfolio, she has actively pursued the craft of writing for the past twenty years. Apart from serving on Writers Guild of Alberta committees and its Provincial Board, she has co-ordinated the Calgary WGA Prose Writers Critique Group these years. In 2008 she was honoured with a WGA Life Membership. She works in several genres but prefer to write short stories, novels, and some poetry.

Her other works include *Hypothermia,* and *Outhouse Memories and Other Cottage Poems.*